THE VOYAGE OF CARLO SARFE

THE JOURNEYMAN TRILOGY, BOOK TWO

J.W. WEBB

Acknowledgement for:

John Jarrold, for editing

Roger Garland, the late Tolkien artist, for the illustrations

Ravven, for the cover design

Chris Kocher, for proofreading

Crystal Sarakas, for book design

For Linda,

Your gorgeous fantasy art has been such an inspiration for my muse. Especially Winter, The Huntsman who rides above my desk.

Thanks for all your support and encouragement over the years, and for the wonderful maps you created for the series.

To view Roger and Linda Garland's Art visit Lakeside Gallery:

lakeside-gallery.com

Would you trade your soul to save your life?

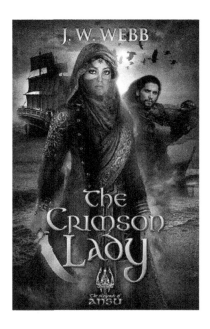

The Crimson Lady knows that her soul may be the price she has to pay to get revenge.

If you enjoyed *Blood Feud,* you will love this new tale, *The Crimson Lady.* It's available free for newsletter members only. Don't miss out! Join our fun newsletter the JW Webb VIP Lounge. *Subscribe today!*

The Voyage of Carlo Sarfe

PART I

DREAMS

1

TORRIGAN'S TAVERN

MAREI WATCHED the four men playing cards at table. She didn't like them and couldn't guess their origin. Rough soldier types. Big and surly, their accents harsh and strange to her ears. The leader had eyes like congealed gray glass. Cold as an adder, a short scar dipping below the left one. He glanced at her sometimes. That made her shudder. *Where was Garland?* She hoped he'd stay away. These men were trouble, and he would want to intervene should they start anything.

Best she kept busy. Dafyd was outside in the yard hauling goods from the last delivery. The city wagon stopped by once a month. Something new, after Garland had crossed the mountains with Dafyd and met with some of their merchants. Garland was proving quiet the diplomat. Her son worshiped the journeyman. Marei loved him, though feared he wouldn't stay. His home would be calling him, she felt certain of it. In the six months he'd been here, Garland had helped her, with not only the running of the tavern, but gaining new custom from the village and, more importantly, the great city in the east.

The road was busy again—the first time in years. And the Hall remained quiet. That was good. Perhaps those inside had moved on. They did that from time to time. Marei hoped that was the case. Throughout the weeks, she'd seen merchants and soldiers moving through. All heading for the coast and on, either up north to the other places she'd heard them speak of, or out to sea to seek their fortunes, or fight the Kaa. Some of the city folk were just curious and hired vessels from the villagers. Rosey's kin kept boats.

These four strangers were different. Killers of the worst kind, no doubt about that. The leader caught her eye again before she'd turned away. He grinned, signaled her over with a finger. Marei shuddered, chewed her lip. She put on a brave smile and dusted down her apron.

I've handled worse than you.

She walked over calmly, still wearing her customary smile. The men studied her body with oafish transparency. She ignored their grins. The leader grabbed her shoulder rudely as she stood over them.

"Where are your menfolk, wench?"

"Around," she said, her eyes hinting outside.

"They must be sorry fools to leave a pretty lass like you all alone."

"Why would that be?" Marei met his cold gaze with an even stare. "I run things here."

"There could be trouble," the leader said, gazing at her legs. "You're not young, passed your best, I'd warrant. But you do have certain charms."

Marei resisted the temptation to spit in his face.

"We've been on the road a long time. You could oblige us." The leader's smile was a crooked smear. The others laughed as he reached out and gripped her thigh. Those smiles faded when the knife appeared in her hand.

"You threatening me?" The leader barked a laugh. For an answer, Marei deftly flicked the knife into a fist and jabbed it up under his eye, just left of the scar, touching the skin but not piercing. He wasn't laughing now. "Are you?" The gray eyes had narrowed to dangerous flints.

She withdrew the knife and returned to the counter where she poured an ale, a faint smile on her lips. Glass Eyes stood up and walked across.

"I asked you a question, woman."

Marei passed him the full mug of ale. He looked at it for a moment then nodded. Took a long swig. "We'll leave you be," he said, winking back at his friends. "I was just joking, lass." Marei nodded, but she had the knife in her hand below the counter. "Name's Shale," he said, trying to make his sloping smile look genuine.

"Marei," she replied. "This is Torrigan's Tavern. It's usually crowded, though tonight we're quiet. I expect the regulars will be in soon."

"We don't want trouble—I told you," Shale said. "Just lodging and more ale. It's good." He sipped again.

"The rooms are occupied with paying guests," Marei said.

"Empty them," Shale said, wiping froth from his mouth. Marei stared at him coldly and he laughed again. "She's a feisty one, hey, lads?" The men grinned. The skinny one made a lewd gesture with his fingers.

"You cannot stay here. There are no rooms for you." She gripped the knife and felt the sweat trickle into her palm.

"We'll see." Shale shrugged. They'd eaten the stew she'd made and consumed several tankards. They weren't drunk, but this could only go one way. The crossbow was in the kitchen fully cranked. That would deal with Shale. The other three …

She changed tack. "Are you from the city?"

"Hmm?" Shale's lip quivered with slight irritation.

"The city across the mountains. We have soldiers moving through from there, making for the wars far away."

"Don't know it," Shale said, his face had turned serious. "We're from the Hall."

"Graywash Hall?" Marei felt her stomach lurch. "No one comes here from there."

"Well, we have, darling—and a fine welcome you've given us. You should be nicer to your neighbors, Marei."

"You can't be from the Hall. Its gates haven't opened in months. Word of your leaving them would have reached me from the village. I know a lot of people around here." She held his gaze, tensing like pulled wire.

At that moment, the door swung open and she saw Dafyd standing laden with logs. His eyes were wide, gazing at the strangers.

"Who's this?" Shale's glassy gaze swept across the room.

"My son." Marei nodded at Dafyd. "Leave the logs outside and see to the beasts, will you?" He nodded, recognizing the code Garland had told them to use. He turned away and dropped his load in a pile, before vanishing outside again. Marei noted how Shale and the others rested hands on their swords.

She brought them more ale and they turned quiet for a time, whispering amongst themselves. She needed to know who these people were and what they were up too. Shale and his men could cause trouble in the village. They must be from the city. Where else was there? Doubtless they'd heard about the Hall. Rumors would have reached that far. There was only one man who had been inside that place and lived. Garland never spoke of what he'd seen.

She watched them talking, leaning close in their cups. Marei withdrew to the kitchen and carefully scooped up the crossbow. She reentered the taproom, placing the weapon under the counter. None had seen her move. She rolled the knife inside her apron and waited.

The door swung open, and all their heads turned that way. Garland stood with broadsword thrust into the straw. Shale rose to his feet, the others following. "Your husband?" He flicked her a sharp lance.

"*Sir* Garland is a friend,' Marei replied. She turned and smiled at her man. "These gentlemen claim they're from the Hall," she told him.

"I doubt that," Garland said, his calm gaze studying Shale and his cronies.

Shale's smirk broadened. "Sorry to say, but I'm going to kill your friend, Marei. He looks like a troublemaker. Can't be too careful these days. Once he's bleeding out, I'll strip you naked, and me and the boys will take turns. You had your chance. We're done being nice here." He blinked at a shadow. Marei saw Dafyd frame the door with nocked bow in hand, the bowstring pulled taut.

Marei hoisted the crossbow from behind the counter and leveled it at Shale.

"Shoot those men, you pair," Garland growled. "I deal with the leader." With a speed that made her blink, he swung his broadsword across in a furious arc. Shale was quick, too. His shorter blade met Garland's with a clash of sparks. His men remained frozen, their anxious eyes on the bowman and Marei's aimed crossbow.

Shale slid his sword from Garland's blade and jabbed low, aiming to gut him.

Garland blocked, stepped back to make room for another swing. Shale jumped toward him, stabbing out a second time.

Garland blocked that too. "Shoot em, Marei!"

She couldn't do it. Neither could Dafyd—she glimpsed his blue eyes twitching with concentration. Like her, the boy wasn't a killer. They were angry, but shooting men like ducks in a row—and so close—was no light matter.

The skinny one grinned. "She hasn't the bottle—neither the boy." He reached for a knife as Shale stabbed out at Garland's eyes.

Garland blocked again, but this time he stepped forward, switching grip. Grabbing the sword on its leather band below the cross-guard, the other hand on hilt, and ramming the round pommel hard into Shale's face—a trick that worked well. The crunching blow knocked Shale backwards, but he kept his balance. His face was bleeding badly.

The knife man yelled and raised his arm back. He screamed as Marei's crossbow twanged and the shaft pierced his shoulder. She cranked another bolt before anyone had time to register. The wounded man staggered and almost fell. He held out his good arm, and one of the others supported him. Shale glared at Garland, who watched him calmly.

"Shoot again, Marei," Garland said.

"No need," Marei replied. "These fools know they're outmatched." She flicked the crossbow at the door. "You had best leave while you still breathe." She motioned Dafyd at the doorway, and he stepped back to allow room.

The skinny one was gripping his arm trying to staunch the blood from his shoulder, his lean face white as a lily. The other two looked wild, but neither seemed ready to challenge them.

They were shaken and hadn't expected resistance, let alone being overcome. Shale was different. He appeared faintly amused and stooped to wipe the blood from his face with a rag he'd retrieved from his sleeve.

He glanced at Marei, then at Garland. He bowed his head slightly. "As you wish," Shale said to Marei. "We'll leave it here for the moment." He raised a brow at the nearest of his men. "Mikkael, help Brunden and grab Doolen's other arm—he looks a bit pale." He made for the doorway. Garland blocked him but stepped aside reluctantly after a nod from Marei.

"Thanks." Shale smirked as his men followed him outside, the wounded Doolen staggering between the other two and almost blacking out. Dafyd's nocked arrow covered their departure as they shambled from the tavern yard. Garland followed, and Marei stood behind with crossbow aimed.

The four reached the gate to the compound, opened it and pushed Doolen through. Shale turned and nodded, his glassy eyes calm and ironic. No anger there.

"You people have made a bad mistake today," he told them. "I'll be seeing you shortly, *darlin'*." He winked across at Marei. She considered pressing the trigger, but the distance was too far. Garland was right—she should have shot them in the taproom.

"I've killed far worse men than you," Garland said, thrusting his broadsword into the dirt again. "You'd best stay away, lads—for your own sakes. We were only playing this evening."

Shale nodded. "Aye, I'll see you, too, *Sir* Garland. Watch you bleeding and grubbing in the dirt like a butchered sow writhing in its own spilled guts." He wiped blood from his face again. "Best you stay awake at night, good people. Keep the lights on." He turned with a swirl of his heavy gray cloak and left the stockade briskly, his shadow fading off into the dark. Garland followed and, at a nod from Marei, Dafyd trotted after him.

Marei walked behind, taking deep breaths to calm her nerves. She waited by the gate as their shapes faded in the gloom. Dafyd reemerged after ten minutes, his young face paler than before. "They disappeared," he said, blue eye wide. "Vanished."

"It's moonless and almost midnight." Marei waved a dismissive hand. She saw Garland's shadow approaching and caught the grim expression on his face. She suppressed a shudder. *The Hall. Can it be?*

"Dafyd said—"

"—I know ..." Garland held up a placating hand. He slid his sword inside the scabbard and made for the inn. "I need a brandy, Marei. A large one."

"Think we all do," she replied with a nod, and the three of them went inside. Garland placed the heavy bars across the door and shuttered the windows.

"You think they'll return tonight?" she asked him.

"They wouldn't if they were dead." His tone was sharp, and she bit her lip.

"I'm sorry, Marei. Truth is, I don't know what to think," Garland continued eventually. Dafyd uncorked a fat, cloudy bottle behind the counter and poured, filling three large mugs with amber liquor. Garland pulled up a chair and Marei sat beside him, her heart heavy and head thumping. Dafyd remained standing, his eyes edgy and mostly on the door.

Garland took a slow, measured sip. He sighed, sipped again, and smiled wryly at her. Her hand felt for his beneath the table.

"What should we do?" she asked. He shrugged, sipped

again. "They said they were from the Hall. Is that possible? Dafyd said they … *disappeared*."

"Before they got to the road, aye," Garland said. He coughed quietly and gazed about the gloomy taproom, as though someone was listening. "I think it's starting again, Marei."

"What is starting …?" She felt the familiar icy tremor deep inside.

"The *Dance*, she called it. The Emerald Queen. The business with the bow. It isn't over. It's found me here. I thought that it finished with Lord Tam and those witches dying. But that was only part of the thread. Those men looked like Morwellans."

"You're not making any sense, love." She squeezed his hand. Although he'd been here six months, her lover had hardly spoken of his realm or the harrowing time he'd endured, both inside and beyond the Hall. Marei knew that Garland had witnessed things way beyond the ken of most folk. Like most things, she blamed that on the Hall. "You think those men came from your … *world*?"

"Ours is the same world, Marei. We're from different dimensions. But the same shadows flicker through both. I don't understand it either. We mortals can only scratch the surface. Suffice to say, their leader reminded me of an outlaw I encountered long ago. A Morwellan killer called Hagan."

"You think that someone back there sent them after you?" Dafyd asked him, his eyes still on the door.

"It's possible, but I doubt it," Garland said. "I don't know those men, but they resembled the brigands in our northlands. And their accents—though not the same—were similar to Morwellans I've met."

"But we can assume that they're from your homeland,"

Marei said. "But how did they get here, and what do they want?"

"Same way as I did," Garland chuckled and sipped again. "The Crossroads. As to what they want ..." He blew out his cheeks. "I expect that's the same as what all men like that want."

"They didn't seem lost," Dafyd said.

"He's right," Marei nodded. "Shale showed clear purpose and, whether or not they came from the Hall, there must be a connection."

"It does seem likely," Garland said.

"They disappeared, mother." Dafyd shook his head. "Like wraiths in mist."

"I should have shot them," she said to Garland.

"You shot one of them, Marei. They didn't expect that." Garland grinned raffishly and gripped her hand in his. "I trained you well with that weapon."

"I've a sharp eye and quick hand."

"If they can disappear in the murk, they might reappear inside this tavern," Dafyd said, looking miserable.

Garland stared at him. "Get some rest, boy. You did well tonight. Don't fret. I'll keep this trusty blade well oiled. You too, Marei. Sleep, if you can." She shook her head. But Dafyd nodded and took to the bench beneath the window. Outside, the sound of wind buffeting announced a storm approaching. Autumn was fading fast.

The pair sat in thoughtful silence for half an hour, her hand locked in his. Dafyd was sleeping. Marei envied her son his dreams. No sleep for her tonight.

"You shouldn't have returned," she said eventually.

"What ...?" Garland grunted and blinked. He must have been dozing.

"Back here." She let go of his hand and stifled a yawn. "Far better if you'd stayed with your friends. Your men. It was rash to return here, sweet man."

"It was for love that I did it. I've never met a woman like you, Marei."

She chuckled wryly. "You daft bugger. I'm the wrong side of forty winters. You could do better back home, I'm sure."

He shook his head. "I'm fifty-three, far as I can make out. Most men my age are witless fools, or already dust. Back there, and in this land. And my heads a shamble, Marei. It's a wonder I'm sane, I've witnessed so many horrors." He sounded exhausted. She smiled, squeezed his hand again.

"You are strong, my love. In your prime."

He chuckled. "Ah, thanks, but the truth is I'm worn out. You know, after that business in the other castle, the one with the lights. It messed with my head. I told you about that, right?" He didn't seem certain.

She nodded. "I didn't understand fully, but you were trapped by witchcraft? In a haunted castle."

"The Castle of Lights in Rundali. Very strange place. And the end of a fruitless journey. I was charged by Queen Ariane of Wynais to find her missing cousin, Tamersane. A hero from the Crystal Wars."

"Did you find him? You never said."

"Eventually, and only after it was too late. There were three terrible women. Sorceresses, and more. So much more. I was confused, Marei. Shattered. My men, those you mentioned. Some are dead. The forest took them. The others … I don't know. I lost them, Marei. I failed my troop. And my queen. I am a sorry tale, but at least I can help you and that boy. They've a baby son—Dafyd told me this afternoon."

"Daughter." Marei nodded evasively. She didn't want to

think about Rosey and the child. They were too close to the Hall. It hadn't mattered when Rosey was just a girl her son liked. But now she was Dafyd's woman with a newborn. And the Hall right there, a dark shadow looming over their little village. It was almost too much to bear. Marei pushed aside those troubled thoughts.

He looked hard at her concern in his kind blue eyes. "Are you holding up all right?"

"Yes, I suppose so." She smiled. "Just angry. You'll have to tell me about those adventures one day." He had mentioned a castle of lights, but of course she hadn't understood when he'd mumbled about what may or may not have occurred there. Marei had assumed that castle to be another manifestation of Graywash Hall. The place was never the same twice, or so they said. Those rash folks who had ventured near the gates.

"I'd sooner not," Garland muttered. "But I fear you're involved, anyway. The blight has spread. If Shale and his men did come from Morwella or thereabouts, that can only mean the portal has reopened. The crossroads I spoke of. Perhaps someone—or something—in Graywash Hall is summoning aid."

Marei shuddered. "Why do you think that?"

"The piper, Jynn, from the crossroads. A strange being, but powerful. He closed the portals after the Emerald Queen destroyed that other castle." Garland shook his head as though forcing those memories away. He held up a hand, noting her blank expression. "I'm sorry, Marei, I'm bone weary. Suffice to say, I agree with you. This is the Hall's doing. Something's changed."

"What should we do?" She wiped sweat from her face. "We cannot hold this tavern like a fortress and wait for Shale to return. Or hope some decent fellows, or soldiers, drop by and help us. It's been quiet this week. I lied to Shale saying the rooms were full upstairs."

"I'll ride to the Hall in the morning," Garland said, and she felt a stab of cold in her belly.

"Please don't."

"Dafyd wasn't exaggerating," he told her. "Those brigands vanished like smoke. Either they were pulled back to *wherever*. Or—more likely—Graywash Hall has sucked them in. Either way, we need to know what is happening." She saw he was going to add more, but he stopped suddenly, his face blanching.

"What is it?" Marei followed Garland's gaze. Her jaw dropped open as a shape floated out from the fire. A man framed by mist stood before them, his features shifting like the fading flicker of smoke. Almost, he appeared as an etching carved out from the rock, hard to discern and vague with distance. The dark features were handsome, and a curved sword rested at his hip.

Marei stared at the figure in the fire. Clearer now. A fighting man garbed in gaudy colors, a red sash covering his head, the black smoky curls spilling over and around. He was standing with brawny arms folded, the hint of a grin on his handsome face, but she saw the haunted gleam in those nut-brown eyes. The stranger appeared to be moving up and down. Marei heard the sound of seabirds mewling and guessed he was on a ship.

Then the vision faded, the sailor vanishing and the smoke dissipating from the room like venting vapor, leaving no trace. The fresh draft sighed through the gap in the door as the wind cried louder from outside. Marei stared at Garland, whose face had paled to gray.

"That was Carlo Sarfe." He stood shakily, his eyes filled with dread.

"Who?" She'd scarce uttered the word before a loud rapping turned their heads to the door. Dafyd's eyes blinked open. He yawned and reached for the bow.

"Please, help me. Dafyd!"

A woman's voice. *Rosey?*

"Stay back—it could be a trick." Garland unsheathed his sword and approached the door. "Who's out there?" he yelled angrily. Marei noted the sky had paled in the yard. Dawn must be close. At least the storm had passed.

"Let me in, Sir Garland!"

"Rosey!" Dafyd rushed to the door, and he and Garland removed the bars. The girl stood soaked and shivering outside. She'd been weeping, and her red-rimmed eyes were wide with desperation. Dafyd pulled her close in his strong arms. Desperate, she broke loose.

"Rosey, dearest. What's happened to you?" Marei stood with fists on hips.

"They took Dalreen, Marei," Rosey almost screamed the words out. "My poor Dally's gone!"

"The baby?" Garland glanced Marei's way and she nodded, biting her lip.

"Wait, *wait!* Poor child. Come in, you're soaked. Were they raiders, or from the Hall?" Marei asked, as Rosey slumped like a dead thing into her lover's arms. Dafyd glared at his mother, his eyes blazing with rage.

"They came to the village," Rosey sobbed. "Said they were from the Hall. A man with cold gray eyes like smoky glass, and three others. *Bastards.* One was wounded. They snatched Dally from my grasp. Glass Eyes told me he was going to feed her to the Kaa. And that it was all your fault, Marei."

"Fuck this," Dafyd thrust Rosey aside and vanished outside.

"Wait, boy—it's still dark," Garland yelled after him, as Marei comforted the wailing girl.

"We'll get her back," Marei told Rosey. "Sir Garland is an accomplished knight in his own land. And he alone has returned from the Hall. Be calm, Rosey. You must stay calm. We'll wake from this nightmare stronger if we keep our heads. *Yes?*"

Rosey nodded amid sobs. Marei glanced at the door. "Dafyd?"

"He's taken a bloody horse," Garland said, having just reappeared. "Best I follow, catch him up before the fool reaches the Hall."

"What about my daughter?" Rosey wept.

"I'll get the child back," Garland glared at Marei. "And your son too, if he's gone inside."

"We're coming with you," Marei said.

"No, *no!*" Garland held out his hands.

"They've got my granddaughter, and this girl's child," Marei yelled at him.

"I know I can survive inside that place, Marei. But only if I'm acting alone. I'll seek out Earle Graye—he helped me before."

Marei gripped his hand and let go, brushing tears from her eyes. Rosey was weeping again. "What are we to do while you're gone?"

"Go to the city."

"I'll not leave my tavern."

"Go to the city, Marei. Take Rosey, and seek a miller called Randle."

"*What ...?* Who?"

"Randle's not who he appears and will help if you mention my name. Promise me you'll leave." She nodded after a moment. Garland left them without further word, heading for the stables.

"Wait!" Marei rushed after him and caught his arm before he vaulted into the saddle.

He turned and stared at her. "I love you," Marei told him.

"I know," Garland stroked her face with a gloved hand. "I'll find your rash boy and the wee bairn, lass. That I promise."

"I know you will—you're the best of men."

"And it's *best* that you leave within the hour," he told her, urging the beast forward toward the lane.

"Just you be careful, Sir Garland!" Marei called out to him. Garland waved and heeled his horse canter out toward the road threading the ten twisting miles north to the sea, and Graywash Hall, and Rosey's village beyond.

Marei returned to the tavern and found Rosey staring at her, dry eyed and resolute. "We have to leave here," Marei told her. The girl nodded grimly, and Marei went to prepare some fare and fuel for a three-day ride. Like Graywash Hall, there were rumors surrounding the city. Few of them were good.

2

THE ARABELLA

GET OUT OF MY HEAD, damn you...

Carlo Sarfe rolled free from the bunk and struck his head. He cursed and got to his knees slowly, his head thudding and eyes moist.

The dreams were getting worse.

Carlo slowed his breath, gripped the hammock stay and rose to his feet, feeling giddy, and a little sick. Through the porthole, he saw the roll of wave meeting sky, as the *Arabella* rose and fell, over and amidst the wide blue waters of the Great Murmuring.

He was used to dreams, especially after the events of the previous month. But this nightmare had been new. Vivid and savage, a blur of faces and screams. A series of fathomless scenes, morphing together into one congealed horror. In the last instant he'd been standing on a rock with a cold, different sea washing his boots. There had been a square, black, oily castle on an empty hill. A terrible place. He shuddered.

Castle ...? More like an entity.

A living thing, the wet stones breathing, and a billion

baleful eyes gazing down upon his shipwrecked body. The glistening, squat tower had pulsed with black lights. Its foundations clawed at the rock supporting the wet, glistening walls. The nearest tower had risen toward him, sucking him closer. To death, or something worse.

The fierce woman had saved him. She with the fiery hair and tiger-crazy eyes.

Damn these fucking dreams …

Carlo reached for his decanter and poured shakily, allowing the strong brandy settle his nerves and steady his grasp. Nourished, he left the cabin and made his way up the rope ladder to the blue, bright warmth of that summer's afternoon.

Gold Tar grinned at him. "Skipper, you look like shit."

Carlo ignored the skinny bosun and pushed past toward the stern castle, where Dry Gurdey worked the wheel. Gurdey saw his approach and nodded.

"We'll moor by dark, skip," the wheelmaster told him.

"Good," Carlo grunted. "I'm ready for some fresh grog. Tai Pei says the Shen brew a hearty rice wine."

Gurdey didn't respond. "Hmm," Carlo muttered to himself as he gazed at the line of cliffs flanking the south. A week at sea, gliding through soft rolling seas amid summer-hazy days. Seabirds and porpoise—perfect weather. So different than the week before. He closed his eyes, not ready to think about that. The Castle of Lights. The witches. The Goddess and Her bow. And lovely Teret of the Rorshai …

Enough.

Someone shouted, and Carlo turned his head. He winced, spotting the shaggy-haired Tseole clamber on deck amid customary expletives. Carlo wasn't in the mood for Stogi. The Tseole brigand hadn't adjusted well to life onboard the ship.

Stogi had been green for the first three days, despite the clement weather. Almost funny, seeing that tough, scarred face so haggard and pale. Carlo liked Stogi, despite him being both rogue and killer. But today he could do without the conversation that would surely follow.

Then there was the other *passenger*. The Shen wild-cat called Tai Pei. That one hardly spoke at all, but when she did the tone was cutting and razor-sharp. Stogi talked enough for both of them, even when he looked sickly. He was currently shouting, pointing at the shoreline.

Carlo turned and saw the white tower riding the edge of the bluffs. An ink-quill pillar of purest alabaster. It didn't look natural, and after his dream he wouldn't be surprised if the thing turned into a bird, raised its wings and screamed toward him.

The white tower remained put, rising needle-sharp as they clipped closer, the breeze kicking in as the shoreline swelled leeward.

"The Golden Ones built that tower."

Carlo turned sharply. Tai Pei was smiling. The sort of grin a woman wears before she stabs her husband for playing elsewhere.

"You mean the Aralais?" He'd hardly spoken with the girl and was startled by her silent approach. In a way she reminded him of Teret. That thought left him sad. Teret was gone. *Lost.* So much was lost. Tai Pei looked at him for a moment and raised a brow as Stogi joined them. To his right, Dry Gurdey spun the wheel, and Carlo heard Gold Tar yelling up at the boys in the yards.

"They're wizards, mostly," Stogi said, eyeing the shore as though he wanted to swim across. "They—"

"—he knows far more about the Golden Ones than you do, horse thief," Tai Pei said stiffly.

"I don't know that much," Carlo replied with a shrug. The girl looked at him sharply and gazed back across at the tower, already slipping to stern. "This Shen port of yours, how long?" he asked her.

"Three hours." She shrugged, too.

"She has to stay onboard," Stogi said. Carlo looked at him. "She's ... known to the officials of House Xuile. They'll want to question her." Tai Pei glared at Stogi for a moment before barking a laugh and wandering back toward the cabin shelter.

"Are all Shen like her?" Carlo asked the stocky Tseole

"She's the only one I know."

"Your lover?"

"I'm trying," Stogi crinkled his nose, making his earrings jingle.

"Tai Pei doesn't seem to like anyone on this ship."

"She's solid gold, just a little sharp around the edges," Stogi said.

"You haven't told me how you met her."

"In the mines. Northern Shen. Shithole." Stogi sighed. "Tai was a slave. She freed herself and joined us."

"Freed herself?"

"It's a long story." Stogi smiled. "As is yours, Carlo Sarfe."

"That it is," he said, as Gurdey spun the wheel again. "Do you have dreams, Stogi? I'm haunted by the fucking things. Distortions and twisted memories—because of the sorcery in that castle, I suspect."

Stogi looked serious. "I don't dream," he said. "But I remember each passing moment painfully. I miss that daft bugger, Tam. You traveled with his woman, I heard. Tam loved her so much."

"As did I," Carlo said quietly, and Stogi stared at him askance. "We were comrades," he added, feeling his face flush with the memories. He'd shared some sensitive hours with Teret of the Rorshai. Fate had brought them together, only to pull them apart most cruelly. Teret had died in that cursed Castle of Lights, back in Rundali. Those lights had all gone out for him. Carlo blamed her reckless husband, Lord Tamersane. The same sorry soul Stogi called his friend.

"What's the plan?" Stogi changed the subject, his shrewd black gaze noting the sorrow in Carlo's tone.

"We dock at Ta Shen, resupply and set sail. East."

"To Gol," Stogi smiled slightly.

"Eventually, yes. But it won't prove an easy voyage."

"Because Gol doesn't exist," Stogi said, grinning.

"It does. But in the past."

Stogi stared hard at him for a moment, and his grin faded. "You know, a month back I would have dived overboard hearing you say that. But today, I'm all right with it. Just another riddle along the way."

"You heard the piper, Jynn."

"I did."

"You know Gol can be reached."

"Perhaps."

"You and the girl could slip away at Ta Shen. We've garb that will hide her from prying eyes. If you stay onboard, you'll most probably die, both of you. We sail into the unknown, Stogi of Tseole. Not only unchartered seas, but different dimensions. Anything could happen. The pair of you would fare better in Shen."

"Let me tell you about her. She's from House Zayn."

"So …?

"Meaning she's proud."

"You said Tai Pei was a slave."

"Before that, she was a noble-born assassin from House Zayn. Feared by all, until the rival House Xuile conspired with the smaller houses and destroyed House Zayn in a night of knives and whispers. The girl's a … tad bitter."

It was Carlo's turn to laugh. "That's a shame."

"Maybe," Stogi said. "But she likes your ship, Carlo Sarfe, and means to stay. That means I'm staying, too."

"You're in love." Carlo smiled briefly, until he thought of Teret again and his face turned sour.

Stogi looked offended. "I'm a Tseole. We are warrior born."

EVENING FELL, AND THE HARBOR DRIFTED INTO VIEW. Carlo stood beside the wheelmaster as Gurdey guided the *Arabella* between the harbor arms, the lanterns flickering as they passed. Carlo saw men with odd-shaped helms leaning on heavy spears, the blades overly large and curved. He knew nothing of the Shen except Stogi's prattle about the mines. If they were all like Tai Pei, this business had better be concluded swiftly.

Truth was, he didn't want to stop here. He'd prefer making progress out into the open drink, confronting whatever he must. But he needed to adjust the ballast and make room for more supplies, perhaps purchase more sailcloth and ropes. The *Arabella* was tidy as any vessel he'd known, but that could change in the weeks ahead. Fortunately, there was plenty of coin left from the last trade before the shipwreck.

Carlo chuckled to himself. According to his crew, that disaster had never happened. He'd questioned Gold Tar and

Dry Gurdey in detail after rejoining the ship. Like a man waking from a drug-fueled dream, Carlo had walked from prow to stern castle, his hands sliding through ropes, his mind full of wonder.

He'd been shipwrecked and washed up on a foreign shore. Half-drowned. Not a dream. He'd felt that pain. Spewed out like shark bait on a cold, empty beach. Waking frozen and soaked, half-crazed in a different world with an orange sky, and no clue as to how he'd arrived.

Stop thinking about that.

Carlo shook his head angrily as they moored alongside a large Shen junk with dark red sails. He'd seen many such craft as they neared this city.

The harbor was quiet, and he heard distant bells chiming behind the larger walls that enclosed the main city, Ta Shen. Gold Tar ordered the men tie off. Carlo leapt onto the quay and walked toward two soldiers who were watching them warily, their faces squeezed inside those strange, pointed helmets. One of them shouted and hefted his heavy spear.

Carlo stopped, smiled and held his hands out. "We're here to trade, buy goods," he told them. The soldiers looked stiff and irritable. The one who shouted shook his head.

"This is irregular. Your vessel was not booked in."

"We are strangers here." Carlo hung on to his smile best he could. "I have gold coin, and my men are thirsty for ale."

"We will speak with the harbormaster. Wait here, foreigner." The largest of the two stamped his heels, muttered something to his comrade and started marching stiffly off to the distant cluster of buildings and low-sloping roofs. The other stood with spear held out, as if he expected Carlo to attack him with his bare hands.

"What's occurring?" Stogi emerged to his right. Carlo

swallowed a curse as he saw the soldier glaring at Stogi. "Did you have to appear right now?" Carlo hissed under his breath.

"Tseole dog." The soldier shook his spear again.

"Thanks, man," Stogi rubbed his earrings and grinned at Carlo.

"Where's Tai Pei?" Carlo hissed, barely controlling his anger.

"Asleep in your cabin."

"My—*my* cabin?" He didn't have time to ask further, as another shout announced the solder returning with a portly, pot-bellied red-faced official with three broad yellow stripes emblazoned across his tunic. He looked flustered and maybe a little drunk, as though he'd been enjoying his leisure and Carlo had spoiled his evening.

"That's a strange-looking ship," the harbormaster's dark eyes flashed angrily at the *Arabella*. "Three masts and triangular sails. Ungainly tub. I'm surprised it floats with those odd, square turrets and either end."

Carlo felt his mood darken. "She *floats* well."

The man ignored the glint in his eye. "Where are you from? I'll need a report. There will be dockets to sign, and you'll need to come with me. You are the captain?"

"I am. And this strange-looking ship is the *Arabella*, named after my sweet mother. She's sailed far across the world. She'd appreciate some courtesy."

"And I'm usually the discreet one," Stogi whispered beside him.

"Shut up, Tseole," Carlo said.

The harbormaster tugged at his long, wispy beard. Eventually, he nodded. "You are foreign. It's not surprising you've the manners of a goat herd. Why is this Tseole turd with you?"

"I found him along the way." Carlo tried again, forcing a

smile. "Look, *sir*. I'm sorry if I caused offence, but we've been at sea a fair while. My men could use some food and grog. I told your soldiers here that we have good coin to trade for supplies in your city."

"Ta Shen is out of bounds. No traders are allowed through our gates. Any bartering or deals must be conducted in the harbor with the proper officials."

"Fine. Can we at least eat? There must be a tavern in this harbor—it's almost a small town in itself."

"The taverns close at dark."

"It isn't dark yet. Perhaps if you put in a word?"

"Hmm." The fat man tugged his drooping moustache. "This is indeed irregular. But you have an honest face for a rogue, and I'm willing to make an exception. But it will cost you extra." He held out a hand and wiggled his fingers.

"My coin is still in my chest below decks," Carlo told the man.

"You had best retrieve it quickly if you want supper, or else stay onboard and chew your strip jerky and rotten fruit." He looked at the soldiers and they laughed, as though he'd said something amusing.

"I'll go get some coin from the hold," Gold Tar said dourly. Carlo hadn't noticed the bosun standing behind him. Dry Gurdey was there too.

They all stood staring at each other in awkward silence until Tar arrived back with a jingling sack of coin. He tossed it to Carlo, who removed three silver pennies and passed them over to the harbor captain. "What am I paying for, exactly? I don't usually part with coin unless there's something in return."

"Tariffs." The harbormaster smiled thinly. "Harbor taxes. I'll need more than that."

"Greedy bugger," Gold Tar muttered between the gap in his eye teeth. Carlo selected two more coins from the bag. He flicked them high, and the man caught them deftly with his gloved fingers. He bit down on one and stuffed the coins in his purse. He stroked his moustache and nodded ponderously, seeming pleased with himself.

"Barely sufficient, but I'm feeling generous. The Cherry Grove Inn will see to your needs." He barked at the soldiers, and the smaller one trotted off toward the buildings. "I must return to my ... hmm ... studies."

"Drinking and wenching, more like," Gold Tar murmured.

"You need to be back on that ship before the third gong strikes from the city," the harbormaster told Carlo. "Enjoy your supper, you and your men."

"Thanks," Carlo replied drily.

"That Tseole must stay here—his type are always trouble."

"What?" Stogi said. "I've never—"

"—we'll bring you something back," Carlo waved his hand hushing Stogi's protests.

A HALF-HOUR LATER, HE FELT BETTER. HE SAT IN A dockside inn, his men gathered close. More coin had got them several large jugs of strong, odd-tasting spiced wine with food on the way.

A strange tavern. The ceilings were low and crumpled, and square lanterns hung from tall poles in each corner. There was a small fountain trickling in the corner, a cream-colored orchid poking out the top, like someone had shoved it in there as an afterthought. The gurgling sound was distracting. Carlo dared not drink much, or else he'd be relieving himself in the gutter outside. These Shen might not like that. They didn't seem to like anything.

The proprietor was reed-thin and surly. Clearly he was not happy about this *irregular* arrangement. Carlo had paid him handsomely, emptying the coin sack. He told himself they wouldn't be needing more where they were headed, but loathed parting with it all the same.

The food arrived, spicy and very hot. He tucked in, Gold Tar and Dry Gurdey troughing beside him. His first mate, Slim Tareel, joined them after seeing to the vessel and choosing who should remain onboard with the Tseole and the Shen woman. The rest of his crew were seated on nearby tables, and the three nearest the fountain were yelling at each other. The food was excellent and worth the wait. Carlo found himself almost forgiving the pompous harbormaster. The proprietor brought more brimming jugs.

Carlo almost jumped when a distant clang and boom sounded from somewhere beyond the walls inside the main city. "Second gong," the tavernmaster smiled. "You'll need to drink quickly."

"How long have we got?"

"Not long." The tavernmaster grinned at him, and Carlo waved him away, irritated by his manner.

"What do you know about these Shen?" he asked Dry Gurdey, who had always been the best among his crew for gleaning information. A shrewd and affable listener, Gurdey seldom missed anything. Gold Tar was just as sharp, but his surly manner and temper kept him away from most negotiations and trading. Gurdey worked well as Carlo's second.

"Only what that horse thief Stogi told us," Gurdey said.

"And most of that's probably bullshit. I tried probing the girl, but gave up when she swore at me."

"Lucky she didn't stab you." Tareel winked. The first mate was the joker of the crew. Slim Tareel was easy company. Like Tar, he had a temper, but the mate was glib and quick with his tongue—though quicker yet with his jewel-hilted, curved dagger.

The men grew quiet, looking at Carlo as he finished his meal and pushed the plate aside, slurping more wine. He knew what they were thinking. They hadn't asked where he'd gone the days he'd been missing. Weeks for him, but they'd said days. And he hadn't added much after the initial ship-wreck conversation. Their expressions had warned him back, lest they deem him touched by madness. But he couldn't hold back much longer. Even Gold Tar had refrained from his usual sarcasm. Carlo owed them an explanation.

"We'll purchase what we can in the morning," Carlo told them. He flagged one of the crew, who was shouting and had obviously downed too much wine. Tar went over and punched the fellow to silence, or else the harbor guard would arrive and spoil their evening again.

Gold Tar returned, scowling, and slunk in his chair. He looked at Carlo with those gloomy, dark eyes. Dry Gurney coughed, and even Tareel looked serious.

"What's the matter?" Carlo glared at them.

"Captain," Gurdey said, using his formal title, which his three top men rarely did unless they were in trouble. "We're a touch confused." It was a ridiculous understatement. But where to start?

Carlo held up his hands. "I know, *I know*. You've been patient and, I'm grateful for that. But I can't convey what happened back there in plain words. It's too ... *strange* to relate. Imagine being inside a dream, only it's someone else's dream. A nightmare unraveling. If I recount all that occurred, you'll think I'm mad. Lost my wits entirely."

"We've always thought that, skip." Slim Tareel grinned, and the other two chuckled. Carlo smiled. He always let them tease him, but they knew when to draw the line. "But so are we," the mate added. "I mean, we crew sailed out with you, so we must be. Left Sarfania weeks, maybe months ago—hard to know for sure."

"I don't recall much about the departure," Carlo said. "My mind has clouded due to the confusion I endured in that … castle."

"That's the thing, skip." Dry Gurdey leaned forward, his voice hushed. "You've told us nothing except a mumble about being shipwrecked, and no explanation of why you brought those two strangers on board. The lads love you, skip—as do we. As Slim said, we volunteered for this venture. Have only ourselves to blame. Just tell us what has happened to you. You changed after we lost you in that last town when you went wandering off, as you do. Returning days later with dreamy, lovesick eyes and outlandish tales of shipwrecks and steel monsters. We thought you'd been on the poppy."

"Probably helped me if I had. What town was that?"

"Aye, see …" Gurdey looked at the other two. They nodded, eyes serious.

"Our last mooring three weeks ago," Slim Tareel said. "Can't remember the name. You joined us there with Stogi and the girl in tow, after disappearing in the streets for three long days."

"Longer. And that was no town, but a castle," Carlo said, wishing he hadn't as they stared at him unhappily. *Skipper's lost it.* Carlo saw it in their eyes. He sighed, not knowing what to say next that would help them believe he wasn't crazy. "We were—or rather, I was—shipwrecked off a foreign shore. I cannot recall how that happened, or what we were doing there. The *Arabella* broke apart on the rocks. I heard your screams but was washed ashore and tossed on that cold beach like flotsam. A grim place with copper skies. There were steel birds up there circling. Gwelan, she called it. The sorceress we encountered."

They were shaking their heads. Gold Tar was sneering and rolling his eyes. Gurdey and the mate chewed their beards. Happily, his crew were out of earshot, intent in their drinking.

Carlo held up his hands. "Listen, we were separated, I don't know how. And I was deceived, whether by false glamour or sorcery, that you and the ship were gone. Believe me when I say I witnessed the *Arabella* torn apart by storm. Do you think I'd dream up such a horror? I deemed you all gone, and me washed up half-drowned and witless."

Nobody spoke. As though sensing the mood, the crew all looked at him from the other tables, though he'd kept his voice to whispers and the chiming fountain drowned out their questions.

Gurdey coughed awkwardly. "Well, as you see, there was no shipwreck. You went into that town alone, against our advice. Like you were in a fucking trance, or some power was calling you from within those sandy walls. After an hour, me and Slim decided to look for you, but there was no sign, and the locals said they hadn't seen you. We waited. What else could we do? Two—no, *three* days. Finally, you arrived back with the strangers and ordered us set sail, as though nothing was awry. Announcing that we were returning home. What were we to think, captain?"

Carlo rubbed his eyes. "There was a woman."

"Teret." Gurdey smiled softly, and Carlo stared back at him in surprise.

"How do you know about her?"

"Your Tseole friend."

Damn Stogi and his cavern mouth. Carlo was about to explain more when the wicker doors burst open and heavily armed soldiers rushed in, their long-bladed spears leveled at him and his men. Carlo stood quickly and instinctively reached for his scimitar before holding his hands out in protestation. "What's the problem this time?"

The harbormaster strode into the tavern. He shouted at the proprietor, and that one made himself scarce. "Your Tseole friend has been caught fighting in The Dreamy Girl."

"What? Stogi's onboard ship—isn't he?" Carlo looked at Tareel.

"Was, when I left," the first mate said.

"Where is he?" Carlo squared up to the harbormaster, who stepped back slightly, noting the glint in his eye.

"Your companion is detained. We will be hanging him at first light."

"Wait, *no!*" Carlo shook his head. "This is a misunderstanding, sir. I can sort this out, even pay for his release. Let me go see him."

"Th executioner has already been notified." The harbormaster smirked slightly. "It's too late to cancel, I'm afraid." He rubbed his reedy whiskers.

A shout turned their heads. Carlo saw Pastele's face emerge between the Shen guards framing the entrance. The ship's carpenter was shouting, and the harbormaster nodded those men let him through.

Carlo found that he couldn't speak. Instead, he stared until Pastele stood over him sweating and panting. "You were meant to be watch leader," Gold Tar growled at the carpenter.

Pastele nodded. "I couldn't stop her, skip—none of us could."

"What?" Carlo demanded, as the harbormaster's eyes narrowed suspiciously.

"Tai Pei, the Shen girl … she …"

"Go on." Carlo felt his heart thudding like a hammer.

"There was fighting outside one of the taverns," Pastele explained. "Stogi had gone there saying he needed a quick drink and wouldn't be long. There were soldiers—I saw them hitting him. They were spiteful. Next thing, that girl's shot past us lads and runs at them guards, full tilt. She'd killed three, last I saw. I figured I'd best come find you, captain."

Carlo chewed his lip, his blood seething within. The tavern atmosphere bubbled like kettle approaching boil. Even the fountain had slowed to a trickle, as though dammed by mind mud.

The harbormaster's eyes bulged as though constipated or in pain. "Tai Pei? That cursed assassin is here …?" He looked at his men, their hands tensing on those odd-shaped spears. "You people are spies for House Zayn! I should have guessed that immediately." He'd turned beetroot-red and could hardly squeeze the words out. "Kill these pirates!" he yelled at his soldiers and they raised their spears to stab. The harbormaster rounded on Carlo, reaching for his skinny blade. Carlo got there first, his scimitar sliding out from the scabbard and slicing the fat man's throat wide open.

"I'd guess that means we're leaving," Slim Tareel said, reaching for his scimitar.

3

THE LOST QUEEN

QUEEN ARIANE of Kelwyn placed arrow on bowstring and pulled back with one fluid movement. The stag saw her and darted into the brush just as she loosed. The queen muttered a curse and urged her mare deeper into the forest. Her hunters were behind her, with evening falling fast.

A beautiful day in late summer, and she was taking her leisure the way she liked best. Far from the courtroom and their miserable faces. Like her lamented father, Ariane loved the hunt. It mattered not whether the beasts escaped. Sometimes she preferred it when they did, admiring their quickness and survival instinct.

Truth was, she envied those animals. They didn't have to think. That deer, like all the others, lived and would die without any thought to future or past. A life spent in the moment. Flight and food. Mating and breeding. Then, one day, the wolf or sickness. Maybe an arrow taking everything away. Simple.

She rode closer to a knot of pale ash trees. The ground had steepened around her. The foothills rose like gnarled knuckles, up toward the glassy heights they called The High Wall, glinting through the trees to her east. In the other direction, a blue gleam announced Lake Wynais a dozen miles distant.

A noise behind her. Ariane waited as Fassyan, her head huntsman, joined her, passing across the flask for her to drink.

She smiled thanks and took a long sip, allowing the to brandy swill. She never used to partake, but anything helped to relieve the boredom these days. She grinned at Fassyan. "I almost got him."

"That I do not doubt, my queen—superb huntress that you are. Where is the animal now?"

"Gone." Ariane shrugged and passed the brandy back. "As we must—though I'd sooner stay. Lord Calprissa wouldn't be happy were we to linger in these woods." She knew that there were whispers concerning her times spent hunting with Fassyan. Lord Raule had grown cold and distant of late. Her fault, but there it was.

They rode back through the trees, joining her party of hunters, beaters and houndmasters with their long spears, whistles and horns. The troop returned to the city through the back gates as the sun set like spilled blood over Lake Wynais.

Lord Calprissa was in his study reading scrolls when she returned to the palace conservatory, taking a moment to enjoy the stunning views over mountains and lake. Seeing her, he rose and placed the parchment aside.

"Ariane, you've been gone all day." His face was stern, unsmiling. But Raule rarely smiled these days.

She shrugged. "I need a hot bath," she told him. "My body aches far more than it used to."

"You are yet young," he said, trying. *Poor thing.*

"And you look tired, my lord," Ariane told him. "Does your knee trouble you?"

"No more than usual," he replied. "It's mostly because I'm worried about you."

Not this again. She stared at him and raised a wry brow. "Why?"

"Ariane, there is talk. Mostly idle whispers, but still. You are spending too much time on these outings."

"We are queen and shall do as we please."

"The hunt is perilous. Do you forget how your father died?"

"You are saying that to me?" Ariane lashed out in sudden rage, striking him a blow with her fist, knocking her consort off balance. "My father was murdered, Raule!" She struck him again, until he backed away with hands raised in supplication. "How dare you mention King Nogel!"

Raule stood his ground by the doorway, arms folded. Not defeated, but resigned. She let her anger vent as her breathing slowed. He had that mournful old dog look, and she felt a sudden shift of mood. "I'm sorry Raule, I really am. But ours has not been a normal life, has it? I find courtly routine and monotony brings back the memories. The *darkness*," she added quietly. "The escape of hunting and riding takes me back to those earlier times."

He nodded but still looked unhappy.

Ariane reached up and brushed a hair back from his rouged cheeks with a wet finger. "I shouldn't have struck you, my dear. I'm sorry."

"It doesn't matter," he said. "I was thoughtless and over-hasty. But that was only because I've been so concerned about you."

"I am not flirting with Fassyan," she said quietly. "He's raffish, I'll grant you that. But you have nothing to worry about there, my lord. Or anywhere else."

His face was indignant. "I never once thought—"

"—but others clearly do."

"Yes, I believe so. There is idle chatter among your courtesans. Some of the palace guard, too."

"Nothing new there," Ariane chuckled. "And those palace guardsmen are worse than my girls with their tongues wagging. Let it be, Raule. You look exhausted, my love. We'll talk more on this in the morning. I need that bath and some warm wine to ease my bones and soothe my soul."

"You were never a drinker until recently."

She felt a flash of annoyance. He was always so critical.

"Stop judging me, husband. Else I grow vexed a second time in one evening."

"As you wish, Ariane. I'll bid you goodnight." He bowed stiffly and left her to summon the chamber girls.

Ariane stripped and studied her body in the mirror, as she allowed the girls fuss around her and fill the bath with steaming water.

I'm lean and bony. Small wonder Raule has scant interest. *And I've aged.* The face staring back at her was sharp, lined, the cheekbones showing, and her dark eyes were shadowed with dull rings. The neatly bobbed black hair showed fresh streaks of gray.

You look worn out, Ariane of the Swords. A dry, spent stick. What happened to your fire? She waved the girls away and stepped into the bath. The hot water soaked her nicely, while Clarry brought the wine.

"How old am I, Clarry?" she asked the girl.

"My queen, I dare not presume."

"Go on, have a guess. Indulge me."

The girl looked unhappy. "You're very young looking, highness, but ... perhaps *forty*."

Yes, I do resemble that age, Ariane smiled wryly. She was thirty-three. That war had taken its toll. Clarry wouldn't remember much. The girl was perhaps sixteen and would have been far too young to comprehend the enormity of the events eight years ago. Nor would her parents or elders have mentioned it, except maybe as a warning of how lucky she was.

But Ariane remembered. All too well, she remembered. Thought about it every cursed day. Why wouldn't she?

The *Happening*.

That's what they called it in Wynais. The dire event that had changed her life. Everybody's life. Yet hers more than most. A peasant or tradesman could still visit the tavern and conduct his days much as he had before that calamity. But she had to govern and counsel and listen to foolish idle chatter in a realm that the gods had deserted—in a city and land whose brave heart had been torn open and tossed to the winds.

Tosh … this won't do, Queen Ariane.

Bored with the bathing and cross with herself for moping on things that couldn't be changed, the queen stood dripping and dressed herself quickly, not wanting the girls around. Ariane chose her favorite blue silk gown, the one Tamersane had brought back from the east a few years ago. She strolled out to the balcony, allowing the late summer breeze tingle up the tiny hairs on her thighs. Ariane smiled at the sensation, pushing the other thoughts away. She'd brought the wine with her and sipped slowly, allowing her mind go whither it would, and her worries eased back gently.

A quiet tapping at the chamber door inside. She turned her head hearing soft footsteps. Geyla, her head courtesan, stood hovering awkwardly. They knew not to disturb the queen when she was on the balcony alone.

"Well ...?"

Ariane gazed coolly at the tall Raleenian beauty. Geyda was the prettiest of her girls. More importantly, she was both calm and wise, only a year or so younger than the queen. She had that olive skin and large dark eyes so common in Raleen. Her looks had reminded Ariane of Silon's wild daughter, who she'd met several years ago. But that was the only thing they had in common. Nalissa had been a firebrand in her earlier days and caused her father a deal of bother. Ariane had liked her, though, as she did this girl—a distant cousin, Silon had said.

She missed the merchant and former master spy. And dear old Galed, who'd retired to the sea near Kador because the climate there eased his consumption. But mostly she missed Tamersane. That loss was an ache in her heart that wouldn't budge. At least he was at peace—that much she knew, having seen him in the Dreaming, with that Rorshai girl he loved so much. *They have moved on, leaving me alone.*

Ariane brushed the irksome thoughts aside and looked at the girl. "Go on, Geyda. What's wrong?"

"A man is come, highness. From the north, by his accent."

Ariane felt a quiver of excitement. *From Kelthaine? How intriguing?*

"Who?" she asked.

"Does the name Cale mean anything these days?" The gruff voice came from the door at the chamber.

Geyda looked anxious. "I told him to ..." She stopped when Ariane stood and clapped her hands in joy as a familiar face peeped around the corner.

"Cale the guttersnipe! It's been a long time. You are much changed, sir!"

"And you radiant as ever, my queen."

"Leave us, Geyda, and return with more wine." The girl vanished swiftly, after awarding the freckly face an outraged glare.

"That one doesn't like me." The young man strolled out onto her balcony, as though he belonged there. "I've missed this place."

"Why are you here?" she asked. "I mean, obviously it's good to see you. But ... it's no longer safe on the roads, they tell me. And the mountains are worse."

"True enough, and I rode in some haste. From the front. Point Leeth, to be precise. I'm second in command of the garrison there."

"Congratulations on your promotion. From former thief to battle commander—you've done well." She smiled. "How goes the war up there?" She studied his features. The cock-sure lad was still there, but mostly he resembled a fighting man— strong and sharp. He would be twenty-two, perhaps? His hair was as wild, curly and ginger as she recalled. He had a new scar under his lip and a short, ruddy beard. The eyes were the same insolent blue beads she'd known so well.

"It continues to occupy us most days," Cale told her. He took a seat beside Ariane. Geyda returned with a pitcher of wine. "Thanks." He winked up at her as the girl poured.

"We'll need brandy, too," Ariane told her. "And you'd best fetch Lord Calprissa, Gey. Though it's a shame to bother him at this late hour. Go on, off you go." She flicked her fingers and Geyda vanished, after awarding Sir Cale a sharp glance that made him chuckle.

Ariane turned to study her former squire, while coolly sipping her wine.

"You're drinking?" Cale raised a quizzical brow.

"It appears so." She smiled, and he nodded showing his

customary gap-toothed grin. "Why have you risked the long ride to Wynais? Are you not needed at Point Keep?"

"Indeed I am, highness. But this news couldn't wait."

"Do you not have couriers and fast riders?"

"Many. We decided it had to be someone you knew, from … *before*." He shrugged, awkwardly.

Ariane nodded. "I understand." A silence followed as she looked at him. They waited for Raule to appear, talking lightly of this and that. "Are you still with Sorrel?"

"No, she left me for another."

"I'm sorry."

"Nah, my fault. Drinking too much, couldn't perform at night. She went off with a harper. To Kador, I think."

"You have someone now?"

"I've several female acquaintances, though none are as pretty as your servant." She raised a brow, half-smiled and he shifted in his chair. "I'm a fighting man, highness."

"That you are."

Raule arrived looking disheveled, angry and tired, his eyes more concerned than before. He almost jumped in disbelief seeing Cale's freckled face. "You?" He turned to Ariane. "Squire Cale, if my eyes don't deceive me."

"Deputy Commander Cale, and it's good to see you too, General Tarello." Cale grinned at her consort.

"Nobody calls me that these days," Raule said. "I'm Lord Calprissa in this city. Raule, if you must. What's this about, Ariane?"

"I'm hoping that we'll know soon enough." She flashed Cale a grin, and he nodded.

"Word has reached the High King that the enemy are preparing a new offensive," Cale told them. "Our spies and the Rorshai scouts on the steppes say the Ptarnian generals have been whipped into frenzy by their mad emperor god. Callanz has promised his officers immortality if they succeed where the previous ones failed. We fear more will come this time than ever before."

"What has that to do with Wynais?"

"The High Queen …" He looked sheepish.

Ariane tensed. "Is my cousin unwell?"

"Queen Shallan fares well enough, highness. But she has been having visions of late."

"Shallan has the Dreaming, like you?" Raule cut in.

Ariane shook her head. "No. Queen Shallan has other … *gifts*." She turned to Cale. "Tell me about these visions. What concern are they for us in the south?"

"The High Queen has dreamed of the Oracle in the wood. The place where we—"

"—what did Shallan see there, Cale?" Ariane cut in, her face flushed and hair tingling, as though charged with electricity. It had started at the Oracle, after her father's death. That's where she'd first met the future High King. And where Caswallon's vile Groil creatures had found her. That seemed like a lifetime ago. Nine years, no more.

"A darkness," Cale shrugged. "What she said. Like creeping mold or fungus. A reaching of tainted fingers out from the well. Her words, highness, not mine. In her visions, the old Faen, Cornelius Zawn, told her that the Emerald Queen faces a new threat from another dimension. An ancient evil that the mad emperor Callanz has somehow tapped into, thus his power grows daily. Zawn told her that Laras Lassladen itself is no longer invulnerable. It's sacred towers are under attack by an alien force guised in the shape of a black castle, she said. It seeps out into the void, stealing souls. Queen Shallan believes the 'castle' a living entity."

"A castle?" Lord Raule looked at Ariane, who shrugged.

"Apparently," Cale nodded. "And ultimately evil. In the dreams, Zawn told her that the Goddess fears this canker is the stain from the Shadowman's dying breath. In her dreams, the dark place is called Graywash Hall."

Ariane felt a shudder at that name. Had she heard it before? If so, where? And why wouldn't the Goddess reach out to her? *I'm the one with the Dreaming. Why Shallan?* The old rivalry flared up again. She placed it aside. Not important.

"What else does the Cornelius Zawn say in these visions?"

"The Faen mentions you, Queen Ariane. He says that Elanion is too far away to reach you, as she once did. And that this … *blight* or stain is sapping her strength. Even as it swells that of our enemies, the Ptarnians."

"This … castle. Graywash Hall?"

"Aye, the High Queen said it resembles a strong fortress, and like Laras Lassladen can cross through the dimensions, linking past to future. Time and space have no power over Graywash Hall. The Faen told her that too. In the dreams …" He looked at her, eyes level. "I don't know, highness. Beyond my ken, but methinks the Goddess needs your help."

A cough to her right. "Hold on, man. This is the Queen of Kelwyn you're addressing. Ariane has done more than enough for her Goddess, who until recently we had presumed deceased, or missing."

"Hush, Raule." Ariane held up a hand. "I shall journey to the Oracle, leaving tomorrow."

"Absurd." Lord Calprissa's voice was loud. "Your country needs you, Ariane."

"I'll not debate this, my lord. A message that comes from the High Queen herself and delivered by my most loyal servant from those tumultuous days has to be acted upon. There is no room for argument here." He made to speak, but she raised her hand again sharply. Lord Calprissa glared at Cale and chewed his moustache. Eventually, he strode off and stared out from the balcony. Cale looked at her.

Ariane uncorked the brandy bottle and spat the cork over the rail. "I'm ready for the journey," she said with a smile.

"I'll be coming with you."

"What about Point Keep?"

"I'm excused from duties there, at least until the next invasion is imminent. The Crystal King himself intervened on my part."

"Because Queen Shallan asked him to." Ariane smiled wryly. Cale shrugged. Raule was staring hard at her from the other end of the balcony. The queen sipped her brandy and ignored him. She knew what he was thinking.

You are just like your father. Reckless and headstrong.

And he would be right. But the Goddess had always spoken to Ariane. And if Elanion needed help, how could she stay put, despite any rational protestations from her consort?

"We cannot spare any soldiers," Raule said, changing tack.

"I journeyed there with only three men before," she said. "That worked out. So, I'll need two others—no more."

"No doubt Fassyan will be one of them," Lord Calprissa said. She noted the bitterness in his eyes and couldn't blame him. But this was bigger than both of them.

"Yes, I deem that prudent with his woodcraft," she said. "Geyda, go notify my huntsmaster I'll need him ready for a long journey at sun up. And he'll need to source four good horses and a pack pony."

"What about the third man?" Cale asked.

"Go to the barracks and ask for Captain Doyle."

Cale raised a brow. "Isn't that the fellow they used to call Doodle?"

"Yes, and he's recently back from the east. Doyle should prove useful, if he's not a complete drunk these days. Goddess knows the poor fellow has cause enough."

"What happened out there?" Cale asked her.

"I sent six men led by Captain Garland east to find my cousin. Doyle alone returned."

"Is Tamersane …?"

"Yes …" Ariane felt a tear glisten at the corner of her eye.

Sad-faced, Cale turned away. "The Crystal King will be saddened, as am I. He was …"

"We all loved him, but he's gone, Cale. They're all gone."

"We're still here."

She flashed him a defiant smile. "Yes, Deputy Commander Cale, we are. And I, for one am ready for some action."

And so, it begins again …

4

NEW HORIZONS

STOGI FIDDLED with the gold hoop in his left ear and stared at a spider halfway up the cabin wall. The floor rocked as the swell increased, making his legs tremble and belly rumble. Beside him, Tai Pei wore a peeved expression, as though a foul smell lingered under her nose. Captain Carlo surveyed them with angry brown eyes, his fists on table and cheeks puffed out.

"I should hang you myself," he'd said when they'd entered his cabin. He'd backed down quickly enough after hearing Tai Pei's violent hiss. Stogi could see his point. They had messed things up back there.

"It wasn't my fault," he ventured lamely after long moments spent staring at the spider.

"Yes, it was," the girl said beside him. He appreciated the support.

"You're both to blame," Carlo snapped. "You, Stogi, for starting bloody trouble, and her for wiping out half the Ta Shen harbor police. No going back there. Why are you smiling, woman?"

"It was only five men. And they were slow. Clearly, I'm out of practice," Tai Pei said, as Stogi blinked beside her. The spider hadn't moved. He wished he could. He'd never seen Carlo so angry. The captain had always appeared dreamy and casual. Easy company. This was a new side.

"I acquired this Jian from the last one," Tai Pei widened her smile, showing off those neatly filed molars. She tapped the slim silver-hilted sword tugged in her belt. "He must have been high-ranked—it's good steel."

Carlo glanced down at the weapon and shook his head. Stogi shuffled and felt forlorn. The captain stared at them for long, uncomfortable moments. At last, he sighed and sat back in his chair. The sea washed hard against the porthole. Stogi felt queasy observing that water thrashing. He imagined a fish or some scaly-eyed beast gazing in at him.

"What am going to do with you two?"

Tai Pei looked bored, so Stogi stepped in. "We're happy to assist with whatever comes along. We have many skills."

"I'm not sure that I care for your assistance, Master Stogi. You disobeyed my orders."

"I'm Tseole—what did you expect? You're not *my* skipper, Captain Carlo. And we Tseole don't take well to authority."

"And yet, you are on my ship. And that means when I give an order, you obey it. Yes?"

Stogi blinked, and beside him Tai Pei burst out in a raucous giggle and covered her mouth. "You are funny," she said to the captain.

Carlo glared at her, his face reddening. Exasperated, he dismissed them both. "Go. *Fuck off.* Find something useful to do. Either that or hide."

They complied readily enough, the girl with a faint smile,

and Stogi nodding sagely. Carlo watched them leave and closed the cabin door.

Stogi followed the girl up the rope ladder. "Why did you laugh at him?" he said, trying to keep up with her.

"Because he's funny."

"You never laugh at me."

"You're not funny." She glanced at him sideways, a quirk on her lip.

"That's because I'm amorous toward you."

"Don't be ridiculous."

"You're my torturer," Stogi told her. "It's why I needed that drink. You didn't have to get involved. I had things covered."

"You were locked in that brick cell like a fat bug trapped inside a jar. If I hadn't persuaded those sorry fools to open the door, you'd still be there in the morning, when the hangman arrived."

"I was working something out," Stogi assured her, and the girl pulled a face.

"You would be dead, Tseole."

"Well, maybe. But that just proves why I need you around. To look after me, see that I don't fuck up again."

"I've already said you're not funny."

"And I've explained that it's an affliction, and you're to blame."

"Silly man." She flashed him a grin and commenced pulling herself up the rigging above.

"Don't go up there, please, no ..." Stogi's stomach churned as the swell picked up again. He tried looking up, but that made things worse. She'd vaulted over the lookout platform they called the crow and was hanging upside down, supported by her legs.

"Follow me," she called down. "Perhaps I'll let you kiss me at the top."

"I can wait." Stogi staggered over to the larboard rail and spewed noisily. He could hear the girl's laughter blending with seabirds' cries. *Merciless bitch, so you are.*

The wind was getting stronger. Stogi gripped the rail in misery and noticed a pair of boots appear beside him. He squinted to his right. "I'm not well," he said. "Piss off."

"It helps to focus on the horizon," the voice replied with an irritating hint of humor accompanying the gruff tone.

"What?" Stogi squinted until his eyes hurt.

"Where sea meets sky. Keep your gaze constant and your guts will settle."

Stogi did as was suggested, and after several minutes felt a slight improvement. "I don't like this ship," he muttered.

"You shouldn't say that—she might be listening."

"It's a bloody ship. Wood and canvas, with no ears." Stogi slumped onto his rump and stared up at a gap-toothed, scruffy-looking sailor, a small diamond stud sparkling in his left ear. He vaguely recognized him as Slim Tareel, the first mate. The man was apparently a joker. Stogi had been tortured enough already by the girl.

Tareel grinned down at him. "She's the *Lady Arabella*, named after our illustrious captain's beautiful mother. Have a care when you mention her name."

Stogi mumbled something and lurched forward as his stomach churned again.

"It will pass in a few days."

"A … few … *days?*" Stogi groaned and wiped his mouth.

"Maybe three, if you're lucky. And there's no storm."

"Will there be a storm?"

"For certain, but perhaps not until the fourth day." The mate winked at him and made to walk away.

"*Wait!* Tareel, isn't it?"

"Call me Slim."

"Slim. That's nice. Well here's the thing, *Slim*. I'm sorry about the harbor affair, I really am. Got us in a fix and that wasn't helpful. Captain Carlo is upset."

"He'll get over it."

"He looked like he wanted to stab me with his desk knife."

"Don't fret about it."

"What do the men think?"

"Like me, that it was pretty amusing."

"You thought it was funny." Stogi craned his neck and squinted up at the grinning mate.

"Well, yes, until that girl started killing the daft buggers. Things turned a bit serious after that."

Stogi choked, lurched forward and spewed again.

"The horizon."

"I'm looking at the fucking horizon," he croaked, focused and glanced sideways when the lurching sickness abated. "What are you doing?" The mate had kneeled beside him, as though he wanted to share a secret.

"Thing is, Stogi, you can assist me and the lads."

"When I feel better."

"You can talk plenty between honks, old son. It's like this. We don't know bugger all about you, or that ..." his eyes flicked to the rigging above "... woman. And our captain—who I've known most my life—is a changed man. What the fuck happened to him? And how are you two involved?"

Stogi took some long slow breaths and gazed at the distant skyline. "I'm unclear about Carlo's story, but our paths crossed outside that creepy tower. I was trapped in dark corridors.

Horrible place, where I lost my friend Tam. The Jynn and the Emerald Queen—their fault." He gagged and gripped the rail. "Deities or demons. The whole disaster was caused by them. And Seek. That snide bugger was involved for sure."

The mate was staring at him intently. "Skipper described it as being inside someone else's nightmare. Were you there too?"

"Only at the end when I met the others, including your Carlo, and Jynn led us out to your ship like a herd of lost sheep. Lord Tam wanted to rescue lovely Teret from the twisted bastard who'd kidnaped her. We caught up with them all outside the Castle of Lights in Rundali. But I lost them soon after."

"That was the name!" Slim Tareel exclaimed happily. "*Rundali.* The town was called that—I remember now."

"It's a country, not a town." Stogi was feeling better. He risked a grin. "A weird fucking country, if you ask my opinion. Spiteful woods and dangerous jungle mountains to the north. Big cats. And that tower, or castle, where we boarded your ship was one of the queerest places I've encountered."

"There was no castle, Stogi. No tower. Just you and that pale-faced wench. And our captain, looking three years older than when he'd left only *three* days before. Into the town called Rundali."

Stogi barked a laugh. "Look, Slim. You have to take my word, and your skipper's. Things go awry when the bigger players interfere with our lives. That's what happened in the Castle of Lights."

"You mean the gods?" Slim Tareel's face turned serious. He rubbed his diamond stud to ward of any bad fortune.

"Aye, maybe—it's hard to tell. Complex entities that treat the likes of you and me like fleas on a dog's back."

"You should have a care. Zansuat may be listening."

"That's the old name for the sea god, isn't it? They call that deity Sensuata here."

"Whatever they call Him doesn't much matter. It's wise not to bitch about the gods when He might hear you. Unless you want a storm to arrive."

Stogi grunted agreement. "All I can tell you is that we were all tangled up with three horrible women who messed with a lot of people's heads. Especially Lord Tam and his girl … your captain too."

"Teret died," Slim Tareel nodded. "I heard the captain mutter the girl's name, as though she was gone."

Stogi was going to respond, but a second, smaller pair of feet appeared alongside and he winced, seeing Tai Pei grinning down at him.

"You look like a lost puppy," she told him and shifted her gaze to the mate. Slim Tareel's face had paled. He didn't seem comfortable around the girl.

Stogi shifted and pulled himself up, not wanting to appear pathetic in front of the woman. He grinned at her. "This is my new friend Slim." Tareel nodded stiffly, and Tai Pei flashed him an amused glance.

"I'm impressed with your maritime skills," the first mate said to Tai Pei. She glared back at him until he dropped his gaze.

Tai Pei laughed. "You men, you're all so stupid. I'm off to see Captain Carlo. He at least is interesting company."

"I don't think that's a good idea," Stogi said, but she was already making for the cabin hatch.

"What's her problem?" Slim Tareel muttered.

"Lass has been through a lot," Stogi said. He looked at the horizon his queasiness returning. It was darker, and there were heavy clouds bunching. "That stuff about the gods. You don't think …"

"Aye." Slim Tareel glanced at the distant clouds. "Looks like a storm, after all. Cheer up, Stogi. Had to happen sooner or later." The mate slapped his back and left him glaring miserably at the distant storm clouds.

CARLO SIPPED THE BRANDY SLOWLY. IT WAS EARLY FOR grog, but his mind was troubled, and he missed Teret so much.

Stupid to fall in love with the woman, and her married too. But they'd shared so much in that short time together. She'd saved him from himself in that hut on the beach and enabled their escape from the steel-clad Grogan and his foul cage fires. That abomination had perished inside the Castle of Lights, along with Teret's enemy Sulo. But so had Teret and her damn fool husband.

A soft tap at the door. Carlo sighed, not in the mood for interruption.

"What is it?" He half-expected Slim Tareel or his other two officers, but the cabin door opened and Tai Pei stood there.

"You."

She smiled and walked in briskly without invitation. She grabbed the decanter and filled a glass as he watched, unable to find the words. She sipped, sniffed and then downed the contents in one gulp.

"That's good, captain." She smiled, placed the goblet down, and folded her arms.

Carlo rubbed his eyes. "What is it?" he said eventually, moving the brandy flask so she couldn't reach it.

"You're troubled and sad—I see that."

"I don't know what you're talking about." He waved a hand to dismiss her, but she stayed put. "I meant what I said earlier, Tai Pei. You and that Tseole horse thief are on sticky ground. What's to stop me ordering the men toss you overboard?"

Her smile faded, but her eyes remained calm.

"Please," Carlo said, finding this woman impossible to fathom. "I've much to contemplate, about our voyage and other things."

"I can help you with that."

"I don't think so."

"Oh, but I can, Captain Carlo."

He sighed. "Very well then, take a chair. Help me."

She flashed him that fierce smile, and her brow hinted at the brandy. He passed the bottle across, and she poured for both of them.

"Do you honestly expect to make it back to Gol? A voyage through time, as well as distance?"

"I have to try. As I said, you and Stogi should have left in Shen. Now you're as doomed as the rest of us."

"But you believe you can do it?"

"Yes. We sailed from there, so we can return."

"While the conjunction lasts."

"What do you know about that?"

"I'm from House Zayn."

"So?"

"We are the most enlightened family throughout Shen. It's why we are hated and the lesser houses betrayed us. During my childhood, I was taught many things, among them the arts of killing and astrology."

"Astrology? I don't know anything about that."

"Did they not have star readers in Gol?" she asked him. "I once read of an island ruled by sorcerers near there. The scrolls said it was destroyed by the same demon who took your land."

"What do you know about Gol?"

"That it sank millennia past but can be found again while the conjunction lasts."

"I heard something about that in the Castle of Lights."

She nodded. "That's because that shimmering tower was a manifestation of Laras Lassladen, much as Graywash Hall reflects its darker side."

Carlo felt a flash of memory. He sat on a rock, waves lapping his feet and a huge ugly black castle looming over him. A woman with strange eyes and hair the color of fire appeared. The image vanished, and he turned to gaze at the porthole.

"You're having visions," she said, her large dark eyes blazing into his.

He rounded on her. "I think you should leave, Tai Pei. I appreciate you're wanting to help, but I need peace and quiet to work things out." He motioned her to leave and shifted his gaze to the porthole again.

"Teret wasn't your woman. But I can be."

He turned sharply, but she'd already left the cabin like smoke fading in misty rain.

5

SIR VALEN THE GAUNT

As Garland had suspected, the Hall looked different this time. He'd ridden the coast road hard but seen no sign of Dafyd. The boy must be inside.

Too bad. He cursed himself for not acting quicker when Rosey appeared. He could try the village, but Garland deemed that a waste of time. The sooner he entered the Hall, the quicker he could save Dafyd and his baby daughter. They'd remember him in there, though some had doubtless departed since his first visit.

At that time, the place had resembled a grim, dark beast of a building squatting over a fast-flowing stream. This morning, Graywash Hall appeared as a pale fortress standing proud on a low, bare hill—a brave sight that he knew for an illusion. Ten lofty towers rose in neat squares above the walls, their crenulated caps adorned with bright, multi-striped banners and rippling gonfalons flashing yellow and purple in the sunshine. A wide portcullis yawned open at the far end of a thin, gray drawbridge. That rickety wooden structure spanned a misty gurgle of invisible water. Garland couldn't hear the sea, which was odd since he knew it was less than half a mile from the castle.

He rode closer, reining in sharply when a rider emerged like solidified vapor at the far end of the drawbridge. Garland watched as the hazy horseman urged his mount forward. The rider was clad from helmet to boots in highly polished armor. A visor masked his features, and a single scarlet plume lifted proudly from his helmet.

"You return to us as was expected, *Sir* Garland of Wynais." The voice was hollow and metallic. Garland wondered if a man was beneath that steel, or whether this was a sending from those inside. Much like the ghouls he'd encountered before.

"Who is it that addresses me?"

"Sir Valen the Gaunt," the rider said, urging his horse closer. Garland saw a lance appear from nowhere as the figure cleared the drawbridge. The rider leveled the lance at tilt and bid his horse trot.

Garland slid his broadsword free and waited as the rider reined in close, his long lance pointing down at Garland's face. "I could kill you easily," the hollow-voiced knight said.

"Then you had best stop boasting and try, before I hurl you into that moat. It's unlikely you'll float with all that metal."

An odd sound that could have been laughter echoed out from the visor. Done with this charade, Garland swung out with his heavy sword, meaning to shatter the lance but striking nothing but misty air. Sir Valen the Gaunt had vanished.

Damn you …

"I'll see you soon, brave knight." The hollow voice came from somewhere inside the walls.

Garland cursed and dismounted. "Ride back to the tavern, girl," he told the trembling mare. "You don't need to be a part of this madness." He slapped the horse's rump and walked purposely over the narrow wooden bridge that led across to the waiting portcullis without a backwards glance, his sword in both hands. He daren't avert his gaze, lest Sir Valen—or something else—rush out at him.

Halfway across, Garland glanced down and regretted it. He saw fleshy fingers writhing and reaching up from the gurgling, steaming, dark water far below. He clicked his tongue, stifling a shudder, and entered the castle walking fast as he could, passing warily under the portcullis and through a windy gate area.

Once through, a barbican closed around him in deep stony silence. He saw a well, racks of weapons gleaming on walls. A table with three empty chairs, as though the occupiers had had to leave in a hurry. There were dice on the table. A half-filled wine glass, but no bottle. He looked closer, and the dice turned into mice with men's faces that leered up at him. Garland shuddered as they sprouted frogs' legs and hopped from the table.

He glanced about, heavy sword held ready. The wind whipped his face like winter, and above the sky had darkened to inky blue. No one around.

Keep moving.

He walked over a mound of dead grass toward the large square keep tower that dominated the surroundings. That was the real hall, Garland knew. He saw the greenish-yellow aura seeping out from the gates and arrow slits, like a sickly vapor or poisonous gas. He also felt the weight of a million malevolent and curious eyes watching his approach. As if hearing his thoughts, the surrounding walls and towers and barbican all fizzed and faded, as though no longer required. All that remained was the grim keep looming ahead like a forbidding square finger of dark, gray rock.

Past that tower glinted a streak of water. Garland heard the surge of waves brushing the shore. The sound comforted him. It was real, beyond the confines of this place.

Garland approached the keep, the wind biting harder at his face. Off to his right, and high above, he saw a one-eyed owl perched silent and watching him approach from a crenulation. The lone eye probed inside his head. Garland ignored the bird and walked quicker. Beyond the owl, a tall, metallic figure stood on the keep parapet. His armor appeared darker this time, as the blue-gray clouds trawled the skies above. The knight stood in silence with lance raised in salute. Garland heard that strange laughter again, and Sir Valen the Gaunt vanished into the gloom for a second time.

"I would speak with Earle Graye," Garland called up to the keep. He saw yellow smoke drifting out from the murder holes and arrow slots, accompanied by a grating noise. The gate yawned open, venting a long, lazy sigh like a woman caught in rapture as yellow gas seethed out and vanished in the wind. An acrid smell stung his nostrils. Garland saw thin blue light within. It reminded him of the luminescent mildew he'd seen glowing in Rundal Woods—a place nearly as bad as this. He approached the gate, ignoring the fussing of urgent whispers.

Garland focused on his task and shut out their voices. They were testing him as they had before. He half-expected the knight to return and attack him, but his way forward wasn't checked. He reached the gate, took a deep breath and entered.

Stale blue light surrounded him, clawing at his cloak like

wet slippery fingers. Garland heard the gate thud shut behind. He stopped, gripped the sword warily, and circled slowly to make sure he was alone.

He stood in a courtyard, the sound of dripping water coming from a hidden corner. It was dark, the blue light having departed soon after he entered. He could see shapes, some of them moving. To Garland's eyes, they resembled fronds lifting up and reaching out, as though some huge man-eating plant was trying to trip him. He walked forward, and the walls closed in on him. There was ivy coating the stone. Garland watched as it unwrapped itself, twisted, and writhed toward him.

He swung the heavy blade, severing the vines. They hissed and drew back like a disturbed nest of serpents.

A door appeared from that gloom. As Garland approached, it creaked open. He took the hint and entered quickly as the vines and fronds mustered behind him, bunching and popping like bladder rack on a hot summer's day.

Inside, corridors led off in three directions—much like before, when he'd encountered the witch Cille. But she was dead, and Earle Graye had to be here somewhere.

A second door opened like an invitation, and he entered a smoky room. He half-recognized the lone desk at the far end, and the figure slumped over it, as though resting in fatigue.

"Earle Graye?"

No movement. Garland strode toward that prone shape. He saw crows hopping and jumping on the table. One pecked at the figure and snatched something in its beak. Garland noticed with horror that it was one of the man's eyes.

The crows hopped and flapped and squawked at him as

Garland hoisted his sword. They fluttered off to dark corners and glared back at him with beady red eyes.

"Stay away from me," Garland muttered as he gazed down at the corpse. A reedy, thin old man. Hardly recognizable. The body had shrunk into the clothes, and his face was blackened with mold, the cheeks sticking out and bleached skin stretched like ancient parchment. So much for Earle Graye. Garland sighed and lowered his sword. The crows watched him in silence. What now?

I need your help, Sir Garland.

He turned sharply. That voice belonged to a little girl. Garland shuddered. Another ghost, perhaps? There were rumored to be plenty here. He felt a tug at his cloak and looked down but saw nothing.

"Where are you, child?" he asked.

"*Here.* I'm waiting for you."

Garland turned about, sword ready. He paused, seeing the silhouette of a young girl grinning at him from the door he'd entered. "You need to follow me, Sir Knight. There's nothing but death in this room."

"First, tell me what's happened to Dafyd and his baby child. I know they're inside these walls."

"The Kaa has them, silly. You can't save *them*. Well … unless …" She giggled slightly. "Come on, Sir Garland. Wake up. Your challenger is looking for you. Sir Valen's artful and likes his games. He will trap you if he can. Best we move quickly."

"I don't fear that metal scum." Garland almost caught up with the girl as she vanished into the corridor beyond. He could barely make her out in the gloom.

"You should—but you'll learn that soon enough."

"Tell me where they are! I'm sure you must know."

She turned, placed a finger on her lips. "Tosh. Stop moaning. It's not safe to linger here. Follow me, and quickly."

Suspecting this to be another snare, Garland walked close behind the drifting shape of the girl, his broadsword resting easy in his gloves.

"At least tell me what your name is."

"You know it already."

She entered another doorway and beckoned him follow. Garland obliged with a scowl. He stopped in surprise at the sight ahead.

They stood on a broad verandah, the sun streaming down and a wide view of the gleaming ocean ahead. What madness was this? The sea looked warm and reminded him of Laregoza. A lure, no doubt. And there were palms swaying over golden sands. Garland rubbed his eyes. At least this was a pleasant illusion, unlike those he'd encountered with Cille.

"Where have you led me? And why?"

The girl laughed. "You're looking into the past, Sir Garland. This place no longer exists in your time."

He could see her clearly at last. She was pretty, perhaps nine years old. Her long blonde tresses were neatly braided, and her immaculate blue dress was spotless in the sunshine. Her beady blue eyes mocked him, as did that easy smile. There was something familiar about the child.

"We are standing on the Ledges," the girl told him. "From here, you can see into every corner of the nine worlds. You are fortunate. Very few mortals have stood here. Mother is most particular."

"Who are you, girl?"

"We can talk freely here, Sir Garland. Did you know you're a knight? Knights are special and revered in your Marei's dimension. But not in Gol."

"Gol?"

She shook her head. "We cannot linger. Sir Valen's henchman will be looking for us. Their leader, Shale, doesn't like you. Nowhere is safe from his crew."

Garland grunted. "So that villain Shale came from the Hall, as we feared." At least Marei was safe if those curs were after him. "He is in this Sir Valen's pay?"

The girl giggled, as though he'd said something amusing. "No, silly! Shale and his men are Sir Valen's slaves. He has their souls, and they must do as he bids. He saved them from the ax and noose, and he has promised them freedom if they succeed."

"Succeed in what?"

"Killing my Mother."

Garland rolled his eyes. He changed tack. "Tell me about this place. The Ledges, you called it. Where is that ocean down there? Don't tell me it's the same one as outside this castle—past or present. Graywash Hall clings to dark seas."

She looked at him and shook her head. She seemed bored, fidgety.

"Why have you brought me here?" Garland pressed to no avail. As he looked on, he saw specks in the distance. It was though he'd raised an invisible spyglass to his eyes. The dots drew nearer, becoming more defined, until he recognized them for islands. Two mountains rising from the ocean, perhaps a dozen miles apart.

They stood proud like stone ships, remote and tall in their lofty solitude. There were seabirds circling the crown of the nearest island. The farthest peak was smoking. He sensed a terrible power residing within. An alien heat seeping out from some deep cavern within.

Before Garland could enquire further, the scene shifted

and blurred. This time, he saw skinny ships ploughing at speed through dark, churning waves. Again, his vision brought the ships closer. The lean craft bore a single triangular sail the color of spilt blood. There were blue-faced men rowing at oars. Garland could discern their cruel tattoos covering cheeks and brow in dark spirals. He heard the cries of prisoners being lashed below the decks.

"Those are slavers," he spat.

"They are the Kaa. They have the child you seek."

"What of Dafyd?"

"Perhaps they have him too." The girl shrugged, as though that was irrelevant. She cocked her head hearing something. "Best you get after them, Sir Garland, while you still can."

"How? Where?"

"Down there, silly. The Ledges will lead you to the beach. You'll find a boat that will carry you across to the Alchemist's Isle, providing you can pay the ferryman's toll."

"Where? What about those slavers?"

"That's the nearest island you saw," she replied, ignoring his question. "Best you avoid the smoking one. Once you reach Alchemist's Isle, you can seek news of the emerald bow."

"Kerasheva? The Goddess has that."

"It was stolen from her."

"How?"

"You must find Kerasheva, or Dafyd and his baby are lost. And you have to find it before Carlo Sarfe."

"Sarfe? But how do I get there?"

"Time will tell …"

The girl giggled and clapped her hands three times. She vanished, as did the hall. He stood on the Ledges, a warm breeze lifting his hair

"I like you, Sir Garland," her voice called out from

behind. "Brave knight, you are. You're not as funny as Corin, but it's early days. Go quickly, you must. Sir Valen hunts! The faceless knight and his men are scouring the corridors with death hounds. They will scent you out if you linger. Go! Take the boat. I cannot help you more than that—my Mother needs me."

Garland stared at the spot where he'd last seen her. What to do? Had she been part of the illusion caused by the Hall? He didn't think so. Was he still inside?

No. I'm somewhere else.

Whoever that girl had been—and she was familiar—she wasn't from the Hall. Suddenly, a thought grabbed him.

Corin.

She'd mentioned the High King's name. What he was called before he became the Crystal King. *Who was she?*

The distant sound of baying hounds and blast of horns snapped his thoughts away. The girl had spoken truthfully about that much. Someone was hunting, and doubtless he was the quarry.

He sheathed his sword and walked over the edge of the flat rock, gazing down and feeling a lurching feeling in his belly. *I'm to climb down that?*

The drop was almost sheer. Perhaps three hundred feet, and every fifty feet a ledge thrust out, each one more prominent than the last.

It was desperate—it'd be suicide clambering down there. He gazed about as panic seized him. Howls and horns were much closer. He could see things moving in the hazy dark beyond the ledges—the place he must have left to get here from the Hall.

He walked the length of the rock, seeing nothing but a sheer drop down to the next ledge. The howls were accompanied by shouts. He turned and saw a rider canter onto the ledge. Valen the Gaunt blew three notes on his metal horn, and a dozen huge white dogs emerged from the gloom.

Garland couldn't kill all of them. Better to fall than be torn apart. He ran to the edge and glimpsed something out of the corner of his eye.

A rope?

He blinked to make sure, and grinned in relief. A thin, shabby cord dropped from the corner of the ledge down to the next one.

Garland didn't hesitate. He sheathed the sword, sprinted over, and jumped, catching the rope, even as the nearest hound leaped after him. That dog fell barking. Garland saw its body tumble and snap open on the ledge below. The other hounds snarled and yapped above as he worked his way down the rope, hand over hand, fingers slippery with sweat.

Looking up, he saw Sir Valen the Gaunt's steel vizor gazing down at him. The knight vanished, and the sounds of dogs and horns trailed off.

Garland dropped onto the next ledge. He saw the broken body of the hound. As he stood shaking, getting his breath back, the beast decomposed and crumpled into yellow smoke before his eyes. He looked up but saw nothing but clear sky and the shadow of the ledge above.

He made for the edge again, spotted a second rope descending down to the next ledge. Garland grabbed it and lowered himself the fifty feet or more before he jumped onto the third ledge. This one was bigger. A great, flat slab awarding wider views of the seascape beyond. At its far end, a stream cut through, spilling from above. Garland walked that way and reached down, cupping the cold clear water in his hands and drinking deeply.

Exhausted but refreshed, he rested for a time before finding the next rope and climbing down to the fourth ledge. Once there, he stared out. The beach was close. A hundred yards below. The surge and sigh of gentle waves blended with the palms. It was hot, and he wiped sweat from his brow. He saw large white pelicans winging low above the surf, a long column that faded northwards. Again, the sight reminded him of Laregoza.

The sun was lower—it must be late afternoon. He could see the islands clearly, the higher smoke-wracked one half hidden by its twin. Garland rubbed his tired, sweaty face and looked out at the horizon. What a fool he'd been to think this was over—that he could settle happily with Marei and shut out all the horror.

He laughed softly. Was it his fate to go mad? Chased by spirits or demons, or rogue knights? And now impish girls too? Driven mad, until at last he was caught and slain?

Fuck that.

Annoyed, he pushed such useless thoughts aside. This wasn't about him. There was a child to save, and Marei's brave young son.

But what to do? The answer was simple. Keep moving— don't overthink. It had worked for him during those earlier trials. He'd survived red Cille and the spirits of Rundal Wood. He'd walked unscathed from the portal he'd jumped through, after leaving the Castle of Lights. He'd fought the basilisk and survived that encounter. It wasn't his destiny to fail. Garland knew he still had a part to play.

That joker child knew his value. Who was her mother? Garland guessed that he knew that answer. Kerasheva, the same emerald bow Teret had used to slay the basilisk, had been stolen. But how? Didn't matter. He was needed again.

And Carlo Sarfe. Why was he involved? He'd known the man so briefly in that cavern but had liked him. Now he had to stop Sarfe from finding the bow? Didn't make sense. *Keep moving, stop pondering. Actions lead to discovery. To dither is to perish.* He said the words over and over until his mind settled. He found the rope and descended, quicker than before, and hardly stopped at the lowest ledge before resuming and half-sliding down the last rope to the beach. He landed with a thud in soft, dry sand. The palms waved at him. Beyond the sea, the sun fell crimson.

He walked the dunes, seeing the skiff beached dry under the shade of palm trees. He approached and looked down, spotting two oars, a bundled sail with dismantled mast, and a small, round object that he guessed must be a lodestone for navigation. Looking closer, there was something else. A parchment, crumpled and stained. A map!

Garland scooped up the chart in his hands and studied the contents. It looked ancient, and the text was faded and blurred. He looked for Laregoza, Rundali, and next for Port Wind and the Kelthaine coast. He recognized nothing. He was about to place the chart back in the skiff when he noticed a faint line tracing a coastline at the corner of the map. A town was marked there, surrounded by what appeared to be swampland.

Reveal harbor. He could just make out the words. Garland searched his memory. He'd never been one for history but knew that Kael, the first ruler of Raleen, had come from a swampland called Sarfania in Gol. The main city of that land was hidden in marshes. Reveal had been its name. Carlo Sarfe had sailed from Reveal. Perhaps this chart was his?

He looked up. The long, eerie note of a harp drifted

through the palms. Garland felt a shiver. He knew he was being watched. With a curse, he pushed the skiff down toward the waves and clambered aboard once the vessel was afloat. He grabbed an oar in each hand and rowed out into the deepening blue of the evening water.

The islands had vanished below the horizon. He'd need to study that lodestone and struggle with the sail. *I'm not a bloody sailor.* Time, he learned. And how about a plan?

Survive, follow the clues. Find the bow and save the child.

How?

No fucking idea.

Garland laughed at the absurdity of his situation as he rowed toward the setting sun. Before light faded, he'd stowed the oars and erected the mast, catching what breeze he could with the sail. Next, it was time to study the lodestone, else he washed up somewhere even farther from his destination. The place she'd called Alchemist's Isle.

Marei draped the cloak around her shoulders to keep out the mountain chill. They'd been climbing all day, the two donkeys weighed down with food and vittals. Rosey was sleeping, hunched on the third beast. The girl had succumbed to exhaustion and despair.

Marei determined she'd not fall prey to either. Her face grim, she struggled to light a small fire that night in a fold of woodland to keep out the worst of the cold. She'd never been this far south into the mountains. As Rosey sat hunched, Marei warmed the broth and they sipped quietly from the bowls she'd brought. Beasts howled somewhere close.

She had the crossbow and a dozen quarrels—her knife,

too. No beast would trouble them tonight. She thought of her tavern and home where she and her long-dead husband had built their life together. She'd lost him during a winter storm, and now Garland and her son were gone, too.

As the girl slept beside her, Marei watched the flames crackle and felt the trace of a tear wet her cheeks. She snatched what sleep she could. By dawn, they were ready to climb higher. Another long day should see them over the snow pass, and by night fall tomorrow they should reach the city. Once there, she would ask around for a miller called Randle.

6

ACROSS THE BORDER

ARIANE REINED IN ABRUPTLY, seeing the smoke-wracked sky ahead. It was late evening, and stars glinted through gaps in the clouds.

I'm back in Kelthaine.

She had vowed never to return. It felt strange—made her uneasy. She sniffed at the wind and waved her gloved hand, bidding her party ride on after their brief pause. She'd had scant time to gather her thoughts. But thinking seldom worked, as it brought everything back.

Darkness fell as they passed empty fields. The moon rolled from a horse-shaped cloud chariot. Her heart skipped a beat as the city slowly revealed itself as a twinkle of lights in the north. Her men sat their horses silently beside her. Cale alone looked content. Doyle was troubled, and her huntsman's eyes were grim. They cantered closer.

"Are you ready, gentlemen?"

Ariane flashed them a brave grin as the walls rose higher at their approach. She masked her emotions well, but all three could surely guess how this must feel for their queen. Eight years had passed since last she'd seen this city.

Kelthara.

Cale was born in the slums, she recalled. She'd refused to go north since, unless it was to Car Caranis, and that only in a crisis. There were too many memories here.

The Happening.

That was the name they gave to the day everything changed. The portentous event when the gods destroyed each other outside that city's walls.

And He came. The wicked one, clad in white. She saw her goddess fall. Doyle had witnessed it, too, as had Garland, her brave captain. Lost forever in the east lands. They had been saved, and the Enemy of the World broken. But Ariane knew part of her had died that day. She'd blocked Kelthara from her mind, telling herself it had been Wynais where that terrible event had happened. But she couldn't hide from the truth forever. Now she'd returned. A new game had started.

The Crystal King had rebuilt the city in defiance of the atrocity. But he had not been there that day—he'd joined them soon after, having won the war in the northlands, claiming his crystal crown and putting an end to evil. Or so they'd believed for a brief time.

"Ya!" She spurred her mare pick up pace. *Ride harder, don't dwell on the past.*

They approached the high walls, and clarion trumpets announced their arrival. A tall, mustached captain met them at the gates. He bowed low, and he politely bid the queen and her three men follow him to the palace at the north end of the city.

Ariane hardly recognized Kelthara. That made her feel better, dispersing some of her earlier dread. She noticed

Fassyan glancing around in wonder, and she recalled that he'd never spent much time in Wynais itself and had never ventured beyond their borders. A true countryman. Until today.

Cale was grinning and obviously approved of what the High King had done to his old home. He'd been a cutpurse sewer rat. Half-starved, but clever. A survivor who had charmed the queen into making him her squire.

Even Doyle seemed more relaxed, though his eyes were haunted by memories. Poor Doyle. She flashed him a smile as they were escorted through the palace doors. Doyle grinned back, which made him look younger. Doyle was much changed since his return. They'd found him in a tavern, as she'd expected. In sorry state, as was so often his wont. The newly promoted captain hadn't recovered from his ordeal in distant Laregoza. She knew he partly blamed himself for Garland's rash actions. He'd begged her to allow him to return, but she'd forbade it.

"Garland's fate, and that of his men, was my responsibility, Captain Doyle. Not yours," she'd told him. He'd joined them happily enough after sobering up but had proved a terse companion, despite Cale's easy banter that had clipped away the miles.

A week's ride. Now they were here. In Kelthara. Where her goddess, Elanion,

had been torn apart.

King Corin met them in person in the crystal throne room. The Tekara throbbed and pulsed where it rested on a table by the throne, both raised high on a dais. She knew he only wore the crown occasionally, lest the pulsating aura drain him.

He smiled warmly as they approached, her men bowing low, herself dipping her head slightly. *Almost we were lovers.* Had that really happened?

The High King bid servants bring them food and ale. He turned to her. He was clad in simple dark trousers, tunic and cloak. Knife at hip. A plain fighting man's garb.

"You look well, my queen." He smiled at her again, and Ariane noted how he'd aged. As though the responsibility of high kingship and war had stilled some of the fires she remembered so well.

"As do you, my lord."

"Thank you for coming." Corin looked briefly at Cale, who nodded and whispered to the others. The three made themselves scarce at the far end of the tables arranged for his warriors. There, they were brought flagons of ale and hot food. She saw Cale grinning at the girls who served them.

And now …

Ariane studied her overlord's face. The old scar above his brow made her smile. The long hair was graying and his face thinner, more lined than before. The wildness. She saw it lurking beneath those haunted blue-gray eyes. *We were so young!* She accepted a glass of wine from a servant and chuckled at his surprise.

"No tea?"

"I still drink it," Ariane told him. "But often prefer something stronger these days."

He accepted a glass and toasted her. "How fares Lord Calprissa?"

"Aging too fast. It's my fault—he worries about me."

"Hmm, that's understandable. Raule's a good man. It

took resolve, your coming here, Ariane. Believe me, I didn't want to involve you in this. You who have endured so much."

"No more than you, or the High Queen." Ariane looked around, as though half-expecting her cousin to appear, as radiant and dazzling as she remembered her. "We were all broken and rebuilt crooked by that war. Queen Shallan … is she …?"

"In Vangaris."

Ariane felt a guilty tingle of relief. "She is well I trust? The dreams …"

"Have troubled her deeply, yes." He rubbed the scar, a habit she remembered. A gift from his old Swordmaster. The man had attacked him during that first campaign in Permio. He'd killed him, and nearly hung for it. The start of a lusty career as a mercenary and reprobate. Until the war with Caswallon had brought them together, in the wood at the Oracle of Elanion. That place where she must return.

"How much do you know? Did Sir Cale explain everything?"

"Yes, and I was surprised that the Dreaming hadn't found me. That the Goddess, or someone, reached out to poor Shallan instead." She didn't add how resentful she'd felt. "Cale hinted at something about a new otherworldly threat, or the same evil returned in different guise. A castle, or hall—if that makes sense?" He nodded briefly, and she continued. "He said that the old Faen creature, Cornelius Zawn, came to her. The same being who died outside Grimhold Castle in Leeth. Her *father …*"

"I was there when Zawn died," Corin said softly. "A noble being. Like many now lost." He stared long and hard at Ariane. She matched his stare, studying his face again, feeling the old chemistry welling up inside her. At last, she averted her gaze.

We would have been bad for each other. I should be grateful to Shallan.

She wasn't.

Ariane had always loved this man, and nothing could change that. And he had loved her, too, when fate forced them together. The rogue and his feisty foul-mouthed queen. But gorgeous Shallan had drifted in like a dreamy butterfly and swept him away, in that gleaming white villa the merchant Silon once owned. *Memories.* She looked at him again, and he smiled awkwardly.

"I'm sorry, Ariane. I make for poor company these days. The war ..."

"The responsibilities make boors of us all," she replied and smiled back, sipping her wine. "I hate being a queen. I liked it better while we were fighting. When I could cuss and barrack like the men. Back when I was Ariane of the Swords. Governing from a courtroom is not my favorite pastime. I miss the action of the old days. I take after my father in that."

"You are not your father, Ariane. I met him once—did you know that?"

"I didn't—you never mentioned it."

"I deemed it unwise when first we met. Later, I forgot. He viewed me as a brigand, a troublemaker up from Raleen."

"Which you were." She grinned, feeling a lightening between them.

He smiled. "I miss those days, too."

"How are your daughters?"

"Trouble, mostly. But the brightest lights in my eyes." He sighed, looked at her again. "You don't have to get involved, Ariane. I'd sooner you didn't. Wynais is your domain. I wanted to impart the news and am happy that you've come. I need your counsel, you see. Nothing more. The Goddess ..." He shook his head.

"Is out there somewhere, and needs me. Her conduit."

"I always thought that was my role. The conduit—the Crystal King."

"You are tied here."

"As are you, in the south."

"No." She placed her glass down softly. "We have no children. Lord Raule and I ..." she shook her head. "Truth is, I want to help in whatever way I can. I *need* to. I sent my captain, Garland, with a troop east to find Tamersane—which was reckless. Doyle returned alone." She craned her neck toward where the three sat talking quietly. "I should have gone instead."

"And Tamersane and Teret? Was there any news from Caranaxis?"

"No. But he's gone, Corin. They both are. I know that now."

The High King nodded, his eyes filled with sorrow. Tamersane had been her favorite cousin, but he'd also been Corin's companion during the war in the desert, leading up to the time he'd met the Rorshai girl.

"They're together," she said. "I feel it, you know, like the Dreaming. Deep inside."

Again, he nodded but said nothing.

Neither of them spoke for several minutes. He glanced at Doyle dicing on the far table, his brows knotted as though trying to remember who the man was.

"So be it—you'll ride to the wood," he said eventually. "Enter it as we did before. No Groil this time, hopefully." He grinned.

"And no wild hero with the longsword to butcher them."

"Bleyne was the hero, as I recall."

"You both were."

Bleyne was the mysterious archer who'd joined them after destroying Caswallon's sendings. Gifted to them from the Goddess. He'd vanished after the war, as had his woman, the wild-eyed killer Zukei.

"Send Cale to report back."

"I will, and gladly."

"I cannot express—"

"I know." She smiled. "The war keeps you here."

"The Tekara acts well as a bastion against the mad emperor. But, like ants, they keep coming."

"Cale informed me that the Ptarnians are planning a new offensive, goaded on by that maniac."

"Aye, Callanz has tapped into some ancient evil. Perhaps it's an Urgolais renegade. I'm sure that some of those twisted devils survived. And their ancient home was near Caranaxis, beneath the mountains. Even if it's not the Urgolais, something's feeding the Ptarnian ruler, fueling his lust to destroy us. His captains are more resourceful than the early lot. They're proving tenacious and hard to beat. I thought that we were done with war, after the Happening. We had … what, a year, maybe two?"

"Ours was not meant to be a peaceful time."

"No, it wasn't." He nodded and grabbed her hand in his own. "It's so good to see you, Ariane." She felt a tear well at the corner of her eye.

"You had best tell me everything in detail," she said quietly. "We'll ride out at first light."

"As must I. Back to the front at Carranis."

She nodded gravely as servants brought plates of piping

fish and meat. They ate mostly in silence, the odd word seeping out. She felt overwhelmed. Both sad and warm, remembering how she'd been drawn to his rawness eight years ago.

It feels like eighty. Best we don't meet again, Crystal King.

"What of our friends," she said later that evening. "Do you ever hear from Barin, or King Ulani?"

"I've heard nothing from Ulani in years," he said. "The Yamondons have their own share of troubles with their neighbors the Vendeli. But Barin was here just last winter. That one hasn't changed." He laughed quietly. "The grizzled old bear told me he was planning on sailing to the rim of the world with Taic and Fassof, and some of his old crew. To get away from his daughters. I know how he feels." He chuckled, but then his face turned serious again. "I've heard nothing of him since. No word from Valkador."

"Knowing Barin, he did just that."

"Aye, I wouldn't be surprised."

THE FOLLOWING MORNING, THEY RODE OUT EARLY AFTER a brief farewell. The High King led his company north toward the distant Gap of Leeth, where he'd join the garrison at the huge fortress called Car Carranis and there await news of the enemy. Their eyes had locked briefly. She had stared into those troubled blue-gray orbs. In her heart, she knew she'd never see him again. Corin an Fol—the only man she'd ever truly loved.

They rode west for three days. Passing the ruins of Kella City, where the sorcerer Caswallon had perished amongst his schemes, torn apart by the same vile creatures he'd summoned up from Yffarn. Beyond that dreadful place, they'd entered

wild country, riding up through hills she remembered. They'd
been attacked by the Groil at Waysmeet village—flesh-eating
ghouls sent by Caswallon to trap them. Corin had emerged
wielding his sword Clouter, like a man dispossessed of his
wits. That was where it all started, outside the Lady Wood.
She'd been there with her champion, Roman, and Tamersane
and Galed. The first two were gone forever, and Squire Galed
suffered ailments and had recently retired to the coast. He'd
been Cale's best friend, she recalled.

The dark line of forest loomed ahead. Ariane gazed at her
companions. *I won't let these good men suffer as my old friends
did.*

Cale flashed her a reassuring grin as they reached the
deserted, ivy-choked walls of Waysmeet village. Cale knew
what had happened here, though he hadn't joined them until
they reached Kashorn on the coast. The boy had been working
for Hagan of Morwella. He'd changed his loyalties and swum
out to join them, as they sprung that brigand's trap. The boy
had served as her personal squire after that, and during the
war with Caswallon, taught by Galed. And now the former
guttersnipe was a commander in Point Keep.

At dusk, they entered the wood and rode through the
broad paths, cut and paved by the High King's pioneers after
the last war. Even though they'd believed the Goddess gone
forever, he had wanted to make the Oracle of Elanion acces-
sible for all. A place of hope, as the Ptarnian shadow rose once
again in the east.

They reached the oracle at dusk. Ariane dismounted and
bid her men wait with the horses outside the grove of elm
trees and stone circle that surrounded the sacred well. She
entered the stone ring alone, the stars watching her through
the shadow of tall trees above.

Ariane reached the center and knelt by the well, much as she had at that distant time. She spoke the words, over and over, chanting softly. This time, no one answered. She crouched in silence with hands clasped for what seemed like hours. The trees leaned closer, as though listening with her, hoping like she did that the Goddess would return. The tall stones reflected starlight. A mist rose, as night deepened and settled in the hallowed grove.

At last, Ariane sighed and stood slowly. She could see the others outside the circle seated by the horses, playing dice. She made her way back with heavy heart, stopping when a shadow brushed past, flitting from left to right. She felt a gush of emotion, seeing the owl settle on the nearest stone. Its gold-green eyes were familiar. Ariane guessed its true identity and felt her heartbeats quicken in excitement.

Vervandi appeared like smoke drifting through the trees as the owl faded. The tall, willowy woman stared down at her, not unkindly. Ariane could see right through her.

"Are you real, or a dream?"

In a sense—I am both.

The voice reached her and clung to her as the woman's smoky form shifted and dissembled to shift back whole again.

"The Goddess?"

Our Mother needs your help, queen.

"And I am here, as you bear witness, Vervandi. Tell me what I must do."

The woman gazed at her for a moment, then nodded slowly.

You must find the emerald bow. It was stolen from Us.

"Kerasheva? One of the Aralais treasures, was it not? I know nothing of its whereabouts. I'd thought it lost in the east." A memory stirred inside. Doyle had mentioned the bow.

Kerasheva must be recovered, or this new evil will prove unstoppable.

"Where can I find this bow?"

On an island in the ocean. Near Gol.

"*Gol?* That place no longer exists. It's a myth, a land lost beneath the waves millennia past."

An island near Gol, the wispy woman repeated, her tones sonorous. *And you must find the bow before the lost voyager, Carlo Sarfe.*

"Who is Carlo Sarfe?" Ariane had shouted the words without realizing. She heard one of the men call out and saw them coming her way. The spirit, Vervandi, had vanished. She saw the owl watching her from a branch above. The eyes blinked once, and the bird disappeared.

Cale reached her first, fumbling his way through the stones. "We heard you shout."

"Vervandi was here—I'm certain it was her. A ghost, no more."

Cale's mouth dropped open. Fassyan emerged beside him, his dark eyes wide, rough hands gripping the longbow. Doyle must have stayed with the horses.

"Come on," Ariane told the men. "We've a new journey to make."

"Might we enquire where?" Cale asked her, as they wandered back out through the maze of stone circles and rejoined Doyle, who was standing anxious with the horses tethered and cropping the dewy grass.

"To Gol." Ariane grinned at their stunned expressions. Cale's jaw dropped again.

"I thought that was just … er, stories. I mean, does Gol actually exist?" Fassyan asked.

"It did once, and must again—as we need to find it," she

said. "Or an island close by. The place where the thief took the bow."

The three exchanged bewildered glances.

Eventually, Cale laughed. "Hadn't you better explain to us fools what actually happened inside that mysterious ring?"

"I will," she said, climbing onto her mare's saddle. "But first we need to get moving. We've a long voyage, gentlemen. We must ride north to the coast at Vangaris and find a good ship."

"To go where? *Gol?* A legendary land from the past?" Fassyan blinked.

"Welcome to my life." Cale winked at him.

"West over water," Ariane patted her horse's neck and allowed the beast lead her from the glade that shrouded the Oracle of Elanion. The men rode close behind, she could hear their baffled whispers accompanied by Cale's harsh laughter.

Sorry, Raule. I don't think I'll be back in Wynais for some time.

7

STRANGERS ON THE SHORE

STOGI HAD BEEN FEELING BETTER the last few days, almost happy. His sickness gone, he'd enjoyed watching the dolphins dance off the prow as the hot sun blazed from above, melting the tar on the stays.

During that brief, joyful time, he'd studied the crew. Carlo had nine sailors besides his three top men. These were friendly enough, and none seemed to hold a grudge after the unfortunate events in Shen. Some even thought it hilarious, like his new friend the first mate.

The top men were the bosun, first mate and the wheelmaster. Of the three, Slim Tareel was the most approachable. The wheelmaster, Dry Gurdey, seemed a decent enough sort, though by his expression Stogi could tell he was not on Gurdey's approval list.

The wheelmaster might not approve of him, but Gold Tar had taken an instant dislike to Stogi. The ship's bosun was an ugly, moody, skinny-boned, foul-mouthed, miserable turd. Stogi could think of several other dubious qualities to add to the pile. He didn't much care for Gold Tar. Alone of the crew, the bosun had mocked him while he was ill. Stogi never forgot things like that. He'd keep an eye on Tar.

But it wasn't important. The skipper seemed to have forgiven him. That was the only thing that mattered. Moving forward, he would watch and wait, hope that any storms passed quickly and without too much calamity. Why, this morning, Stogi had even started smiling. That hadn't lasted long.

The storm hit them like a herd of ghostly cattle trawling the dark clouds in heated stampede. He'd spent that entire afternoon retching and clinging on the larboard rail, as the *Arabella* rolled and bucked and bounced like a discarded bucket descending a flight of stairs. He'd endured floggings from Ptarnian out-rangers during his cattle raiding days in western Tseole that left him less forlorn. Mercifully, the storm abated at dusk. Slim had told him to expect more, and most likely soon.

"We're riding the Sea God's chariot," the gap-toothed joker had said. It was fully dark by the time Stogi managed to stand without his legs shaking. He was looking out across the star-studded water of a calmer ocean when Carlo joined him.

Stogi felt awkward at first, but the skipper was smiling and had regained his former friendly manner. He stood beside Stogi, leaning out from the rail.

"Beautiful, is it not?"

"Aye, perhaps. When it's flat like this," Stogi grumbled.

"You'd soon get bored with calm all the time. Trust me—the doldrums are worse than days of storms and rain and thunder. The endless monotony can loosen a man's wits like a canny whore loosens his laces. I like storms, Stogi, they make a man feel alive."

"I'm happy for you."

"You'll adjust. It takes time. Some of the lads suffered badly when first we set out from Gol. Whenever that was." He added the last words as though asking himself a question.

"So your first mate told me."

"Tareel should know—he was green for days. Doubt he told you that."

Stogi shook his head. "Captain, I've been meaning to apologize—"

"You let us down in Ta Shen. That said, I partly blame myself. I should have known what to expect from you and that feisty lass."

Stogi looked at him for a moment and nodded. "What's next on this voyage—an island? Maybe a sea monster?"

"I'm hoping for the first, since fresh water is always our prime concern. I've never encountered the second, though I've heard tales from some who have, long ago. There was a one-eyed beggar fellow in Rakeel harbor. He'd seen a thing or two. Used to talk about a great serpent, how it emerged quickly and sunk his ship off the coast of Xandoria. He lost everything that day and ended up a pauper begging in the quay. I always felt sorry for the chap."

"Don't tell me anymore. I'd rather know what you're planning next, captain. How far away is—or was—Gol? I'm trying to get my head around what you're hoping to achieve, and how you mean to do so."

"Did you not experience strange events during your recent travels?"

"Aye, lots." Stogi winced at the memories he'd tried to stow aside. "I was too busy with Lord Tam and that sly bastard Seek to think about them much. We were trying to survive day to day and find Tam's missing lass. Recently, though, I've had plenty of time to ponder. What happened at the Castle of Lights? And why were you separated from your men? Slim's worried, the others probably more. You need to explain best you can to those men."

"I know, but how? You witnessed some of the quirks brought about by those dreadful women. They tampered with time itself, Stogi. Or maybe that was the Jynn? Doesn't much matter, because here we are."

"Here." Stogi looked about. "Sea and sky."

"I don't understand the mystery any more than you," Carlo said. "All I know is, I witnessed my ship torn apart on rocks that had not been there before, heard the dying screams of these same men—my crew and friends. I was spared, tossed onto an alien beach. After that ..." He sighed. "Things got even stranger. But wondering doesn't help us. We sailed out from Reveal in Sarfania, a province of Gol. That can't have been more than a few months ago. Since then, I've somehow been thrust into the future and heard of my home's ruin. Impossible, but there it is. I mean to return, warn my kin of what is to come. Save my family. What else can I do?"

Stogi stared out at the ocean. "We'll have to cross some kind of dimension, like you must have before, and Tam and I did when that Jynn fellow tricked us at the crossroads. That's the sort of nonsense Seek jabbered on about. And here I am believing it."

"We'll sail east and see what happens. That's my plan, Stogi. Keep things simple while we can."

"That's not a very satisfying answer," Stogi replied.

"What more can I tell you?" Carlo waved a hand. "We are in the hands of the Fates. Sometimes you must have faith, Tseole. We've survived this far. I, for one, believe this is meant to be."

Stogi stared at him. "I still think you need to talk to your men. Some of them, like that bosun, are already grumbling that you lost your mind back in that city they keep talking about."

"I will, and soon. First, I need to ask you about something else."

"I'm listening."

"It's someone, actually. Your girlfriend, Tai Pei."

"She's not my girl … I told you that. I would never presume, especially with her."

"But you're fond of her."

"I admire her spirit. Who wouldn't? She's a fine woman, though a tad impetuous."

"Tai Pei approached me in my cabin a few days back. She said …" Stogi raised a quizzical brow, and Carlo shrugged. "Never mind, I'll work it out. There are far more important things to think about. You need to get some food in your belly, Tseole. Before Zansuat's mood shifts again." He clasped Stogi's shoulder and wandered off to join the dour-faced wheelmaster. The two men gazed back at him from the wheelhouse before turning their attention to the ocean ahead.

"What was that about?" Stogi muttered to himself as he watched the ocean sparkle. He was hungry now that food had been mentioned. Still grumbling, he made his way below and sourced the galley, where the cook Shorty gave him some dried jerky and a mug of cloudy grog.

Tai Pei wandered over and seated herself neatly on a stool. She was wearing that superior smile. "You look better, but there's more rough weather to come, Shorty tells me. They'll be reefing the sails on all three masts. You'll have to try and keep that food down, else you weaken badly. I don't want to have to look after you."

"I thought you're already doing that for the captain."

The punch hit his nose with a thud. Stogi saw stars as he tumbled from the stool, his face bloodied and nose hurting like it was on fire.

"*Shit … whoops …* sorry about that, Stogi," Tai Pei said, leaning over him. "It was meant to be a playful cuff, but I forget my own strength sometimes. You shouldn't pry. I go where I wish, talk to whom I please."

"I think it's broken." Stogi grumbled, after getting a modicum of blurry vison back. He wiped snot and blood from his mouth and coughed up more.

"I can fix that."

"No! *Fuck off.* Stay away from me."

Before he could react, she'd pounced on him and grabbed his tortured nose, wrenching it sideways with a cruel twist of thumb and forefinger. Stogi yelled as the bone crunched back into place. Again, his eyes watered and the cabin whirled like a spinning top. "It's straight," the woman said. "Now … tell me what were you hinting at?"

"Augh, by the Gods, woman, you're torturing me. 'Tis but this: The captain came to see me, just now." Stogi coughed and spat goo on the floor. He could make out the cook glowering at him from the galley, as though this was his fault.

"So?" Her dark eyes narrowed evilly.

"Carlo asked me about you."

"Me?" Her upper lip quivered with interest, and she looked pleased.

"He wanted to make sure that you weren't my woman. I told him I'd rather eat worms. No, don't hit me again, I'm not at my best right now."

Instead, she burst out laughing. "Carlo thinks we're lovers?"

"Stranger things have happened."

"Oh, Tseole, I could never be your lover. You're far too ugly."

"It's a moot point."

"But I'm your friend, and will always look out for you. Believe me when I tell you that you're better off that way. You wouldn't want me as your lover, Stogi. I doubt you'd survive."

"Would Carlo fare better?"

"He interests me, nothing more. Are you jealous?"

"Just curious. None of my damned business."

"It isn't." She kissed him lightly and stood smiling, for once with genuine warmth.

Stogi blinked in surprise. "What was that for?"

She ignored him. "He needs broth," she told the red-faced Shorty. "And a cloth to clean his face."

The cook obliged ungraciously, passing her a damp towel that she used to clean Stogi's face. Minutes later, she spooned hot broth into his swollen mouth. "That's better. Try to get some sleep before the weather changes. Shorty says there's bound to be a swell coming soon."

"Don't think the cook likes me," Stogi said, feeling exhaustion taking over and closing is eyes warily.

"He doesn't have to like you, or me—as long as he doesn't poison us. And if he does, I'll cut out his liver and feed it back to him with ground beans and garlic. Poison doesn't affect me. During my assassin training in Pol Shen, I sampled everything from digitalis and death cap to hemlock and heart bane." She grinned at the cook, who'd turned his face away as though he wasn't listening and was making busy in the galley.

After she'd gone, Stogi stretched out on the cabin floor and drifted off. He woke with a thick head when the sun glinted bright through the porthole. The galley and cabin were empty. He heard someone shouting above deck.

No more storms yet. Stogi felt better for the rest. But his nose hurt badly, and he was more than a bit cheesed off with Tai Pei. Baffled might be a better word. But he was confused about everything, so might as well include her too. The wench was trouble. Carlo Sarfe was welcome to her.

More shouting above.

Best I go see what's occurring.

He clambered up the rope stairs awkwardly until his head cleared the deck. Another beautiful blue day, the sea flat as a Shen lily pond. Mirror clear and calm. These seafarers were doubtless teasing him about storms. He yawned and stretched. Another shout.

Stogi saw the island.

It had risen from nowhere. A twisted spike jutting a hundred feet above the water. Narrow and steep, a lone pinnacle marking their passage like a warning finger. To Stogi, it seemed as though a giant must be lying beneath the water, one broken digit thrust out as he drowned.

Stogi joined Slim Tareel as he stood with the bosun, who awarded Stogi a cold stare, which he ignored.

"An island," Stogi said.

"It does appear so, yes," Tareel answered.

"Don't look natural," Gold Tar said, before shambling off to join the captain and Dry Gurdey by the wheel.

"What are those?" Stogi saw dots drifting and darting like dragonflies up near the spindle-thin peak.

"Birds. Any more stupid questions?"

"Well, if they are birds, there must be more land nearby," Stogi said patiently. "I can't see the bloody things perching on that gaunt finger for long."

"Doubtless they fish," Tareel said. "But I concur, there's most likes another island close by."

As they inched toward the island, a breeze lifted from nowhere and Carlo ordered the men un-reef the sails.

"Blessed be," Slim muttered. "Some good wind at last."

"You told me there was another storm coming."

"There's always another storm coming, Tseole." The mate grinned at him. "But not today. Just breeze. Zansuat's changed His mind. He does that often."

The *Arabella* lurched as her sails trapped the breeze, and the crooked finger isle loomed closer. Stogi could see the birds clearly. Huge white darts that folded their wings and dropped stone-swift into the water.

"Gannets," Slim Tareel told him. They passed the island, and, as Stogi had guessed, it wasn't long before the lookout above spotted more land.

Another crooked finger cracked out from spilling waves, and beyond that he saw a third. The ship cleared these, and more appeared until they were surrounded by the twisted, broken fingers. Stogi feared some would come alive and grab the vessel as she sailed between the shallows, the water glassy and swirling around.

"I've never heard of a place like this," Slim Tareel muttered. He looked edgy and went aft to speak with the captain. Stogi followed and was joined by Tai Pei, who'd jumped down from above.

"I've been on the crow's nest with the lookout," she told him. "It's like a maze we've entered—there's no end to the rocks."

"Let's hope we get through to the other side," Stogi said. Even as he watched, the channels of water were becoming treacherously narrow and convoluted. Were the rocks moving? He hoped not, but he had to keep looking to make sure.

Dry Gurdey steered through one channel entering the

next, his face locked in concentration. The *Arabella* followed a jagged course of churning white waves until a larger island filled the sky ahead. This one had three broken spikes reaching skyward. As they approached, Stogi saw that the island resembled the face of some long-dead giant. Unlike the others they'd passed, there were stubby bushes at the base of the three spikes. A thorny forest clung to the giant's broken three-pointed crown.

"Looks like a cove," Dry Gurdey pointed to the far end of the island where Stogi saw a stony strand of beach wedged between fat gray rocks.

"Let's go see." Carlo bid the wheelmaster guide the *Arabella* close, until they entered calmer water trapped in that lee. Here they tossed anchor. Carlo ordered the skiff lowered.

"Want to come?" He grinned at Stogi. Tai Pei had already climbed into the smaller craft, along with Slim Tareel and two others.

"Not really," Stogi said, but joined them and squatted uncomfortably as the skiff drifted out from the *Arabella*'s hull. He watched as Tareel and Tai Pei worked the oars with the other two crew. Carlo was seated at the prow, his gaze intent on the rocky strip of shore.

"There might be rabbits," Tai Pei said, to no one in particular.

"I doubt that, unless they've got wings," Stogi said. She ignored him. They beached the craft, and Carlo leaped ashore. The others followed, and Stogi—last as always—got soaked as he waded across to the shingle.

Not much to look at. Steep sides of rock and a dreary beach of sorts. He didn't know why Carlo had wanted to stop here. Water, perhaps? That said, it was good to feel dry land under his feet again. He doubted this would prove a long stay.

Tai Pei and Carlo were already at the far end of the strand when Stogi saw what appeared to be the ashes from some dried-up fire. He stooped and looked closer.

"Someone's been here recently," he said, and shouted across waiting for the others to join him. He crouched, felt a faggot, and as Carlo kneeled and joined him, passed it across.

"Still warm," Carlo said. He looked about. "What kind of men could dwell in such a desolate place."

"Perhaps they're not men," Tai Pei said helpfully. "Could be any kind of djinni out here."

"We need to explore further. There are bound to be caves under all that rock," Carlo said. "You, Stogi, stay with Slim and mind the skiff. We don't want to be trapped here. The rest of us will go see what we can find. Tai Pei, how are your rock-climbing skills?"

For answer, she flashed him a grin and trotted off to the nearest cliff wall.

Stogi watched them leave as Tareel produced something from a bag at his belt. "I've been saving this bacci. Do you partake, Tseole?"

Stogi grinned, seeing the pipe, and watched as the mate struck tinder to flint to create a spark. They sat and smoked contently for a time. Stogi almost drifted off, the rhythmic sound of the waves having lulled his senses. He opened his eyes in alarm when a shadow blocked the sun.

A man stood over him. A second fellow had his arm locked around Slim Tareel's neck. Where had these two come from?

"Who the fuck are you?" The shaggy-haired, rangy one looking down at Stogi spoke with a familiar accent that reminded him of Lord Tam.

"I'm Stogi," he said, smiling up at the man. He carried a

knife and had a long bow slung over one shoulder. He was tall
and lean in build, fair-haired, his face hard. A seasoned
warrior, he appeared. Brown eyes. Tough, but not cruel. The
other man had let go of Tareel, guessing they were safe from
attack for the moment.

"How did you get here?" the tall one asked Stogi. He
pointed to the *Arabella* anchored close by, and both
strangers blinked in surprise. "You sailed her through the
Crantocks?"

"If you mean those finger islands, yes. We're on our way to
Gol," Stogi said happily, receiving a harsh glare from Tareel.
"We might as well tell these lads our plans," he told the mate.
"They look harmless enough."

"I'll give you fucking harmless," the second one said. His
face was grimmer than the tall one, hair darker. He stared
coldly at Stogi, as though wanting a fight.

"I meant no offense." Stogi shrugged. "But we have no
idea where we are, and … it's always nice to meet some fellow
travelers when lost."

Tareel was looking at the far end of the beach, as though
he expected the captain and others to return. Stogi kept his
eyes on the strangers. He had his curved knife, but not much
else.

"As I said, we're sailing for Gol," he explained.

"There's no such place," the grim one said.

"Try convincing this boy." Stogi slapped Tareel's shoulder.
"He was born there."

The second man looked hard at his companion. "What do
you think, Tol? Are we still dreaming? Lost in those fucking
woods. None of this is real."

"This talkative fellow appears solid enough." The tall one
smiled slightly. "You're not a figment of our imagination, are

you, Master Stogi? It's just, we've been through a rough time lately and have learnt not to trust what we see."

"Were you at the city?" Tareel asked suddenly.

"What?" The tall one glared at him. "This one speaks as well," he said to the other.

"Rundali," Tareel said. "My friend Stogi says that's a country, but we were recently in a city of that name, when our captain disappeared."

The other one nodded slowly. "They are from Rundal Woods. Demons, like those that did for Pash. We should kill them quickly, Tol."

"We're not from any fucking woods," Stogi said, feeling irritated, as Tareel reached for his dagger. He stopped when the tall one flicked the knife deftly between his fingers.

"Relax," Tol said. "Taylon here had a bad time in Rundal Woods. Compared to him and the rest, I got off lightly."

"You were at the Castle of Lights?" Stogi said. The two men stared at him. "That was where the witches almost destroyed us. In *Rundali*. Lord Tam and I. His beloved Teret, and that fellow Carlo mentioned, Garland."

"What did you say?" The one called Tol crouched and, lightning quick, pressed the knife blade against Stogi's throat. "Is it as my friend suspects? You're spirits come to mock our sorry plight. What do know of our captain?"

"How would I know your captain?" Stogi slipped his finger around his dagger and inched it from his belt. He'd need to be quick, but he'd achieved similar things before.

"Garland. You just mentioned his name."

"A good fighter who I would have liked to have known better." Stogi was relieved to see Carlo appear out from behind a rock. Beside him, Tai Pei had a knife held ready. "You're Garland the Journeyman's men?"

The two looked startled by Carlo's appearance. But Tol nodded, the knife dropping away. Stogi took some deep breaths. "You know of our captain. How?"

"I was with him in that castle in Rundali. Together, we two and brave Teret fought and slew the steel Grogan."

"What happened to our captain?" The other man, Taylon, glared at Carlo. These two were hemmed by Carlo's sailors. Tareel stood and joined them.

"We were separated," Carlo said. "Garland jumped into a vortex after fighting the basilisk that Teret shot. He said there was something else he had to do."

Tol looked at Taylon, while Tai Pei raised a questioning brow at Stogi. "We're friends here," Carlo said eventually. "And like you, we have been trapped in a maze of deceit and witchery."

"You're saying Captain Garland lives." Tol folded his tanned arms and glared at Carlo.

"He did when last I saw him," Carlo said. "How did you two strays end up on this island?"

They looked at each other and shrugged. "We were in Rundal Woods," Tol said. "Things happened there that I'd sooner not talk about, and some of us were worsted. We lost our captain. His second, Doyle, had already departed for Wynais to report back to the queen. There was trickery, sorcery. The whole place stank of beguilement. Pash and Kurgan died in the woods. That left us two."

"The Silver City," Tai Pei said suddenly. "I've heard mention of the place. Wynais lies in the uttermost west, beyond the World's Edge Mountains."

"It was our home," Tol said mournfully.

"But now we're lost," Taylon added, venturing a hesitant smile.

"As are we." Stogi grinned up at him.

"You lads look handy—best you come aboard my ship," Carlo told them. "There's fresh grog and good, hot food. What say you?"

"That if this is yet another enchantment, it's one I'm happy to risk," Tol said.

"As am I," added his friend, and they helped Stogi and the sailors push the skiff back into the water.

On the way across, Tai Pei stared at him.

"What now?" Stogi asked her.

"You almost got yourself in another fix there, didn't you? I can't be your nursemaid every waking minute."

"I had things under control."

"Yeah, it didn't look like that from where I was standing."

8

THE URGOLAIS

GARLAND OPENED his eyes and blinked in surprise. He must have been asleep for some time. Although it was dark, the shadow of the nearest island rose sharp to his left. He could see the shifting patterns of smoke spiraling high above.

Steer clear of the smoking island.

He cursed and grabbed the oars, started rowing hard and working the boat out from that shadow. He rowed for almost an hour, until his arms cramped and he slumped back to rest. It was a starry, deep night. The second island hovered like a brooding beast in the distance.

He rowed on, arms working hard. The breeze picked up after he cleared the first island's lee. Sail trapped wind, and he guided the skiff best he could in that gloom. An hour or two later, he was pleased to see the sky paling ahead. The island was close, its sides rising steep and clean from the pinking waters surrounding.

As he approached, Garland saw an ancient harbor, clearly abandoned, the stones in disarray. There were vines and scrub wedged between them. His sharp eyes saw a faint path zigzagging up to what might be buildings at the island's crown. Ruins. Like the harbor walls, half-buried by green.

The Alchemist's Isle.

Garland felt a shiver along his spine. There was something sinister about the island. He didn't feel the trepidation he had from the first island. But there was a feeling of menace lingering. Here it was subtler, like someone or something lurked, waiting, or expected his arrival. And why wouldn't they, with everything that happened over the last few weeks?

Eyes scanning, he entered the harbor and rowed the skiff alongside the broken mooring stone. He found a capstan and tied off, staggering onto the quay as his legs adjusted to dry ground. He slung the sword over his shoulder and gazed around.

Early morning. The sea, shell-pink and flat. A large fish jumping out from the water. Perhaps a dolphin? He turned and looked up at the broken path winding up. A steep stiff climb to warm his muscles. He wriggled his tongue to swallow saliva. Thirsty and tired. He'd best climb up there before it gets hot.

Hope there's water.

He made for the path and stopped abruptly. The urgent peel of harp strings rose from the knot of bushes surrounding the harbor.

"Who's there?"

Garland felt a cold tingle crawling up his neck. He unsheathed his sword and tied the scabbard to his belt. *Come on—I'm not playing games.*

Silence. Breeze and shifting ferns. He wasn't alone.

Up yours, whoever you are.

He took the path and walked steadily, panting at the exertion. His mind was weary and confused and full of foreboding. What if that imp child had tricked him? She'd been in the Hall, as had the faceless knight. Perhaps they were in cahoots, though he didn't think so.

As he climbed panting, Garland cast his mind back to the harrowing events in the Castle of Lights. Six months ago? No, that was Marei's home's time. In her dimension, things moved quicker. *Gods, I'm tired.* The memories were returning. The basilisk. The three witches, how they merged into one and became the goddess. Did he witness that?

I saw something. The bow Kerasheva. The harrowing events were a murk in his mind. Marei had kept them at bay. But they were creeping back inside him. The bow Teret had loosed to kill the serpent he was fighting. Kerasheva. Lost, as Teret was lost.

Garland forced the thoughts away by repeating his mantra. He reached a summit. Behind him, the sun had risen promising a warm, bright day. Vines smothered the stones all around. Ruins of buildings long abandoned.

He gripped the broadsword tighter, sensing wickedness. An ancient malice seeping out from those haphazard stones. The harper, perhaps? Garland ignored the chill in his bones and gazed out at the watery horizon, turning slowly until he'd studied a full circle. The smoking island hovered close, seeming almost reachable from that high place. He felt the danger like hot raking claws reaching across to him, before dissipating as vapor in the blue morning.

In the opposite direction, Garland saw a line of dull brown cliffs vanishing into the morning haze. A mainland. Gol? *No.* Records in Wynais had mentioned another continent. Far bigger. Gol lay beyond that. *Gods,* if only he'd studied his history more.

He rubbed his eyes and rested for a time, hands on the

crosspiece of his sword. "I don't care for this place." He must have spoken out loud, because someone had heard him.

Garland turned sharply and stared into the maze of ruins. His ears detected what might pass for throaty laughter. The ghostly harper?

"Show your face!" Garland swung the blade in a circle.

"No one likes this place." The voice was cold and raw, like the north wind ripping through dead trees. Garland felt a shudder. Perhaps the faceless knight had caught up with him. Instead, a shadowy, twisted shape emerged through the tangle of vine.

A manlike creature. Short in stature and crippled, leaning heavily to its left, a carved bent staff supporting it. The face was a horror of torn, stale, blackened flesh and broken black teeth exposed in a horrific grin, the mouth half-rotted away.

"Who ...?" Garland choked the word out

"Gruden Zorc." The creature barked the name at him. The horror hobbled forward and rested its hideous body on a rock. "That's what they used to call me. *Zorc* will suffice."

"*What* ... are you?"

"I was an Urgolais wizard, fool. But that was before the world changed."

"That explains the stink on this island. The Urgolais were evil."

"You have no idea how irritating that simplistic answer is on my battered ears." Zorc spat black phlegm on the dirt at his feet. "You know nothing of our history, mortal. How we were betrayed by our golden kin. Those connivers made us out to be wicked, but it wasn't that straightforward."

Garland lowered his sword wearily. This creature, whether malicious or insane, seemed harmless for the moment. "You alone here, *Zorc?*"

Zorc made a gurgling noise that might have been a laugh. "Mostly, though at night the Burnt Ones come pay visit."

"Who are the Burnt Ones?" Garland wondered if he should walk up and skewer the thing with his sword. Save time killing it later, when it had filled his ears with lies. He'd read about the Urgolais, or Urgo Lords as they were sometimes called. Malign sorcerers from a bygone age. But one, at least, had survived. He recalled vaguely how the usurper Caswallon had summoned Urgolais help during the Crystal Wars. The vile Groil had been their creatures. He'd fought Groil on the western slopes of the High Wall mountains.

"It's hardly important that you don't like me." Zorc was staring at him, the ugly cavern-shaped mouth gaping slightly.

"How do you come to be here, fiend?" Garland hefted the sword again and noticed Zorc's dark gaze following its steel. The eyes were coaly black with weird golden pupils, which expanded and shrank as he talked.

"I like it here," Zorc said with a rasp. "There are few places we old folk can hide these shallow days."

"I had thought your kind all perished with the Shadowman."

"Mostly we did. But that was Morak's fault."

The name Morak was familiar. He'd heard that mentioned before. Back in Wynais, or maybe during the mountain campaign when the Crystal King joined them in fighting Caswallon.

"Morak was your leader, I remember."

Zorc spat at him, the dark eyes flashed violent gold. Garland raised the sword, but the danger passed, as Zorc started coughing and holding out a feeble blackened hand.

"Don't anger me, fool. I'm not your enemy today, but the rage lies close below the surface. Morak the Cursed was a traitor who betrayed our people, even as that pompous prick Arallos deceived his Aralais kin. The two leaders wanted to continue with their age-long feud. Morak's lies led us to fight the Golden Folk, knowing we had no chance of winning without the Shadowman's help. It was Morak who sold us to Old Night, thus damning our souls to eternal midnight."

"I'm sorry to hear that." Garland sighed, lowering the sword. This could go on a while. His stomach rumbled, and his eyes hurt in the glare. The sun had risen high above his head. The morning passed swiftly, and he was achieving nothing here.

"You're not sorry—don't lie to me."

Garland shrugged. "I seek a bow. I believe it might be on this island."

Zorc coughed the laugh again. "Kerasheva is not here, *Sir* Garland. Nor are the two you want to save." Garland wasn't surprised Zorc knew his name. *Sorcery.* Like the island, this demon reeked of it.

"What do you know about my business? Are you from the Hall, too? And this yet another illusion? Like the mind-maze of Rundal Woods? It's all a bloody nightmare, and I'm trapped within."

"Are yes, Graywash Hall. That's what they're calling it these days. Strange name. I'd stay away, were I you. The place retains …" Zorc turned his head as though someone was listening in.

Garland heard the soft sound of harp music returning and rising from somewhere below. "Do you hear that?"

Zorc didn't respond.

"If you can't help me, stay out of my way," Garland said. "I've work to do, so bugger you and your misery, Zorc. Move!"

He made to brush pass and make for the tumble of stone. Zorc's blackened hand shot up with alarming speed to catch and tug his arm.

"I want to help you."

"How? *Why …?*" Garland stared down at him, almost choking at the stale odor coming from his breath.

"To avenge my people. Clear our names. It can't end like this."

"The Urgolais were evil," Garland said. "You're spinning me a web of lies. You know my name and are most likely partnered with those other fiends in the Hall. You and the girl child. Sir Valens. That villain Shale. All manifestations of the same fucking nightmare."

"Shut up and listen!" Zorc's strange eyes blazed into his as Garland shoved his hand away. "Graywash Hall is a mirror reflecting the darkness that cannot penetrate Laras Lassladen. Light and dark, Law and Chaos. Or good and evil, if you want to be simplistic. You cannot have one without the other. The coin must spin as it will."

Garland turned his back on the cripple, half-expecting Zorc to rise up and stab him. Either way, he was done talking with this creature. He left the Urgolais crouched on his rock and went searching through the ruins.

It was a couple of hours before he'd completed the survey, having walked and crawled through the undergrowth and thicket wrapping the dry, broken stones. At the center, he'd seen a huge dome, cracked open like a giant bird's egg, its green roof crumpled from where it must have fallen. He gazed about half-expecting to hear harp music, but instead saw Zorc leaning on his staff and breathing heavily.

"I told you there's nothing here but me."

Garland nodded grimly. "But you know where they are. The ones I seek. And the bow?"

"They are both near and far," Zorc said evasively.

"What?" Garland controlled his irritation. Deranged Zorc's ramble was all he had to go with. Not much, but maybe better than nothing. Worth a listen, if he could keep his temper from slicing the twisted demon in two.

"Near in distance; far in time." Zorc coughed and made a squiggle with his stubby fingers.

"Indulge me."

"The Kaa have the ability to cross the sea portals. A gift from the Shadowman. Unlike us, those reavers have always been His creatures."

Garland stared long and hard at the Urgolais. Eventually, he sighed.

"All right, I'm listening. Let's say I believe you, to make things easy. Where are Dafyd and his baby daughter? Help me find them, and I'll aid you in return. *Happily.* Help you spread the word about the wonderful kindly and misunderstood Urgolais wizards."

"Don't attempt humor—you're not very good at it," Zorc snapped at him.

"I'm sorry."

"You're caught in a web, *Sir* Garland of Wynais. We all are," Zorc chortled. "It's a game played out between the Emerald Queen and Her greatest foe."

"The Shadowman is no more."

"His essence survives in Graywash Hall. His spirit is the Hall. It's not a place, Sir Garland, but rather a being. A continuation. You have to understand that."

"You're saying that Graywash Hall is a living thing?"

"Perhaps, it might be."

"Then I need to go back there and put an end to it."

"Brave Sir Garland," the Urgolais mocked him. "You could try, *knight*. But you'd be going in the wrong direction."

Garland was about to ask more, but stopped when Zorc sniffed the air suddenly and raised his head. "They are here," he said.

"Who—your burnt ghosts?"

"The Kaa …"

Garland blinked in surprise. "The sea raiders who sacked Rosey's village? Where?"

"A small party, perhaps six. Their craft is hidden in reeds at the other end of the island."

"You can see them?"

"With my mind's eye."

"Wait here—we'll finish this conversation later."

"Be careful. The Kaa are most dangerous."

"So am I," Garland growled, and he hoisted his sword as he made for the north end of the island.

He walked warily in a half-crouch until he'd cleared the other end of the ruins. The wind was picking up and he saw seabirds diving close by. The sight comforted him. Something normal in the madness. He reached a ledge awarding views of the shoreline below. He could see the reeds that Zorc had envisioned. Without pondering on whether to trust Zorc's words, Garland started down through the steep rock and dense undergrowth, making sure his body was well hidden from anyone gazing up.

He reached a knot of shrubby bushes where the sound of waves announced he was close to the shore. He crouched, listened and waited.

Nothing.

He walked on, until he saw the reeds swaying in the wind.

Other sounds accompanied them. The soft crackle of fire, and what's that?

Voices?

Garland cupped an ear and listened, ignoring the wind, tuning his ears to pick up the other sounds. At last, he nodded to himself. *Voices.* There were men down there. The Kaa. Notorious baby-killers and looters. Perhaps they had Dafyd and the child. Time to find out.

He waited for several hours, until dusk settled and the fires crackled louder. They would be at ease in their camp, expecting no attack on this deserted shore.

Garland rose slowly and began inching his way closer until he reached a gap in the undergrowth, which allowed him peek through. He saw smoke rising up from somewhere close. Beyond that, the sea combed the shore with constant sighs. Then he saw them. Men seated around a fire. He counted seven.

He entered the reeds, creeping forward on his knees and lying low as he reached a closer point to study these men. They were twenty feet away, their harsh voices barking in some foreign tongue. He could see several faces. The sight chilled his blood.

If these were the Kaa, they truly were the spawn of Old Night. His first impression was how thin they appeared. Gaunt and lean, as though half-starved. The cheekbones stood out on their chins. They were half-naked, ribs jutting, wearing dark trousers. The skin that showed was a mass of intricate tattooing that ran from navel to neck.

The faces were very pale, apart from the spirals and weird shapes that showed, as more tattoos covered gaunt cheeks and brow. They wore bone earrings. Garland made out a rack of fish harpoons stacked against a broken stump. He couldn't see their ship and guessed it was hidden below.

He watched carefully, as night settled and a reed bird called out three times. The voices grew quieter. One stood and walked off to the right. Garland followed the pale figure and heard him laugh. A second sound reached him. A sobbing and whimper, then the cry of pain. He saw the man return, dragging a body, a knife clutched between his fingers, and dark blood dripping from the blade.

Garland saw another man stand up and laugh. He produced a heavy object. Garland saw with horror that it was a cauldron. The first man hurled the corpse on the ground and his comrades turned to their knife work, laughing as they cut into the body, sawing limbs and hacking flesh.

Garland stood up, cheeks burning with rage. He unsheathed his sword and walked briskly forward. They didn't notice him until he was upon them, broadsword swinging.

The one who'd killed the prisoner was the first to turn and see his approach. He yelled a warning that stopped abruptly when Garland's sword hewed half his face away.

The other men dropped their grisly work and leaped to their feet. Two ran for the harpoon stack, while the other four faced him with their bloody knives. Their eyes were very pale blue, and they were smiling at him.

Garland swung hard and fast, hewing the arm from the nearest, while sidestepping and swiping left tp cut through the shoulder of the third.

The two runners returned with the harpoons. Garland ducked low, as one cast the fish spear at his face. The weapon whooshed over his head. A Kaa grabbed his arm and another lunged at him with the knife.

Garland broke free from the first and butted the knife

man in the face, snapping his nose. The man he'd butted gripped his legs, knocking him off balance, while the second spearman approached and reversed his weapon, ramming the butt into Garland's face as he tried to rise.

Garland cried out at the pain and reached for his sword but it was kicked away. A face hovered in front of him, as his vision blurred. He guessed this was the leader. The Kaa said something, and Garland felt his arms pulled apart. The leader kicked him hard in the groin and he stumbled to his knees.

Fuck you.

The leader laughed at him, as he rammed the spear butt down into Garland's face a second time. Garland crumpled, and the world turned black.

9

THE COMING OF THE KAA

GARLAND WOKE to blinding pain and realization. He was a captive of the cannibal Kaa, and soon to be devoured. He had failed Dafyd and the child. His Marei was gone forever.

He couldn't see properly, and his face felt wrong. The mouth was leaking blood. He couldn't shut it, and guessed his jaw must be broken. His lip was split, and one of his eyes filled with blood. He struggled but discovered his arms lashed cruelly behind his back.

He heard a laugh. Tried to turn, but a boot struck the back of his face and he sprawled. A second boot stamped on his back. Someone else laughed. Garland heard a watery sound and realized the first man was urinating on him. Job done, he kicked Garland hard in the ribs and left him be.

It was dark. He must have been out for some time. He could hear the sound of bubbling water. He shuddered. What a way to die.

I'm sorry, Marei.

He'd done for three. But what did that matter? He'd been foolish indeed giving in to rage. He was a better soldier than that. The prisoner was already dead. Why had he attacked them? Unprofessional. Far better he'd learned more about them and sought help. Too late.

I'm delirious.

He almost laughed. Who would help him here? Garland pictured the little girl's grinning face. *Help me.*

Nothing.

You can't leave me here—you need me!

No answer. Garland stifled a sob.

I'll not fucking die like this.

Out the corner of his good eye, he saw the leader amble casually toward him, a long knife gripped in his left hand. Garland tensed. But the leader dropped the weapon in the sand, point down. He folded his lean skinny arms and smiled, showing neatly filed teeth capped with steel. The Kaa saw Garland watching and spat in his face, before kneeling in front of him, hovering close and staring at him with feverish blue eyes, the tattooed face inches from Garland's.

"You, warrior ..." The man struggled with the word. "Kaa eat you soon."

"Where's Dafyd?" Garland forced the words out between his broken mouth.

The Kaa tilted his bony face sideways and stared at him, much like a beady crow surveying its prey.

"I'm going to kill all of you!" Garland spewed the words between his lips.

The leader reached out and grabbed Garland's mouth with blood-stained fingers, wrenching it open. The pain almost caused him to lose consciousness again. The Kaa let go when Garland heard a vague, familiar sound somewhere close.

A harp.

Help me!

The Kaa leader must have heard it, too. He stood sharply and gazed around, cruel eyes worried. He clicked his tongue nervously. Garland craned his neck and saw the other three sprinting across to join their leader. All four Kaa stared down at Garland. One held a harpoon and leveled it at him, a half-grin on his tattooed face. The leader hadn't moved. He seemed hesitant, as though expecting newcomers or another attacker.

The sound of harp music rose up like an orchestra pealing all around. An angry tingle of random notes that grew louder before trailing off and fading again. Garland suspected he was losing his mind, perhaps dead already. The Kaa muttered to each other. The one with the harpoon turned to the leader, who shook his head.

Garland felt his mind slipping away as the harp song drifted in and out, like noisome flies around his eyes. He heard the leader bark an order and blinked as sudden cold rain dampened his face. He heard their boots moving away, then more harsh voices. The haunting harp song followed them, then faded …

Silence.

He closed his swollen eyes, but half-opened them again, his senses realizing someone else was here.

"I told you they were dangerous."

Garland noticed a vague shape crouched before him. Zorc had come to investigate.

"The Kaa?" He worked his mouth best he could.

"Gone for now. I have something for the pain."

The Urgolais produced a small vial and scooped up some dark unguent with a filthy, blackened hand. Garland turned his face away, but Zorc tutted and leaned close, rubbing the greasy stuff into his bad eye and all around his mouth.

He voiced a silent scream. The gooey ointment stung his

eye like a thousand wasps. He wriggled and shook as the pain lashed his face, slowly subsiding. The bastard had come to torture him, finishing what the Kaa had started.

Fuck you …

Exhausted, he blacked out again.

NEXT TIME GARLAND WOKE, THE SOUND OF CRACKING fire and roasting meat teased his nostrils. He no longer felt any pain, just badly dazed and giddy. He could see Zorc working over the same cauldron the Kaa had used.

"They cooked … people in—"

"—you hungry, or fussy?"

"Not hungry," he lied.

Zorc looked at him and shook his ugly head. "Mortals," he scoffed, stirring the pot. "Too damned principled. We Urgolais aren't so fussy. A pot's a pot, no matter what's been in it before. Besides, I've tried man flesh more than once. Not bad, though I prefer chicken. What I'd do for a nice plump hen."

Painfully, and very slowly, Garland shuffled to his knees. Zorc watched him while he reached inside the pot, oblivious of the bubbling heat, and pulled out a flesh-covered bone. Garland daren't think where that came from. Zorc crunched down hungrily and spat the remains on the sand.

Garland felt his stomach churn. He leaned forward and vomited. Zorc wandered close, checked his eye, and handed him a bladder of liquid. Garland glared at it.

"'Tis water, Sir Fussy. Best you drink—and slowly, mind, else you puke again."

Garland complied, and the warm, brackish liquid settled his stomach. He waited a few moments and drank some more, feeling a modicum of strength return. He moved his mouth and was surprised to find it no longer hurt, and he could speak easily.

"You fixed my jaw?" The eye was better, too—he'd felt so sick he hadn't noticed.

"Your face is healed, Sir Garland. You're still ugly, but I'm not a miracle worker."

"Why are you helping me?"

Zorc's weird eyes gazed into his. "I want you fat and healthy so I can eat you later."

Garland gathered that was some kind of joke. He looked across and saw his sword resting against a stump. He stood shakily and walked over and picked it up, managing a relieved smile. Zorc watched him without much interest.

"I am grateful for your help," he told the crow-like figure squatting by the cauldron.

"You should be," Zorc snorted. "Were it not for my intervention, you'd a be a stewing bag of bones."

"You are the harper."

"No!" Zorc looked around in alarm, as though they were being stalked. "You must ignore those noisome sounds. They are perilous and will lead you astray."

"The harp song saved me, Zorc. Not you. Though you've restored me, and for that I'm truly thankful."

Zorc didn't respond. Garland decided he needed an ally and might as well learn what he could from this hideous creature. He only knew what he'd been told about the Urgolais. Unlike the Crystal King, and his own beloved Queen Ariane, Garland had never seen one. Only the Groil creatures they summoned from Yffarn to aid Caswallon in the war.

Zorc reminded him of those creatures. But the Groil he'd fought had been taller, vicious but dimwitted. They'd carried serrated swords. Zorc didn't look like the sword type. Neither was he stupid. The way he understood it, the Urgolais were the clever conjurers and the Groil their foot-soldiers and sorcery-dulled chattels.

His mind wandered back and forth, churning through the haze of worry, hunger, and distress.

I'm in shock.

He needed his strength back. Time to move on. He sat on a wet rock, the sea brushing his boots, his stomach rumbling and head throbbing. He looked over at Zorc and managed a lop-sided grin.

"I'll help you, Zorc. If I can. I promise. First, you have to tell me all you know."

"*All* … I … know?" I'm almost four thousand years old."

"That's old. Small wonder you're ugly. Tell me the recent stuff."

Zorc glared at him. "You mortals are so peculiar. I'll never understand how you came to rule our world."

"We aided your foe, the Aralais, when King Kell the Conqueror crossed from Gol. After it sank." He added the last bit quietly, thinking of Carlo Sarfe determined to return there.

"Bollocks," Zorc said.

"What?" Garland raised a brow. This was obviously a sore point.

"Another falsehood fabricated by Aralais propaganda. Both our races lost that war. The Aralais were shredded, as were we. Spent and juiceless and hung out like drying seaweed after high tide's withdraw. A thousand-year conflict does that. And the sorcery backfires eventually. All thanks to fucking Morak and Arallos. Damn their blighted souls to eternal Yffarn. You humans were a rag-tag band of refugees who turned up when all the fighting was done. Arallos was desperate, so figured you might prove useful. He was almost broken, and he retired to that lonely tower in distant Fol and set about plotting how he could use you."

"Arallos?" Garland registered the name from somewhere. "You mean Zallerak the Mage who helped us defeat the usurper, Caswallon. What happened to him?"

"The same bastard. A vile conjurer. And I wish I knew, so I could stab his glowing eyes out."

Garland let that go. He'd encountered the Aralais wizard on the Wild Way, the high mountain track where Queen Ariane's camp had spent that winter, having been driven out of Wynais by Caswallon's invading host. All he recalled was that Zallerak had been very tall with hypnotic blue eyes, and he had disappeared when needed most.

Garland changed the subject. "Who stole the bow, Kerasheva?"

Zorc shrugged. "Does it matter? The thing's missing. Elanion's mad as hornets on honey."

Garland tried to remember the chaotic events within the Castle of Lights. He'd attacked the great serpent and nearly perished. Teret had shot it with the emerald bow, killing the basilisk as it had unraveled around him. Carlo Sarfe had been there, and some others. The witches had … fused into another, more powerful being. The Emerald Queen had taken back Her bow—and lost it again. Seemed careless, especially for a goddess. He laughed slightly.

"Tell me about the Kaa."

Zorc shifted awkwardly and wriggled his crooked stick. "They are woeful creatures. Products of Chaos. It's strong on the Outer Worlds."

"Where is that? You're saying the Kaa aren't human?"

"Perhaps they are. I doubt it, though they share your

people's ugliness. They come from one of the far planets. The cold places. Like the steel Grogans, the Kaa slipped through the dimensions after the great calamity."

Garland suspected this creature might be mad. But his only choice was to learn all he could. "You mean the Happening? When the gods destroyed each other outside Kelthara?"

"The world fabric was ruptured by that strife. Still is. The order of the universe thread got tangled and ruptured during the process, and the lightweight gods weren't around to mend the tear. Things got through from the Chaos realms. Unpleasant creatures who usually only frequent your darker dreams. The Grogan you battled was one such being, the Kaa raiders are another."

"How do you know about the steel Grogan?"

"You were quite talkative in your sleep, Sir Knight. The drug I gave you told me all I needed to know."

"You drugged me with that ointment?" Garland felt a sudden wave of panic flood his veins. *He's poisoned me …*

"Saved your body and restored your wits—so shut up. Yes, I drugged you."

Garland glared at him. *I wish I could believe you, fiend.* He opened his mouth and closed it again. It would be good if something made sense in his life.

"You're telling me those Kaa scum broke through from another world and are trapped here? That's insane, and yet … doesn't matter, once they're dead. How do I find them, Zorc? Is there a camp or fortress?"

"Trapped here?" Zorc chuckled. "Hardly. They surf the nine worlds easy as whores passing from tavern to tavern. Sea and space pirates. The Kaa sleep mostly on their skinny ships. They are dimension rovers and rarely stop anywhere for long."

"That's too bad, because I need to find them and kill

them. Or at least, the ones who took Dafyd and Rosey's baby girl. And Dafyd, too, most likely."

"That won't be easy."

Garland kept his temper despite the irritation he felt. "Obviously. But you know where these Kaa might be and can help me find them."

"Yes, to a point."

Garland rubbed his eyes. They were sore, but the wounds had dried up quickly without infection. "Good, and thanks. We had best return to my skiff, and you can tell me where to sail."

"Not yet."

"Why?"

"Because we need help."

"From whom? No one here but that harper you won't speak about. Besides, I thought you knew what to do?"

For answer, Zorc sniffed and motioned up the wooded slope with his nose. "The Citadel," he muttered eventually.

"There's nothing up there except burnt-out ruins. And ghosts. Wait a minute, you're not thinking …?"

"The Burnt Ones might help us."

"Spirits, and especially those who died badly, might not prove over-generous to people disturbing their rest."

"The Burnt Ones don't rest. I can summon one, make an offer."

Garland stared at the Urgolais. "You're serious, aren't you?"

"Do you want to see Marei again? Rescue her grandchild and son?"

Garland guessed he must have been talking a lot while he slept. He nodded grimly.

"The Kaa move around, as I said." Zorc waved a scrawny hand. "But it's not just where they go. It's *when*. The Kaa and the steel Grogans can manipulate time, too. Bend it like a bow, so that past and future merge into present. It's an uncanny knack they have. We Urgo always envied them that. The Kaa go where they can feed. And they're always hungry. I daresay a few will be raiding yonder coast." He nodded toward the distant line of cliffs. "The Great Continent that was. Not much remains, but if they go back a few centuries in time ..."

Garland scratched his head. "You mean the Burnt Ones are the warlocks, the same who ruled the Citadel in the distant days of Gol? What happened to them?"

"They burned." Zorc offered what might have been a grin, but it looked more like a demon scowl. "Or were scorched to cinders by the demon the renegade Ozmandeus summoned. A fire Elemental. One of the most powerful. Ashmali. Sly Ozmandeus had been cast out of the order and wanted revenge. He used the trapped Elemental to kill them. A few warlocks escaped and fled to the east lands. Most didn't."

"I thought Gol was destroyed by water."

"Fire played a key part. The Elemental, Ashmali, proved too strong for its master and devoured Ozmandeus. The Sea God Himself intervened and drowned everything. A nonce heavy-handed, but the High Gods always overreact."

"But why would one of those scorched warlocks help me?"

"Let's go find out," Zorc replied. "It's nearly dusk. Best we clamber back up and steal quietly among the ruins. Wait for one to come by."

Garland stared at him, his mouth open. He was weak from lack of food. The thought of climbing back up to the ruined Citadel was not appealing.

"You have a better idea?"

"I don't."

"Cheer up, Sir Garland the Valiant. I have some snared

coney in my cave, close by the ruins. We'll pass by there first, get my summoning gear and feed your stomach. It might prove a long night ahead."

THE CITY WASN'T WHAT MAREI HAD EXPECTED. SHE'D imagined a splendid array of towers and stone, high banners blazing in the sunshine. Proud, cloaked knights riding out and ladies clad in colorful, dazzling gowns. What she saw was a dull brown road leading toward shabby gates. And in front of those, a pot-bellied soldier in a broad brimmed straw hat, seated with legs sprawled akimbo, sound asleep.

When she and Rosey approached, the man blinked and squinted up at them.

"Who be you?"

"We're seeking lodging in the city," Marei said.

"The city?" The man chuckled, as if she'd said something amusing. He stank of stale ale and sweat, despite the chill wind. "You hear that, Monsy? These two lasses seek lodging in *the city.*"

A bleary-eyed rangy guard appeared from behind the gate. Marei could tell he'd just woken from a doze. Quite the pair, these two. The second guard stood blinking in the morning sun.

We've scant time for this. Marei was cold and hungry, and Rosey needed rest badly. She'd not suffer fools today.

"Aye, the city, if that's where we are. Can't say I'm over-impressed, so far. We need a place to stay for a couple of nights."

"Hmm, daresay we can let you in," the fat one in the hat

said. "Make for the market square, pretties. Plenty of inns there—one should take you."

"We're looking for a miller," Rosey said, but Marei hushed her. These fools didn't need to know their business.

"Where you from?" the other one had recovered from his nap and seemed more curious than his companion."

"Over the mountains," Marei replied.

"The coast, near the Hall," Rosey said, unnecessarily.

"What Hall is that?" The curious one frowned at them. "No one comes over the mountains. They came over the mountains," he repeated to his chubby companion, as though he hadn't heard her too.

"'Tis irregular, for sure," the other one said.

"The market, thank you." Marei motioned her head, and the fat one waved her through.

"Does the city have a name?" Rosey asked as they walked through the stone gates.

"Yes," said Monsy, and the pair laughed as they returned to their idle repose.

"Wankers," Marei muttered under her breath as they entered the grubby street ahead. She glanced at the girl beside her. "Mind you tongue, Rosey. These people are not to be trusted. Leave it to me to ask any questions. Got it?"

"Yes, I suppose so," Rosey replied irritably.

10

TWO QUEENS

A<small>RIANE</small> <small>REINED</small> in as the hills parted and a wooded vale yawned a gap in the trees, allowing the road to wend through. She saw roofs, smoke rising, the distant glimmer of ocean. She chewed her lip and swallowed a grumble. She'd wanted to avoid Vangaris. Cale had persuaded her the Morwellan city was the best and quickest place to secure a ship stout enough for a long, arduous voyage.

She'd known that of course. It was just … *Vangaris*. Things had happened here, too. Bad things. It was Shallan's home, and the High Queen was here. She would, of course, have to pay a visit—though both of them would doubtless find that irksome. They'd never been friends, Queen Shallan and she. Araine had tried, especially in the early days. But failed easily, not caring overmuch.

Cale said the High Queen had proved difficult of late. Ariane had stifled a laugh. Shallan had always been difficult. But the third child's birth had given her problems. She'd withdrawn from duties, fretted that her husband was doing too much and resented this new war—as though it was a personal affront to her. Ariane knew Cale loved Shallan. All men did. She was the most elegant and beautiful woman Ariane had ever known.

My cousin.

They reached the gates, as a low sun glinted through ash trees. Guards bowed when they recognized Ariane. She ignored them as she guided her mount through the cobbled streets. Vangaris was much changed. The High King had ordered the entire city rebuilt after the destruction caused by the murderous Northmen of Leeth. But to Ariane, the soul of the city had died. She remembered the kindly Duke Tomais. Shallan's father had been good to her on the many visits north as a child. But the duke had died in the Crystal Wars, and his daughter was a colder fish.

They reached the palace. The guards filed out, and grooms grabbed the reins of their horses. Ariane exchanged a wry glance with Cale and dismounted. He accompanied her, while Doyle and Fassyan stayed with the soldiers.

The palace wasn't large—more of a fortified courtroom. Vangaris was a working city and the biggest port in all four kingdoms. Everyone traded here, from Yamondons in the far south to Northmen from distant Hraggland—a new country, like Rethen to the east of Leeth. The docks had even attended spice junks from legendary Shen. Cale had reported sighting the odd-looking ships moored neatly in the massive harbor. Trade with the east was a new thing. He assured her that there would be a craft in that harbor they could use, for enough coin.

She'd nodded without comment. Were they really doing this? The Goddess needed her help. Meant to be. Ariane sighed. *Let's get this part over with.* She'd keep it brief. Shallan had prompted her journey, so should prove accommodating.

A fawning page led her up through twisted stairs leading to a long corridor. Double doors opened at the far end, and a tall guard bowed low. Cale nodded to the soldier, who saluted briskly as Ariane swept through and entered a wide room with large arched windows awarding stunning views of city and harbor. Beyond these and wrapped around, the broad, curving estuary of the mud-brown River Falahine dwindled into distant ocean, the woods surrounding hemming that sludgy fuzz with autumn's dappled yellow and sweeping russet browns, lifted by the occasional glint of maple red.

A tall woman stood with her back to them, her hands resting on an oak desk. Ariane remembered that as the duke's favorite spot. She was gazing down at the harbor, the long, chestnut curls almost reaching her hips.

Ariane coughed and shuffled her feet.

The woman turned, a half-smile on her face.

"I'm most grateful you're here, cousin." She dipped her head in a half-bow. Ariane curtsied, and Cale kneeled and brushed the floor with his fingers.

"Sir Cale, you may leave us for now. We queenly cousins have secrets to discuss." The High Queen's violet eyes flicked at the warrior. He stood swiftly, bowed again, and made himself scarce. Shallan stared at Ariane and held open her arms. She walked forward and hugged her cousin awkwardly.

"It's been too long," the High Queen said.

"You, cousin, are as beautiful as ever," Ariane said. It was true. And the lines on her face and dark rings shadowing her eyes strangely enhanced that beauty. She looked paler than before. Thinner. *Drawn*, and yet still she had that eldritch beauty. A gift from her father. The real father, not the poor, lost duke.

"Hmm, don't lie. You were never good at that, Ariane.

Truth is, I'm fading. A hollow shell of the woman I was. The past demanded a heavy toll."

"It did on all of us, my queen."

They parted arms, and Shallan gazed at her frankly. "You look good, coz. Still the warrior queen! A sword at each hip. One curved, the other straight. Ariane of the Swords is back." Her smile was genuine, though she looked tired.

"I still practice daily," Ariane said, smiling, "but my reactions are slower, and my back aches constantly."

"Don't mention aching—the damp in this city seeps into my bones."

"Do you still shoot?"

"Haven't in years," Shallan told her. "Ours is a dreary role these days."

"You are the mother of future kings—yours was the hardest task."

"Ha, maybe. I love them, but never took well to motherhood. My husband … we just saw it as our duty. You know he still loves you, Ariane?"

That caught her off guard, but she kept her lips together. "We were always close," she responded smoothly. "Good friends, that is all, cousin. You were the only woman he's ever truly loved. I know this."

"And yet, here we are. You full of life, and myself a stale shell. No matter. I'm happy you're here. Truly. And you'll need a ship."

"Yes."

"You remember Taic?"

I do … *vaguely*. A Northman, related to Barin?" Ariane felt a lurch of panic. Not *the* Taic?

"His nephew, the one who was always fighting."

Everyone remembers that Taic.

"I met him but briefly," Ariane said. "After we freed Calprissa. But you knew him well, did you not?"

"A dear friend, and somewhat reformed." Shallan smiled. "Taic has a new ship, and he's got Barin's wanderlust. The Northman nearly jumped at the chance of a long … unusual voyage. You'll find him at the far dock awaiting your arrival."

Ariane didn't know what to say. She stood stiffly, as Shallan walked over and returned her gaze to the city below.

"We'll have food and wine brought up," the High Queen said. Ariane noticed how she clenched her fist at her sides. "It was hard coming back here, Ariane. Vangaris has echoes and shadows of memories waiting for me wherever I turn."

"I can imagine."

"He is everywhere."

"The late duke?"

"Him too, and my dear lost mother. *Ghosts*, cousin. I visit the oak grove every morning. Can't help myself."

Ariane knew that was the place where Shallan had first encountered the Faen creature, Cornelius Zawn.

"How long are you staying in Vangaris?"

Shallan turned and stared hard at her for a moment. Ariane almost flinched, seeing the pain in her eyes. "I don't know, another week, maybe two? Truth is, I'm tired, Ariane. I feel a kind of peace here, despite what happened. And my children like being closer to the ocean."

"I saw Corin. He looks well, I thought."

"He looks older, as do I."

"All of us—that damn war."

"Gah, I'm sorry, cousin, I'm poor company these days. I shall rally but need rest and sleep. And an end to this conflict. Curse that mad emperor, Callanz. I would have my children live without the shadow of war."

"They shall. The crazed dog in Ptarni will implode, I'm certain of it. This new offensive of his will break on Car Carranis walls like every other army."

Shallan nodded, but her eyes were far away. Those dreamy blue-gray orbs that lured men like moths to fire.

"How did you cope with the Dreaming?" she asked eventually.

Ariane shook her head. "I didn't, really. It was always there —my mother had it, too. The Goddess speaking to us, or rather through us. Hard to decipher. Dazaleon always understood them."

"Another victim of the war."

"And much missed."

Dazaleon had been Ariane's high priest and councilor. A man she'd loved who'd been murdered by the treacherous Yale Tolranna, Tamersane's older brother. Tamersane had killed Tolranna in Wynais during the war. That terrible deed changed her favorite cousin forever, resulting in his departure to Ptarni a few years back. Strange how things turn out.

"Are you well?"

"Forgive me—just thinking on old friends."

Shallan's eyes were kind. "Come, Queen Ariane. Dearest cousin, we shall eat and share a cup of wine, and you shall inform me of your plans."

If only I had some, Ariane thought wryly as she accompanied the High Queen to her private chamber, where a buffet of dry meats, wet fish and honey breads had been left for their leisure, together with a carafe of vintage port and a squat bottle of brandy. Ariane raised an eyebrow seeing that.

"I heard you enjoy the odd tipple these days," Shallan smiled.

"I do that." Ariane laughed as she opened the bottle.

They ate and drank for a time, and walked out onto the wide, windy balcony. Cold in this city, so unlike her expansive views of lake and mountains. Morwella was a bleak country. The river below churned with small waves lapping the harbor arms. She shivered and again questioned her wisdom undertaking this quest. *I am the Goddess's vassal here on Ansu.* What else could she do?

As they gazed out at the Falahine in silence, Shallan reached across and gripped her arm. Ariane turned, surprised by the urgency in her cousin's eyes.

"What ails you, Shallan?"

"It's mere foolishness. A fleeting trouble that assaults me from time to time."

"You who've been through so much, it's hardly surprising. I led an army to war, but mine was an easier challenge than yours."

"If anything happens to me, I want you to look after him."

"What?" Ariane almost dropped the brandy glass. "Don't be ridiculous."

"I mean it, Ariane. The shadow. It ... Just say you'll do it."

"I ..."

"For me, sweet cousin. I need this solace."

"I will always serve and love the Crystal King, as my ruler, my dear friend, and ... whatever else might happen. But this is nonsense—"

"Thank you, Ariane. I know we were never friends, but for my part I wanted it. You were just too fierce and, well ... I couldn't keep up with you."

Ariane felt a wave of sorrow and regret. *I should have tried harder.* "And I always thought you disliked me, found me coarse and harsh. I looked up to you like an older sister. The most beautiful woman I've ever known."

"Ah, such times, Ariane. What webs we two have woven. You'd best leave soon, cousin. Taic will be waiting. He's a good man, grown up since the war. Barin even speaks to him these days."

"Shallan ..."

"Farewell, brave Ariane. I doubt we'll meet again."

"Cousin?"

Shallan waved her away as she turned and gazed out at the sea. Ariane could see a tear welling at her eye. She took the hint.

"Your highness." She curtseyed and left the chamber, as dampness settled in her own eyes. Curse that fucking war.

An hour later, Queen Ariane stood with her three men on the deck of a stout ship. The biggest in the harbor, though smaller than Barin's legendary *Starlight Wanderer*, the brigantine she'd voyaged on back in the war with Caswallon.

Taic's ship, *Kraken Girl*, had two masts but only five sails, unlike Barin's fourteen. Painted blue and gold, with an iron ram guised as a golden-haired maiden figurehead, sprouting out from a writhing kraken comprised of brass and steel. A sturdy-looking craft, *Kraken Girl* made for a gaudy sight among the drab fishing boats, skiffs, and merchant traders up from Raleen.

The crewmen were typical rough-looking Valkador sailors with earrings, scars, shaggy hair and gruff, coarse manner. Taic had been one such. The worst, apparently. But he'd changed.

Hmm.

Where was he?

It would be dark soon. If they were leaving, they'd best do

it right away. A crewman approached them, and Doyle tugged his sleeve.

"Where's the captain?"

"Skipper's saying goodbye to the keg, I reckon," the scruffy Northman said. "We got plenty of ale, but why drink our own when there's fresh grog in port."

"Going to be an interesting voyage," Fassyan muttered wryly.

"It always is with Northmen," Cale added.

"You know you're addressing a queen?" Doyle snapped at the sailor, not seeing the funny side.

Ariane heard a shout and turned her head, seeing a big, long-haired ruffian jump onboard. She vaguely recognized Taic by the blond mop and smiling eyes. He had a few extra scars and limped slightly.

He grinned at Ariane and Cale, ignoring the other two.

"Hello, queen."

"I've missed Northmen," Cale muttered under his breath.

"Taic," Ariane replied tartly. "Your men have been waiting for your orders."

"Here I am, and ready for anything. Where are we sailing, highness?"

"You don't know?" Doyle looked shocked.

"That's probably a good thing," Cale added. "Because neither do we."

"We're sailing far, Taic," Ariane said. "Until west meets east. I hope your men are all right with that."

"Very happy," Taic said, smiling. "Uncle Barin's been talking about doing that for years. He's too old and fat these days, so we'll do it instead."

"I thought the world was flat," Fassyan said nervously.

"It's round," Cale told him. "Trust me. We won't roll off.

If we keep sailing we'll reach the coast of Shen—maybe in a year or so."

Ariane could see that Fassyan did not look encouraged. She left them to natter as she joined Taic below decks. Once they were out of sight of the men, he winked at her and closed the cabin door.

"I have to act like a drunken lout, highness. It's Valkador tradition—why the men follow me. But the High Queen sought me out herself and begged me to undertake this voyage."

"It could prove your last, Taic."

"Same as any voyage. And I'd not refuse Queen Shallan. I love that bonnie lass. Me and Sven fought with her, you know? Quite the archer she was."

"In Calprissa." Ariane smiled. "I was there, too, remember? We were trapped outside the east wall, while you were defending the west one."

"Old memories are always the best," Taic said. His shrewd blue eyes narrowed. "What's the plan? Any charts? Queen Shallan didn't elaborate."

Ariane laughed wryly. "We need to sail until we find a land that no longer exists, and recover a bow that's been stolen from the Goddess. That's it."

Taic stared at her intently. "Not the answer I expected, but it sounds intriguing. We've plenty of grog, and I've brandy for your good self. And the boyos are up for some frolicking misadventures. This is a good day."

Ariane chuckled. "You Northmen. Does anything get you down?"

"Only when the ale runs low."

"You have no further questions? Most sensible skippers

would scurry back to the taverns and hope I found someone else."

"And miss all the fun?" Taic beamed at her.

"There's more than that to you, Taic. What's the real reason you offered your ship and crew?"

"Aye, well, we Northmen love sailing. The Goddess Herself spoke to Queen Shallan. And now Ariane of the Swords is on my ship. Of course I'd volunteer. Aside from the Goddess and Her Norns, you two queens are the finest women in this world. Who am I to question your wisdom?"

"Thank you, Captain Taic. I appreciate that." Ariane gripped his hand.

"I'm going up, get us out the harbor and river. Once we're at sea, I'll pop back and we can discuss this more. Have you eaten?"

"Yes."

"Brandy? Would you like me to pour you a glass?"

"I can do that myself, Captain."

He nodded and smiled. "See you shortly." Taic ducked his head and vanished outside into the main cabin.

Door closed, Ariane sat quietly for a time. Her head was dizzy, but the brandy helped. What had Shallan meant? She hadn't looked sickly, just tired.

And we're all damned tired.

Why had Elanion channeled into her cousin instead of her? Ariane knew how to absorb the Goddess's visitations, enduring the stress and headaches they brought on.

"Here we are," she said to herself, before sipping and swilling the warm liquid around her mouth. "Elanion, Beloved Goddess. If you're listening these days, please give me some direction."

AN EXPLANATION OF SORTS

CARLO SAT in his cabin as the waves buffeted the hull. It was stormy today, and he'd ordered the sails reefed to the nine yards and boom as they glided and crashed through the chop, rain lashing the decks. His cabin porthole was sprayed by misty fret.

Carlo didn't mind the weather. Storms made him think. They cleared the head, and there was so much to chew over. They'd left the finger islands—or Crantocks, as Tol had called them, after dreaming the name apparently—behind three days ago. Since then, they'd been sailing through clear, wide water, no land in sight. The sea birds had vanished, as had the glassy, calm waters, replaced by a steady monotonous deep-ocean roll that wore on body and mind. The storm arrived this morning and worsened as afternoon faded into evening.

Gold Tar and Gurdey had the wheel, and Tareel was up aloft with the incorrigible Shen girl, keeping an eye out for islets and rocks, lightning, and other hazards. Tai Pei never stopped moving. The girl was another trouble on his mind, but one he was happy to put aside. There were far more pressing matters to consider. Tai Pei had won over most the crew, and the recent castaways seemed to like her, too.

Tol and Taylon, Garland's lost strays. Carlo had spoken with them on that first day. Taylon was dour and quiet, but the younger Tol chatted more than enough for both of them. He seemed a decent sort and reminded Carlo of Slim Tareel with his easy banter.

The poor sods had been caught up with the same witchery that had assaulted him in the Castle of Lights. They'd lost their captain and friends but were relieved to learn that Garland still lived. Or had, back then.

Taylon had an old wound on his arm that still troubled him. Tai Pei had seen him scratching it and pounced on the man before he could blink. She'd rubbed some salve on the arm and he'd slept for two days. The girl was a wonder. She was also a nightmare.

Stogi had kept a low profile, especially now that the rough weather was back. Slim had reported this morning that the clouds were darkening, and this could blow all night.

The perfect time to think.

The lads were busy aloft, the passengers sleeping or dicing with off-duty crew. He was left alone with his thoughts. Mind clearing at last. The troublesome dreams had faded as they left the mainland. He was grateful for that—and his mangled memories of Rundali seemed but part of them.

Carlo pictured Teret's blue eyes and her strong, tanned features. He'd loved her, a stalwart companion and friend. They're shared a journey through hardship, mystery and horror. But she was dead. Or gone—he wasn't really sure which. Lost to him, because of her husband, Tam. The man Garland had been charged by his queen to find.

And yet, paradoxically, none of this had happened yet.

Teret's world was in his future. Stogi and Tai Pei, Garland's lost men—their time yet to be.

He'd sailed out from Gol that bright summer morning, his mother and father watching with young Kael. Estorien, his older brother, had been away attending some important wedding in Galanais. The vile Barolans were involved. Carlo had warned him not to go—sly Galanians being what they were, and Baron Barola rumored worse. But Estorien had a glib tongue and had assured him he'd be fine. He wasn't sailing west like a fool into dreams and nothing.

And why did I leave them?

He tried to picture his mother and father. Teret's face was hazy in his mind, but his parents were gone. It was like their memory had been erased from his head. He'd seen twenty-five winters and never lost that wild craving for adventure—his crew, too. Restlessness. A need to explore. Not for him the sleazy sinister politics of Gol's six bickering provinces. Estorien had thrived in that world. Carlo was a plainer man.

He and Gurdey had built the *Arabella* over three summers. They'd corked and tested her in rough waters, hewed the trees for lumber, and raised the masts, even set needle to thread on sailcloth.

They'd reworked and added ballast while she lay up for winter, dry and safe in Reveal harbor. Bench and oar, cabins and galley. The two men, and Tareel and Tar, with occasional help from others, had made it their passion, until the *Arabella* took shape that bright spring morning. They'd been drunk in a tavern when he'd come up with the wildest notion.

"We'll sail as far west as we can," he'd told Gurdey and Slim, his closest friends. "Find fresh continents and discover new peoples. We know they're out there. They must be."

Easy, and yet …

Baroness Arabella had wept seeing her son guide the ship he'd named after her through the reeds and mangrove enclosing Reveal harbor. He'd waved back at her, and she'd turned away. The vague memory stirred inside. Had that been a year ago? Two? He had no idea.

A tapping at the door brought his thoughts back to the present. *Not again.* He wasn't in the mood for Tai Pei.

"Who's there?"

"Taylon. Garland's man. I'd like a word if I may, Captain Carlo."

Carlo blew out his cheeks and bid the man enter. He was surprised to see Taylon's arm in a sling. "She did that?"

"Fixed it proper," Taylon grinned, showing broken teeth. It was the first time he'd seen the man smile. "Been giving me jip since we left the Laregozan border country."

"An accident?" Carlo enquired without much interest.

"An arrow. Gifted from a Ptarnian raiding party. That Shen woman ... she's—"

"—I know." Carlo smiled and motioned Taylon take a seat in his study. He poured brandy, and the man slumped back in the chair. "You've been through a lot."

Taylon gave him a level look and nodded. "As have you, captain."

"How can I help you?"

"I don't know, some guidance perhaps? This journey ..."

"... doesn't make sense to a rational mind." Carlo sipped brandy, folded his arms and leaned back in his chair. The cabin rocked gently—his ship knew how to ride a storm. Outside, water thudded and washed against the porthole, smearing the view as the cabin timbers creaked and rattled. Tareel was right—the gale was worsening. "What have my crew told you?"

"Not much." Taylon shrugged. "The few I've asked seem as confused as Tol and myself. Though he's happy enough. Tol always believes things happen for a reason and it will all work out. I don't share that view. I need to know what you are hoping to achieve, and how I can find Garland. If, like you implied, he's not dead."

Carlo sighed and nodded slowly. "You're right, Taylon. And I've been hiding this from my crew for too long, using one excuse or another. Enough said. Enjoy your brandy, man. We'll wait for the storm to abate and I'll address these matters on deck, say at first light."

Taylon nodded. "That works for me."

"We're sailing into the past." Carlo awarded the hard-faced soldier a frank stare.

"That's what I've been hearing."

"Insane, isn't it? Were you not tempted to jump overboard?"

"The thought occurred to me, albeit briefly. You're not mad, as first I deemed. And … me and Tol. We've seen things that change a man. Bad things. I'm willing to accept that there are phenomena that simple folk can never grasp."

"Good. *That's good.* I'll see you in the morning. Here, take the bottle. I'm done for the night. Help you sleep through the weather." He smiled passing the fat bottle across.

"Thank you, captain," Taylon accepted the brandy and left him be, closing the cabin quietly behind him.

Carlo closed his eyes. He'd been dreading this. He gazed at the small, round window, letting the rhythmic thud of wave on glass lull his senses. He had to forget Teret and all that happened back there. That past had gone. Or had it been the future? He laughed, feeling slightly drunk, and closed his eyes. That foray was over like any other dream. Gol was another matter. A past that lay ahead. How to convey that to his men?

Crossing dimensions, sailing through the gods alone knew what. To a homecoming, before that home was swept away.

It's a wonder I'm sane.

He slept fitfully for an hour, before waking and writing a few notes on parchment with his quill. Dawn brought a calmer sea. Carlo went aloft and smiled in the sunshine. He approached Dry Gurdey at the wheel.

"Rough night."

"We've known worse."

"You want me to take over for a stretch?"

"I'm good," Gurdey said. "Do this in my sleep."

Gold Tar appeared yawning, and Carlo bid him summon the crew and also wake the passengers.

"What's up?" Tar asked.

"Just get everyone, saving the lookouts."

Tar disappeared. Carlo heard his shouts below deck and watched as the bleary-eyed crew emerged, yawning. Most had spent the entire night fighting the weather and looked grumpy.

Next came the two newcomers with Tai Pei between them, laughing at something Tol had said. She seemed to laugh more of late. Last up, a green-faced Stogi staggered through the hatch. He glanced around warily, seemed satisfied the sea had calmed down, and hobbled over to stand close to Tai Pei and Garland's pair.

The crew lounged on benches as Dry Gurdey handed the wheel to Slim and joined them, amidst mutters and shoves. Gold Tar stood with brawny tattooed arms folded, his face grim, watching from the stern.

"Will this take long?" the bosun said. "Boys need their kip."

"Not long," Carlo replied, and Gold Tar leaned against the second mast, striking flint to stone, lighting his clay pipe.

Expectant faces gazed up at Carlo, as he stood with feet braced beside Tareel. He smiled at Slim. "Where to start?"

The mate shrugged. "At the beginning?" he suggested.

Carlo nodded, turning to face the crew and passengers.

"I know you all have so many questions. You, my loyal lads, found your captain wandering aimlessly in a strange town. And you four—our new friends—have experienced different versions of the weirdness I've seen.

"Suffice to say we left Gol, our home …" He looked at Stogi, Tai Pei and the other two. Tai Pei alone gazed back at him with a grin. Stogi was scratching his ear thoughtfully. Tol looked half-asleep, and Taylon intent with his dark eyes on the horizon.

"… about a year ago according to my reckoning." He glanced at Gold Tar and the crew. Some shrugged, others shook their heads.

"It's only been a few months, skip," Slim whispered in his ear. Carlo chose to ignore that.

"Don't know about you boys, but I can't recall much of that early sail. We'd called in at Cazea, or one of Island States. Can't remember which. At some point, we entered a terrible storm. Far worse than last night's blow, Master Stogi. It was during that deluge that disaster struck and the crew and myself were parted. Or so it was shown to me."

He noted Gold Tar scowling at him.

"Shipwrecked, I was washed up half-starved and wretched on an alien shore. A different world entirely, it turned out. The sky was wrong, and I thought I was in Yffarn. There was a woman …"

Slim chuckled beside him and some of the men grinned, causing a release in the tension.

"There always is with you." Dry Gurdey spat tobacco from his mouth.

"And a witch," Carlo continued. "Three, actually. And a steel warrior." They were looking worried again—except Tai Pei, who was nodding her head sagely, as though she knew exactly what he'd experienced on distant Gwelan.

"The woman, Teret, told me many things. She helped us escape the metal monster's traps. She was very brave and was seeking her husband, after being kidnapped by a brigand. A man she later killed in the Castle of Lights.

"We escaped that awful place, Gwelan. And left Elerim's lair—an uncanny forest sounding like the Rundal Woods you mentioned. Perhaps the same, hard to guess." He nodded to Tol and Taylon.

"We travelled south on mountain roads. From Teret, I learned that I had somehow slipped through time. Ha, I know …." He looked at their hushed faces and chewed his bottom lip. "We … or at least I, was in our distant future. Yes. And Gol, our home, had been destroyed by a demon one thousand years ago."

He stared at them bleakly. No one spoke. Tai Pei was still grinning. Beside her, Stogi looked wary, as though expecting trouble. Garland's pair were nodding. At least he had their support. But the crew looked edgy.

They think I'm touched, or cursed. This could go either way.

Gold Tar hawked and spat tobacco over the rail.

"Things came to a head in the Castle of Lights," Carlo continued, despite their narrowing gazes. Again, he glanced at

Tol and Taylon. "That's where I met your leader Garland, and Teret was reunited with her husband. Things occured there that I'd sooner not mention, nor is it relevant. But a strange being called Jynn guided me to a shore, where I saw my ship waiting and you lads all unhurt. I thought I'd lost my mind, and perhaps I had."

"How long do we have to listen to this?"

Carlo ignored Gold Tar.

"We need to hear this, Tar," Dry Gurdey said, and nodded to Carlo.

"Stogi there, and Tai Pei, had travelled with Lord Tamersane, brave Teret's missing husband." They nodded back at him. "And you two warriors from Wynais had journeyed east with Garland to find Tamersane, but like myself were assaulted by all manner of bewitchery."

"In Rundal Woods," Taylon said gloomily.

"One thing came out of it all," Carlo continued. "One certainty. We have to go home. Save our families and our country. Change our future, before it becomes their past. Back to Gol. The only way we can do that is to sail through the dimensions, crossing time itself—crazy as that sounds. Despite that, I know we can—and will—achieve this. We have to."

Gold Tar laughed out loud. Some of the crew were shaking their heads.

Carlo persisted, despite his worries. "The bow Kerasheva was lost in the Castle of Lights. I saw Teret shoot and kill the giant serpent Garland so valiantly engaged in battle. It's all I remember before the blasting and arriving on the shore, with Stogi and Tai Pei, and my ship a feast for starving eyes. Jynn saved us. So it seemed to me."

"You think Garland is in Gol? Trapped in the past where you came from?" Taylon asked.

"I doubt that," Carlo replied, shaking his head. "Your captain seemed to know exactly where he was going. How, I've no idea. Just another factor of the warping inside that castle. That said, I believe we will encounter Garland again. Call that a hunch. This *game* isn't over—far from it. I know enough in my heart to feel that we are all connected and will be brought back together."

"A hunch? We're sailing towards the rising sun and backwards in time, all to save a land drowned a thousand years ago? What's next? Dragon racing?" Stogi raised his hands. "Don't get me wrong, skipper, I'm happy to be here. But I don't think you've thought this business out properly."

"Shut up, you fat fool." Tai Pei nudged the Tseole in the ribs. "Sometimes you have to have faith. Captain Carlo knows this is right. If you were from the past and discovered something bad had happened, you'd want to get back too."

"I'm only saying ..."

"Well, don't bother—it isn't helpful." She winked at Carlo, who felt like he was sinking, watching their eyes. More of his men were shaking their heads. Tar was scowling and spitting. Garland's two looked baffled and worried. Stogi's eyes were on the horizon, as though sensing more storms. But Tai Pei was still grinning at him like a playful cat.

"That's it," Carlo said. "Best I can do."

"Not like we have much of a choice, is it?" Gold Tar muttered.

"Don't you want to go home?" Gurdey glared at his friend.

"Of course, I want to go home," Gold Tar said. "But that means sailing east and finding it. I'm sorry, skipper, but I think you've lost your marbles. Whoever these strangers are, you're caught in their fucking web. We lads found you witless and wandering inside that city. Rundali, the locals called it.

Confused and blabbering nonsense. Then this rogue and that slant-eyed killer wench turn up like stray cats. Now these two castaways. And they all know the people you know. I say this is bollocks, captain. But as long as we're sailing in the right direction, I'll keep my mouth shut."

Tai Pei glared at the mate. "That's just as well, if you want to keep breathing." Tar avoided her gaze and disappeared below, followed by a few of the men.

"That angry fellow reminds me of Pash," Carlo heard Tol mutter.

"Aye, history repeating itself," muttered Taylon.

"I'm done," Carlo said. "Wake me if you must—I'm for sleeping a few hours." He left them to it and climbed back down the hatch to his cabin, his head buzzing and mind troubled. He wasn't surprised to see Tai Pei waiting for him by the cabin door.

"I'm not in the mood for further discussion," he told her.

"There's going to be trouble," she said. "That Gold Tar, some of the others. They won't be able to handle what's coming. They're weak."

"And what is coming, Tai Pei? How is it that you alone seem to know the future?"

"There is no future. Or past, captain. But we do have this moment."

"Please, no riddles—I really need to rest."

"I can wait," she said, and stepped sideways allowing him through.

CARLO MUST HAVE DOZED OFF, BECAUSE THE SUN WAS high when an urgent rapping shook sleep from his eyes. He rolled from the bunk. He was angry with himself. He'd said too much and confused them. Far better, he'd just allowed they were sailing home, but were lost and it could take a while. He hadn't wanted to lie, though. They deserved better than that.

"We will get back to Gol." Carlo said to himself as he slipped on his deep boots, strapped scimitar to belt and ventured back on deck.

"What is it?" Carlo asked Dry Gurdey at the wheel.

"That." The wheelmaster pointed north to a dark speck of land surrounded and hooded by eerie cloud. "Goskin spotted it emerging from mist."

Another island at last, perhaps a dozen miles away. They could divert easily, seek fresh provisions. Maybe hunt some game. Be good for the lads to get some fresh meat, particularly after he'd bungled things this morning.

"What do you think?" Carlo asked Gurdey and Slim as the mate joined them. Most the crew were busy, and the others sleeping below deck.

"Looks a tad gloomy," Slim Tareel held the spyglass to his eye. "Like those dark clouds are attached to it, like the hood on a cloak."

"Dark clouds mean rain. And rivers. Fish ..." Carlo grinned.

"Aye, and probably beasts we can hunt," Gurdey said.

"Fancy a forage?" Carlo grinned at his friends. He felt more positive—they had something fresh to focus on. "Let's take a look."

"Aye, skip." Gurdey turned the wheel, and Slim Tareel shouted orders to those aloft

12

THE HOODED ISLAND

"I DON'T LIKE the look of the place," Stogi said, twenty minutes later, as the skiff buffeted through chop to the gloomy rain-washed shore.

"You could have stayed put with Tol and the other one," Tai Pei told him.

"You'll need skilled hunters," Stogi told her. "That's if there's game to be had, which I doubt."

"Come, Tseole, it's not like you to be pessimistic," Carlo said, as he worked the tiller. "I thought you'd be happy for a chance at dry land again."

"I'm just saying that place has an unsavory look. Those clouds worry me. We Tseole have a nose for such things."

"Tosh, you're losing your edge," Tai Pei said. "You've been a mess since we left Ta Shen. And you should have stayed on the *Arabella*—I can catch anything with these." She held up a sling and small bag of stones, which she'd somehow acquired during their brief stop in Ta Shen harbor. She also had a crossbow, courtesy of Carlo's rack. Stogi carried three knives and a short hunting bow. He said he wasn't taking any chances after getting caught out at the Crantocks.

Carlo had his scimitar strapped to his waist. He'd decided to go alone, mainly because he wanted time away from the crew—for their sake as much as his. He'd changed his mind and told Slim and Gurdey to keep an eye on Gold Tar, reporting back any sly comments they heard. Tar was an old friend, but people change. He couldn't afford the crew to take a set against him. The mate and wheelmaster had been disappointed but agreed their friend needed watching.

Carlo gazed at the approaching land as they drifted closer.

Dark woods smoldered into gloomy haze as he furled the sail and grabbed an oar. He was enjoying himself, the two still bickering at the front of his smaller skiff. He smiled at their nonsense and worked the oars, guiding the craft as she crashed through breakers and emerged on a damp, stone-washed beach.

Stogi helped him push the skiff onto dry shingle, while Tai Pei stretched like a cat and gazed up at the dark trees, hanging like dripping fingers over the landward side of the strand.

The rain had ceased, and a pale mist occluded what he'd marked as low hills from the *Arabella*. Looking back, he could see her sitting proud in the sunshine.

Stogi grumbled, while Tai Pei started trotting toward the dripping trees.

"She never stops," he said. Carlo nodded, his mind on other things. It felt good to have a break, especially after this morning's disaster.

"Go catch her up," he told Stogi. "I'm heading for that stream." He pointed to a dark crack of rock, where clear water could be heard crashing out onto the shingle. "Could be I'll tickle a salmon or two."

"Be careful, captain," Stogi told him, his dark eyes showing genuine concern. "There's something not right here. I feel it. Whistle if you need us. Three times. I'll do the same."

Carlo nodded and waved him away, slightly irritated by Stogi's timid behavior. Tai Pei was right—he'd been gloomy of late. He waited until the Tseole had caught up with the girl, who was gazing up at steep rocks. He saw them pointing and arguing.

Carlo shrugged. *We all need some space.*

He found the stream, a narrow, rock-squeezed half tube, funneling water out in jetty squirts. He scooped down to wash his face but stopped when the water's iciness sent a shiver up his spine. The water's touch felt that dead man's fingers. He shuddered and glanced up, sensing movement.

"Who's there?" he asked, reaching for his sword.

Whooooos there … there …. theeeere … An echo drifted back to him. Carlo shook the shiver away. Damn Stogi and his misgivings. He was imagining things now.

"Get a grip, man," Carlo muttered under his breath and moved on.

He walked up the shale-crumbly crack, taking care and keeping his boots clear of the water. The stream's path led down from a steep, stony bank. He saw ferns shifting in a breeze he couldn't feel. It was muggy, stifling even. His eyelids felt heavy as he clambered up, and the higher he got, the wearier he felt.

Carlo cursed and staggered onto the ridge of stone, where the stream met the rock slide. Beyond that, a dark pond seeped into murky, weed-covered banks, its coal-black surface cloaked by dead-looking bulrushes. The water stank and clogged his nostrils. He looked around and saw a track of sorts skirted the right side of the pond.

He could make out what looked to be steps of stone winding up into the low-hanging cloud above. Perhaps he could get above the cloud and mist? The hills' crowns had been clear when last he'd seen them from the *Arabella*, the rain having passed.

He took the track skirting the rancid water, but stopped again when he heard a shrill call to his right. Carlo blinked and saw a large, black bird settle on a nearby tree. A raven. It watched him in silence. He shook his head and moved on, following the track toward the broken steps. These he took two at a time, pausing often and peering up through the gloom. The weariness was draining him, and he felt a compelling urge to give up this climb and rest in the bracken framing the edges of the steps.

I'm tired, that's all.

It must be the rank atmosphere of this place. Perhaps something large had died in that pond and was decomposing. Carlo wiped sweat from his face. He regretted coming here but felt determined to make the visit worthwhile. If he could get high enough, the air would be fresher. There would be prey up there. With all this water, there had to be. Once he could see, he'd whistle to Stogi and the girl. He didn't want them to choke in the pond's foul fumes. He hoped they were having more luck—maybe Tai Pei had found her rabbits?

He forced a smile to his lips, *I'll turn this day around yet.*

A soft sound to his right. Laughter? He heard it again.

Someone's watching.

And a third time. An ironic chuckle, as though a hidden eavesdropper had heard his thoughts, as if he'd uttered them out loud.

Damn this.

Carlo slid the scimitar free of its scabbard. He circled

slowly, gazing back down the steps. He could no longer see the pond or stream. Neither could he see the ocean beyond, the steamy fret having gotten so thick.

There was movement below. He was certain of it this time. A vague, shapeless figure was inching up the steps towards him. Carlo felt an overwhelming sense of dread as his gaze remained fixed on the apparition. Stogi had been right. They should never have come here.

It was rising slowly like smoke, its form shifting and changing, until he saw what looked to be a man with the face of a boar, a single horn protruding.

Carlo forced movement into his trembling legs and turned to start climbing, as swiftly as he could, up through the mist. He didn't stop or look back, but sensed whatever it was closing the gap behind him.

He could hear a hissing sound like the venting of a kettle. The creature's breath? The pig thing was gaining on him fast. Carlo broke into a panicked run. He reached a crest and tripped as the loose stones rolled under his feet.

He sprawled on his face and tried to roll and lift the sword, but a heavy boot pinned him to the spot.

"We have him," a dry, hollow voice said, and Carlo blacked out as something hard struck the back of his head.

STOGI CHEWED HIS LIP AS HE GAZED ABOUT. TAI PEI HAD vanished in the gloom, despite him yelling for her to wait. He couldn't find her, or even the path she'd used to get up there. He heard grunting and saw movement in the brush over to his right.

A large animal. He reached for his bow, nocked shaft to

string and waited. Perhaps a boar? If he were careful, he could catch it with an arrow when it broke loose of the under-growth. He waited. Nothing. Then a quiet rustle of leaves further away.

Stogi cursed under his breath. The pig—or whatever it had been—was gone. He'd seen the bushes shake as it faded back into the darkness beyond the trees. He felt sweat trickle down his face. Damn that woman, and Carlo. This entire island was a trap, he felt certain of it.

"You'll have to save them, Stogi. This could be your big chance."

The voice had been that of a young girl. He could still hear her shrill laughter trailing off.

"*Who* ... where are you, spirit?" Stogi turned slowly, the bow string pulled back. Sudden movement to his right. He released the string. The arrow thudded through a shadow and disappeared. Stogi cursed his wasting a shaft.

"You'll have to do better than that." Her laughing voice was closer this time.

"Show yourself, wight." Stogi fumbled with another shaft and nearly dropped it, his fingers greasy with sweat.

"You three are in danger," she said, chiding him with mocking tones. "Not wise, coming here. But you knew that, and still came. *Love* does that— makes a man a loon." The voice was right behind him. Stogi turned slowly and saw her at last.

A young girl wearing a short blue dress, with two blonde pigtails tied neatly with bows, and a big smile; the eyes were birds'-egg blue. The child was seated on a branch a few feet away. Her bare bruised legs were crossed, and her grubby fingers steepled beneath the chin.

"What are you?" Stogi's hand trembled on the bow. He

eased back the tension, somehow knowing he couldn't shoot this specter.

"I mean you no harm," she clasped her hands together. "And I came to help. Explain a few things. You have questions, I'm sure of that?"

"Who are you?" Stogi pressed.

"I am Urdei, child of the Past. Innocence. Birth and growth. One of the Three you men call the Fates. Or Norns, depending where you're from. We have other names. Too many. My gift for you today is to guide you through these nets."

"I don't believe you. You're a spirit, and ill-wight who intends myself and friends harm. I will fill you with arrows drow, if you don't step aside. Move! I have friends to find."

The girl shook her head slowly in disapproval. She folded her arms and tutted. Stogi made to pull the strings back, but she'd know he was bluffing. It was hopeless—she had him hooked. He couldn't hurt a little girl, be she illusion or not.

Damn you. Stogi placed the arrow in his belt and leaned heavily on the bow.

"Say I believe you, for the moment. Why help us—and where is this shitty place? *And* … how do you know my name?"

"I know everything about you, Stogi Tseole. I'm Urdei. The gatekeeper of what has already happened. My province is the past. Big sisters Present and Future are currently working on other projects. We three like to keep busy. I've been away from Ansu a while, but your new friend Carlo Sarfe has been making noises and caught my attention—and that of some very unsavory types you'll encounter soon."

"Where are my friends?"

She ignored the question as if he hadn't spoken. "You

mortals can't expect to stomp about and dabble with complexities you don't understand without waking things best left alone. There are always consequences. The universe is complex, a finely tuned machine."

"My friends?" Stogi tried a second time.

Again, she ignored him. "You see what I mean? Captain Carlo's wanting to return to the past. That's dangerous for humans. Hazardous for anyone, really, but especially your lot. Some things you just don't attempt without the right preparation. But … I'm here to help." She rubbed her hands together and grinned down at him. "Well …?"

Stogi scratched an ear. He heard crashing somewhere close. It sounded like a large creature out hunting. Bigger than the pig he thought he'd spotted earlier.

"Do you know how to get to Gol?"

"Of course I do, silly. But it's not just getting there, is it? It's surviving the process."

"I don't know. Hope so. I gate-crashed this adventure, having fallen off the last one. Tam—"

"His story's over." She looked irritated. "You're in Carlo's tale now. Maybe Queen Ariane's too, if you hang in there and don't get killed—though, of course, I can't be certain, as I am not my sister."

Stogi tensed, hearing a scream trail off somewhere in the tangle of trees above. He looked past the girl, who waited with her smile and a finger poised neatly under chin. The scream again. *Tai Pei?* It didn't sound like her. Then who?

"I've got to get moving," he told her. "I don't like this place, and my friends could be in trouble."

"Carlo certainly is."

"*What?* Where is he, can you see him?" Stogi made to push past the branch, but the girl swung down gracefully and caught his arm with an iron-strong grip. He turned and saw her gazing intently up at him.

"Listen, Stogi of windy Tseole, I know you're not a fool. Although you can be a joker—and I like jokes. They make me giggle—so I want to help. But you need to listen to what I have to say. Yes?" He nodded reluctantly. "Captain Carlo is in big trouble, and your sweet Tai Pei will be very soon too. I'm impressed with her skills, and that she's avoided them so far."

"Who is *them*?"

"Sir Valen the Gaunt and the hunters from the Hall."

"All right, enough said. Step aside, Urdei, *please*, and let me go find my friends before these bad people—"

"Shut up and listen!"

Stogi's mouth froze half open. She was standing right in front of him, one small fist rammed into her waist, the other pointing a finger at him, her pretty freckled face set in a deep, angry frown. Stogi sensed an uncanny power in that gaze, but there was no malice. She didn't feel *wrong*. But neither was she what she appeared. That much was obvious. He didn't buy the nonsense about Present and Past. She was an imp, and had somehow got the scoop on him. He slumped his shoulders in defeat.

"Best you start helping right away," Stogi said, gazing around through the dense brush and trees. It was lighter but still hard to see clearly.

Her blue eyes narrowed mischievously. "Do you remember Seek?"

"Unfortunately, yes. The shaman was a blight on my community."

"Well, perhaps, maybe so. But the *Seek* you thought you knew was someone else. A sly trickster who would sow seeds of discord. He's been watching your progress, all of you onboard that dead ship."

Dead ship?

Stogi's mind glazed over the last words. She'd put a spell on him. He needed to get moving, but doubted he could without her permission.

"Seek the shaman is in Tseole, or was last I saw him."

"No. He is here, or lurking close by. And wearing a new guise. He's invested in your game and means to stop Carlo from getting home."

"Why would Seek do that? He's never met Carlo Sarfe. He's a shaman from Dunnehine."

"The conniver I'm talking about stole Seek's form. Killed the real one. Yes, Stogi, the old Seek's dead. Torn apart. Bird food. That's what happens when you pry too much. Especially if you're mortal. But it's also good too, isn't it? As you didn't like him."

Stogi's mouth was open. There were no words.

"Hmm ..."

"This replacement Seek is an older, far wiser entity than that vain, foolish shaman," she continued. "*This* Seek means you harm because you're breaking his rules. That's bad, isn't it?"

"Sounds bad."

"Trust me, it's disastrous bad."

The scream again. Further away this time.

Stogi swallowed an urge to run past her. Try at least.

"I don't know any Graywash Hall."

"You should," she smiled. "Because you and your friends are trapped inside its deepest chamber."

The moment she spoke, the last words the atmosphere changed. Shifted, and darkened further. The trees faded back to black. Almost, he saw pale faces looking out, with eyes cruel as executioners. He glimpsed what resembled dark dirty walls, leading off to a door.

"Sorcery." Stogi spat the word out.

"Of the worst kind." He heard her voice, but could no longer see the girl.

"Not you're doing, imp?"

"Don't make me cross! Follow me."

"How can I, if I can't fucking see you?" It could have been his imagination, but the walls seemed like they were closing in to crush him.

"Don't be vulgar. Shut up, and follow this light." Her voice came from ahead, nearer the door.

Stogi blinked when a tiny glow appeared from nowhere. A giant firefly, or will O' the wisp. The light hovered and drifted back, circling in front of his face. Before gliding away and floating off down the dark corridor, bouncing off the half-visible walls like a child's discarded illuminous magic ball.

Stogi gulped. He tried to hold on to his reason as he followed the flickering dancing light toward the distant door. The walls were shrinking. As he passed, he sensed more than saw paintings on the walls. The cruel faces were framed, their eyes watching and weeping black liquid as he hurried by.

"What is this foul place?" He called out to the light.

"Keep up!"

"Tell me!"

"Graywash Hall lies outside your understanding." Her voice floated back to him, as Stogi rushed closer to the dancing golden glow. Unlike its shrinking sides, the corridor seemed to stretch on forever. The door slipped further back, withdrawing as though baiting him. The one time he'd dared look back, he thought he saw a greenish figure on a horse wielding a spiked mace on a chain. Too dark to be sure.

"There's something back there."

"The Faceless Knight—you'd best keep up."

"I'm right behind you. What is—"

"Think of the Hall as an entity. A living, breathing organism, or a substance that resembles a building."

Stogi was about to ask more when the light flickered and went out. He quelled his panic, surrounded by silence and utter dark. It was stuffy, hard to breath, and with a cloying stale stench made him want to retch.

Got to move.

He blinked, shouted her name and pushed forward, stopping abruptly when his face struck a wall, and icy cobwebs clung to his nostrils.

Fuck this, Stogi wiped the sticky mess from his nose and sneezed.

A noise behind.

He turned, his eyes adjusting far too slowly to the pitch. He spotted the horseman riding silently toward him. An aura? Still some distance away. A steel rider wearing a tall helm with a long scarlet plume. The armor glowed a faint, sickly green. The knight's features were hidden by helmet and visor. The morning star and a long sword were belted at his waist.

You're not real.

As the apparition approached, Stogi saw the knight whirling something new over his head. A net. He almost choked. Turning about, he scurried on through the dark, panicking. He stopped abruptly when Urdei emerged from the gloom standing braced, with arms folded.

"This way," she said, her face serious again. "You need to take that door."

"Where?" He couldn't see anything apart from her shadow standing beside him, and the steel warrior riding his horse slowly, the armor shimmering dark green, and the large net swaying toward them.

"Who is that fellow?"

"Open the door, silly!" her voice shrieked inside his head. Stogi stumbled blindly forward, and his fingers slid over something round. He gripped it firmly.

A handle, thank goodness.

He turned the knob and fell inside.

13

THE CAULDRON

CARLO WOKE and found himself chained to a wall, his feet dangling high above a huge cauldron that bubbled and vented steam.

No way ...

He struggled at the chains and almost fainted from horror. How was this possible? Who had attacked him, and why? Was it the Grogan? The steel giant in Gwelan where he'd met Teret? That brute had liked his fires. No, the Grogan was dead. Perhaps another had tracked him to this horrible place?

"He's awake. We can start."

The hollow voice croaked out over the bubbling hiss below. This wasn't happening. Carlo closed his eyes. *I don't accept this as reality.*

"Oh, but it is, Carlo Sarfe," the dark voice said.

He craned his neck and saw a tall, reedy thin figure watching him from a platform beside the cauldron. He wore a flat, square black cap and dark-red cloak. Emaciated, his features were shrouded in gloom. Beside the cloaked man stood another figure. Bigger, and covered in glowing green steel. A tall warrior, leaning on a heavy broadsword. Steel gauntlets resting on the cross-guard. The face was hidden by a highly polished visor and mirror helm that reflected Carlo's stricken gaze. A scarlet plume crested the helm and appeared to nod toward him.

"Who are you people?" he croaked the words out. "What madness is this?"

"You should have listened to the Tseole," the thin man in the cap said. "Too late. Stogi and the girl will join you soon as we prepare the feast."

"Yffarn take you."

A dark chuckle. "But this is Yffarn, Carlo Sarfe. Or can be, if we wish it so. Graywash Hall can be anything. Its people are not restricted by movement or time. You crossed through the dimensions coming here. Alerted the Orb. It's how we noticed you and lured you inside. Did you not hear the harp?"

"This is not happening."

"You are an offering to the Lord of Chaos. Our master. The essence that surrounds us here Is the stain of his majesty."

Carlo craned his neck the other way. Dimly, he saw movement beyond the two figures. Someone was shouting obscenities. He recognized Tai Pei's voice and called out a ragged warning. He strained, trying to see her. Over there were deep grooves cut into what appeared to a be very large caverns, or pits oozing spurts of flame.

As Carlo looked in horror, he could just make out the tiny figure of the girl running toward the giant cauldron, the sling in hand, whirling as she ran. He saw other figures, perhaps a dozen or more. They were running to cut her off. He croaked another warning, but she was too far away to hear him.

The steel warrior was watching her, while his companion

clapped silently with soft, white leather gloves. "And here she comes—such bravery," the thin one said to the other.

Tai Pei weaved and danced across the cavern base, the dark figures chasing. Carlo saw bridges spanning fire trenches. This must be Yffarn. The island's demons had drawn them inside. He shook the chains, wriggled, and tugged. He was stuck fast as a bug in warm honey. He watched in despair as they surrounded her. Large men with strange-looking heads, hefting crooked spears.

Tai Pei broke through their ring, tripping one fellow and diving between another.

"Carlo!" he heard her yell.

"Get away!" he shouted back and saw her look up at him, her pale face and dark eyes stricken with horror.

"You bastards!" Tai Pei whirled the sling, catching one of the men chasing her in his eye. He tumbled, disappearing into smoky vapor. "I'm going to kill every one of you," she yelled. The men caught up with her again and cornered her as she ran toward the bubbling cauldron.

"Save yourself, Tai Pei," Carlo yelled across. She'd lost her bow and seemed out of stones. "Run!"

One looked his way, and Carlo saw with horror his head resembled that of a fox. A second stood beside him, face blurred and distorted into some horrible fish parody. They didn't look like helmets. He could see them better where they surrounded her. A dozen brutish figures, their faces covered in hideous animal masks. They were goading Tai Pei with spears.

One got too close, jabbing at her. Tai Pei danced aside and got behind the rat-faced spearman. Deftly, she slipped the sling around his neck and tugged hard, lifting Rat-face off his feet and releasing, kicking him forward into the next man. Carlo watched, his mouth numb, saw them circle her, forcing her back until she was pinned against the cauldron with nowhere to go.

"Bring her up here," the thin man in the hat said lazily. "We'll cook her first. The Kaa will enjoy digesting this one."

Carlo saw Tai Pei fending them off with her fists and boots. Punching, jabbing. She gouged at a fish face with her fingers, ripping out his huge, round, lidless eyes. That attacker dropped and exploded into smoky cinders. These were not men, but demons, Carlo realized in horror.

Tai Pei fought on despite it being hopeless. They were playing with her. Most had abandoned their spears and were reaching for her with brawny, leather-clad arms. She threw punches, clawed and gouged, spat and shrieked.

He saw her kick out, catching a weasel face in the groin, and simultaneously jabbing backwards with an elbow as a bird-face reached for her from behind. They bunched closer, about to rush at her. She sliced out with her fingers, ripping off a badger snout, then spun around in dazzling speed and scissor-kicked a fox-face in the neck.

But it was over. They fell upon Tai Pei and bore her down, smothering her body and stifling her yells as Carlo screamed rage, his throat dry and red.

The thin man rubbed his gloves in glee. "Here we go," he said, cheerfully. The narrow face tilted toward the place where Carlo hung. "You've got the best seat, Carlo. Once she's tender, we'll start on you."

Carlo spat bloody phlegm. "Fuck you. This isn't happening."

He saw the tall warrior turn and stare across at him, point and make a sweeping chopping motion with his steel gauntlet. Unlike the Grogan he'd encountered, there was a man inside that armor. What kind of deviltry possessed these people?

Carlo heard a hollow sound like laughter coming from inside the gleaming helmet.

He heard shrill shouts below. Tai Pei! She'd broken loose again, rammed her fingers into a dog-face and ripped his broad snout open. The thing crumpled like ancient parchment fading into dust. Carlo saw her staring up at him.

"I'm coming up," she shouted hoarsely, as a shadow loomed behind her.

"No, Tai Pei. Run!" Carlo yelled back, seeing the shadow rise higher. A giant figure with the face of a bull, the huge horns curving out sideways. Tai Pei turned too late. Bull-face reached down with huge steel gauntlets and lifted her over its head before tossing her up onto the platform as though she was a parcel. The warrior and cloaked man watched her wriggle and spit. The thin one motioned his steel companion forward.

The faceless warrior walked over and kicked Tai Pei as she struggled to rise, knocking her prone again. He stood on her back, stamping down hard with the steel boots. He turned and looked at his companion.

The thin man pointed a pale glove. "Toss her in."

"No!" Carlo yelled, as he saw the warrior reach down and lift her one-handed, scooping her up easily, as a man lifts a small bag of salt. She screamed and spat in the mirror visor. Carlo heard the hollow laughter again. The knight held her high over his head, the steel fists glinting in the orange glow and merging with his sickly green. He walked over to the narrow platform that reached out to the middle of the caul-dron, much like a ship's gangplank, tottering high above the bubbling water.

She was screaming and struggling, held fast in that iron

grip. Carlo's voice was raw and bloody as he retched and bucked in his chains. "Tai Pei, I'm so sorry."

A shudder hit the walls of the cavern.

Carlo heard a shriek of rage. He saw the warrior turn in confusion, dropping his offering. Dazed and bleeding, Tai Pei crawled out between his steel legs and crawled off the plank.

Another thud, followed by a long steady boom, and what could only be the eerie tingle of harp strings fading off.

"I've lost my mind." Carlo closed his eyes, and his head started spinning. He opened them again, and gasped. He felt sick and weak as wilted lettuce.

Carlo saw the thin man staring at someone, his voice making mewling sounds as though the torturer couldn't move his lips. Carlo watched in horrified wonder as the surface of the cauldron became still, the water cooling fast, and freezing over.

"Kill them!" The man in the hat worked his mouth, forcing the words out with spittle that trailed off from his mouth. The warrior looked up, tilting his visor toward him.

Carlo beckoned him forward. "Yes, up you come, shit-head." The warrior was walking toward the wall where Carlo hung, his sword slung loose over a shoulder. He stopped, as another thud shook the platform. The thin man tumbled on his knees. The warrior tottered and thrust his sword point down to anchor himself.

The harp sang shrill.

Carlo heard the chains snap and blinked as sparks exploded in his face.

I'm free …

He felt his body drop, plummeting stone-swift toward the frozen water. As he tumbled face-first in stunned silence, the ice cracked open and Stogi's shaggy head burst free.

Carlo struck the freezing water and sank below the surface, his mouth too numb to swallow. A strong grip caught his wrist and tugged him up. Carlo gulped air as Stogi pulled him free. The two climbed out of the cauldron, the ice breaking and melting around them. Even as Carlo tugged himself free, he glimpsed the water heating and bubbling again.

"Someone's on our side," he choked, and seeing Tai Pei on her knees, ran over to join her. The warrior watched them in silence for a moment before flickering and fading from view, the hollow laughter trailing off.

The torturer looked terrified, left alone. He pulled a curved dagger from his cloak and stabbed out at Stogi, who'd been staring at the knight. Before Carlo could shout to warn him, Stogi turned, caught the thin man's wrist, and twisted the knife out of his glove. The torturer screamed as his wrist-bone snapped like a twig. Stogi pulled him close and butted his face, knocking him backwards into the bubbling water. The thin man screamed again and was pulled below by slimy fingers reaching out above the surface.

"This way, you three."

Carlo, dazed and half-deaf from the continuing booms, found himself staring at a little girl's grinning freckled face.

"Who …?"

"The sinkhole, quickly!" The blonde child pointed at a large, smoking orifice that had yawned open beyond the cauldron and apparatus. "You must dive inside," she said. "I cannot hold the Void back for much longer. The Orb searches. Run now!"

"Do as she says." Carlo saw Stogi glaring at him, before turning and running toward the yawning pit. He blinked, felt a small hand grip his own and saw Tai Pei glaring up at him.

"Come on," she said, bravely showing a smile. Together, they ran full pelt for the crack. As they sped, the cavern exploded into boulders crashing down around them. They reached the edge, Stogi waiting for them with eyes wide. Carlo couldn't see the child.

"Jump!"

He heard her voice and stepped forward into the chasm, his hand gripping Tai Pei's, and Stogi leaping at the same time.

They fell.

The cavern vanished, and a swirl of gases blinded him. Tai Pei's hand was wrenched from his grasp, and he heard Stogi shouting. Carlo reached out in the gas, seeking her hand, but a jet of hot air struck his face, knocking him backwards. He heard the wild random notes of the harp spinning around his head. The din assaulted his ear like tiny biting flies. He struck a hard object and fell over something else, crashing onto what felt like wood.

Bruised and panting, Carlo carefully opened his eyes and discovered he was back in his cabin, the sun shining through the porthole.

"What the…?"

Carlo heard someone laugh behind him. A child's chuckle. He turned and saw the blonde girl seated neatly at the end of his bunk.

Carlo blinked at her. "You … saved us from … that island …" He couldn't speak properly and felt sick again.

"Stogi saved you," she said. "I merely acted as a guide."

"Who are you, child?"

"I'm Urdei," she told him smiling. "She who owns the Past. *Your* past, Carlo Sarfe. I've come to take you home. Back to Gol. Are you ready for the ride?"

Carlo closed his eyes, blacked out on the floor.

End of Part One

PART II

DIMENSIONS

14

CADZARILLO

Zorc held his crooked stick and hissed at the flames. His tongue was clicking and making sounds that put Garland's teeth on edge. It was late. The night sky was a smother of dark lumbering clouds that trawled over his head like heavy silent ships. Occasionally a beam of starlight filtered through, settling graveyard pale on that dreadful hilltop.

Garland held his nerve as he chewed his moustache, his eyes tired and face taut with worry. At least his stomach was full, and he felt stronger. There were no lasting effects from his fight with the Kaa, and Urgolais witchery had brought him back to life. He dreaded to think what Zorc had used to make that unguent. No matter. It had worked.

They'd entered the Urgolais's damp cave on the other side of the island. Garland had screwed his nose up at the stale odor and pile of skulls and clutter rimming the cave wall. A low fire crackled at the rear. Zorc had roasted two coneys and, as promised, they'd eaten well. A short rest, and after that the climb back up to this tumble of weed-choked broken stones and crumbling walls.

Zorc gargled a strange noise and spat on the grass at his feet. Garland shivered. He saw something vague flicker past his head. He thought of the Castle of Lights and Rundal Woods—all the sorcery he'd endured on the fruitless quest to save Tamersane.

His men, Pash and Kurgan, had been taken by sorcery in Rundal Woods. Garland wouldn't forget that. His fault. He'd led the men there despite the rumors. Pash had spoken out against him. Perhaps Pash's angry shade would join those the Urgolais summoned.

He forced the useless thoughts back inside his head and switched them off. The only way he could survive this, and find the lost ones, was to keep his mind focused on what he understood. However difficult, or almost impossible that task proved.

I'm a soldier.

Not his job to ask, but to carry on through and get the work done. He thought of Marei and the brief happy time they'd shared together. If joining forces with this Urgolais meant seeing her lovely face again, he was fully committed. Zorc—whatever he really wanted—was an ally, if a tenuous one. Though watching the humpback twisted vile creature gargling and spitting and making symbols with his crooked fingers, made that choice all the more challenging.

"Are you getting anywhere?" Garland hissed. He'd seen odd shapes shifting but put that down to plant shadows moving in the night breeze. That, and his imagination torturing him.

"Shut up," Zorc hissed back, without turning his head. Garland complied. He wiped sweat from his face and went over to a rock, where he sat staring out at the dark water far below.

The chanting and spitting continued through the night. He must have dozed off for a moment, for a brush of wings past his ears snapped his eyes open. Garland stifled a shout seeing a large owl settle on a bush nearby.

It's just a bird, you fool. The owl stared at him in silence.

Garland stood wearily. He slid his sword free of scabbard and started working the blade with the whetstone he always kept in a small bag at his belt.

"Stop that! We're at a crucial point." Zorc's croak paused his hand. Garland placed the stone back and walked over to where the Urgolais sat wrapped in cloak, claw-like hands gripping the rod.

"Yes, here it comes," Zorc hissed triumphantly. "One of their leaders. I did us proud."

As Garland watched in morbid fascination, he saw a vague shape drifting toward them from one of the broken walls. The hairs tingled up his spine. Garland saw the shape shift and change, blur and reappear, until a vague man shape stood there, his features badly burnt and hair stuck to broken bits of blackened scalp. The eyes, though corpse-glazed, were full of hatred.

"Who dares summon Archmage Cadzarilo?" The voice was a drone resembling the distant dark waves on the shore far below. Garland thought he saw insects drifting out from the specter's ruined mouth as it spoke the words.

"I am Zorc. An Urgolais, who your people once called friends. We schooled your academy and funded this citadel, helping your order get started. Do you not remember, Cadzarilo? You were young and bright. I recall your zeal to learn our craft. Your peers called on us to deepen your knowledge and lore."

The Burnt One's eyes flickered, the malice replaced by a

woeful stare. Garland was breathing heavily as he leaned on his sword. Mercifully, the specter didn't seem to have noticed his presence, its dead eyes focused wholly on Zorc.

"We remember you, Stunted One." The voice was scrape raw, a dry blunt saw cutting knotted lumber. "It's true that you helped us long ago. But we repaid that by harboring you from the Golden Ones. I owe you nothing."

"Ingrate. No matter. I have powers that can help—or hinder—you," Zorc said. "I can make you whole again, Cadzarilo. Or not. Bring you back among the living, your flesh healed and spirit repaired. Or return you to the pyre."

"No being can do that. Not even a god. You are an imposter, Urgolais. I will summon the others. Together we will blast you and this man from our Citadel."

He sees me. Garland lurched forward and gripped the sword, readying to swing as Cadzarilo's dead eyes fell on him in fury.

"Fruitless is your quest, Journeyman. It ends here tonight." Cadzarilo raised a blackened, withered nubbin. Zorc emerged between them and struck the ruined digit with his staff. The wood shimmered slightly as it passed through Cadzarilo's hand. Garland heard the soft tingle of bells and saw weird lights flickering among the darkness of the ruins.

Cadzarilo's ghost faded back into nothing, the cold voice screaming out, *Save me. Don't send me back there!*

"And you'll agree to help?" Zorc shook the bent staff above his head. "Join us and find the Kaa? Unite your spell craft with my lore and this man's sword?"

"I do. *I will* ... Just don't send me back there."

"Very well." Zorc slammed the staff into the ground and uttered a terse command. Garland felt a gush of cold wind batter his face. He glimpsed the forgotten owl shrieking and gliding off over the stones before vanishing up into cloud.

Garland covered his eyes from the horror emerging. He heard the rip and tear of oozing flesh, accompanied by screams and choking.

"What is happening?" He covered his ears as the din grew louder and finally ceased. Garland took a deep breath and turned. He was expecting a horror, or ghoulish apparition. Instead, he saw a tall man staring back at him with flat, sardonic violet eyes. Zorc was crouched low, his ugly face showing broken black teeth in a ghoulish smile.

"Archmage Cadzarilo will help us," Zorc told Garland, who wasn't convinced.

"Or you'll return him to the burn pile?"

He looked at the tall man, currently dusting down his garments and gazing wide-eyed at the ruins of his ancient Citadel.

A handsome, stern figure. The charred specter had been replaced by a proud-looking individual with hooked nose and deep, intelligent eyes that blazed at Garland like amethysts. His skin was olive brown, the beard neatly trimmed into a trident. His black hair was long and oily, tightly curled and shiny as the eyes.

Those violet orbs were studying Garland like a hawk watches a wren. His shirt and trousers, and muscular frame, were covered by a long crimson cloak, with intricate golden circles traced along the edges. These glowed and shifted in the dark, the symbols moving up and down. Beneath his cloak, the baggy trousers were tugged into soft suede crimson boots. The shirt was a deep blue velvet, and a jeweled dagger and golden bag were pinned to his belt at either side of his waist. He glared at Garland.

Garland stared back unflinching, his gloves on the heavy sword. The man smiled slightly, raising a brow at Garland's defiance. He turned to Zorc, still watching from his wary crouch.

"This is a bold fellow, Urgolais. He dares match my gaze. Few could, even among my own. Perhaps I am not fully recovered."

"You are. I saved you, Cadzarilo," Zorc said. "You have to keep your side of our bargain, else I send you back down to Ashmali waiting in Yffarn. I can do that as easily as I brought you here."

Cadzarilo's dark eyes flashed angrily. He nodded. "Urgolais lore. I will do what I can," he said, glancing at Garland again. "But it's best you don't test me, soldier."

Garland said nothing. He had no idea why this former sorcerer harbored such dislike for him. Zorc had brought the archmage back to life to help them both. The man should be grateful. He let it go.

"What happens now?" he asked Zorc, ignoring the other's cold gaze.

"Cadzarilo finds them," Zorc said, and the tall man nodded.

"I see the Kaa, and the little ones they snatched," Cadzarilo said. "There are many captives. They mean to feed well tonight."

"Where are they, ghoul?" Garland gripped the sword, barely holding back from swinging it at the former Burnt One.

"Close … and yet …" Cadzarilo smiled at him. "… out of reach."

"You had better get them in reach. And sharpish. Else

Zorc—or more likely my sword— sends your cindering arse back down to whatever Yffarn he pulled it from. You don't scare me, magician. I've dealt with far worse than you. Tell me where Dafyd and the baby are, and how I can reach them. And do it fucking now."

He heard Zorc chuckling quietly. Garland's full attention was on the violet-eyed man staring back at him. Cadzarilo was probing him, those clever eyes gleaming like freshly polished jewels. Garland's cheeks burnt under that acerbic gaze. He imagined tiny ants running over his eyes.

He's using sorcery.

His legs trembled and flesh started to smolder and split.

An illusion. I must hold out.

"The archmage is testing you." Zorc's croak reached him as Garland felt his lips crackle and spit blood.

Enough.

He lifted the sword and stepped forward. Cadzarilo clapped his hands together. The pain and heat dissolved immediately. Garland stopped in mid-swing, the sword thudding into the soil.

"There ... You have a tiny inkling of what it feels to burn. You *are* the Journeyman, I see that. The one chosen for this tumultuous task. I'll not bait you any longer, *Sir* Garland. You have the strength."

"I don't give a damn—"

"—he had to test you," Zorc interrupted. "I told him you were the Champion, the man She chose."

"I don't know what you're gibbering about—either of you. Help me find that baby and Marei's lad, or get the fuck out of my way."

"Tell him," Zorc said.

"They are in Zorne. Their ship's anchored near a village on the coast. The villagers are either slain or captured."

"Then we had better get sailing to Zorne."

"You can't sail there in your skiff," Zorc said.

"I can and will," Garland told him. "Those cliffs are scarce a dozen miles distant. We can get there by daylight, if I row hard. You can use your tricks and guide me to that village."

Zorc chuckled again. "We could, but that wouldn't help overmuch."

"Why?" Garland held back another urge to hit both of them with his sword, his patience all but done. "Where are they?" He hissed the words through his teeth.

"It's not *where*. It's when," Cadzarilo said, his arms folded and expression grave. "The Kaa you seek dragged their prisoners back through time, emerging shortly before the fire demon Ashmali was summoned by the traitor who betrayed us. To achieve your goal, you'll also have to undergo a voyage into the past. Back to the days when the Citadel held more power than your simple soldier's mind could imagine."

"This is madness," Garland said. "I'm trapped in Graywash Hall, and the Kaa are there, too." He stopped, seeing a stricken look on the archmage's face.

"Do not mention that name again," Zorc said in a hushed voice. "The Orb searches, and we cannot let it find us. The child guide helped you escape it once, the Goddess Herself before, when She was posing as Cille the Witch. A third time would seal your ruin."

"What is the Orb? Part of the Hall? I don't understand."

"Fret not, Sir Garland." Zorc cracked that ghastly grin. "Your journey leads back into the past, and the one advantage we retain is that we can time our arrival to coincide with the Kaa. You will save that child! Cadzarilo can tap into time thaumaturgy, while I can create a forcefield that will protect us."

Garland gazed at each of them. "Best you get on with it."

"Stand here," Cadzarilo told him and reached out for Zorc's arm. "We need to link. The Urgolais and I will channel. You, Journeyman, need to hang on to both of us. This will not be pleasant."

Garland shook his head. He couldn't believe he was entering their game. But what else could he do? A long-dead magician and a sardonic crippled demon were his new allies. The only chance he had to save Dafyd and the child.

Bugger it ...

He slammed the sword back in its scabbard and reached over, grabbing Zorc's filthy arm and the archmage's hand. Zorc held his staff and shook it three times. Cadzarilo chanted words that made no sense. He went on for a time until Zorc started yelling and thrust the crooked stick in the sky.

"Nothing's happening," Garland said. He was about to break loose when the ground lurched beneath him and fell away.

Shit ...

Garland felt his body squeezed into a throbbing, warm hole that sucked him through, and along, a wailing, windy tunnel.

"Don't let go. Unless you want to spend eternity in the Void." Zorc's voice reached him through the whistling wind. Garland hung on to both of them as tight as he could. He tried to yell back, but the air screamed at him and filled his throat with bile.

"Watch and learn," Cadzarilo's proud voice came through. Why could they speak, while he could not? "There are patterns in the Void a lore-wise man can translate. You will see visions, *Sir* Garland. Some true, others false. The concepts of past, present, and future have no meaning here. Nor have distance and dimension. Here there are no rules."

The tunnel sucked him down, twisting his body and squeezing hard, until his chest stung with pain and breath came out in choked gasps. He felt sick, and on the verge of blacking out, when the tunnel fell away, and Garland felt his body floating through colorless air.

He was caught in a vacuum. He gazed down at his hands and panicked.

They're gone, left me.

Garland heard Zorc's voice: "We are here—you have come through the first stage."

"Where are you? I can't see anything."

"That's because there's nothing to see in the Void until your mind lets the visions in. Watch and wait. Enjoy the dance …" Zorc's croaky laughter faded around his ears.

"Zorc?"

Garland imagined himself spun in circles by some invisible spider, his body lifting and drifting through featureless rooms. He smelt sulphur, and his nose stung.

I think I'm dying.

The stench grew until he gagged and shook his body as best he could. He saw an object appear through growing mist. A castle glistening with weeping black steel. The walls dripped metal, and tall knights stood gazing down from battlements, their black visors and armor covering them head to toe. The knights wore helms fashioned as birds and insects. As one, they turned in silence and gazed across at him. The nearest held a long black spear. He pointed this down at Garland, who yelled in pain as if feeling the spear pierce his flesh.

"Close your eyes, that will release you—not all your visions will be bad."

Zorc's distant voice was urgent. Garland buckled in pain but forced his eyes shut. The searing agony vanished. He drifted on like a leaf in autumn. Moments passed—he wasn't sure how long. Drifting, floating. No pain. Nothing.

He blinked one eye open. The slimy black castle had gone. Instead, a horseman waited for him on a small round grassy hill. He recognized Sir Valen the Gaunt by his glowing green armor and scarlet-plumed mirror helm. He was surrounded by huge white hounds that bayed and yapped and circled around his horse.

Sir Valen bore a long lance tilted high and reaching back, a blood-red tassel hanging from the tip. He turned his head slowly in Garland's direction and nodded. Garland saw other men appear and stand beside the faceless knight. He recognized Shale and his men. But there were many more.

Shale's pale eyes locked on to him and he smiled. "You'll never see them again," he called across. "Your woman's mine now."

"I'm going to kill you." Garland worked his mouth, and the words drifted across. But as he spoke, the cruel vision passed and a new one emerged.

He cried out, seeing Marei walking up a dry mountain track behind a hard-faced man shouldering a heavy-looking metal cylinder. The man had to be one of Shale's thugs.

Your leave her be!

Neither the warrior or Marei heard or saw him. She looked tired, drained. There was no sign of Rosey.

"I'll find them, Marei—I won't let you down. But don't let him hurt you!" He saw her stop and gaze about. *She heard me* … The stranger stopped, too, and stared at her questioningly.

She shook her head and spoke to the stranger. They moved on, fading and merging into another phantasm.

Marei!

Garland wanted to follow her and tried pushing his body. Instead, he spun in sickly circles and heard Zorn chuckling somewhere.

"You cannot reach her from here. These are things that may or may not come to pass. What you do once we're through to the other side will affect everything you see …"

Zorc's voice faded again. Garland blinked as he saw a ship riding a glassy flat ocean. The vessel had three masts. He counted nine triangular scarlet sails drooping in the calm.

Garland drifted close and glided like a bird. He saw the prow rising clipping waves, and the aft poop covering the castle deck at stern. Closer, he saw the figurehead. A woman's handsome face carved in gold, the eyes smiling at him. Garland gazed at his arms. He gasped, seeing wings there instead.

He flapped, fell. Steadied, and glided. His mind softening, registering this but part of the illusion.

I'm a bird—so fucking what?

He dropped stone-heavy and felt his wings steady the descent, settling on the ship's high poop. A man stood gazing out to sea. His tanned hands gripped the spoked wheel, and his brown gaze was far away. Garland recognized Carlo Sarfe. He reached across with his feathers. Carlo and his ship disappeared.

"They are close," he heard Cadzarilo's voice for the first time. "That ship's about to pass through our wormhole. You see how everything's connected. He's making for the Island States."

Garland tried to shout back, but his body was sucked

down another hole, his yell swallowed by silence. He fell for seconds, or half an hour. Perhaps weeks? No idea.

As he tumbled, faces loomed out at him. Some were kindly, other coarse and cruel. He saw Pash and heard his screams, and he watched as the ghoulish Solace smiled at him from the glade in Rundal Woods.

He fell.

At last, a dim blue light rose up to greet him. His body slipped warmly inside that glow, its embrace soft as down. A chrysalis or shell closed over him, smothering, then let go. In another vision, he was in a forest of golden lanterns. There were beautiful, wise-faced people gathered all around him.

A tall woman approached, her eyes glinting green and gold. She smiled warmly and placed a brown hand on his shoulder. He recognized her from somewhere.

"You *are* the Journeyman," the woman said, her voice honey-rich and smooth. "Your road is long, Sir Garland. Courage alone will see you through to the other side."

"Marei needs me, I must get back there."

She shook her head. "Follow me."

He obeyed in silence, his mind in a trance. She was lovely, vaguely familiar. A memory flickered, but he couldn't catch it. She led him in silence through the shadowy veil of trees. A golden lantern swayed in her hand, and countless others hung from the crouching misty branches.

They entered a grove, a single standing stone glinting in moonlight. She placed aside the lantern and beckoned him to follow. He complied, and she reached in and grabbed the stone, speaking in words he couldn't understand.

She smiled. "You must enter, and the others will join you soon."

"The stone?"

"It will take you back there. A dark way lies ahead. But you, champion, have allies. As does Marei. Soon you will be united with someone else you love. Enter quickly, while there is still time." She reached across and he saw the stone face peel away, as though it were aging parchment revealing a gaping rent. Inside, he saw stairs glinting with starlight and disappearing down into gloom.

The woman nodded and urged him hurry. Garland entered the hole in the tall stone and started descending the stairs. The stone thudded shut behind him, and he quelled panic as darkness surrounded him.

He walked down, calling out Zorc and Cadzarilo's names.

I've lost them.

But something in the woman's smile had given him courage. He'd been through so much, it wasn't time to ponder. He reached a level platform and blinked in surprise as a sultry breeze ruffled his hair. He stood on a high cliff overlooking a stone harbor, the rising sun blazing at his face. Far to the south, he thought he recognized Carlo's crimson sails emerging from mist and clipping across bright waves in the morning sun.

You are through, too.

A chuckle behind him.

Garland turned and saw Zorc. "Welcome to the past!"

"We're ... through?" Garland blinked at Zorc, his mind adjusting to the new reality.

"Yes. Impressive, isn't it? Sorcery's not all bad. Just a matter of correct application, and lots of patience." Zorc showed his ghastly grin.

"If you say so." Garland felt empty and drained. All the juices sucked from his bones.

"I do. Come wake up—the archmage has alerted his

people. The Citadel lies above us. We will join Cadzarilo shortly. He won't let us down. Knows he has a chance to avert disaster, if he plays this right."

"Where are the Kaa?"

"Patience is needed. They haven't arrived yet. We timed this perfectly. In the meantime, this will keep you occupied while we wait." He produced a long cylindrical object and bid Garland hold it close to his eye.

"Look away from the sun." Zorc said. "See that distant speck? Another ship sailing the dimensions."

Garland placed the eyeglass to his head and cursed as his vision went fuzzy.

"It takes a minute," Zorc said. "I brought it with us through the portal. Thought it would come in handy. An Urgolais farglass allows you see through all five dimensions, and time. It pulls images from both the past and future. What you see may have already happened, or is yet to pass."

Confused yet again, Garland relaxed and felt his eyes adjust to the glass. He saw the island's western slopes breaking off into sharp rocks and the creamy sea stretching out beyond.

"There's nothing out there."

"Give it time."

He kept looking, ranging from left to right. He was about to hand the farglass back when he spotted a dot on the horizon. "There's something …"

"Twist the end until it finds focus."

Garland fumbled, and the dot disappeared.

"The other way, you fool."

He twisted again and found the speck, twisted more, turning the cylinder at the tip of the glass. It started spinning through his fingers. He worried that the end would drop off.

"That's it!" Zorc said behind him. "Look. See who's here, too."

Garland thrust his eyes harder into the bulging glass. As he watched, the speck swelled and became another ship. A smaller, faster looking vessel than Carlo's. It bore two masts and five blue sails. He saw three decks, and at aft a balcony jutted out, with two large lanterns glinting in the sunshine. He saw the words *Kraken Girl* carved beneath. A gaudy, sturdy-looking vessel. But whose?

He kept spinning the farglass and the ship grew larger. He saw men watching from the prow. A fair-haired, rough-looking Northman stood alongside a tall, stern figure, leaning on a bow. Close by, a youngish fellow with curly ginger hair lounged against the rail, his lips raised in a crooked smile. Garland nearly dropped the bow when he saw that third man.

"That's Cale. The Queen's former squire. A man grown. How ...?"

"Keep looking."

He did, and gasped when a newcomer joined them to gaze at the morning.

"Doyle!"

They were sailing to find him. Doyle must have reported his failure. And they were coming.

"That's my ..." He turned to Zorc

"Look, or you'll lose the fucking focus!"

Garland slammed his eye back in the glass and watched as a smallish woman walked briskly up to join the men on the balcony. He saw the tall man with the bow dip his head respectfully. The woman had her back to him. Her dark hair was cut in a neat bob, and she wore a long green cloak. Her feet were covered in dun-colored suede boots, neatly folded over at the top. Cale smiled at her. He saw Doyle nodding and answering something she must have said.

She turned and gazed directly at Garland, as if she could see him watching. He felt the glass slip through his trembling hands.

It was Ariane of the Swords. His queen. She'd crossed through time to find her lost captain.

15

SHIFTING WATERS

CARLO WATCHED the distant sparkle of wave meeting sky. It was boiling hot, and the sea had leveled to a soupy, mesmerizing calm. As he gazed from the prow, he saw tendrils of mist lift and drift, like vapor wraiths fading up into the sun. A week had passed since they escaped the hooded island. His mind still struggled with what had occurred there.

Too many questions.

Afterwards, he'd woken on the floor of the cabin and reached for the brandy. It hadn't been much later when he'd heard urgent knocking on the door. Slim Tareel and Gurdey had needed to talk. He'd steered away from any mention of the island, other than it being infertile and devoid of fresh water. They knew he was lying, but that was too bad. Stogi and the girl had backed up his account. Those two had been badly shaken. Even Tai Pei had kept a low profile all week, staying mostly below deck.

As for himself, he'd shunned company. Sometimes taking the wheel, or else spending hour upon hour watching out from the prow, his mind on many things, but especially the blonde child who said she was going to guide him home.

Urdei.

He'd believed her a dream at first, a residue from the nightmare before. But Stogi had insisted she was real. As had been the harrowing events on that terrible island. They were a long way out. Far away, but the shadows still reached his heart. And how far had they come? Were this his own time, the craggy coast of Zorne or the sun-bright Island States should be visible in days.

As morning seeped dreamily into afternoon, Carlo watched the horizon, wrapped in his thoughts. He saw porpoises leaping and large birds skimming the glassy surface, off to port. Pelicans. There must be land nearby. He felt a surge of hope mixed with dread. More illusions, and traps? The girl, Urdei. Where was she? Why had she helped them, and could he trust her? He shook his head.

Keep sailing—we'll get there. We have to.

It was almost evening when Slim Tareel joined him, his gap-tooth, kindly face concerned.

"You all right, skip?"

"I'm fine," he lied. "Perusing and planning."

"The crew's worried about you. Tar's been jabbering."

Carlo sighed. "I'll speak to them again, Slim. Or could you? Truth is, I'm bone-weary. Something happened on that island that I can't bring myself to mention."

Slim nodded. "Stogi hinted as much. He's been close all week—even the Shen girl's on edge. I saw her lurking in the saloon plying dice with Tol and his mate. But don't worry, skip—I'll handle Gold Tar and any other whining bugger."

"Thanks, Slim."

"Are we going to get home, captain?"

"Yes, we are."

"That's all that matters." The mate smiled, then grabbed Carlo's arm and pointed. "What's that haze? It doesn't look natural?"

Carlo looked where he pointed and saw the horizon had darkened to a fuzzy blur of orange, the sky above reflecting the sunset's sheen behind them. He shrugged, and the two watched the colors shifting. Carlo heard a distant sound like the thunder of drums on a battlefield.

"We're in strange waters." He smiled at his friend.

"Aye, that we are, skip."

As they drifted through that calm, the sea ahead changed hue again from green to blue and darkening to purple before turning almost black. Both sky and water shimmered and sparkled. He saw choppy waves brewing and what appeared to be whirlpools, as they approached the shifting waters. Slim shouted as a waterspout rose, tottered and belched up at the clouds. Carlo smiled. They were riding on the Whales' Path.

"It's the Copper Ocean, skipper. Beyond lies the Shimmering Sea. See the colors changing again, fading back to blue. We're almost home!"

Can it be?

Carlo pictured the blonde girl's grinning face.

You promised. Don't let us down.

LATE THAT NIGHT, CARLO SIPPED BRANDY IN HIS CABIN as stars glinted over the black shiny water, the shifting hues having settled as night moved in. The *Arabella* rocked lazily, her timbers and strakes creaking, as he tried in vain to rest.

The knock was quiet.

Carlo rubbed his eyes and opened the cabin door. Stogi and Tai Pei stood outside. Both looked sober. Her eyes were downcast.

"Good to see you." Carlo welcomed them inside his cabin and poured a large brandy for each. Stogi grinned as he chugged a swallow. Tai Pei swirled her glass and sniffed before taking a hesitant sip.

"This is good," she said. "Strong."

"I'm nearly out of bottles," Carlo shrugged. "Been drinking too much. Think we should finish it tonight, we three."

"Works for me," Stogi said, and pulled up a rocking chair. Outside the porthole, a silvery gibbous moon floated like a ghostly face above the lapping water. It was tranquil. Dreamlike. But Carlo was tired of dreams.

He stared awkwardly at his guests and sipped in silence. Even Stogi looked cagey and kept swallowing brandy. Tai Pei avoided his gaze.

"We've reached the Copper Ocean," Carlo told them to break the uneasy silence. "It lies to the east of my country and merges into the Shimmering Sea, beyond the Island States. Or it did, when we sailed forth." He turned quiet again.

"The girl ..." Stogi said eventually, placing his glass on Carlo's ebony table.

"Urdei." Carlo nodded. "She's ..."

"Guiding us," Stogi said, nodding his head sagely.

"She said you saved us from ... *that*." He shook his head. "The horror we endured. I haven't come to terms with what happened on that fucking island, and I feel bad that I didn't thank you. Either of you."

"Urdei saved all three of us," Stogi said. "For her own reasons, I expect." He sniffed. "She said there'd be a price.

She's one of the Fates, you know. Past." He said it so casually, Carlo almost laughed.

"She told me she was *my* past and was going to get me … *us*, home. It's beyond my comprehension, but that's nothing new. What price did she mention?"

"She didn't, exactly," Stogi said. "But there will be one."

"You're avoiding the issue," Tai Pei cut in. "Urdei wants to stop her Father—they've always bickered, that lot." She sipped her brandy carefully. Her pale cheeks had reddened. She seemed more relaxed, happy.

"Her … father?" Carlo looked at Stogi, who shrugged.

"Must be a Shen thing," he said.

"You two are fucking clueless. Everyone knows that old Oroonin is Urdei's father. And Elanion's her mother. Those two deities have been carrying out a personal vendetta for eons. We of House Zayn know our mythology, history, and lore. We are not clueless yak-shaggers like you, Stodge." Carlo saw the teasing smile on her lips as Stogi's moustache drooped.

"It's a moot point," he said, flashing her a grin.

"What you're saying is we're caught in some personal argument between two of the old gods?" Carlo gulped and almost belched a laugh. "The same entities that supposedly perished in that Happening you always talk about?"

Tai Pei nodded, and Stogi's face turned serious. "You saw the Emerald Queen rise up in that castle, did you not?" he asked Carlo.

"Elanion. With her emerald bow, yes, I did. But lots happened in that castle that made scant more sense than …" He didn't want to mention the hooded island.

"Elanion's bow is missing again," Stogi said.

"Kerasheva? How so? I saw Teret use it to kill the serpent.

The Goddess—if that's who that giant green woman was—
gave it to Tamersane."

"And Teret shot the basilisk, I know."

"You weren't there, Stogi."

"Yes, *no*. Doesn't matter. We two have worked it out."

"What?"

"There was a man called Seek. A miserable shaman from
Dunnehine," Stogi said. "Turns out, he's dead and his soul
possessed by—"

"The god Oroonin." Tai Pei cut through his words like a
scimitar slicing rope.

"Yes ... that one," Stogi added lamely.

"Has used a mortal thief to steal Kerasheva. He's been
tasked with shattering the stalemate between the Crystal Kingdoms and their enemy, Ptarni."

"What are you talking about? How do you come up with
these wild theories?"

"She's a thinker," Stogi said.

"Shut up." She waved them be silent. "Tol said they've
been fighting for years. Oroonin's angry, and a warmonger.
The warmonger. He wants revenge against those mortals
involved in the Happening. We've been caught in the
crossfire."

"You're not talking sense, either of you." Carlo's head was
hazy. *I'm getting tipsy.* How much brandy had he consumed?
He didn't care—he needed more.

"It's complicated." Tai Pei smiled at him. She went on to
excitedly explain how she'd learned a lot from Tol and Taylon
while beating them at dice, asking about the Crystal Kingdoms, the Happening, and why it happened. And the war
with the wizard that led to that calamity. Her face was flushed
and eyes dreamy. He'd never noticed how attractive she was

before. Those black eyes shone like jewels. Her skin was flaw-less in the lamplight.

Stogi glanced sideways at her, then at Carlo, and nodded wryly. "Urdei told me…"

"What did she tell you?" Carlo found his gaze drifting to Tai Pei's ankles and moving up. She was smiling at him. He wrenched his thoughts back to their conundrum.

"Your turn, Stogi." Tai Pei grinned silkily at Carlo. She shifted on the divan where she'd perched, her black hair gleamed long and silky. She'd pinned it back tonight. Carlo forced his gaze away and listened to what the Tseole was saying.

"After the Happening, the gods were blasted to the far corners of the universe by the Weaver. They'd let Him down twice before. Most perished, but some endured."

Carlo blinked and stifled a yawn.

"You feeling all right?" Stogi asked him.

"I'm fine," he said, avoiding the girl's gaze. "Continue, it's fascinating."

Stogi nodded. "Oroonin survived through cunning and kept changing guise to stay ahead of His angry Father. The Maker blamed His second child almost as much as the Shad-owman. For the harrowing conclusion of the Crystal Wars. Elanion's always been a bigger fish, despite Her husband contending that."

Carlo nodded, his eyes closing.

Stogi persisted. "Urdei said that Ansu, this *planet*—she called it a planet—was her Mother's world. Gifted to Elanion by the Weaver at the dawn of days. Shifty Oroonin stole it from Her when He first bedded Her."

Tai Pei kicked Carlo's shin, and he jolted awake.

"Go on, I'm listening."

"You need to," Tai Pei said.

Stogi grinned. "Elanion took Ansu back from Oroonin shortly afterward. And so it went. Throughout the ages, husband and wife, god and goddess, brother and sister, squabbling endlessly over this green rock we call Ansu. But Elanion's the rightful guardian. So Urdei said. Her Mother wants to cherish Her estate. She loves its myriad peoples, Urdei told me. Not sure if that includes us."

Tai Pei smirked. "You're good, Stodge. She loves the ugly ones, too."

Stogi ignored her. "Whereas," he continued as Carlo held back another yawn, "Oroonin the schemer wants turbulence, to spite Her. The old sky Wanderer's stirring up war. Stoking fuel into the Ptarnian emperor's greed for conquest. Callanz, he's called. A deranged lunatic, according to Tol. Believes he's a god, and yet a real one's helping him. Ironic."

"Seems petty, for so terrible a being." Carlo rolled brandy around his tongue to help him concentrate.

"That's the old gods for you, especially Him. Can't leave anything alone. Why he took Seek's form—the two seem much alike to me."

"There's a third player," Tai Pei added quietly, her eyes misty.

"Who?"

"Not a being. A *place*. Well, maybe a being of sorts. Graywash Hall."

As she spoke the words, a dark shadow cloaked the porthole and Carlo's candle flickered and popped. Her eyes were wide, and Stogi looked tense.

"Any more brandy?" Stogi asked.

Carlo passed the almost empty bottle across. "Are you thinking what I'm thinking?"

"We were there and escaped," Stogi said.

"But it's hungry to catch up with us again," Tai Pei whispered, as shadows drifted from the cabin. "It's you, Carlo. Something inside that place needs you."

"Why do you say that?" His weariness had gone replaced by a quivering inside.

She took the bottle from Stogi's shaking hands and drained it. "Because it's true." She stared hard at him until Carlo felt his legs quiver.

"Think I'm done," Stogi said, belching, and left without another word.

"You leaving, too?" Carlo asked the girl.

She raised a brow. "Perhaps," she said.

ARIANE SAW THE DARK LINE OF CLIFFS PASSING TO THEIR south. Clouds scurried past, and the sea churned angry gray below. It was rough. The wind buffeted her face and stung her eyes. She smiled, enjoying the solitude and freedom. Her thoughts drifted back to an earlier voyage, when she and her friends had sailed to find the lost prince, Tarin. After her first journey to the Oracle in the wood.

It seemed so long ago. Nine years? Perhaps only eight—she wasn't certain. Hard to be sure about anything these days. Cale and Fassyan joined her to watch the sunset fade beyond the westernmost cliffs of Fol.

Corin's home, she thought sadly, as they watched the cliffs slip to stern. She glimpsed a tall broken tower on the highest point. That had been Zallerak the Aralais's sanctuary before the war. Now a home for seabirds and echoes. So much had been lost.

Eyes moist, she turned. Ahead lay empty water until they reached Crenna. They'd stop for supplies, Taic had told her. She'd had misgivings after her last visit to that island. But he'd assured her the last of the pirates had been found and hanged by the new administrator—a former Wolf officer and one of the veterans of the Kelthaine army. Appointed personally by the High King. Crenna would be their last stop before ...

Cale grinned as he accepted a mug of ale from Fassyan. Taic had been generous, and their voyage had started well. "I can't believe we're going back to Crenna," Cale said.

"You can stay onboard. I certainly shall," she told him. "Let Taic and his men do what they must."

Doyle appeared with a mug. "What's our timeline, highness?" He joined them in watching the afterglow, as the dark mass of land slipped behind, finally fading out of view.

"I've really no idea," she answered. "I mean ... I've thought about it. What to expect? There's got to be land thereabouts. The Great Continent was not completely destroyed by the demon, Ashmali. Nor was it consumed by Sensuata's floods. Zansuat, as the ancients called Him." She felt a deep shudder after mentioning the sea god's name.

She'd made a promise once, long ago. A bargain with the Lord of the Oceans. He'd saved them from a kraken and pursuing ships, but he had demanded a price for that help and she'd accepted. Except the Sea God had perished in the Happening, as had His kin. Only Elanion survived, as a shadow or the mist of whispers.

Enough!

She pulled her thoughts back to the present. Cale was staring hard at her. He'd been there, and he knew of her sacrifice and vow.

"We sail boldly westward and greet what awaits," Cale

grinned, easing her mood. That old charm always worked. "I'm glad to be away from the front for a time. Taic's up for anything, and he's more generous with the ale than Barin was. That guzzling giant used to glug it all."

"I miss Barin," Ariane said. "I'd feel safer were he with us."

"I'll wager he wishes he was," Cale said. "Instead of weighed down by his responsibilities in Valkador, and those troublesome pretty daughters."

"What are your thoughts, Doyle?" She turned to the quiet one. "You've traveled farther than any of us."

"I believe anything is possible, highness. There'll be a way of finding Carlo Sarfe, and my captain. Garland's out there," Doyle said. "We must search and see what appears. Stout hearts will win through."

"I agree." Ariane smiled at him. "I'm glad you joined us, captain. I know it wasn't easy for you."

"A journey into the unknown, with Queen Ariane of the Swords herself, and her valiant new champions," Cale grinned wolfishly. "How could anyone refuse that?"

"I'm honored to be invited," Doyle said, managing a smile before dipping his head. He was awkward in her presence. But he'd never known her like Cale or confided with her as had Fassyan on their many forays into the woods. Instead, Doyle was haunted by the last journey he'd made accompanying Captain Garland.

"Good to hear," Ariane said, after a pause. She turned to Fassyan, who alone knew none of those names mentioned. Her huntsmaster was patient as ever, his calm, brown eyes content on the voyage. "I'll need your hunting skills to find that bow," she told him. "We must catch the thief and win this war."

"First, we need to find him, whoever he is. Or *her*." He

smiled at Ariane. "That won't prove easy. A thief who steals from a goddess must be both clever and brave."

"And dangerous," Cale added. "The adventure starts after Crenna. Eventually we'll reach those lands you mentioned. But what happens then?"

"We'll seek a harbor, see if folk still live there," Ariane said. "I know Rakeel was destroyed, but surely some of what was Xandoria and Zorne must remain—their peoples, too. They were huge countries, according to our legends. Both had empires once."

"They could well prove hostile," Doyle said. "We should be prepared for that."

"We will be," Ariane told them. "Now excuse me, gentlemen, I'm for my cabin. I'll leave you three to discuss this further." They bowed and she smiled, leaving them to their cups as the sky darkened and the high cliffs of Fol vanished to stern.

Ariane entered her spacious cabin and wandered out onto the balcony. Taic had generously given up his captain's quarters. She'd marveled at his taste. This older Taic loved his comfort and had furnished his cabin well. The private lamplit balcony allowed her what solace she could gather. She was tired and sat out there for a time, gazing at the water passing below the strakes. The golden lanterns flickered either side of her rocking chair, and the sea's constant thudding lulled her senses. Comfortably hemmed by silk cushions, she dozed for a time.

When Ariane woke, it was pitch dark.

The skies were occluded by heavy cloud, and a soft drizzle

dampened the balcony. Ariane shivered. How long had she slept? The lanterns had burned low, and her cabin door creaked open, slamming shut again behind her.

A draught shivered up her arms. She made to get up and go inside, stopping when a shadow brushed past and a soft plop announced something entering the balcony.

She froze.

I have a visitor.

Ariane turned very slowly.

A strange woman sat poised on the balcony, her long wet hair and glistening naked flesh glinting and shifting from blue through greenish yellow. Her eyes were milky white and without pupils. The face and ears were pointed, though oddly beautiful. Her long fingers were linked by translucent webs of flesh, as were the toes, the nails broken and grimy. The sloping, milky eyes gazed coldly at Ariane.

"I am Rann," the woman told her in a voice that surged like stormy seas. "I bring a message from my Father to the woman who deserted Him. Sensuata has not forgotten your promise, queen. You should never have returned to the ocean. You are in Our domain now."

"Sensuata perished eight years ago," Ariane hissed the words out. "He's gone, and you're an ill spirit. A nicor, or nix. Nothing more."

The strange woman smiled cruelly.

"We will meet again soon, Queen Ariane. Nothing is ever forgotten. You mortals may have short memories. We of Telimantua do not."

The woman stood gracefully and blew her a cold kiss with her pale wet palm, smiling cruelly before slipping over the balcony rail without a sound. Ariane lurched to her feet and gazed down at the rushing water. There was no sign of the woman.

Rann, eldest daughter of the Sea God. Could it be possible?

Heart thumping, she staggered inside and cracked open a wine cask.

16

THE MILLER AND HIS BAG MAN

MAREI STARED through the smeared glass of the inn window at the crowd of people gathered outside. She watched horrified, seeing wooden gallows being set up, the carpenters hard at work sawing the lumber, and an overseer with a tall hat watching on and scratching notes with parchment and quill.

Rosey was dozing in a deep chair beside her. She saw no reason to wake the girl. At least the innkeeper had proved generous, offering them a room and taking no more coin than she'd been willing to part with. He was scrubbing the counter and talking lazily to a gaunt-faced fellow, leaning over a brimming tankard of dark ale. The proprietor saw her looking and nodded, wiped down his apron, and walked over to join her.

"Said I'd help you, if I could." The innkeeper showed a grubby smile as he leaned over the divan where she sat with the sleeping Rosey. His breath stank of garlic. "I put a word out."

"Thank you," Marei said, crinkling her nose. "What's going on out there?"

He arched his bushy brows. "Is it not obvious? First day of the month, which means it's swing-'em-high time. It's when we hang villains for all to see. It's what makes this city special, my dear. Vagrants and rogues are not tolerated on our streets."

"I suppose that's good. The miller, Randle. Any word back?" Marei asked him, trying to shut out the shouting and grind of saw cutting timber.

"Give it time."

She nodded, hoping he'd leave her alone. Instead, he lingered, hovering too close, his eyes studying hers. She chewed her bottom lip nervously, not liking his expression.

A click. He turned away, gazed over at the door. "Seems you're in luck. Here's someone entering. Looks like Randle's bagman has found you first."

Randle's bagman?

Marei turned her head and saw a tough-looking individual enter. A big man in a dark blue coat, he carried a cudgel in one hand and lantern in the other. His hard blue-gray eyes swept the room and rested immediately on her and the girl.

"That's Dunrae Tarn," the Innkeeper whispered in her ear. "He cleans for the miller."

"Cleans?"

"In a manner of speaking. I'll not say more." Marei saw the newcomer nod warily at the innkeeper, who responded with a nervous grin and fidgety fingers.

He fears this one, Marei thought.

"Best I leave you be. Dunrae Tarn will take it from here." The Innkeeper walked off briskly without a backwards glance.

Marei gazed at the big stranger as he walked coolly toward them. His eyes were calm, and she noticed a short sword strapped to his waist, half-hidden by his coat. Could this be another Shale? He looked like a mercenary. Perhaps the miller had tricked Garland into thinking he was a friend. No. Garland would see through a liar. She placed aside those useless thoughts and forced a welcoming smile to her lips.

"You work for a miller called Randle?" Marei asked, as he pulled up a stool, and gazed at her frankly. Rudely, in her opinion. She met his stare, and he smiled slightly. His eyes were a stony blend of slate-grayish blue. The hair was brown, thick, and scruffy, with a stubble of growth showing and a faded scar circling the shadow beneath his left eye. Perhaps forty, maybe younger. Difficult to tell. The tanned face was hard. A killer, the eyes shifting carefully across the room, noticing any movement or sound.

"What do you know about the miller?" Dunrae Tarn said eventually. His accent was rough. Strange. A commoner, but she suspected not from the city. The voice was deep and gravelly, as though he smoked a pipe too often.

"My ... *friend*. Garland of Wynais, a soldier. A noble knight. Do you know him?"

"Could be, I do."

"Garland sent me, and this young lady to seek Randle. Says your master knows our business."

"I'm my own master."

Marei shrugged. "That's your concern, not mine. Will Randle help us?"

Dunrae Tarn stared at her for a moment, the half-smile rising at a corner of his lip.

"He'll do what he can," he said, gaze shifting to Rosey. The flat eyes softened, until something akin to pity showed. "She all right?"

"Tired. She's been—"

"—I can see that," he cut in, his hand reaching across and grasping Marei's, with a speed that made her jump in alarm. She tried to pull away, but he pinned her wrist with the other hand and held it firm, but not so much that it hurt. He was very strong, she noted. "Shorty sent me to fetch you, Marei," his voice had dropped to a whisper.

"Who's that?" She guessed it was someone else in Randle's pay.

"Himself. Randle. What I call him. A nickname—he doesn't like." He grinned slightly. Marei didn't know how to take this stranger. Those cool eyes were probing hers as he spoke.

You're testing me. She mustered calm and held his gaze until he nodded, the eyes hinting satisfaction. "My friend spoke well of your miller."

"He's not only a miller, as I'm not who I appear, either. We two are not liked here. And I have to get you back ere dark, else they'll be hindering our plans."

"Hindering? Who? And why is that innkeeper scared of you."

Dunrae Tarn's eyes flicked to the innkeep, who'd been slyly watching them, and quickly feigned a sheepish smile.

"All good there?" the innkeep called across.

"Aye." Dunrae dismissed him with a wave. "We'll speak on the road," her told her in a low voice. "There is danger for you in this city. Like us, it's not what it appears. You can't trust these people. They live too close to the crossroads."

"The place where the trickster called the piper lurks?" Garland had mentioned a man with a flute who'd popped up by a crossroads. He'd turned out to be someone quite unusual. He'd been cagy about the details, but she recalled he'd said the man's name was Jynn, and he'd been involved with Garland's witches. And that meant the Hall. Marei stared hard at the man. She was on to something here. "Am I not wrong?"

He didn't respond, his eyes probing her. Beside her, Rosey yawned and shifted, opened her eyes. She saw the man staring at them and covered her mouth in fear.

"This gentleman is Dunrae Tarn," Marei whispered gently. "He works for Randle the miller and says they'll help us."

Rosey nodded, her eyes wide. "Getting dusky."

Marei glanced outside where the workers hammered. The light was fading fast. Strange, she hadn't thought it that late.

"That innkeep says they're hanging people this evening."

"We best get moving quietly," Dunrae Tarn said. "The buggers will be looking for more poor sods to string up."

Marei gazed out at the workers. The scaffold was almost erected. One man was testing the ropes, another stringing lanterns around the timbers. She shuddered.

"This city … it's …"

"Not now, Marei." He glared at her, eyes narrowing. "Follow me, *please*—both of you." He stood casually, swept his steady gaze across the room again, gathered the lamp and heavy stick, and without further word made for the tavern door. Marei saw the proprietor watch with relief as he left.

"Come back soon," he said with a smile as she and Rosey followed. She waved a thanks and took the door. Rosey stared at her with worried eyes.

"Come on, don't fret," Marei said. "We'll know more soon, and I see no reason to stay here any longer."

The man in the blue coat led them through a maze of dusty lanes, his lantern glinting and throwing back shadows. Marei told Rosey to walk behind her, so she could protect her, should any footpads be lurking. She had her knife hidden in her belt, and the small crossbow primed and ready in one hand. She'd kept that well hidden in the tavern, but she suspected Dunrae Tarn knew she had the weapon. His sharp gaze seemed to miss little. But If he knew she was armed, he showed no sign.

Night fell silent and still. No birds, or dogs barking. She picked up her pace and urged Rosey do the same. They entered a wider street, twisting up to a long, low building draped with a smoky thatched roof, the smoke hanging low and framing the house.

She saw small, diamond-crossed windows and a thick oak door painted black with a brass knob for a handle. A lane barred by an arched gate led through freshly clipped roses, their scent reaching her even from this distance.

"This way," Dunrae said gruffly, without waiting to see if they followed. He opened the gate and left it swinging for them to enter.

"Who is he?" Rosey asked in a whisper.

"A servant or bodyguard, I suspect. This Randle character probably needs men like him."

"I don't care for this place, Marei. The city."

"Me neither, and hopefully we won't be here long. Look now, he's entering that house. We'd best follow quickly, else people see us. He says we can't trust the folk here."

"Let's start with him—he don't appear trustworthy to my eyes," Rosey said as they reached the heavy oak door, Dunrae holding the lantern high and working a jingle of keys.

They joined him, as he pushed the door ajar with a shoulder, allowing warmth and yellow light rush out to greet them.

"In you go, lasses." Dunrae Tarn motioned them to enter. Rosey glared at him, and he raised a wry brow. Marei let the girl go first and swept the room with her eyes. It was smoky. There was a large gray cat lounging by a blazing hearth. Its green-yellow eyes watched the fire without much interest. Tallow lanterns flickered on the whitewashed walls. She saw beams; the floor looked uneven. This place looked older than her tavern. She caught movement. A smallish man was seated on a shabby chair. He wore thin, round spectacles and appeared to be sleeping.

Dunrae shoved the door shut and reached across, placing two heavy bars down into iron brackets mounted for the purpose. Those bars concerned Marei. Perhaps Rosey was right to be worried about these people. She drummed her fingers on the crossbow hidden inside her cloak.

I'm ready for anything, she told herself.

"You won't need that weapon here, sweetheart," a warm voice said, as though its owner had read her thoughts. She froze, her fingers gripping the crossbow. The round-faced man in the specs had one brown eye open and was grinning broadly at her. "The crossbow you've been carrying so carefully inside that cloak. Must be heavy, poor girl. You won't need it tonight. You're safe here, Marei. You too, Rosey. Time to relax, you pair."

Rosey glared at him. "How do you know our names?"

His smile broadened. "Take a seat—go on. Are you hungry? You must be. I doubt that tight-fisted Golman overfed you at the Draper's Arms."

"The innkeeper was kind to us, and yes, we've eaten," Marei responded stiffly, dropping her hand from the crossbow and allowing it to swing from the tie at her belt.

"Well, good. Please come and take a seat in the chairs here. You look tired, and full of questions. We'll sup some ale. Tarn, old lad, would you be so kind to—"

"—get your own fucking ale," Dunrae Tarn responded

harshly, before the spectacled man could finish. Marei stared at both of them, and Rosey tutted with disapproval.

"Don't mind Tarn," the man said, grinning again. "He looks gruesome, I know. But he's as friendly as Camfaleese there, to good folks anyway." He motioned at the large yawning cat, who was yet to acknowledge their presence. Marei stared at the cat for a moment before returning her gaze to the seated man and Dunrae Tarn standing behind him. They both watched her, as though waiting for an announcement. The big, dour one stared back at her with those brooding eyes, his coat discarded and abandoned over a chair. The small, round-faced smiler's spectacles glinted in the firelight.

"I assume you must be Randle?" Marei asked, urging Rosey take a chair. No point them standing gawping at each other.

"It's a name," he said. "Works well enough here." He rubbed his chubby hands together and steepled his fingers.

Suddenly she had a thought. "If this is a mill, I didn't notice a stream or wheel."

Randle grinned at her and didn't respond.

Rosey nodded and stared at her with worried eyes. "I don't trust these two, Marei. We should run."

"Bless this child—she's got spark." Randle motioned Marei take the wooden rocking chair beside the girl. "We're friends, Rosey. I'll not tease you any longer. We can help—you have my word on that. Garland of Wynais is a colleague of ours."

"He's only been here the once," Marei said. "How is it that you're so well acquainted with him? Did you encounter him at the crossroads?"

Randle's grin faded. "Let's not speak about that place

tonight. Garland stayed here for a couple of days while he was purchasing goods and resting his ponies. We got on famously. He's a good man, and fond of you, I dare say."

Marei chewed her bottom lip and wondered what this smiling man's game was.

"You don't believe me?" His grin broadened. "There is a mill hidden down the lane beyond this house. A river, too, winds around the back. It's where I grow my watercress. I own the mill, not the stream. I'm sure Tarn has informed you that this isn't our real business."

"He hinted as much."

"Good, I was hoping he would. Makes things easier." He glanced at the big man currently slumped in an armchair, his eyes half-closed. Randle smiled and stood, rubbing his hands again as though cold, despite it being stifling so close to the fire. "I'll get us some wine, and we can talk candidly."

Rosey glared at Marei, as she watched the short man leave the room. She heard him humming and objects clattering for a few minutes before he returned. Dunrae Tarn's eyes were fully shut. Rosey's looked wild. The poor girl was half-mad with worry and terror for her husband and child. Marei sighed. These two had better prove helpful, else this could be a long night. Randle placed two fat wine sacks on a table and grinned.

"Strategy is thirsty work."

"Strategy?" Marei raised a quizzical brow. "What did Sir Garland tell you about us?"

"Aye, that," Dunrae Tarn muttered without opening his eyes. Rosey was about to blurt something angrily when Randle stopped her with a warning finger.

"Dafyd is in great danger, yes, we know. Garland, too— though he can handle himself well enough."

"What about my baby?"

"She's unharmed. We still have time, Rosey. I'm mostly worried about your son, Marei. He's out of his depth entirely."

"How do you know all this?" It was Marei's turn to be angry. "Are you telling us falsehoods?" She looked down at the wine glass. Was it drugged? Rosey had already drained her glass, her hands shaking with rage. Randle was gazing calmly at her.

Damn you and your smirk, man.

Were these people playing with them? Had they come from the Hall, like that villain Shale? Perhaps that garlic-breath innkeeper was in with them, too?

Randle held her challenge with a measured stare. "We are not from Graywash Hall, Marei," he said eventually. "I understand why you would suspect it were so."

"Then who are you, and how do you know about this poor girl's child? And my son?"

"I make it my business to know … many things."

Rosey started sobbing, the wine working on her quickly. "Where is Dafyd?"

Marei felt like getting up and knocking those spectacles from the smug man's face.

"The Kaa has the babe." Dunrae Tarn winked open an eye. "And Sir Valen, your boy. That lad was rash to enter the Hall. Bravely done, but foolish. Garland, too, but at least he's a professional and had help waiting as he's been inside before."

"I want my daughter!" Rosey yelled, standing and hurling her cup at Dunrae Tarn's face. He dodged, and the cup hit the wall with a thud, staining the white with crimson. Forgotten, the cat stretched and blinked. Its green-yellow eyes opened wide and gazed directly at Marei. She shivered under that uncanny stare.

"You've woken Camfaleese," Randle said, as though that was important. Both men ignored the mess.

Marei stood and comforted the weeping girl. "You need sleep, Rosey. These people will help us, I'm sure of it." She wasn't. She looked to Randle. "Is there a bed for her?"

"Of course." He nodded, his face kindly but the smile fading. Marei took a long sip. She felt her anger diminish as the wine warmed her belly. It was strong and good, and she was so damn tired.

"Come, Rosey," Randle said. "I've a cozy chamber in the back, fresh clean sheets, and pillows of the softest down. You'll sleep so well, and we'll talk more in the morning. Don't fret— your loved ones will be safe. Leave that to us."

Rosey glared at Marei, who nodded slowly. "Come on, he's right. You're exhausted, and you'll get sick if you don't rest."

Marei followed Randle as he led the girl through a long, low corridor, with doors leading off on either side. The cottage was far bigger than it had appeared from outside. She'd glanced back and seen Dunrae Tarn watching them leave the room with careful eyes. Again, she wondered what their game was.

Randle opened the last door on the right and pointed to a large bed with four carved posters at each corner. "You can both sleep here," he told Marei. "There's a basin for washing and an urn for night soil in that cupboard."

"Marei ..." Rosey stared at her.

"Rest. I'll find out what it is these men can do for us."

Rosey nodded and made for the bed, while Randle reached over and lit a candle by the latticed window. "Your dreams will be kindly ones tonight," he told the girl.

. . .

BACK IN THE MAIN ROOM, DUNRAE APPEARED ASLEEP AS
they returned. Marei knew he wasn't. She sat poised with
questions and accepted another cup of wine. Where to start?

"Why would you help us, even if you know about our
situation? Can you get me inside the Hall? I need to see my
son. And what about the babe?" Marei asked, rushing her
questions, her tired mind unravelling as anguished thoughts
crisscrossed through her head.

Randle and the cat were staring at her. There was something peculiar about that cat. Maybe it was the wine, but the
animal seemed to read her thoughts, too. She shuddered,
gazed down at her drink, and fiddled the mug through her
fingers.

"Well ...?" she pressed.

"Your brave knight, Sir Garland, will find the Kaa and
save the child," Randle said quietly. "I've no doubt of that.
He's crossed already and has ... aid from an unlikely source.
The Journeyman—that's what we call him—will endure
because he has to. Rosey's girl will be fine. The Kaa are not
invincible. But rescuing Dalreen is only the first of many
hurdles you'll have to overcome to defeat them. Tarn here can
help with Dafyd. He knows how to navigate Graywash Hall
better than most."

Marei turned and stared at the big man. He was snoring
soundly, his head slumped back in the armchair. The cat was
still watching her. Marei ignored it and returned her weary
gaze to the miller. "What are you proposing? Tell me about
this *strategy* of yours."

"I'll keep it simple to begin with. Rosey stays here where
she's safe."

"No way. This man told me this city isn't safe. I'll not part
with my daughter-in-law."

"You have to. Rosey cannot go near Graywash Hall. They'll sense her desperation and alert the Kaa. And don't worry about the people outside this house. My property lies in a different dimension from the city. They can't get in here."

"Then why bother barring the door?"

"A habit of ours—we're old school." He smiled, arched his fingers again. "Be patient and I'll try to explain. Enjoy the wine—it's good, isn't it? Help you relax." He sighed and gazed at the cat. "How do I start, Fenglegrim? You could help me." Marei saw the cat switch its gaze to the man and back again, the yellow-green eyes probing into hers.

"I don't like your cat," Marei said, shuddering and staring hard at the fire.

"Ha, did you hear that, Grim? She doesn't mean it. You always upset them. You know too much, that's your problem. She has two names, you know. One for each soul. Camfaleese Fenglegrim is not your average cat."

"What about my son?"

For an answer, he stood and walked over to the fire, his chubby face serious for once. The cat purred loudly and hopped across, jumping up onto the sleeping man's lap, its uncanny gaze still on Marei. Again, she ignored the animal.

"There are things happening you'll never grasp, Marei. Ancient events and the reactions countering those events. The cycle repeats itself, time and again. The worm-eaten thread never stops spinning. Be satisfied we three are on your side. And Garland's. It's in our interest to help the Journeyman, thus you and the girl, too."

"Why do you keep calling him that?"

He ignored the question. "Inside these thick walls, we can resist the evil seeping out from Graywash Hall. The same wickedness that defiles this city. The Orb. A spider stain that cannot be washed clean. The people here are under its spell, poor fools. They would have come for you and the girl, had Tarn not reached you in time. Few will mess with Dunrae Tarn. Even the Grogans dare not confront him alone."

"Graywash Hall. What evil does it hide?"

"A canker that reaches far and wide. Seeping poison, caused by the Orb. I'll not say more—those inside have a way of listening in when mentioned."

"But this is a safe house?"

"It is, I promise you. Rosey stays with me, protected, until you return—or, more likely, we come to you. Tarn will accompany you back to Torrigan's Tavern. He'll sweep away any lurkers. There are bound to be some of Valen's thugs around. The Faceless Knight will be scouting the area. That one knows Garland's a threat to their plans.

"Once you're back home, Tarn will help you plan the best moment to enter the Hall. Probably in a week or so. Dafyd is safe for the moment. We have spies inside the Hall, you see. My team are doing what they can. My master spy, the Firefly, informed me that Valen is holding your son for bigger bait."

"I don't understand what it is these vile people want."

"It not a matter of understanding, Marei. We're talking about an ancient evil. A shifting residue, circular in shape. We call it the Orb. His stain. A substance that returned from the Outer Void from whence it was cast. Plucked from the Chaos Realms beyond the ken of mortal folk. There are dark places out there that even I cannot reach. Though once I did, when I was young. No matter—I digress. You'll learn more than you care to, soon enough. Go rest up, else you'll be as distraught as that poor girl."

Marei nodded, the wine was making her drowsy. Despite

her many questions and concerns, she wouldn't hold out for much longer.

"You'll leave at dawn, so go get some good rest. Your eyes are barely open, my dear."

"One last question." Marei stood shakily, gazing deep into his soft brown eyes. Behind her, the cat purred loudly, kneading the sleeping man's lap while watching her with those hypnotic, lamp-bright eyes.

"Go on …" Randle folded his hands and gazed up at her.

"What's your real name?"

"Shorty doesn't have a real name," Dunrae Tarn said quietly, one eye blinking open.

I knew you weren't sleeping.

Randle smiled at her. "It's true that I have small use for names. For I am many things, Marei, and not just one. Names are like garments. They can be discarded and reclaimed at any time. But tonight, Marei. Tonight, you can call me Jynn."

"You're the piper from the crossroads." Marei felt panic rising inside. "The trickster who Garland had mentioned." This was a trap, after all. She reached inside the cloak for the crossbow but stopped when Dunrae grabbed her hand.

"It's all right, Marei," he said, the hard eyes intent, but kindly. "We're on your side, love. He likes to tease, does Shorty. There's a war going on you know nothing about. On one side, it's the Hall and them what live within. And their allies the Kaa, Grogans, and worse—Sir fucking Valen the Gaunt and his ghouls and hounds and such other trash. They worship the Orb. They're the Shadowman's people, girly. The Orb's His stain that remains."

"And you two are…?" Marei blinked up at the big man.

"We're the other team, Shorty and me. He's … what he is. I'm just an old freebooter with too many secrets."

"And what are your secrets, Dunrae Tarn?"

"Not important. Shorty here knows far more than I do about what is. But I've some tricks, and the three of us mean to dismantle Graywash Hall. Unravel the Orb thread. Destroy its malign force completely."

"You said *three*. Who is the other person?"

His eyes flashed to Jynn, who shook his head. "Later, Tarn."

"The Goddess and Her husband are at it again," Dunrae continued, after a gruff nod at the other. "Her younger, watery brother, too. The old team are back and have got out of hand. They're mad as hornets in a hurricane. The dimension plates are shifting back in place after the disruption caused by the last Happening." He looked hard at Jynn. "You're too soft with them. It's why he's back here too. Shorty left things alone and they messed it up. *Again*. Frigging useless, that lot."

"Yes, and rather badly this time, I'm afraid," Jynn added. "The lost sailor, Carlo Sarfe, will soon cross back into the past. His ship will return to Gol, where he'll attempt changing what cannot be altered. Fortunately, Garland's back there, too. Our stake at the table, if you like. Soon, the third thread in this jolly tangle will arrive and join the fray.

"Queen Ariane means to recover the bow Kerasheva. It was stolen from Laras Lassladen by a master thief who contracts out for those in the Hall."

It was too much—she was fading. He saw that and urged Dunrae Tarn escort her to the chamber, lest she end up collapsing on the floor. "I'll bid you goodnight, Marei." Jynn-Randle grinned at her, as the big man gently ushered her from the room.

"I'm too tired to ask anything else," she told Dunrae as they entered the last chamber. Rosey's head showed past the candle. Marei smiled, seeing she was fast asleep. At peace, at least until morning.

"I'll wake you before dawn," Dunrae said softly. "Good night."

Marei grabbed his arm and stopped him.

"What is it?"

"Just promise me we can trust you, Dunrae Tarn. You and your clever little friend."

He smiled for the first time. "I swear it. This is an old fight, girl. You're caught right in the middle. But don't fret— we're seasoned campaigners, and I'm not one for losing. Sleep soundly. We'll talk more on the road."

"One more question?"

He turned, his dark face shrouded by lamplight.

"You mentioned someone else. Who is this missing member of your team?"

His smile was genuine, and she saw humor sparkle in his eyes for the first time. "I expect you'll soon discover that without my help."

He turned and made for the door. She watched him leave and closed the door. She doffed her cloak, unclasped her belt, and allowed the weapons clatter to the floor. Lastly, she wriggled under the sheets and blew out the candle.

Eyes half-closed, Marei glanced at her sleeping companion.

It's going to turn out all right, Rosey. Whoever these men are, they're on our side.

Something in Dunrae Tarn's moody eyes had reassured her. She felt better, less afraid.

"Bless you," she whispered, kissing Rosey's cheek and turning her gaze to a dark line shifting beneath the door.

"Who is there?"

The door creaked open, and she saw small paws enter. Camfaleese Fenglegrim's yellow-green eyes shone up at hers, like jewels on fire. The cat cleaned behind his ears and jumped up onto the bed. Marei was too tired to shoo her off. She closed her eyes, her consciousness fading, as the cat's loud purrs drummed like an attacking army in her ear.

17

THE CLIFFS OF ZORNE

GARLAND SAW the tall form of Cadzarilo walking down the slope. The archmage looked different. Prouder, and maybe even taller. Alive. A powerful man in his prime. Hard to imagine him as the burnt horror from last night.

He was smiling in the sunshine as he joined Zorc, dwarfing the stunted Urgolais. They made quite the pair, Garland thought grimly as he shook his head and tried to make sense of the madness engulfing him.

He was in the past, standing on an island filled with scheming sorcerers.

Gods, but I'm weary of this.

But another thought troubled him more.

Ariane was here, or soon will be if Zorc's farglass wasn't lying to him. His queen must have abandoned her land because Doyle had begged her to help find her lost captain. Somehow, she'd found a way back through time as well. All because of the man who had failed to bring back her cousin, Tamersane. Why else would she be here? And how was it possible? How was any of this possible?

His head hurt thinking about what had or hadn't occurred. Cold beings far wiser and cleverer than humans were playing games, with him stuck in the middle. What choice had he but to keep moving forward, hold on to his hope that he'd see the other end, and Marei would be waiting? A dream to focus on while the nightmares kept coming.

He wished Doyle had stayed in Laregoza, or at least retired in Wynais and kept his mouth shut. But this wasn't down to his lieutenant. Loyal Doyle had acted as he should—doubtless reporting his worries about his captain after the mutiny by Pash and the others. Garland had failed. He'd lost Kargon, and Tol and Taylon—all of them. Only Doyle survived, and he'd come back. Far worse, he'd brought the queen.

I'm in the shit.

Zorc stared at him, the ugly leer smudging what remained of his lips. Cadzarilo's gaze was far away. Garland didn't want to guess what that one was thinking.

"You have a promise to keep," Garland vaguely heard Zorc say to the archmage. "I can send you back there anytime. Don't think that I can't."

"You can trust me." Cadzarilo's cold eyes settled on Garland.

"And you need to stop moping," Zorc told Garland, as though he'd read his thoughts.

Garland felt his face flush, so tired of being played for a fool.

"What I need is to know how my queen arrived here, and at the same instant we did? And Carlo Sarfe, too? What's the connection?" His glare switched to Cadzarilo, gazing coldly down at him. "Don't answer—I'll find out eventually. I'm sick of your secrets. Just get us a boat, archmage. I'd sooner not linger on this island of yours."

Cadzarilo shrugged. "I've not yet consulted with our Order. We'll need a mandate to cross—everyone does before leaving the Alchemist's Isle."

"What is he talking about?"

"He needs a spell-guided boat, and therefore a key." Zorc scratched his ruined nose. "There are invisible spell-mines surrounding this island that will blast any escaping boat to cinders without the correct release code."

"I don't understand." Garland felt a flood of exhaustion wash through him.

"In the upper chamber," Cadzarilo said. "Follow me, we're done talking. If anyone spots us loitering, you'll be slain. I'm your protection here."

"And I hold your leash," Zorc said, receiving a withered stare from the archmage.

"Never mind, Zorc, I'll gut you open if you let us down," Garland added.

Cadzarilo's eyes flickered brief anger. He nodded slightly and smirked, turning away. Zorc glared at Garland. "Have a care with your tongue, Journeyman. Let me handle this."

"As you wish," Garland muttered. He didn't trust either of them, but Zorc had his reasons to want to help. He glanced out at the ocean, seeing no ships or disturbance. Perhaps Zorc had tricked him, and that glass was all part of some new contrivance.

No. Ariane was here, as was Carlo Sarfe. Caught in the same trap. And Zorc needed his help, as did Cadzarilo—the only way to divert his horrible fate.

Don't think. Act.

He started walking, heart-heavy but determined. There was nothing he could do about Ariane or Doyle. Too bad.

Once clear of this island, he could focus on finding the Kaa. Plan an attack that wouldn't end in disaster like the last one.

I've got this.

The stone path chiseled into rock, winding in concentric circles around the rugged outcrops. There were no trees. Garland guessed the ones he'd seen in the future must have been planted long after the Citadel's destruction. By whom? Didn't matter.

He saw crooked towers leaning toward him, glanced at roofs with strange stone gargoyles crouched on each corner. Getting nearer, Garland glimpsed ornate gilded gates, a maze of buildings beyond, and a huge golden dome rising dreamily in the heat of that afternoon.

The gilded gates were closed. He saw no guards. Cadzarilo approached them, raising a finger. Garland heard words he didn't understand.

The gates opened without a sound. The archmage motioned them to follow.

Zorc grinned at Garland as they walked inside the Citadel. "You should feel honored. Few untrained souls have seen this place—except slaves and sacrificial victims."

Garland ignored him. He glanced around but saw no one. The entire Citadel had a eerie vacant quality. It felt like a trap. He'd preferred the ruins with the burnt ghosts.

Cadzarilo led them over a thin arched bridge that spanned a deep crevasse. Garland glanced down, seeing a stream running far below. Some kind of volcanic tear. How had he missed that before? Perhaps the wound had healed by his own time? He almost laughed at the thought.

"Where are his fellow enchanters?" Garland muttered to Zorc as the tall figure walked on ahead.

"Doubtless at their studies," the Urgolais said. "Mages

enjoy solitude, only conferring on special days. Clearly this is not one of those."

"Happy to hear it."

They crossed a row of low buildings linked by gilded cloisters and deep alcoves where single lamps shone on rich carpets and ornate tapestries. Cadzarilo stopped suddenly to catch his breath. He stood for a time gazing at one of the alcoves.

"What's the matter?" Zorc asked, as Garland stepped up alongside. He glanced in and saw a youngish, hawk-faced man seated at study, his dark aquiline features reading some ancient parchment. The man looked up curiously, as though sensing they were watching. Garland was grateful he couldn't see them from his position. He had long black hair and a close-cropped beard. He was staring right at the place where they stood. Garland sensed an unhealthy hunger behind those dark eyes. No one moved. The man smiled faintly and returned to his studies. They walked on, and Garland released a slow breath of relief.

"It's him," Cadzarilo spat the words out after they'd left the cloisters behind.

"Who?" Garland demanded.

"Ozmandeus," Zorc said, and hissed him be silent. "The traitorous mage who released the demon that destroyed Gol. The one responsible for burning this Citadel months before that happened."

"Then let me go back there and stick my sword up his arse. Save a continent, as well as my sanity. Maybe after that, we can all go back to our own little worlds."

Cadzarilo was moving on and hadn't heard, but Zorc glared at him.

"Were you to do that, you would lose everything, Sir Garland. Your life, your *soul*—your very essence. You would

simply *disappear*. There is one thing the universe doesn't toler-
ate, and that's someone fucking with its order. That's why your
queen is here, and us. Her Goddess knows Carlo Sarfe cannot
reach his home. Were he to do that and warn them … try to
alter what will be …" Zorc shook his head. "Disaster."

Before Garland could respond, the Urgolais urged them to
catch up with Cadzarilo, who was already approaching the
great domed building.

After closing the gap, he watched as Cadzarilo traced his
fingers along the doors to the great chamber. They opened
wide, and he entered.

"You two need to stay here," he told them haughtily.

Zorc squinted up at him. "Remember your pledge."

The archmage nodded stiffly and vanished inside.

"He'll betray us," Garland muttered.

"He daren't. Knows I'm not bluffing. Cadzarilo will help
us, however unwilling. And I cannot do this alone. You need
me, as I do you. And we both need that sorcerer's power."

"What about Ozmandeus, back there?"

"We avoid him, and any others we encounter. An old
Ulgolais trick," he added smugly. "My cosmic-crypto calcula-
tions timed our arrival a year before Ozmandeus betrayed the
Citadel. We most likely just witnessed him planning that
treachery."

Garland didn't respond. He was thinking of the task ahead
and how impossible it seemed. Even if those Kaa were the
same ones who had the child and Dafyd, how could he save
them in time? And even if he did, how to get them back safe
to Marei?

His thoughts were interrupted when the doors opened and
Cadzarilo stepped out. He held a rod in his left hand that
glowed dull red. Garland looked questioningly at Zorc.

"Code spanner—we can go now."

AN HOUR LATER, HE WATCHED THE CLIFFS DRIFT PAST AS Cadzarilo worked the tiller on the borrowed skiff. They approached a landlocked cove that had been hidden until they'd got close.

"We'll disembark here," he told them. "It's where the slaves were—or should I say are—rounded up and brought across to our Citadel. There's a track leading up through a split in the cliff. We can access the coast road from there. Once on that, we'll get a good view of any coast-huggers, though I suspect the Kaa will have preyed on the first village they found."

Garland swallowed his anger, thinking of the poor souls waiting in chains to be dragged off to Alchemists Isle. Gods alone knew what horrible fates awaited them there. He helped the archmage drag the skiff up the shingle as Zorc watched on, whispering a concealment spell.

Garland followed the other two up the beach. He glanced back to the warm sea and was shocked that the skiff had gone. "You did that?" he asked Zorc.

"Easy enough when you know how," Zorc chortled back. "But I had to keep it quiet. Spells make invisible waves that travel through the atmosphere. The stronger the enchantment, the bigger the wave. We cannot afford to draw any attention. The Kaa, though not adept at sorcery, can detect interference through the dimensions."

"A simple 'yes' would have served well enough," Garland muttered, receiving a bleak stare from his stunted companion.

They climbed the steep stairs leading up to the clifftop. A

rope allowed good purchase, and Garland steadied himself as he crested that rise. He looked back over the sea. The two islands seemed to float on green steam, the first almost reachable and the other one half-hidden behind a thin trail of smoke inking the skies above. He looked for ships and thought of Ariane.

He shook his head and turned away.

Garland followed Cadzarilo along the track until a wider way opened ahead. The road ran smooth and even, the cliff edge scarce twenty feet to their right.

Zorc stumbled beside him, working his staff, his stunted legs struggling to keep the pace. Garland thought about asking Cadzarilo to wait or slow down, but part of him liked seeing the Urgolais struggle. His race had been Caswallon's mentors, and that vile despot was Queen Ariane's bitterest foe.

They walked for several hours, the archmage stopping occasionally when Zorc grumbled loudly enough. By late afternoon, they'd reached a turning point where the path veered west from the southerly direction they'd been heading.

Ahead, he saw something flapping. As they approached, Garland chewed his bottom lip in distaste. Three dry, rotted corpses creaked in cages hanging on a gibbet, their limbs half-eaten and eyes missing. A shoe hung by a lace from the remnants of the nearest one's foot.

"Escaped slaves?" Garland asked Zorc, his anger still focused at Cadzarilo.

"Outlaws, more likely. Gortez Castle is close. That's Ozmandeus's ancestral home."

As they passed the wretched gibbet and cages, Garland saw another track veering off toward a break in the cliffs. Out of curiosity, he dropped back for a moment, as Zorc focused on keeping pace with the archmage.

Garland wandered the track for fifty feet until he reached a sign with a symbol he couldn't understand. The random scrawl of a madman, it seemed. But the meaning was plain enough: *Stay away.*

Past the marker, the lane descended through bracken and scrubby woods, emerging into a steep, verdant valley with the beach and ocean just visible beyond.

A grim castle stood at the head of the valley—a black square of metal on rock. As he watched, Garland felt the tiny hairs tingle up his neck. It was though someone was staring back at him. He pictured a face in his mind. Deep, dark eyes, close-cropped beard. The moment passed when something hit his leg. A stave. He turned and saw Zorc panting and staring up at him in disbelief.

"Are you always this stupid?"

"I wanted to take a look, make sure we weren't followed."

"I told you who owns that castle."

"Yes, but Ozmandeus is in the Citadel."

"His body, aye—but that mind could be roving anywhere. Rumor was Ozmandeus always set spell snares on approach to his home. You're lucky I caught up with you. That's another one you owe me."

Garland glared at him. "Thanks," he said ruefully and followed Zorc back toward the coastal road, the Urgolais hobbling faster than he had all that day, clearly anxious to be away from this spot.

Cadzarilo stood on the road, his proud eyes full of contempt as they joined him. He said nothing, turning about with a swirl of his cloak and renewing his pace. Zorc didn't speak either. Garland suspected they'd been swapping insults about him in their witchy heads. Not important. Hopefully he'd be done with the creepy pair in a day or so.

By evening, they reached another turn. Here, the path veered left, and a long string of coastline revealed they were standing on a headland, a faint line of cliffs marching eastward into murk, where graying water met sky. He saw the distant twinkling of lights, but miles away—too far to walk.

"What is that city?" he asked Zorc.

"Aketa. It lies across the river in Spagos."

It was almost dark when they reached another sign, badly faded with a dull arrow and name Garland couldn't read, indicating another track leading off.

This one they took, climbing down for over half an hour until they were swallowed by rooky woods, the birds perched silent and watching them pass. Cadzarilo stopped at a turn.

He smiled and folded his arms. "Here you are. I've done my part and brought you to them. You can release me from my vow, Urgolais."

"Not yet," Zorc told him, and the tall wizard scowled but didn't respond. "I'll keep an eye on this one," he told Garland. "You go and see what's down there." He tilted his head toward the dark trees below.

Garland nodded and tugged his sword free of its scabbard. He didn't like leaving the two sorcerers behind him, but what choice was there? Whatever hold Zorc had over the archmage, he clearly had to be near him to maintain the connection.

It was good to be alone again. He walked briskly down through the tangle of wood, stopping once when a bird called out in a shrill voice. Twenty minutes later, and much further down, he spotted torchlight glinting up through the trees.

He crouched and watched for a moment before moving on. Taking care to avoid stepping on twigs, Garland followed the track until he heard the murmur of distant water and made out the faint outlines of a lean, skinny ship, a single sail furled tight. He descended slowly, heart thudding in chest.

He reached a huge oak and hid behind the trunk gazing down. He could hear ugly voices, their laughter carried up on the breeze. A woman screamed. Garland had to force himself not to run down there again. He couldn't afford to get this wrong.

He crouched in his hideout and watched until a crescent moon slid free of cloud rack and spilled silver light on the Kaa camp and ocean beyond.

For ten long seconds, Garland had a clear view of every-thing he needed. He made a mental note. Perhaps thirty men gathered around a fire. Prisoners off to the right, a dozen at least. Some women and children, though he'd seen no infants. They'd been lashed to a tall post and stood weeping. Beyond that, three odd-shaped ships bobbed gently in the night breeze. He shivered as the clouds swallowed the moon and the woods closed in.

Time to get back and report what he'd seen. He stood slowly and froze as the soft notes of a harp floated up through the trees. The harsh voices below went silent. Garland was filled with an overpowering feeling of dread. He withheld the impulse to run, standing slowly instead and turning, making his way back up the road while imaging knives digging into his back.

The two sorcerers were crouched by a low fire when he joined them panting and sweating.

"How many?" Zorc leered up at him.

"I counted thirty and a dozen prisoners. There's something else down there."

"I know," Zorc said slowly. "This will prove tricky, but the

Kaa and their allies are always stronger at night. We'll pay them a visit at dawn. Cadzarilo's going to help me create a distraction, while you attend to the main task. Don't be senti-mental—you won't be able to save them all. Get the child and the man, if he's there. Then run back up here, where we will await you."

"What makes you think he'll stick around?" Garland glared at Cadzarilo, who stared back at him, eyes hooded.

"We had a frank discussion while you were creeping about in the woods," Zorc said. "Don't worry about us—you'll have enough to fret on. I suggest you get some rest while you can."

Garland stared at the Urgolais and switched his gaze over the archmage. They both looked at him, their expressions unreadable. He wouldn't sleep with these two ghouls breathing over him, but it made sense to rest his body.

He made for a swathe of bracken a few yards distant and stretched out, his eyes resting on the clouds shifting through the branches high above. An owl called out once. He thought he heard the harp again, further away. He must have slept at some point.

18

THE GAP BETWEEN WORLDS

CARLO OPENED HIS EYES, sensing a shadow at the corner of his bunk. It blurred, moved, and became a person. The cabin was dark, his lantern burnt low. He rubbed his eyes and blinked. She was back.

Urdei.

The child smiled at him, the blonde locks glistening in the lamplight. The wineskin was empty on his desk—he must have drained it and crashed.

"Are you real?"

"What kind of a question is that?" Her blue gaze mocked him, and she kicked his leg, making him sit up. He blinked again and strained his eyes as she faded and reappeared.

"A reasonable one, given the circumstances."

"You should be grateful, Carlo Sarfe. To have friends like myself … and Stogi. And Tai Pei."

"I *am*. But I'm also confused and very angry. You know more than I can imagine, so help me again, *please*. I'm sure that's in your interest, or you wouldn't be here."

"You shouldn't get drunk every night. Makes you grumpy.

It's not my fault you lost Teret. She wasn't your woman, but I know you wanted her. And your poor crew are worried about you again. Show some leadership." She poked him in the ribs.

Carlo glared at her, summoning what little patience he could muster. "Let me understand what we're up against here, and what you need from me. All I want is to get my ship home in one piece and save my kin. And if I can, warn of the catastrophe you all speak of."

"You could stop Gol's ruin if you had my Mother's bow." Urdei grinned impishly. "That would be most interesting, I'm tempted to encourage you. But no. I'm loyal and dutiful, as good daughters should be. And She would be *so* angry." She started giggling and wiped moisture from her eyes. "Uncle too, *Him* particularly. And He gets violent when crossed, as your beloved Sarfania is about to find out. Father would encourage it, however. He's been following your every move. I expect He'll show up in due course."

"The gods." Carlo stared at the porthole, trying to shake off his anger and confusion.

"The High Gods, actually. Big fish. Three out of four, anyway. And we don't mention the fourth one. Elanion, Sensu-ata, and Oroonin. My family. All are invested in your fate."

"I was told they were dead? I know the Emerald Queen has returned, but the others ..."

"They were *punished*. We all were—though I, of course, was innocent. But no one truly dies, you foolish man." Urdei giggled. "They get remolded. Softened, like useless dried-up clay. Shaped into something new. Recycling, they call it in some of the worlds I've visited. Souls move around, big or small. Doesn't matter. They are starlight drifting through time and space. Void's full of their voiceless shouts. We three sisters are the door wardens. Without us, Chaos would seep through."

"All right, *good*. I'm impressed. But *why* me?"

"You should ask my gorgeous sister that. Vervandi's thrown her cards behind Queen Ariane, who our Mother has charged with stopping you reaching Gol. You see, Mother doesn't think you're reliable."

"Garland's queen? Teret spoke about her often. How can she possibly do that? Is she following us, and if so, how?"

Urdei nodded. "In a sense, they all are. Pieces on a board, drawn out like slow, weeping wounds. Garland the Journeyman included. He's a knight in Marei's realm."

"What?"

"They're posh warriors that like to rescue cats." She snickered again.

"I'm not understanding you."

"Joke. Too early for sarcasm?"

"I don't know what time it is."

"You would if you didn't drink so much. Now listen." She poked him again. "The World Thread is thin here out on the mid-ocean. You should know that, after all you've witnessed. And the *Arabella* is about to cross the dimensions, allowing her return to your time. You have me to thank for that, as does *Sir* Garland, who you met briefly. You will learn more on the other side."

"Again, why me? I left my home to find new lands, and somehow got caught up in ... Why pick on my ship? And why the fuck was I washed up on Gwelan, of all places?"

"Don't be vulgar." Another prod. "The answer to those questions lies inside the phenomenon that is Graywash Hall," she told him, addressing Carlo as though he were the child and she the grownup. He nodded, noting that her laughing eyes showed concern for the first time.

"There is a war raging that you mortals know nothing about. A continuation of the Happening witnessed outside Kelthara, where the gods supposedly perished. What you experienced in the Castle of Lights was yet another thread."

"I still don't understand why I'm involved."

"Sssh." She placed a finger on her lips. "The Great Enemy has returned in a new form. Much weakened, and yet still stronger than you could imagine. You see, the Maker cannot unmake or destroy something He's put into the world. Ironic, isn't it? Grandfather created the beast that could devour Him. His Firstborn son. Proud Saan, who you men call Old Night, or the Shadowman. You know your mythology?"

"Vaguely."

"Well, you'll need to study and stop drinking. Big Bad Uncle Saan has morphed and evaded the ultimate punishment. Annihilation. He keeps His soul—the Orb—in a place resembling a castle or manor house. That's Graywash Hall. You know what I'm talking about—you saw it when you met Savarna. Remember that dream?"

"I ..."

"The Hall, as men call it, crosses through time and space, mirroring Laras Lassladen, and draining the lifeforce from my Mother's ancestral home. You see, where there is light, there has to be darkness."

As she spoke, Carlo pictured a wild-eyed redhead glaring down at him while he rested on a rock, with a huge, pulsating black square slab of a castle looming behind.

"Savarna ... yes. What happened to her?"

"Doesn't matter. That's the place." She tapped his ribs again. "Graywash Hall is the soul-sapper. Its fly-sticky webs are drawing all that is evil back into the universe. Pulled in by the Orb, that dark rotating thread is all that remains of Uncle Saan."

"The Shadowman." Carlo chewed his lip. His head felt fuzzy, and he doubted his senses. Perhaps he was dreaming again. *She's not real. None of this is real.*

"I'm real, and you're awake." Her eyes flashed with annoyance, making him jump. "Start paying attention—it might well save your life, fool."

"Sorry."

"Saan's damaged soul's unravelling the Weaver's recent tidy-ups. Worse still, my absentminded Mother's bow was stolen. Things are getting messy."

"You still haven't answered my question. *Please,* indulge me …" He smiled.

She nodded. "It's plain common sense. You, Carlo Sarfe, having sailed further west than any before, were exposed on those vacant waters. It's where the gods conduct most of their experiments. More space, fewer casualties. Scant noise to draw attention. You sailed right through Their playground and got caught in the wobble that affected all nine worlds."

"The Happening."

"That jolt from that calamity resulted in your hazardous arrival in Gwelan. You're lucky it wasn't the Void. Unfortunately, Gwelan's a bad place these days. The Jynn was made aware and acted promptly to steer you to Teret, knowing the witch Elerim would be after fresh victims and Teret couldn't be one of them. She was needed for part of my Mother's plan."

Carlo's mind clouded again. He visualized a terrible, glistening rock—a castle with dripping walls and lightless windows. A faint memory. The place where he'd met the red-haired woman, Savarna. He'd thought it yet another dream.

Urdei smiled at him and nodded. As he stared into her eyes, his mind cleared, the flashbacks returning.

"I remember Savarna as a bad-tempered redhead with strange eyes. Like a tiger, I thought at the time. I was outside a black rock. Stranded. A castle, maybe. *Lost,* again. It's all coming back to me. Savarna, and that—"

"—Graywash Hall is seeking you," Urdei told him sternly. "Those within want to goad you into upsetting the cosmic balance by bidding you use Kerasheva's magical power to stop the demon Ashmali and divert Sensuata's wrath. Change time itself."

"The Emerald Bow? You said it's been stolen. Kerasheva can save my country, my people? How?"

"By destroying everything else." She smiled, but her cheeky eyes were serious. "Father wants this, as does the Orb. They both revel in strife, especially kin-strife. You will be tested and must refuse the bow when offered. This will be your greatest challenge. Your Enemy is guileful and can be very persuasive. Already His hounds are on your tail."

Carlo laughed. "I don't see that as a problem, as I've no idea where that bow can be found. Rather, I think I'm losing my mind. You're most likely just part of another dream, but at least I can argue back in this one."

"I'm on your side, silly."

"Perhaps you might be. I'm sorry for being churlish, but I'm so tired of this ... beguilement." He looked at the port-hole again. He was sleepy, trying to hang on. "Why was Savarna outside Graywash Hall? Is she caught in this, too?"

"In a sense, yes. Your paths crossed briefly. These things happen when the alignment is wobbling. Their time is not your time, or even Garland's. But perchance you'll encounter her and the hero, Jaran Saerk, again while outside the confines of time. After all, you fought alongside their friend Finvar Droll on that beach."

"I did?"

Her gaze rested on the darkness outside the porthole. He saw lightning strike the water. He hadn't expected a storm tonight. She stood hovering, her face paling to shadow.

"Are you ready, Carlo Sarfe?" Her voice was a whisper.

"For what?"

"*What lies ahead.* Terrors and temptations your mind cannot imagine."

She faded back to dreamy dust.

"Stay! I've more questions!" His eyes were closing with exhaustion.

"We're out of time. Rest, while I guide you through."

"I'd sooner have answers."

"*Sleep!*"

Her face blurred and vanished. Carlo blinked and felt his body slump on the bunk. He closed his eyes and drifted.

STOGI STARED AT THE HORIZON MOODILY. HE FELT EDGY tonight. Something big was brewing. As he watched beside Taylon and Tol, he saw the clouds shifting, changing colors from deep inky blue through red into violet.

"That looks like one bad storm out there," Taylon muttered. The two castaways had taken to Stogi, the only man here from their own time. Stogi suspected Tai Pei scared them. Even talkative Tol was taciturn when she appeared, though for her part she'd been friendlier towards the pair. They played dice but always let her win. He didn't know where she was tonight and didn't much care, not being in the mood for her sharp retorts.

"It doesn't look real," Tol said, leaning heavily on his bow. "Unnerving."

"Gives me the creeps," Taylon replied, and he jumped as a thick vein of amber lightning ripped out from the clouds in three jagged spirals.

Tol's jaw dropped. "*Shit.* That was close!"

Stogi gripped the rail. He felt nausea brewing like a steam kettle inside his stomach. "This isn't natural," he told them. "We're entering a time shift. A *morphing.*" He turned and saw the blonde child Urdei waving at him from beneath a sail. Her eyes were huge, and the long pigtails whipped up in the sudden wind.

Her shrill voice reached him like a whisper in the wind. "Do not fear, Stogi—I'm here to guide you through." Beside him, Tol cried out, seeing the girl for the briefest instant before she vanished.

"Who was that?" Taylon barely choked the words out, his face stricken.

"You don't need to know," Stogi said.

"Bu you do?" Tol asked him.

"Oh, aye, and I wish I didn't. Still. She's on our side, I suppose."

"What's he going on about?" Taylon glared at his friend.

Tol managed a queasy smile. "Our friend Stogi's in the know and won't share. Come on, Stodge. Who was that peculiar child, and how—?"

"Her name's Urdei, and she's taking us back there." The voice was Tai Pei's. The woman stood with hands in fists, her hair pinned back and a fierce expression on her face.

The two men went silent, but Stogi rounded on her.

"Where have you been?"

She didn't respond, her gaze at the flashing aura beyond the clouds.

Tol coughed. "You're saying that child was real and she's taking us to Gol, back to Carlo's time? How is that possible?"

"Did you learn nothing stranding on that Crantock island? Idly scratching lice on your bellies, assuming you'd arrived there by chance. A random misfortune. You daft twats, it's part of the pattern. We're in another vortex, as you were back there." Tai Pei laughed, shielding her eyes from the glare. As Stogi watched, the sky shimmered deep velvet green as thunder rumbled and boomed, like steel barrels crashing down a hillslope.

"That was sorcery," Tol said, avoiding her gaze.

"Hadn't we better take shelter while we can?" Taylon asked nobody in particular.

"There's no avoiding this," Stogi said. *The passage through.*

"Stand fast, craven lads—you're about to witness a wonder," Tai Pei added, grinning. Stogi winced. She was enjoying this. *The woman's unhinged.*

He watched the clouds billow like sails, swelling and bulging into vast mushrooms of vapor. They were moving forward quickly, as though on wheels, rolling, colors shifting, a flashing wall of light racing toward the *Arabella*. Stogi thought he saw great chariots riding the clouds and the faint outlines of giant warlike figures high above.

I don't feel well. He tried shutting his eyes, but that made things worse.

Beside him, Tai Pei yelled out. Stogi blinked and saw the sky turn orange as a noise like a thousand wasps droned around his ears. Stogi gripped the rail as tight as he could and trembled, legs shaking badly. He half-noticed Taylon's shadow vanishing below deck. Past him, the duty crew were staring white-faced next to Slim Tareel, who manned the helm. There was no sign of Carlo Sarfe.

"Are you certain we'll survive this?" Tol yelled at Tai Pei as the rolling chariots turned red through green and back to amber. The thunder echoed. The harbinger clouds reared like frothy towers above their heads. Further out, Stogi counted a dozen water spouts dancing and whirling, drunken acrobats spewing spray up into the mustering cloud racks.

The sky turned black.

The deluge hit them first. He hung on, barely, as a wall of rain struck the ship's decks and more splattered in jerky spasms, the brine rising and spilling down.

Tai Pei laughed beside him, her face a parody of rapture.

"We're crossing the dimensions," she yelled at him. Tol had disappeared, and Stogi wished he could, too.

He tried yelling at her, but seawater filled his mouth. The rain shifted past swiftly and the residue of water was sucked from the decks by a huge vacuum of trapped air. Stogi felt his hair whip around his face and jerk back, as though an enemy attacked him from behind. He gulped and shook his head free as the suction faded back.

Next came the wind.

The *Arabella*'s reefed sails bulged to bursting point, some tearing, as a distant roar rose to screaming pitch. The rising gale took on form. Stogi saw the tiny figures of blueish-green people jumping about in the air. They were calling out to him. They vanished, and the wind died back as though some vast being had shut a cosmic door.

A calm settled. The sky paled and rippled, like a wall of curtains waiting to open on the next scene. He heard Tai Pei muttering expletives. Excitedly, she grabbed his face in her hands and kissed his mouth. Before he could blink, she'd returned to her scrutiny.

Dazed, Stogi saw the sky chariots roll past, each one a flashing aura of multicolored light. He saw the figures clearly, a thousand feet above. Stern-faced men and women rode on the cloud-wrought platforms as horned beasts pulled their chariots high overhead.

The giant figures faded as a second lull took hold. The sea turned oily black and calm as silk. Stogi stared at Tai Pei, who looked worried.

"What's next?" he asked her.

She shook her head. Far out, he saw a fret rising. A small ball of green fog moved this way and that, sometimes hovering close or fading back to the horizon.

Silence. The *Arabella* creaked and drifted, her sails limp and torn. Stogi saw Tareel leaning on the wheel, his white face terrified. The other crewmen had vanished. It was just the three of them on deck.

The silence became a throbbing in his head, induced by expectation and dread. Beside him, Tai Pei gasped and pointed. Stogi saw another ship drifting toward them out of the ether.

"Steer away!" she yelled at Slim Tareel, who'd seen the ship and was working the wheel like a madman.

The vessel loomed close, its sides draped in fog. He saw faces staring across at him. Dead faces, pale and emaciated. As he watched, Stogi saw the flesh crumble from some of them. He gasped as he spotted Seek among the dead. The shaman was calling out his name.

The dead ship drifted past, and Stogi retched at the vile stench of the corpses.

He heard a faint musical sound. It grew resinous, the peel

of harp chords scaling up and down. Like noisome, swarming flies, the harp notes pounded louder, spinning around his head.

Stogi saw a face, too blurry to make out. A small figure. Man-shaped, carrying a large green bow, clad in yellow and red-checker trousers and tunic. He was laughing cruelly, his face hidden by a jaunty three-cornered hat, small golden bells hanging from each tip. The manikin held the bow aloft in both hands as the scraping harp music battered Stogi's eyes, like the rain had earlier.

The manikin vison passed, and the music drifted off. He felt the entire ship shudder and rock. The decks creaked below his boots, as though about to splinter.

The clouds shifted and a gap emerged, allowing a liquid rainbow blaze multicolored sparkles on the water as the *Arabella* was buffeted like a balloon in yet another gale.

The gap closed, and skies darkened again. Stogi thought he saw claw-like hands reaching out for them from the gloom. Beyond these, a darker oily mass rose. A square rock resembling a castle, with turrets and window slits gasping open in belching yawns and venting sickly green smoke. He saw a shadowy drawbridge lower in silence and watched spellbound as a helmeted rider covered in green armor guided a dead horse out over the waves. Behind him were warriors shouting and a dozen huge white dogs, their pointed ears the color of blood.

The steel rider swung a huge morning-star mace around his head. He hurled the weapon towards the *Arabella*, and it exploded into ash. Stogi turned and saw Urdei standing with her palms stretched out. Her child's face was angry, and her eyes lightning-bright and filled with alien power.

The rider vanished, as did his train and warriors. The

black, groping void slipped back out of sight. Stogi let out a long, slow breath. The sky paled to a hollow silver. He stared down at glassy water, seeing things writhing and darting below.

Again, Tai Pei shouted a warning. Stogi saw a huge mass of tentacles emerge from the ocean, writhing around. Beyond the kraken, a great serpent reared its head. He saw its coils looping and bunching, a mile to stern.

He barely heard Urdei's voice calling out in a strange tongue. For the briefest instant, Stogi saw Tamersane, his old friend, staring through the clouds.

"Be careful, Stogi," Tam called out to him. "Keep an eye on Carlo, if you want to survive." Tam vanished, and Stogi heard distant thunder trailing off to his right.

The danger had passed—for the moment.

Gods, I'm giddy as a May Queen at the cider keg.

He clung to the rail and, gazing back, saw the crew had returned. Dry Gurdey had relieved the exhausted Tareel. Gold Tar stood scowling and shaking, pointing off to larboard. Stogi saw another ship matching their pace before fading into the glare.

"That's the Kraken Girl," Urdei appeared beside him. The child was smiling again, as though very pleased with herself. "Thanks to my intervention, Queen Ariane's made it through, too. I pulled them into the void, on my Mother's request. Now it's your turn, Stogi."

The child vanished, and instead Tai Pei was staring at him in alarm.

"Are you hurt?"

"No," he said, managing to rise. "Just soaked and frozen, half-deafened, and daft."

The sea was calm, the monsters having disappeared. A blue

sky shone above, and the *Arabella*'s ragged sails trapped the edges of a kindly breeze.

"We're through, Stogi," Tai Pei said. "We've crossed the Void—safely passing through all five dimensions, arriving one thousand years in our past. Some accomplishment."

"How do you know that? It could have been sorcery—like the ordeal on that cursed island."

"No. This was different. Urdei and her Mother, the Emerald Queen, guided us through. They need us, Stodge. That's the thing. But we've got to keep an eye on Carlo. He's going to be trapped, else."

"What do you mean, trapped? And the child hinted the same?"

She placed a hand on his arm. "Why do you think I've been paying him so much attention? Carlo's in the shit. He wants to save his home but cannot prevent its destruction. Nor can he save his kin without disrupting the cosmic order. It's bad luck."

"How do you know all this?"

"Because I'm a magician, or at least have studied enough astrology and thaumaturgy and doodad to comprehend the stakes involved here. The darkness we saw was the Orb they call Graywash Hall. The same as the cavern in that island—the whole island, actually."

"You never fail to impress me."

She grinned. "Graywash Hall sent a thief out to steal Elanion's bow. You saw the checkered joker?" He nodded. "That sly player will offer Kerasheva to Carlo, knowing he won't be able to resist. With the bow, Carlo can bend time and alter history. The Aralais treasures are powerful artefacts, none more so than Kerasheva. If Carlo does that, none of us from his future will survive."

"Magician or not, I don't understand how you can know all this?"

"Magician's the wrong word, but it suffices. Be satisfied that I do, Stodge. It was part of the reason why I accompanied you on this voyage. The challenge. That shaman, Seek. He spoke to me, as did the white tern—the bird he became afterward. That trickster's on their side. We can't let them win, Stogi. Urdei told me that it's down to the three of you to stop Carlo accepting that bow."

"Three of us?"

"Queen Ariane, Sir Garland of Wynais, and you, Stogi the Tseole."

"Me? What can I do?"

She'd turned away. Stogi was about to ask her again when a shout went up from the lookout above. Stogi turned, seeing a distant dark line rising above the waves.

"Land ahead!" Dry Gurdey called out from the wheel.

19

THE LEGEND OF DUNRAE TARN

MAREI WALKED behind the big man in the coat, her mind busy with questions. Despite what Dunrae Tarn had said back at the cottage, he'd revealed nothing during their journey.

They'd left the city in the early morning, as mist wrapped the walls. The guards had slunk back into their sheds liked scolded dogs as Dunrae Tarn strode past. She'd wondered what hold he had over them.

Two days out, they'd crossed the mountains and entered the fertile valley outside her home. They camped in woods that night, the moon riding above trees. Dunrae Tarn refrained from lighting a fire.

"I expect your inn will be watched," he told Marei.

She was tired—he'd pushed her hard, setting a tough pace. But at least he'd brought blankets, and she'd had slept well at night. The exercise had held her questions at bay. And she felt stronger, less afraid. Ready to face what she must to help get her son back.

She climbed into the blanket and watched him staring at a gap in the trees. Beyond, the moon hovered like a huge silver eye. He lit the small pipe he always carried and leaned back, blowing smoke rings up into the trees. She felt her eyes closing and had almost drifted off when his gruff tones brought her back.

She sat up, the blanket draped around her shoulders. He was leaning forward, the dark, shabby coat giving him the appearance of a crow, his hard face gazing across at her.

"What's wrong?" Marei asked, stifling a yawn.

For an answer, he stowed his pipe in a pocket and smiled gruffly.

"You're good lass, Marei. I can see that. And I'm sorry your caught up in this … *bollocks*. Your man Garland should not have returned here. Him doing so has put your little family in great danger."

"You're saying this was Garland's fault? How? And your friend Jynn promised me that Garland will save Rosey's baby. That he has help from someone."

"I reckon that's so, as he has far more important tasks ahead."

"What could be more important than saving a child from those flesh-eating monsters?" She was wide awake now, and cross at his manner.

Dunrae Tarn shrugged. "Save your anger for the men we'll meet tomorrow."

"You mean Shale?"

"Nah. Old Glass Eyes is most likely with Sir Valen. Shale runs the hunt, owns the dogs. Bad lad. But Valen will have left others from his crew near the tavern. It's why we camped here."

"Why not continue tonight, catch them unawares while they're sleeping?"

"Because after dark is when they're strongest. The power

from the Hall's Orb spreads out to those fools who sold their souls. We'll leave at sunup. You'll stay hidden in the woods, while I'll do some cleaning." He smiled slightly.

"What about Rosey—will she really be safe? I worry about her."

"Safer than any of us. Even those devils in the Hall can't hurt Shorty. He is outside their power."

"Who is he—a wizard?"

Dunrae Tarn smiled. "Ah, that's some question, that is. Not sure I can answer that without spinning your head, girl. The master, Jynn, is many things."

"Hmm, I'll let that go. But while you're so talkative, you can tell me about yourself. Why were those guards and other men, like that shady innkeeper at the city, frightened of you?"

He stared at her for a moment and nodded. "They know my legend."

"Legend …?"

"*Curse*. I cannot die, Marei. I'm immortal."

She almost laughed. "You're … a god?"

"No. *Fuck* no." He stared at her harshly. "I'm a man, nothing more. Always have been. But one who was doomed, millennia ago."

"*Doomed?* That sounds drastic. You appear hale and strong from where I'm sitting."

"Appearance isn't everything, lassie. My doom, or fate, is to live forever. Or until the Maker takes us back to the beginning. I can almost die, have done that several times. Not pleasant. And I can suffer hurt and weariness and agony and sorrow. Everything bad. But can never take the final rest. The big sleep. That's my doom."

"That's horrible. What happened to you?"

"I lived in a place where wars raged endlessly. All I knew

was fighting, killing. I was a soldier of fortune, Marei. Good at my trade. Pitiless and lethal. Without honor. Back then, I had no concept of the word. Times were hard. We were hungry and desperate. But I fought for the wrong side and was punished by the victors. One of whom was the clever sod you know as Jynn."

"Jynn punished you? Why?"

"He had his reasons, and I deserved it. Bad things happened on that world, and I was held accountable. And punished harshly, as was my companion at arms. A warrior knight I'm destined to slay. He, like myself, cannot be killed by mortal steel or sorcery. And his punishment was far worse than mine, for he was the instigator. Whereas I, merely a willing participant."

"Who is this wretched fellow?"

"They call him Sir Valen the Gaunt. He has no face, as it was ripped off in the last battle. We were good comrades once. Cruel warriors. Rich, and greedy to be richer. But Sir Valen chose evil forever. And I, though not forgiven, was given a second chance by Shorty."

"You call that punishment a chance?"

Dunrae shrugged. "The faceless knight was kept alive, spared from torment, and given powers by his new masters. They made Sir Valen a terror, but the price was his soul. I've still got mine, though it's ragged as banners ripped in a storm. Sir Valen became a soulless entity empowered by Chaos. A hollow man. Emotionless, and crueler than any other."

"And this Sir Valen the Gaunt leads Shale and his men?"

Dunrae nodded. "They are his chattels. Shale is devious, hence useful to him. The others, nothing. Mercenaries from various worlds scooped up by the darkness."

"But not you?"

"*Almost.* Shorty alone forgave me. The others wanted my head. He persuaded them I could yet prove useful, and he tasked me with seeking out my former friend and destroying him. Crossing any time and dimension. We two have no bounds. Sir Valen knows I hunt him, and he seeks to steal my soul, as only he can. If he succeeds, I will be his creature. The stakes are high, and I will know no rest until I prove the victor."

"That seems a cruel punishment indeed."

He smiled bitterly. "As I said, I deserve it. I'm four thousand years old, woman. I can't bloody well die, and I seldom sleep or rest. Shorty has employed me to stop the power of Graywash Hall creeping into Ansu, as it already has Gwelan and Galenki, and several of the other worlds on the Outer Fringes."

Marei's tired mind was spinning, trying to take this all in. "I don't understand. Jynn said the Hall was a living thing, not the castle it resembles."

"It's both."

"The remnant of the being Garland referred to as Old Night?"

He nodded. "The World Breaker. Graywash Hall is the Shadowman's lingering spirit, if you like. A black shapeless mass. His dying breath. The *Orb*, Jynn calls it. The part of Old Night even the Maker couldn't reach."

Marei stifled a yawn. She had so many questions. "Garland spoke of a war in his realm, where the gods destroyed each other, Old Night included."

"Everything is connected," Dunrae Tarn continued, as though he hadn't heard her. He seemed lost in a dream, perhaps looking back down the centuries at the wreckage of his life. She felt sorry for this grim-looking man. Whatever evil he'd been part of, why was he alone made to recompense?

"I'm sorry," she said softly.

He raised a brow and almost smiled. "The nine worlds. The gods. The Void and Chaos swirling outside. *Connected.* It's a constant spiral within a spiral that never ends, or starts. A continuing. Take your man Garland, for an example."

"What about him?" Marei felt her pulse quicken.

"Poor bloke got tangled in the webs as he quested after lost Tamersane. The loopy witch Ysaren pulled him in. Shorty helped Garland at the crossroads, as he did Carlo Sarfe and Stogi, despite knowing that Carlo could ruin everything for us in his attempt to get back to Gol."

"So you are using my friend?"

"Garland was our insurance. By sending him to your dimension, he came face to face with the menace of Graywash Hall. That needed to happen. He is the Journeyman appointed, and therefore the Hall couldn't destroy him. It tried to trap him inside instead, first by using the witch Cille, and more recently Sir Valen himself. We are pieces on a board, Marei. All of us. But as Shorty said, we two are on your side."

"Why do you keep calling Garland the Journeyman? What journey is he undertaking? And what do you people expect from him? He's just a man."

"Like myself, your gallant *knight* has been chosen for a specific task. Unlike me, Garland's not being punished—though he'd probably contest that." He laughed gruffly. "Poor sod was chosen by his naïve queen, who consulted with her Goddess. Hence Elanion Herself got involved and decided to move him forward as her new champion piece. First, to help Her defeat the three arrogant Aralais witchy-bitches who'd angered Her. Next, to stop Carlo Sarfe from destroying this world. Which he will do if he accepts the bow Kerasheva from the joker who nabbed it."

"A thief stole the bow? Garland told me the Goddess took it from the witches, when he was in that strange castle."

"And lost it again, promptly. She's scatty, that one. Bloody deities—they're overrated. You need to sleep, girl. That's enough of me jabbering for tonight. We'll speak more on this before we enter the Hall."

"I'm going in there with you?"

"Don't you want to see your son?"

"You know I do!"

"Sleep ..."

She glared at him for a moment and stifled another yawn. It was obvious he wasn't going to say anymore, after opening up on so much. He sat hunched against a tree stump, his eyes half-closed.

"One last question," she said, seeing a blue-gray eye glint open.

"Make it quick. The night draws in, and the spirits will be drifting out from the Hall searching for soul-heat."

"That cat, Camfalis. Not an average cat, Jynn said. He's the third member of your team, isn't he?"

"It's *She*, not he. Camfaleese Fenglegrim," Dunrae Tarn corrected her. "Use her proper names. There's one for each soul. We call her Camfey, or Grim for short. Like Shorty, Camfey's not who she appears. And who do you think's looking after Rosey? Jynn never stays put for long."

"You pair left a damn cat to look after that girl? What madness is—"

"Hush! Stop fretting, woman." He raised a finger to his mouth and pointed to the moon. "Rosey is safe, as I told you.

Grim the Puss will make sure no harm comes to her. Rest your weary bones, and for fuck's sake, *sleep*."

She slept.

WHEN MAREI WOKE, THE SUN SPANGLED GOLDEN through beech trees on a rise to the east. She rolled free of the blanket and saw the man standing with pipe in hand, watching the shadows depart from the woods.

"I trust you slept well?" he asked her without turning.

"I did, very well. Like you put a spell on me. Did you?"

He turned and glared at her. "I'm no sorcerer, lass. Hate those oily bastards. But I have learnt some tricks, aye. 'Tis a small benefit of being immortal. Are you ready?"

"Yes."

"Good." He picked up his cudgel and threw the heavy coat over his shoulders. "We'll stop a mile or so from your inn. As I said, you'll wait out of sight as I go explore."

They walked in silence as she followed him along the windy track. They soon left the woods behind and descended further into her valley. She almost wept when she spotted the gray slate roofs of Torrigan's Tavern. At his signal, they left the road behind and approached the inn, via more woods. He made her wait in a hollow. It felt colder than it had a few moments ago. She shivered.

"Be careful," Marei said, receiving an ironic stare back. He was reaching inside his heavy coat and tugging something.

"What are you doing?"

He winked and, reached in further, yanking at a mystery object, much like the fairground magicians who pulled rabbits and such from their hats. The man produced something impossible from inside his coat. Three, maybe four feet in length. She had no idea how he'd managed to conceal such a large object. Dunrae Tarn was full of secrets.

"What's that?" Marei watched him unfold a neatly tied blanket covering the long cylindrical object. It had a spade-shaped handle at one end and tapered narrow, before ending in a fluted circular hole. There was a brass handle of sorts, and a finger tog. Black metal, badly scorched in places. A weapon —had to be. It looked heavy. He shouldered the long, metal object and turned to face her.

"Bessy," he grinned.

"What, *who?*"

"She upsets the crows," he said. "'Spect you'll hear them carking soon enough. That's your signal the Cleaning's started."

Without another word, he turned away and vanished into the trees.

MAREI WAITED FOR OVER AN HOUR, HEARING NOTHING, the worry returning. She felt an icy dread creeping into the hollow.

I'll not linger here like a helpless victim.

She left the trees behind, taking care to not be seen. Just visible to her right, the road ribboned down a hill toward her garth. The cottage and inn were shrouded in mist. It must have rained heavily here last night.

There's no one around.

She expected Dunrae Tarn would return soon and decided, as it was her home, she had every right to venture inside without his permission. She reached the road and smiled, emboldened by her action. She stopped mid-stride when a booming blast exploded off to her right, shortly followed by another to her left.

"Stupid woman—I told you to stay in the woods!" Dunrae Tarn's angry voice reached her from further down the lane. "Dive low, else you get caught in the crossfire."

Numb with fear, she complied, dropping on her belly painfully and crawling fast as she could across to the overgrown verge. She covered her ears as the blast sounded again. As he'd predicted, crows circled above, calling out in outrage at the racket. And who could blame them?

Silence returned for a few minutes. She dared a look up through the dead grass but quickly ducked again at the sound of footsteps approached at speed. Laying low and well hidden, Marei saw two rough-looking men running down the road toward the spot where she lay hidden. She recognized one of them as Shale's man, the one Garland had wounded.

They were getting close, and the nearest had a crossbow cranked and ready. She fumbled for her own weapon, until now forgotten at her belt. They were scarce a dozen feet away when the blast roared again. Marei gasped as the one behind buckled and twisted like a mangled corn doll, vanishing into the verge as if he'd been gored by a two-ton bull.

His companion veered off the road, eyes wild, but another blast resounded. Marei saw his body ripped open and thrown back onto the lane like discarded meat. The torn torso thrashed for a moment and lay still, half the face gone and one leg missing.

Dunrae Tarn's gruff tones reached her: "All clear, lassie."

Shaking badly, Marei staggered to her feet and hobbled toward the mangled corpses, her mouth covered in horror at the sight and stench. She stopped, seeing Dunrae Tarn emerge casually from bracken, pipe in mouth trailing smoke, a wry grin smearing his craggy face.

The noisemaking contraption was hoisted over one shoulder. He glanced down at the corpses as he passed, absently kicking the nearest. He joined her with a shrug.

"Those two clowns won't come back," he told her. "Dear old Bessy. The blunderbuss is from my old world. It don't take prisoners."

"That exploding tube tore those men apart. How did you—?"

"—it's half cannon and musket," he interrupted. "What I clean with, mostly. Keep the long knife for close-quarter work."

He tapped his belt, where the bone handle showed behind his coat. She'd thought it a sword earlier, but it was the biggest knife she'd seen.

"You see, lass, a sword and such ain't much use against Sir Valen's boys. Bessy does 'em nice. Though, I daresay I'll need something special to do for him. Come on, don't fret so, girl. Ignore the crow feed. We'll get a blaze on at your hearth, and you can cook me something hearty. Keep you busy, stop the thinking."

He winked at her, shouldered the blunderbuss again, and whistled off down the lane. Marei followed in silence, her head still aching from the din. She shuddered at the mangled corpses and soon left them behind. She turned once and saw that the crows had already settled to feed. She gagged, choked back bile, and looked forward again.

I'm so glad he's on our side.

. . .

They reached the stockade. All looked as it had when she'd left with Rosey. Shale's people hadn't burnt it down, despite her worries. They had obviously decided to wait for her to return first—rightly guessing that she would. Marei cursed herself for a fool.

Inside the inn, Dunrae Tarn lit the fire while she worked in the kitchen preparing a meal. He grinned, watching her, and poured himself an ale.

"Oh, that's good," he told her, wiping his mouth.

It wasn't until late that night she dared question him again. Her mind was a maze. The man was almost merry, having consumed over two bowls of broth and three pints of her brew. He sat by the fire, his flat, blue-gray eyes on her as she joined him, her own smarting at the smoke from his pipe.

"I knew you wouldn't stay in them trees." He showed a lopsided grin. "Spirited lass like you."

"This is my home," she said.

"Yeah, they knew that, too. Next time, do as I say. It's going to be much trickier once we're inside the Hall. I need you sharp, Marei. That's if you want your boy back."

"What's your plan?" she asked him, pouring herself an ale and him another. She'd decided on drinking to calm her nerves, still shaken by the blunderbuss racket and the carnage it had created.

"Simple enough. We enter Graywash Hall, find your boy, and get the fuck out."

"What about you and this Sir Valen character? Will he be waiting for you?"

"It's not my time to kill him yet."

"How do you know that?"

"Because I do," he said, his eyes warning her the matter was closed.

"All right … say we rescue Dafyd, and Garland miraculously returns with the child. What happens next? Won't Shale, or this faceless enemy of yours return again?"

He stared at her for a while. Eventually he smiled, that rare kindly smile she'd seen before taking the bed in Jynn's cottage. "The game will have moved on by then."

"*Game*? This is a game to you?"

"Everything's a game to them who makes the rules. The hunt's about to shift to Gol. You will be safe here once I've cleaned. Because the Hall will move on."

"I don't understand."

"Graywash Hall never stays long in one place."

"It's been there all my life."

"That's not long. You're what, thirty?"

"Forty-three."

"Wearing well." He grinned at her. "Believe me when I tell you that the place will move soon. Its ultimate goal is catching Laras Lassladen and the Emerald Queen who lurks there."

"What is Laras Lassladen?"

"The opposite side of the coin. A place similar to Graywash Hall, in that it can move through time and the five dimensions. Once ruled by a giant warrior queen called Scatha. She trained me several millennia ago. Quite the woman, was Scat. Giantess with a hearty appetite. I was hard-pressed leaving that island. You will know her as the Emerald Queen."

"The entity Garland mentioned at the Castle of Lights? He spoke about that place but kept most of what happened to himself."

"The daft bugger took on the Chaos basilisk and nearly got killed. Man's got grit. Both Elanion and Jynn were quite impressed. Me too, when I heard about it. Reason why he got this second job. It's what happens when you're useful."

"I cannot grasp how you know all this."

"Jynn needed to keep me in the loop. He called me across from another job. Told me it's vital we help your man."

"These are gods—deities from his world?" Marei chewed her bottom lip and sipped the beer, her thoughts fuzzy.

"Yeah, I know. Don't expect you to understand any of this. For me, it's easy. I've lived so long, I take these situations for normal. Suffice to say, every half-millennium something big happens. This time it's bigger than usual. A cosmic fuckup, and you're stuck right in the middle. Let me protect you, get your lad back, and we'll worry about what's next afterward. Agreed?"

"Yes, I suppose. And I never thanked you for your help. I was a fool ignoring your warning. I would have walked right into their trap. I'm indebted to you, Dunrae Tarn. However bad you've been over the centuries, I for one will call you a friend."

His reaction shocked her. Almost he seemed at the edge of tears. "That means a lot to me." He walked over, placed a rough hand gently against her cheek. "Can't tell you how much. Sir Garland's a lucky bugger. I'll make damn sure that he gets back to you."

She didn't respond, feeling awkward, as though she'd found some fragile corner to his damaged soul.

"How do we get inside the Hall?" she ventured eventually, changing the subject.

His expression had changed back before he reached the chair. The slatey eyes were hard again. "Call me Dunrae," he smiled. "Jynn always using Tarn makes me feel like his servant. Which I am."

"Dunrae it is. *Well?*"

"We leave at dawn again. We'll arrive in full light and enter without issue."

"I have ponies in the stable."

"I'd sooner us walk. The beasts will give off fear as we get close. I can shield you, but not them, too. You see, Marei, the denizens of Graywash Hall smell fear, as decent men sniff freshly cooked meat. They can't detect me, as I'm fearless." He laughed, as though he'd said something funny. Fearless, he was. And yet seemed oddly vulnerable behind those dark heavy brows and cynical smiles.

Marei nodded eventually. "I'll leave it to you. Where will they be hiding Dafyd?"

"I won't know that until we're inside. There are ways of finding people in the Hall. The place never stays the same inside as well as out. Not only does it cross the dimensions— the five planes, as Shorty calls them, and he's the code master. Graywash Hall turns in on itself, like a snail inside its shell—it morphs and shifts."

Marei didn't know how to respond to that.

"And this lost voyager, Carlo Sarfe, is causing the problem? Garland spoke well of him."

"Yep, well, he's likeable according to Jynn. Another good old chap caught with his skivvies down. What would you do if you discovered your home, family, everything you ever loved was about to be destroyed so completely that it would only survive as a myth?"

"I would try to stop that happening. I would stop it!"

"That's Carlo's conundrum. He's desperate, and they know it. The enemy has Scat's bow. Elanion. The Emerald Queen. Same goddess. Kerasheva has strange powers, Marei. One of them is coercion. It's not just a bow. None of the Aralais weapons had single functions. Those twisted golden fuckers were clever. But their maligned cousins, the Urgolais, outwitted them."

Marei was lost again. "Why can't Carlo Sarfe save his kin and land, since he's discovered a way of returning to his own time?"

"Because in doing so, it buggers up the cosmic order. History is altered, meaning everything is changed. That would draw the attention of the Weaver like nothing else. He would be unable to stop the madness ensuing. Chaos would seize the advantage and tear up this world, as it did with Gwelan and the others. That's what those in the Hall want as they serve Old Night. The Lord of Chaos. Another name." He smiled.

"Who is helping Garland?"

"I don't know. Shorty wouldn't tell me."

Marei said nothing. She looked at the door. The wind was getting up. "Will more of Shale's men come back tonight?"

He grinned "If they do, they're in for a nasty surprise,"

She nodded, then yawned. "That's good to hear. I'm for sleeping, Dunrae. I'm past feeling confused and worn out."

"Yes, go, *sleep*. I'll wake you at first light, and you can get us some breaky."

She nodded and turned for the door, taking the stairs, her head whirling and the wind picking up as rains lashed the windowpanes.

Marei heard voices in the night. Distant shouts. Nothing more.

20

THE BEGUILER

"You had better get ready."

Zorc's jet eyes glinted at him. Garland rolled to his side, reached for the sword lying there. He grabbed it and crouched before standing, his hands resting on the cross-guard. He glared at Zorc, angry with himself for drifting off.

"I'm not your enemy, you fool." Zorc's glare matched his own anger. "I asked if you're ready."

"I'm leaving right away."

"Best you eat something first." The Urgolais passed a dark, folded parcel across.

Garland stared suspiciously at it. "What is that?"

"Sustenance, from my cave—it crossed with us. Knew it would come in handy. Stop staring—it's nothing bad. Honey cakes and cinnamon rolled with ganjura."

"Ganjura?" Garland accepted the parcel, unraveled it, and stared at two small doughy bundles. He sniffed. It smelled very good, and his stomach rumbled.

"It's an Urgolais spice. Rare and expensive, and almost nonexistent due to the Aralais bastards stealing most of it. I saved the last fraction of mine for you. See how caring I am? It will give you strength and clarity. You're going to need it. Now eat the fucking cakes."

Garland bit into one and crunched. They were delicious, and he realized he hadn't eaten for some time.

"Thanks," he said, wiping his mouth as the Urgolais watched him. He had a worrying thought "Where's Cadzarilo?"

"Keeping watch."

"You trusted him with that?" Again, Garland berated himself for falling asleep. Was he losing his edge? He'd better get that back sharpish if he wanted to see Marei again. *The change starts now.*

"I told you last night that he will help us," Zorc said, looking around as though Cadzarilo was listening.

"I wish I could believe that."

"We need to get going, else they'll move on." Zorc snatched the empty parchment off him and tugged it inside his grubby tunic.

"What do you mean—move on?"

"The Kaa seldom stay in one place long after dawn. They are creatures of limbo."

"Why didn't you tell me? I'd have gone earlier!"

"And died, after they'd played for a time. Come on." Zorc started walking toward the track that he'd taken last night. Garland cursed and shouldered his sword. He saw Cadzarilo waiting at the edge of the trees.

"I trust that you slept well?" The archmage said, smiling coldly as Garland caught up with them. "I'll lead the way," he told Zorc. "I sowed concealment spell-seeds all along the path. They'll not see you approaching but could still sense a presence, *if you're noisy*." This last comment was aimed at Garland.

Up yours, too.

He followed the tall sorcerer, his thoughts grim and mind anxious. Zorc hobbled behind, again dropping back as the archmage moved quickly down through the trees. Garland turned and beckoned Zorc to hurry, but the Urgolais waved him on urgently. These two were up to something. If he could believe it was to assist him, he'd feel better. But Zorc needed him, and there was no point stewing endlessly over these matters.

Cadzarilo reached the tree bowl where Garland had watched from last night. It was foggy below. He couldn't see anything of the beach or water, nor were there lights glinting down there.

Damn this fret. It would be light proper soon. Garland didn't want to wait any longer, but he couldn't afford to act rashly, like he had on Alchemist's Isle.

"You certain they can't see me?"

"I told you as much."

"Good, you and Zorc make sure they don't. I'll go get this done."

He pushed past Cadzarilo, who smiled slyly. The man was plotting something, and Garland was convinced it wasn't what Zorc or he was expecting. He heard Zorc whisper as he joined the archmage.

Time to forget his irksome companions. He'd soon know if the Kaa would spot him. This wasn't like before. *I'm prepared,* he lied to himself.

Garland jumped down through the last jumble of rocks that opened on the stony strand. The camp was somewhere off to his right.

Can't be far.

The fog was thick and delaying morning. He thought he could hear voices and walked briskly in that direction.

The sounds trailed off like fading whispers. He heard more voices coming from the other way. He cursed and changed direction, the fog swirling like tendrils around his face, its clammy touch making his skin sheen with sweat.

The voices faded again. Garland stood on the beach. There was no sign of anyone having been here.

What's that sound?

He thought he heard harp music drifting across from somewhere. He clenched his teeth and hefted the sword. The eerie notes faded like a muffled scream.

Curse this damn fog.

Nothing this way. He turned again and made back to the spot where he'd left the track, but he couldn't find it and instead entered a narrow strand where rocks reached out into the ocean. Why hadn't he seen this shoulder last night? The moon would have made the sight clear.

He heard another sound. A horn, three long notes drifting off.

Edgy, Garland shook his head and walked on, stopping when he heard voices again. This time, they came from out across the water.

And what was that? Dogs yelping?

Again, the sounds faded. Garland's hair tingled at the nape. Someone laughed behind him. He turned sharply, but saw no one there.

Show yourself.

Movement caught his eye, off to the right. A figure cloaked in gold? More likely the morning rays fooling his vision, piercing the fret at last. But there was no doubting what he heard next. A warning sound— a peel of harp notes drifting and rising, surrounding him, even as the mist departed with uncanny speed.

The mystery harper had returned. To help him, or hinder?

The sun had risen fast and glinted in his face. Garland shielded his eyes and glanced around, quelling the rising panic he felt. He stood on an empty beach. The Kaa had gone, vanished like wood smoke in sunshine. Ghouls of the night. He saw no sign of their camp. *Nothing*. Nor were ships out there on the open water. Garland wiped grime from his face.

I'm so tired.

Had he been hoodwinked again—either by Cadzarilo or some new malice? The mystery harper perhaps? But the harper had saved him from the Kaa the last time. Why work against him now?

I've failed again.

Fighting off despair, Garland walked back along the beach. Maybe somehow he'd gone too far and overshot the camp? They'd been here. He'd seen those prisoners. That hadn't been an illusion. Or if it had, he could no longer trust his own senses. No, they were here. And even if they'd crossed dimensions, the camp should still be visible.

It didn't matter, because they were gone—vanished like the hope in his heart.

What was that?

Garland heard new voices. Commanding, clear tones—as if someone near were issuing orders to a troop of soldiers. That had to be the Kaa. They were close, around the shoulder of rock. He must have walked through the camp in the fog. The only explanation.

Here goes.

Broadsword gripped tight in both hands, Garland

rounded the corner and stopped again, his teeth slamming together.

The was no sign of the Kaa. Instead, three imposing figures stood in a triangle facing each other. They were garbed in long, dark-blue cloaks studded with golden stars and crescent moons. The one in the middle wore a tall, conical silver hat. It trapped the sunlight and dazzled him, hiding the man's face.

"Tell me you're real, not a figment of my restless mind." Garland shifted position, until the reflection faded from the middle one's hat. He walked forward and stopped before them, his eyes challenging the three strangers and hands resting on the crosspiece, ready to swing out.

The one in the glimmering hat pointed a warning finger his way. Garland felt a sudden dizziness, and the sand trembled and shifted at his feet. On impulse, he ran forward yelling, the sword swinging.

The three disappeared as he got near, their laughter echoing off up into the trees.

"Damn sorcerers. Come back!" Garland yelled. "Let me poke this sword up your arses." Furious, he sprinted on along the beach but soon stopped again, hearing a deafening crash and thud behind him.

He turned and shielded his eyes. Rocks had broken loose from the main shoulder and crashed down to block his retreat, the water spilling and frothing around them. A hard swim to get around that. To his right was the ocean. The other way was shadowed by unassailable cliffs. He was trapped, or as good as, and he saw no sign of the woods or track he'd left to reach the beach. Sorcery had assailed him yet again.

"Zorc!"

Nothing. *I've been betrayed.* But what had he expected?

Garland bit into his lip and stabbed his blade down onto the wet sand. What to do? He leaned on the cross-guard, got his breath back and channeled his rage. He had to face this, to find a way out.

The Kaa were here, so I will find them.

He walked onwards, between the wedge of rocks and lapping water. The cliffs rose higher to his left, while ahead he saw another spot where strewn rocks covered the water. No way through without drowning. *I'm stranded by design.*

He turned warily and wasn't surprised to see any retreat was cut off by yet more falling rock. He stood on a shrinking beach. The water lapped his boots, informing him that the tide was coming in fast. *Damn you, Zorc!* He glanced at the nearest rocks and saw what appeared to be a post sticking out like a buoy or a depth-warning marker.

A white post. On closer inspection, an oar that had been thrust handle down deep into the sand. Something red had been nailed to the top. Garland cursed, recognizing a severed hand. A message, and no doubt for him.

"You cowardly fuckers!" Garland shouted at the water closing in on his boots again. The tide was rising too damn quickly. He'd be swimming soon. No way of climbing those cliffs.

Garland swung out with the sword, slicing the oar in two, his rage reaching bursting point inside. He hacked again but stopped hearing casual laughter behind him. He turned, sword swinging wide.

The warlock in the polished metal hat was back. Two shadows flickered beside him—his companions.

"Where's the Kaa, conjuror? Are you in cahoots with that scum? Tell me." Garland gripped the sword in both hands and advanced slowly toward the central figure in the moon-and-stars cloak and conical hat.

"They don't have Rosey's baby." The voice was lazy and filled with contempt. "You've been duped again. *Slow* Garland. You're not the sharpest instrument, are you? She could have done so much better. It's almost a disappointment. *Hmm.* You'll have to try harder in the future than you have in your past."

"Where's the child, specter? Speak before I cut you in two."

"That's no longer your problem. The game has shifted."

Patience exhausted, Garland charged, swinging out, meaning to hack this vile creature in half. The sword passed through nothing but air, making him lose balance. He turned and saw the warlock standing behind him.

"You can't hurt me, you fool. But Sir Valen's dogs will tear you apart if you linger. You're trapped, *Sir* Garland. They are coming for your soul. A bad end to a foolish errand. Marei will never forgive you failing her."

Garland tensed as the sounds of hoofbeats drummed the beach behind him. He glanced back and saw a steel-clad horseman galloping along the waves, the sun glinting off his sickly green armor. Dogs bayed and jumped around the rider. He raised a horn to his lips and blew three times.

Garland saw the sorcerers fade in the sunlight. He ran, making for the rocks ahead. They were closing fast, the hounds snapping at his heels. He could hear the warlock's laughter.

"I want him alive."

Garland scrambled onto the wet rocks, his legs slipping, and arms sliced and scraped by the barnacles. He glimpsed the rider pointing as the huge white dogs jumped and bounded upon the rocks, again snapping at his heels.

He leaped from that slippery stone and crashed onto another, further out. The sea churned and soaked into his boots. The dogs yapped and circled on the other rock.

The sea was closing in. He had no choice but to swim for it, to try and get past the shoulder before the dogs caught him.

He made to dive, but stopped when the lead sorcerer emerged, gliding through the water toward him, the hat glinting silver in the sun. Behind him were men carrying metal nets. He recognized Shale among them.

"At least I can kill you before they take me." Garland balanced precariously on the rock and swung the sword across at the sorcerer.

"You, mortal, cannot resist Us, let alone harm Our majesty."

"But I can—while you're still broken."

Zorc, soaked and battered, shuffled past, glancing sideways at Garland.

"You were right—we shouldn't have trusted Cadzarilo." Zorc traced a symbol in the sky. The sorcerer disappeared and the din of horns faded, as did Shale and his men from view. The white dogs disappeared a moment after. Garland saw the green rider raise a gauntleted hand in salute before he, too, vanished.

He was back on the beach, dry and unhurt. The enchanter in the hat had returned and was gazing contemptuously at Zorc beside him.

Garland blew out his cheeks in relief. Drowning seemed off for the moment. "You trusted Cadzarilo, but I didn't—remember?" he told Zorc.

"You think this one's going to help you? An *Urgolais*?" The man in the hat was smiling again. "You'd fare better siding with Sir Valen and his hounds. You're out of your depth, Journeyman. Poor choice She made."

Garland watched the stranger's hypnotic gaze switch to Zorc hobbling toward the figure, making signs in the sky with his ruined hand. Despite his hauteur, the conjurer seemed wary of Zorc. Garland found himself forgotten as these two spellcasters confronted each other like familiar adversaries. He saw the golden auras reappear on either side of the warlock, congealing until the two figures he'd seen earlier stood next to the leader.

"You dare crawl back from limbo, Urgolais?" the man in the silver hat sneered. "I'd deemed your pathetic race all stoking flames in Yffarn. How did you crawl out?"

"I'll tell you that if you reveal what you've done with Cadzarilo and the Kaa—it was you who warned them, I suspect."

"That your hero was coming to kill them all?" The man in the hat clapped his gloved hands slowly. "Her side's losing this war. It intrigues me that the goons put trust in a Urgolais. Your people always worked for Us."

"Who is this cockroach?" Garland asked Zorc.

"You're better off not knowing."

The man smiled slightly. "Let him work it out." He laughed, a harsh sound like carrion settling to feed, and removed the hat from his brow, tossing it at Garland's face. He ducked as the metal hat exploded into blackbirds' feathers and drifted down like molten ash, settling around the spot where Garland stood shaking with rage.

Dust and feathers disappeared. Garland stared back at the enchanter, making out his features for the first time. These shifted and blurred, the other two mirroring his movement.

They had the same face as his. Pale, shimmering mirror-reflections of his image. A master conjurer. Garland knew he'd seen the face before. Dark, intense eyes and close-cropped beard. Handsome, with a power resonating outward.

"You're Ozmandeus," Garland said.

"Wrong," the sorcerer laughed.

"You're looking at the darkness rising inside Ozmandeus," Zorc muttered. "Not the man himself, but the instigator. The *Beguiler*." Zorc's voice was cracking worse than usual. For the first time since he'd known him, the Urgolais sounded afraid.

"This fool can help Our cause." The man who looked like Ozmandeus smiled across at him as he addressed Zorc again. "*Slow* Garland came too close to Our lair. There were vibrations. He escaped us before, due to that vain bitch Cille's intervention." The cold eyes glinted at Garland. "We almost had you the second time, before Her child intervened. But scatty Urdei has forgotten you for the moment. Hence, you are vulnerable again."

"Yffarn take you, demon."

"I rule Yffarn, you fucking fool."

"Damn you, anyway." Garland chewed his bottom lip until blood seeped through his teeth. Those terrible black eyes were working on him, seeping his resolve. The gaze switched back to Zorc, and Garland shuddered with relief.

"And you, *Urgolais,* messed up when you summoned Cadzarilo's rotting corpse. You're predictable. We got to him first, and he led Us to you. We left poor Cadzarilo's shredded mind wandering nearby. The body …"

"What did you do with him?" Zorc asked, his tense eyes flicking across to Garland, a message in them saying, *Let me handle this.*

Happy to.

"Does it matter? Cadzarilo's dead. And I mean *dead*, this time. We have his soul. The past is returning. Our renegade's first fell deed shall soon be accomplished at the Citadel. You, *Sir Knight*, may have heard rumors of what happens after that." The eyes had flickered back to Garland. The lips smiled as that cold gaze swept upon him. "Best you light a candle at night. We will visit again *soon*."

"This isn't real." Garland said, sweat beading at his temples. He wiped blood from his mouth. "It can't be."

"You're right, in a sense." Zorc, clearly agitated, traced another urgent sign in the sky. The three figures vanished, the leader still smiling. He raised a gloved hand toward them, his fore and index fingers protruding like horns. His laugher trailed off like gallows bird's lifting in a gale.

21

THE GIFT OF GANJURA

"WE NEED TO LEAVE THIS PLACE," Zorc hissed at Garland.

You think?

"What about the Kaa?"

"Gone. The timing's out. Not my fault, as He's involved. The Kaa got caught in His illusion too."

"That trickster who stole Ozmandeus's guise? The Beguiler, you called him. Who was that, and how can he possibly know Ozmandeus will unleash the fire demon?"

Zorc's mouth seeped black ooze. He looked unwell, even by his shaky standards.

"What is it?" Garland glared at him.

"A new development. Not good. He must be getting stronger to reach us like this."

"Who was that bastard?"

"Can't you guess, human? Seriously? You witnessed an illusion spun by Ozmandeus's new master, the Orb. That one's defiled, questing mind has reached out, having sensed us crossing the Void. Cadzarilo will have told that entity everything. No one can withstand the Beguiler's talons."

"Again, *who?*" They needed to move. Garland, badly shaken, vaguely noticed saltwater soaking his legs and lapping around his knees. They'd drown soon. The beach had shrunk to a ribbon of sand.

Zorc seemed oblivious of their plight. He stared like a battered crow at Garland, the black eyes resembling cracked puddles in muddy ice

"The Beguiler must have entered Cadzarilo's soul while I summoned him on the island," Zorc said. "His darkness has travelled with us since, planning our destruction on this beach."

"Ozmandeus?"

The sea was lapping above his knees. Strangely, it didn't seem to matter, like his mind wasn't his own anymore.

"No, you dolt. That was a tease. Ozmandeus is another tool. I'm talking about the real enemy."

"Speak plainly, goblin. Who?"

Zorc glanced down, noticing the rising water for the first time.

"That will be sorcery for you," he muttered. "The apparition we witnessed was none other than Saan Himself. Or his shadowy reflection. Old Night, the Shadowman. The fragments of His mind that endured to became the Orb. The soul of Graywash Hall. The god's essence that escaped the Weaver's chastisement."

"The Shadowman?"

"Yes, in part. Were it the whole being, we would be cinders."

Garland chewed his beard. They had two, perhaps three minutes before the tide cut them off again.

"That's not possible. Old Night was destroyed along with His armies. Outside Kelthara. I was there."

"Mostly, yes, but a remnant has survived. I've told you this. The Kaa must have sensed His approach and departed. Even they dared not linger where His shadow settles. We must flee, too, for He'll have left traps. It's what He does. I used to work for His crew, remember."

"What about the child—I have to find her?"

"I suspect she's still in Graywash Hall."

"Then I'm going back there." Garland stared at the ocean rising around his legs. He slung the sword over a shoulder and started wading toward the wall of cliff.

"Good luck trying," Zorc said, following him, finally realizing he would soon be swimming if he stayed put.

Garland reached the cliff edge and staggered to his knees, head jolted in shock, as a sudden boom shook his body. To the west, he saw bright orange light, and the roaring sound of flames towering up into the sky.

"As I said, the timing's wrong. We're late and had better leave."

"What's going on?"

"Can't you tell? The Orb has intervened. We've lost our advantage. *He's* moved the thing forward. The real Ozmandeus has already freed Ashmali and unleashed the Elemental on Alchemists Isle."

"How can we fight that?"

"The Orb? Old Night's ghost? We have to try. Were that the god himself, our souls would be shredded into bacon strips. His Orb must have caught me prying at the Citadel and followed us here. We dare not linger a moment longer. We must shift dimension again."

"How? We'll be drowned in seconds!"

They were hemmed between rock and ocean. No way they'd scale that rockface.

Beside him, Zorc glanced at the water and clicked his tongue. "We make for Gol. No other choice, is there? Reveal harbor, to be precise. We have to stop Carlo Sarfe."

"Why?"

"Grab my arm."

"What?"

"Quickly!"

Garland reached across and gripped Zorc's ragged shirt-sleeve as a huge blast of orange light exploded off to the west. The brine-soaked sand shook beneath his feet. He felt a sickly lurch in his guts as he was pulled up and sucked dry, into the cloudless sky above. He tried to yell, but his lips were pressed together and face stung as he hurtled through space at blinding speed.

Zorc's insane laughter filled his ears. "Welcome to Urgolais magic! It's good to be active again."

I'm losing consciousness.

Hold on … Garland's mind drifted through a surreal multitiered universe where he watched a mirror image of himself spiraling out across distant stars.

"The possibilities are endless out here. And we have help coming at last." Zorc's voice rose like a gibbering maniac beside him. "The Orb missed a key factor. Dunrae Tarn is back."

"Who …?" Garland felt his body slow and drift. The universe vision passed and merged into gloom.

"The Cleaner."

Zorc's cackle subsided. Where was the Urgolais? Garland saw a wall of light ahead. He closed his eyes as his body sailed toward the glare. He heard Zorc's croaking and gasped as scorching heat tingled his nose.

First water, now fire.

The vision past.

Next, he was sinking in wet mud, cold fingers pulling him down. Choking, being buried alive.

Dying.

A gruff voice grunted, and the sucking slime let go. Garland felt his arms gripped firmly from above. Someone hoisted, pulling him upwards and free to sprawl face-first on solid ground. The mud reached out for him, changing shape, becoming a huge red serpent. The basilisk spat venom at him.

"Fuck off, snake," the gruff voice said.

Garland blinked as light flashed in his eyes and a loud boom assaulted his ears. The basilisk had vanished. For the briefest glimmer, Garland saw a big, hard-eyed man standing over him in a shabby dark-blue coat. He carried a heavy cylindrical object over one shoulder and stared down at Garland like a butcher surveying his meat.

"I'll save them, boy, don't fret. You go stop Carlo the sailor, while the other side's distracted."

"Who …?"

The stranger vanished. Garland gulped and staggered to his knees. He saw his broadsword thrust point down in long green grass. Beyond it, Zorc sat by a crackling fire.

"Good trip?"

"What in Yffarn is going on?"

"The ganjura took hold of you. Saved you from yourself."

"It's you, isn't it? This entire buggeration is caused by your wickedness. You're from the Hall. The only thing that makes sense."

Zorc spat in the soil. "I'm really looking forward to your gratitude one day. I saved us back there. Yes, I *miscalculated*, and badly. Granted. But I got us away the only way I could, knowing the ganjura would protect you during our hectic passage. Those dimension trips can get rough without a guide.

"Who was that man in the blue coat?"

"Dunrae Tarn. An old acquaintance. Once my enemy, but fortunately he's on our side. As I said, while we traveled. We have help. The Orb's appearance sent out vibrations, and Her people heard."

"Stop jabbering nonsense and tell me, where are we?"

"Xandoria, near Xenn City. We need to get to Rakeel and across to Gol. You have to keep your side of the bargain."

"What bargain?"

"The one you made with Dunrae Tarn during our flight here."

"I never spoke with that man."

"You didn't need to."

22

THE ISLAND STATES

CARLO HAD SLEPT late after the tumult. Tai Pei had woken him with a soft nudge. She must have snuck into his cabin again. He was groggy and confused. How long had he slept?

"What is it?" He shook the sleep from his eyes.

"Islands. Your crew are excited."

Carlo stared at her. "I'm not sure we should risk another expedition."

Tai Pei was about to respond when Gurdey and Tareel emerged behind her.

"We're back, skipper," Gurdey said.

"What do you mean, *back*? Islands, she said?" He was irritated at sleeping so long and glared at Tai Pei, who stared back at him with cat-cool eyes.

"Aye, and she be right, captain," Slim Tareel grinned at him.

"What is funny?" Carlo switched his annoyed gaze to the mate and on to Gurdey, smiling too. "Well …?"

"We're almost home, skipper," Gurdey said, emotion

cracking his voice. "Duty watch spotted familiar shores after that last storm abated."

Storm? Was that how you'd describe that?

"Go on—I'm listening."

"It's Cazea."

Carlo blinked, his wits reviving for the first time since they'd escaped from the hooded island. "You're reporting that we've reached the Island States?"

"Aye, so I am. The two of us, and Gold Tar, climbed up and stared out from the crow. It's Cazea all right, skip. I saw the west tower and harbor walls. We're back in familiar waters."

So Urdei had brought them home after all, when he was sleeping. Carlo bid them leave while he dressed quickly, his mind a whirl. He stopped, noticing the girl had stayed.

"Would you?" He motioned the door.

"I like it better here," she replied.

Carlo ignored her, reached for his garments and his sword, dressing quickly. "I've a ship to run." He pushed past her and made his way up the ladder and out onto the deck.

"Try convincing your men. They've been wondering when you'd show up on deck. Lots been happening while you were sleeping."

He ignored the jibe, deserved or not.

The Island States. Can it be?

He reached the prow and gazed for long moments at distant hills and buildings nestled tight around a palm-swept harbor. To their right, a short round sandstone tower glinted in the warm sun. As they got closer, Carlo recognized the green-and-silver banners flapping above the tower, and the sandstone castle revealing itself behind.

A white conch shell on a green background—the emblem

of the Island States. The free trading confederation that lay south of Lamoza on the Great Continent. Two hundred miles west of his own province, Sarfania, in Gol.

The men were right—they were almost home. And yet, were these the same Island States they'd stopped by months ago? Or were they still in the future? He dismissed that worry. The Island States had vanished when Gol was destroyed. That must be true, or he'd have heard Tai Pei or someone else speak of them.

The *Arabella* picked up pace as they clipped toward the harbor, the sun dancing on the calm warm water. Carlo watched, smiling, as dolphins raced to join them and dance beneath the bowsprit.

We've made it back.

They'd rest here for a day or so before taking the final leg across to Reveal. He could scarcely contain his joy. Gone was the stress and mind-fuzz, replaced by a new energy and fire in his heart. Incredibly, they were almost home. They'd crossed through the maelstrom safely returning to their own time, thanks to Urdei. A passage as mysterious as his half-drowned confused arrival into Gwelan.

Today, he wouldn't dwell on that. Carlo determined this would be the first good day in weeks. He liked the Island States. Bright Cazea. Dreamy Dornis, and wild, windswept Trondei, and those other little ones that stretched for miles to the south.

He pictured the tall, graceful, black-eyed women with their sharp tongues and lissome ebony skin. He'd had many a merry time with the island girls when first he'd sailed here as a young man.

They approached harbor, and a horn sounded from the round tower. Slim Tareel stood beside Carlo as he glimpsed tiny figures up on the roof. Tai Pei was above in the crow's nest with Stogi, having finally convinced him to take the climb. Garland's men watched beside Gurdey as the wheel-master guided the *Arabella* past the harbor arms and into a waiting dock.

Carlo saw burly stevedores rolling barrels from another vessel moored ahead. Two men broke away and walked to join them as Carlo leaped ashore. Another fellow sauntered across. Despite the heat, he was garbed in red leather, tunic, and cloak, and he wore a curved, jeweled dagger at his belt. Carlo smiled as he recognized Tisen Garello, Cazea's illustrious harbormaster.

Tisen Garello showed gold teeth. "Captain Carlo, excellent! You're back from … *wherever* you've been." He was a big man, bearded and scarred. He'd been a gladiator once in Xandoria and had even survived several seasons at the annual Gol combat Games in Dovesi. An important man. The Island States shunned rulers and let the administrators, or Tisens like Garello, govern affairs.

Carlo smiled and clasped his huge hands. The black man grinned back at him. "How long has it been?" Carlo asked him as the Tisen's shrewd eyes took in Tai Pei and Garland's men, who'd jumped ashore with Stogi following.

"Several months," he said, his gaze curious.

Carlo saw him glancing at Tai Pei. "We picked up some strays on the way," he said.

Garello nodded. "You'll have to tell me all about the voyage—it's obviously been a great success."

"Mostly it was, aye."

Garello gazed at him for a moment and nodded again. He shouted for more men to help tie off the vessel. Meanwhile, Carlo introduced his passengers as friends. Stogi grinned at the Tisen and his crew, while Tai Pei glared at them. Tol and Taylon stood off to the side, their eyes shifting and wary.

Tisen Garello studied them all as Slim Tareel and Gold Tar yelled at the crew to finish up. Carlo was relieved to be here. Finally, things were looking up.

"I'll have my people bring you grog and fresh meat," Garello called across to Dry Gurdey, who was talking to one of the stevedore chargehands. The two were old friends, Carlo recalled. They'd sailed here many times over the years. "As for your passengers, please all of you join my family for supper tonight. I would learn more about your country."

"That's very kind—thanks," Stogi said, receiving an odd glance back from Garello. Tai Pei nodded stiffly, and Garland's pair offered faint grins.

"Thank you, sir," Tol said, eventually. "We're honored."

THE VILLA SPARKLED IN SUNLIGHT. STOGI STOOD BEHIND Tai Pei, his mind relaxed and lips sipping the strong ale provided by their genial host.

Tisen Garello's villa sprawled over a low ridge awarding stunning views of harbor, castle, and the bustling town below. The highest spot on the island was scarcely sixty feet above sea level. Stogi had spent most that afternoon walking the hillside outside the villa, while Carlo Sarfe and his top men talked with the Tisen like old friends. Tai Pei had stayed with them, but Stogi had joined Tol and Taylon in walking the ridge. It hadn't taken long to get his bearings.

A breezy, green sward of arrow-shaped island dotted with date palms, neat houses, ordered stockades, farms and clear round pools—these were of special interest to him and the pair. An enjoyable afternoon that led to a busy evening at the Tisen's establishment.

He called it a villa. Stogi had never seen the like before. A long white series of connected buildings, the walls plastered with seashells and statues carved out of every corner, most gurgling water into bowls where little gold fishes danced and dived.

The glazed, red-tiled roofs glistened in the sunshine. Amongst these, a bustle of handsome-looking, ebony-skinned people walked and talked casually without any need to hurry. A broad terrace led out to a wide, palm-fanned azure pool topped by fountains and a waterfall where colorful birds chirped.

There were tables and chairs aligned to the right of the pool. Here, servants carried dishes of treats and urns brimming with beverages. The Tisen had bid them take supper in relaxed island style, and he ordered minstrels and dancers to perform their pleasure.

Stogi was amazed by the dexterity of the dancers, whose half-naked, glistening bodies writhed and spun as they entwined in, groped, kissed, and broke away from each other's grip. Tai Pei seemed bored by the whole affair.

After a flute chorus and more lazy eating, the Tisen clapped his large hands, and the tables were cleared. He bid the servants and his family members depart, though a woman Stogi assumed must be his wife stayed put. She had a severe look, and Stogi thought she had disapproved of the Tisen's spread.

"The past doesn't seem too bad," Tol whispered in his ear as the two took seats next to Stogi. Tai Pei was avoiding him for reasons he couldn't grasp, unless she was worried one of those stunning, dark-skinned women would take him away. He chuckled at the thought and dismissed it as unworthy.

"Know anything about these islands? Tales, legends?" he asked Taylon.

"The annals in Wynais mention the Island States as an independent group of tiny countries. An important trading station for Xandoria, Lamoza, and Spagos. They lie south of the Great Continent, so I assume that's our next destination."

"And on to Gol, before it's burnt to ashes," Tol chuckled beside him. "Any suggestions on how we're going to survive this reckless endeavor?"

"No idea," Stogi said. "But we will, as long as we don't think about it too much."

Taylon snorted in his ale. "Makes sense."

Tol grinned at them. "Aye, drinking beats thinking for a worried mind."

Stogi was distracted by a slender woman beckoning him over. She was perhaps twenty and very pretty, with her smiling black eyes and olive skin. He thought his luck had changed, but she was ushering Garland's men too, bidding they all come seat themselves at a table inside, where two burley, tattooed servants waved tall fans.

Stogi would have preferred remaining by the pool, but soon realized he was one of the honored guests. Tol, Taylon, and Tai Pei were seated alongside him. Carlo to his right, then Tisen and the stern-faced woman opposite. Stogi studied her face, noticing the intricate tattoos for the first time. Her eyes were huge and dark, full of mystery. She was by far the most interesting Cazean he'd encountered, though he preferred the smiling girl—presently lurking at the door, awaiting orders.

Dry Gurdey appeared and took a chair alongside his captain. Stogi assumed Slim Tareel and the dour Gold Tar were back with the rest of the crew, most likely getting soused on deck. At least Tar had stopped his whining. Aside from him, the crew deserved a break, the poor buggers. They'd all been through so much. Stogi was happy to forget most of that and enjoy this repast on dry, warm, and fertile land with company that was mostly easy on the eye.

He wished he knew more about this area and its history— but he didn't know any history, so why start here? If Cazea survived the fallout from Gol, it might prove a good option for him and Tai Pei, should they be blocked from returning to their own time. That could easily happen, he suspected. You had to think about these things.

Tisen Garello spoke in depth with Carlo and Gurdey for a while as another girl produced a long pipe on a tray connected to a bowl. This contraption was passed along the table. Each seated guest sucked at the pipe, causing it to bubble.

Tai Pei refused to partake, but Stogi gave it all he could and was rewarded by a spinning head and fit of the giggles, which he disguised as polite belching—that seemed more appropriate in the company. The feeling passed quickly enough, and he tried hard focusing on the conversation at the head of the table.

Tisen Garello was talking to Tai Pei. "Shen sounds extraordinary. How many miles? That far? Amazing—I'd not imagined land out there. The world is bigger than we know. And these fine young fellows are from beyond your land? Astounding."

"Those two are from what we call the Crystal Kingdoms," Tai Pei explained. "The gormless-looking one's a former brigand from Tseole—a rough, rainy, yak-infested region outside Shen."

Stogi wondered what he'd done to annoy her this time. He

noticed the stern woman gazing at him with interest. She was his age. Not unattractive, though fierce with those uncanny eyes, blue spirals on her cheeks and forehead, and the gold stud gleaming under her mouth. Exotic, he deemed her. Most interesting. She wore large seashell earrings that glittered in the sunlight. Her canny dark eyes probed Stogi until he looked away, feeling a sudden disquiet.

"Fascinating." Tisen Garello was talking to Carlo. "And you're returning to Sarfania, doubtless after stopping at Rakeel, before making the crossing?"

"I plan on skipping Rakeel," Carlo said. "I've been away longer than I intended and have learnt some grave news."

Stogi blinked. Was it him, or had the atmosphere changed after Carlo's last words? *Captain, please don't spoil the moment.* He glanced at Tai Pei, but she was distracted by movement at the door.

"It has long been foretold." The older woman spoke for the first time, and all heads turned her way.

"Jenada." The Tisen held up a hand to placate her. She ignored him, her keen gaze on Carlo. "Forgive my sister. She has the sight. It makes her grumpy on occasion."

"The *sight*?" Tai Pei leaned forward and stared rudely at the woman. "You are a seeress? An astrologer?"

"Healer." The woman stared back at her in what appeared a very frank exchange. Stogi chewed his mustache. Things were taking a turn here. But the tension eased as Tai Pei nodded sagely and the woman, Jenada, offered a half-smile. Stogi rubbed an earring, bemused.

"Jenada believes your coming here portentous," the Tisen said.

"No one returns from the west," the woman said.

"Except the illustrious Carlo Sarfe, and with new companions to boot. I am most happy to see you." Garello said glibly, but to Stogi he seemed put out.

"As I am not," his sister said. "For my heart tells me you are the harbingers of a woe we cannot imagine." Silence followed. Stogi held back a belch. Carlo looked awkward, the others edgy, and Garello ill at ease. Stogi switched his gaze to Jenada, watched her scrutinizing Carlo. "Well, captain? Tell me I'm wrong."

Carlo nodded. He stood up, noisily, and held his hands out wide.

"Jenada speaks the truth. There's no easy way of saying this, but … we've returned from the future. Our future." He stared at Tai Pei, Stogi and the other two. "The three men seated here and this woman come from countries we know nothing of."

"How is that possible?" The Tisen's face was serious. He appeared angry, as though Carlo was playing him for a fool. Stogi couldn't blame him.

"The sea changed as we sailed west, leading us into strange waters and beyond to stranger lands. I was separated from Gurdey here, and the crew. I have no idea how. During that turbulent time, I met other folk in those distant lands, including Tai Pei of Shen and Stogi the Tseole." He smiled at them, and Tai Pei nodded. "Both proved loyal friends and stout companions." Stogi grinned, but Carlo ignored him. "We happened upon Tol and Taylon here later, while voyaging back. All of us have been enmeshed in darkest sorcery."

"Are you saying that you've brought a curse upon my island?" Garello stood and glared at Carlo. Stogi gripped his knife under the table. He worried they were going to be seized and slain. He saw Tai Pei's killer gaze narrow dangerously.

"Sit down!" Jenada's words were flat, sharp blades. Garello

glared at her and nodded slowly. He took his seat, battered face taut with anger. "The prophecy," she said, staring at the Tisen. "We all knew it was coming, Garello. The sky has shown its close proximity for years. Not all of us chose to ignore that."

Tai Pei smiled. "You *are* an astrologer."

"I see both forwards and back," the woman replied curtly. She turned to Stogi and smiled. He blinked back shock and wondered what was happening. Ever since he'd smoked that weed pipe, things had taken a peculiar turn.

"Zansuat has been roaming the horizon these last few years," Jenada continued. "Trawling the waters. Searching. Our fishers have seen strange creatures. Telimantua is angry. The long-foretold disaster is about to happen."

"It might not be that bad," Stogi blurted. "I mean, we're your descendants and we're alive. So not everyone in Gol and thereabouts perished."

Both Garello and Carlo were glaring angrily at him.

"What's the matter with you?" Tai Pei said, as Tol raised a worried brow beside him. But Jenada was smiling.

"You're the one I've been dreaming about."

"I *am?*" Stogi felt a worrying hot flush flooding his cheeks. He was in trouble of a kind he couldn't fathom.

The smile faded from her face as she returned her gaze to Carlo. "Sit down, Carlo Sarfe. We are friends, so don't fret." Her eyes flicked to the Tisen, who nodded again. "But your presence here is no coincidence. And you cannot return to Gol."

Carlo met her gaze evenly. "It's my home. I must save my family."

"And destroy everything else in doing so," Jenada told him.

"What do you know?" Carlo asked her, as Stogi swapped a worrying glance with Taylon.

"Zansuat the Sea God stirs in anger. The fiery demon rises beyond Zorne. The stars point the way. Comets and portents." She tucked her fists under her chin and leaned forward, gazing deep into Carlo's eyes. He didn't flinch. Jenada placed a finger on his forehead. "If you go home you will die, captain. As will your crew and these new friends. The Enemy will tempt you sorely. Offer you a gift not His to give."

"What enemy?" Stogi worried she was spinning him a yarn. *But why …?*

"The Deceiver. He wants to divert history to suit His ends. Don't go home. Stay here on the islands. Avoid the temptation." She removed her finger and licked it. Carlo glared at her.

"Makes sense," Stogi offered, deeming someone had to cheer things up.

"I'm going home on the next tide," Carlo told Jenada, and Stogi felt the friction return to the room.

"That might prove sensible," Garello said, his eyes hostile again.

"You cannot stop the prophecy," Jenada told them. "If you try to intervene by stepping off your ship in Sarfania, everything will change. And everyone will die."

"According to my friends, my kin and country will perish if I don't. What choice have I but to warn them?"

Stogi's head was buzzing. That damned smoke. Why hadn't it affected anyone else? If things turned ugly, he needed to be ready. Sharp, not fuzzy and dreamy.

"Will you excuse me," he blurted awkwardly, "I'm in need of …"

"Go," Tisen Garello said, without taking his eyes from

Carlo, looking more and more uncomfortable. The tension was building between them. Stogi glimpsed Tai Pei's raised bow, and he smiled at her reassuringly before taking his leave and walking out under the hot sun.

The pretty girl smiled as he passed, though her eyes were worried. He stopped by the pool, lingering within earshot. The voices died back. The moment of danger seemed to have passed again. A shadow flashed across the water. He turned and saw the woman, Jenada, standing there. She had her plump arms folded and was smiling at him like a lover. This could be bad.

Stogi couldn't help but notice her firm body, the large breasts, and sturdy legs, shown off so well by her deep-cut emerald gown. He masked his admiration best he could.

"Can I help you, lady?"

For an answer she reached out gently and grabbed his palm, lifting it. She gazed down at the crisscross lattice of scars covering his hand. "Your part in this game is key, Stogi of Tseole."

"Game …?"

"*Dance*. A strand of thread that's escaped the Weaver's web. Carlo's voyage is part of something far bigger. Your time with Tamersane and Seek, another fragment. The new Dance is taking shape around us. And your biggest challenge is yet to be."

Stogi locked on to that compelling gaze and felt a shiver inside.

"Who are you, woman? A shaman?"

He gulped back fear as Jenada's face blurred and shifted, fading like smoke.

What the fuck? Stogi gasped seeing the smoke shift into a new shape.

Another woman. A tall, willowy lady now stood before him. They must have put something bad in that pipe. Perhaps Tai Pei had pulled a stunt on him? Just for larks.

He gulped. *All right, you're real. What now?*

He couldn't deny his senses, though he wanted to. Jenada had been replaced by a copper-haired woman with eyes of glittering green and gold.

"Someone who would help you." Her image faded back to smoke, and again he saw Jenada smiling at him.

I should have stayed on the bloody boat.

"What's wrong?" Jenada brushed her fingers against his mustache.

Stogi quivered. "I feel a bit nauseous, is all. Probably the smoking. I was a bit enthusiastic and inhaled more than anyone else." *That must be it*, he told himself.

"Hmm, maybe." Her eyes narrowed shrewdly. "You'll need to watch Carlo carefully, and his crew. Tai Pei is too reckless. You have to take control. They'll feel it most nearing Gol. Beware of Dog Island. I sense a distortion around there."

"Dog Island? Yes, sounds best avoided."

"And *best* you act decisively before the *Arabella* reaches Reveal harbor."

"Why me?"

"Because we like you, stupid."

Stogi turned and saw Urdei smiling at him, her bare feet trailing in the pool's blue water.

"This is such a pretty place. I might stay for a while. Jenada will accompany you instead. I have other matters to attend." The girl looked at the woman, who nodded with a half-smile.

"I'm confused," Stogi said. "That was Urdei."

"My youngest sister, the joker," Jenada said.

"You're not who you appear."

"I'm Jenada, Stogi. But also Vervandi, and sometimes Scolde." The voice was different—he'd heard it before somewhere. "Present and Future are sharing Jenada's life force, as Vervandi and the Crone cannot manifest these days. A regrettable result of the Happening. Wise Jenada is keen to help, for she knows the stakes."

"Which are?" Stogi had decided he might as well embrace this worrying development and learn all he could.

"Laras Lassladen will appear," she told him. "And the thief, and the bow too. Carlo won't be able to resist. He will take Kerasheva from the jester and try to change history. He's a pawn, nothing more."

"Carlo is my friend."

Her eyes turned sad. "Honor that friendship by saving his soul."

"Aren't all men at the mercy of spiteful gods?"

"Not you, Stogi. If you help us."

"You want me to kill Carlo Sarfe, don't you? I won't do that."

"You might have to. The alternative is obliteration. You and Tai Pei, those other two. You'd never exist."

"But why me?"

"Come, walk with me as Jenada."

"I'm worried about my friends in there."

"No need. Tisen Garello might be angry, but he'll not cross Jenada. He knows where I'm going with this. Carlo will sail at dawn, and I'll be going with you. You should be happy about that much. We all discussed this at table after you left to mope by the pool. The Tisen knows that Jenada's word is final on this island."

Stogi didn't respond, but his thoughts turned grim.

They walked through gardens and fields up the hill, stopping to gaze down at the dreamy villa and ocean beyond. A
breeze tussled her hair. He smelled the musk rising from her
skin. She made a strange gargling sound.

"Are you unwell?" Stogi worried that the smoke had
caught up with her, too. The woman had thrust her tongue
out between gleaming teeth. He watched, panicking, as she
rolled her eyes and started shaking badly.

"What's happening to you?" *Was she having a fit?*

She shook and staggered, dropping to her knees in the
long grass. Stogi reached over, but she waved him away with a
warning.

"He is gone. The danger has passed."

"What danger?"

"He was here, watching us." The voice was Vervandi's
again. She pointed off toward the ocean. Stogi saw a white
hawk soaring high and gliding toward them. For the briefest
instant, the bird's golden eyes locked on him as it shot past.
Stogi shivered.

Those eyes belonged to Seek the shaman.

"You'll not win this game, Father," Vervandi whispered
with Jenada's lips.

The bird vanished. The woman shuddered and almost
collapsed again. Stogi leaned over and supported her. She
accepted his help this time. "He's betrayed us." Her eyes
flicked green through gold. There was resentment, fear and
anger in that gaze.

"That bird? You mean Seek the shaman? That was his spirit
creature out there. Tell me I'm wrong?

"Oroonin took Seek's soul and deceived you, as He
deceives everyone. My Father has joined sides with the Enemy.

Because he's bored, I suspect. And hates Mother. Damn His soul to Yffarn." She started shaking again and coughed.

"We should return to the villa," Stogi suggested. "You're not yourself, I'm thinking."

"We will." She sat on a rock, her face flushed and irises dilated. He noticed she was breathing heavily. "I so miss the senses, being able to touch, smell, and feel."

Vervandi's wicked smile quivered on Jenada's pouting lips. "Come here, Stogi the Tseole. There's one small thing you can do for me first."

23

THE CLEANING

MAREI STOOD on the stone bridge, the cold wind whipping hair across her face. She shivered. It took all her willpower to cross that yawning chasm.

"Don't look down," Dunrae growled behind her. "Remember. Nothing you see is real, unless you let it in. That path leads to madness."

They'd left after a quick breakfast and walked the nine miles to the coast. A swirl of mist had greeted them as they neared the sea. Marei had glimpsed the roofs of Rosey's village and held back a tear. The man had set his brutal pace again, but she felt fitter than before, and more determined.

She trusted Dunrae, though she didn't know why. She only had his word, and Jynn's, that they were allies. But there was something about the big man, whether his story was true or not. And why make up such a tale, surely not to impress her?

A war had been waging between his faction and the denizens inside the Hall who had stolen her family. Dunrae would help her, and from what she'd seen of his skills so far, she couldn't think of a better companion.

Tight-lipped, she crossed the bridge, the wind tugging at her cloak and cold voices whispering. She heard his heavy tread behind. A comfort, though not a big one. A greasy dark mass was swelling on the road ahead. The walls appeared as writhing liquid limbs like a sea leviathan, rising and blocking their path.

Marei held back a shudder. "It's changed. I was expecting a castle."

"It's always changing," the man said. "Come on, Marei. Courage, girl! Let's get this done."

"I'm ready," she said, and this time followed his lead as he walked calmly toward the dark mass comprising Graywash Hall, the blunderbuss slung over a shoulder and his heavy blue coat lifting in the gale.

Marei chewed her bottom lip as she approached the arched gate, emerging from steam like broken teeth inside a rotting mouth. A man stood beneath the gates. Tall, reed-thin and clad in a blood-red gown, his features were hidden by a three-cornered cap. He held up a thin, white-gloved hand.

"State your business with the Hall."

"Our business is our own," Dunrae replied. "Move aside, else I toss you over that bridge."

"Dunrae ..." Marei swallowed her fear, seeing the man fade back inside the castle.

He signaled her follow with a casual backwards wave. "Here we go," he said. "Keep that crossbow ready."

She gripped the trigger beneath her cloak. She'd strapped six bolts to her belt along with her knife. She doubted they'd prove much use inside the Hall, but they were a comfort.

They passed beneath the gates. Marei saw figures forming

on the edge of her vision. Soldiers in mail shifted and changed shapes, becoming giant ogres with animal faces.

"Ignore them," Dunrae said. "See the third door at the end of the courtyard?" Marei stared through the shifting murk and guessed where he meant. A swirl of gas opened on three doors lit by dim lights—one yellow, one red, the other blue.

"The yellow door," she said, nodding, and followed him through the draughty courtyard. There were creatures in here. She saw shadows and heard snarling and scraping. She picked up her pace, staying close to the big man's back.

A huge shadow emerged in front of the glowing yellow door. It blocked their way and manifested into a leather-clad warrior with the face of a bull. The warrior held a long-barbed pike and rammed it down at Dunrae.

The man knocked the weapon aside with his blunderbuss and stepped forward, ramming Bessy's butt into the bull-man's chest. The creature exploded into green pus and vanished.

"Inside, quickly!" Dunrae kicked the door ajar and grabbed her arm. She caught a glimpse of other shadows with hideous faces or masks—she couldn't be sure. Among them were fish-heads and weasels, hares and rats.

She entered, and he slammed the door shut behind them with a shoulder.

"Those things …"

"Forget 'em." Dunrae stood staring down a long, faintly lit passage. The door rattled behind them. Marei was about to say something when he laughed gruffly.

"Yeah, I remember. We have to go down, before climbing again. This way."

She didn't ask but kept as close to his back as she could. Glancing behind, she saw smoky fingers sliding around the yellow-framed door. Shouting, snorts and growls came from the other side.

"Stop looking back," Dunrae said, without turning his head. "Never look back, Marei. That's the most important rule here."

"Got it," she said, her mouth dry and voice a squeak.

The corridor was squeeze-narrow and twisted back and forth. Was it her imagination, or were the walls breathing? Closing in? Like they were inside the belly of a giant yet swiftly shrinking worm, shrinking and belching and shuddering as they walked on. It was stifling, and she felt queasy.

"Do you know where we are?"

He didn't respond but had the blunderbuss held ready in both hands with the tapered barrel ranging ahead.

Marei jumped when a long white slug creature emerged and slid toward them. Its slime cracked a mouth, and she saw tiny white teeth. The blunderbuss fired, and the white slug exploded into mush. Dunrae chuckled, and Marei felt sick.

"I hate dimension slugs," he said. Marei choked at the stench and staggered behind him.

It seemed like an hour had passed before another door emerged. This one was round and scarcely two feet wide, more like a hatch.

"Hold back—me and Bessy's got this," Dunrae told her. He tapped the round steel door with the weapon's stock and waited. He winked at her. "Give it a nonce."

Marei gasped as the door flew open and a huge, hairy hand shot out, the filthy claw like fingers jabbing at Dunrae's eyes.

He stepped back. "Hold this." He passed Bessy across and turned again. The blunderbuss was even heavier than it looked. She clung to it with both hands, hugging it close.

"Dunrae, be careful!"

More hands jabbed at him. Dunrae caught the nearest and pulled it toward him. Marei saw a hideous head emerge, goggling fish-eyes and lolling tongue. It gaped at her, just as Dunrae Tarn's long knife sliced into oozy flesh.

He jabbed, sliced, and stabbed until there was nothing left there. He wiped the blade on his coat and grinned evilly, mercifully relieving her of the heavy blunderbuss. "It's clear," he said. "Climb inside." Marei stared at the hole and shook her head in disbelief. "For fuck's sake, do it, will you?"

She gripped the slimy, round rim and pulled herself inside, shutting her ears as the sound of wailing rose from somewhere below. Once through, she turned and saw him pushing the blunderbuss across and forcing his bulk through the hole, cussing when the coat got torn. Once clear, he shut the round door and fastened it with a latch on the top.

"Where next?" Marei said, impressed that she'd managed to speak without shaking.

"Down and up, along again. Not far. You're doing well, girl."

"How do you know where we are?"

He tapped the side of his head and winked at her again. "I do, which is all you need to know, lass. Come on, stay close—we'll see some stairs in a minute."

A short walk led to a gloomy arch. Beyond that, a passage descended at alarming steepness. Calling them stairs was generous. Marei saw broken, worn steps of rotting wood leading down in rickety spirals.

"Will they hold our weight?"

"It's a fucking illusion—didn't you listen to me?"

"Sorry."

"Here. I'll go first. If they break, you'll have to find your own way out of here."

Marei glared at him. "That isn't funny," she said, and started following him down the winding stairs.

She shuddered and tensed, as the wood creaked, and small, glowing-red insects ran beneath her boots. She almost slipped three times and once crashed into Dunrae's back. He caught her wrist and righted her without slowing his descent.

They reached the bottom, and Marei wiped sweat from her face. A wide, airy hall opened out on all sides. She saw lanterns flickering over to the left. There were figures seated there. They appeared to be sleeping, but Marei suspected they would awaken at any moment.

"Corpse Avenue. Careful—this might be tricky," Dunrae whispered as he started walking across the wide hall. Marei followed him, her eyes on the distant lamp-lit faces. They had almost reached the end of Corpse Avenue when the final figure stirred—a woman, her dead stone eyes opening and pinning Marei with a glare.

Marei froze.

"Keep moving," Dunrae hissed. "Don't look at their faces."

She hurried behind him as a sound of whistling breath sighed and drifted toward them. Ahead, she saw three more doors.

"Which one?"

"We'll see."

She was going to ask what he meant by that when the nearest door moved to the right and as the furthest drifted forward and folded, while the middle one turned on its side and floated to the ground.

Marei saw more goggle-eyed faces peel from the walls like rotting parchment. They slid and scraped across the stone flags. The doors spun as they approached. The nearest became the furthest and folded and crumpled, changing arrangement again.

Dunrae produced a lantern from his coat. She had no idea how and why he'd kept that hidden for so long. Too many mysteries. The bright light chased the shadows back to join the dead faces far behind them.

The three doors merged into one, and a huge headless figure barred the way.

Marei stifled a scream.

"Steady, lass. Remember, it's all in your mind. They're playing with us, or at least I'm letting 'em think they are."

He walked toward the door, and she followed hesitantly. She'd almost caught up with him again when a hand grabbed her arm and she screamed.

The stone-eyed corpse woman was smiling at her. She had no teeth, and the stench from her breath was like the gallows tree in summer.

Dunrae swung out with the lantern, and the dead woman vanished. He turned and made for the door, but the huge headless creature was waiting, a heavy cudgel in each of its three hands. It started swinging, and Dunrae Tarn let rip with Bessy. Monster and door shattered into dust. He walked through as though nothing had happened.

Another door appeared. Dunrae snapped his fingers for her to catch him up. He'd lashed the lantern to his belt and gripped Bessy with one hand, the stock resting on his hip. They reached the door.

"Turn the key." He motioned to a large brass lever sticking out of the handle. She did as he said, and the door dropped open. She fell forward into a gaping hole, but Dunrae yanked her out.

"Wrong one," he said. "Come on, there'll be another along in a minute."

Marei felt giddy. She followed him, willing herself not to turn her head as she heard the sound of rushing feet approaching from behind. Two more doors appeared. These drifted and turned on their backs. A third floated down from the vaulted ceiling and hovered over their heads. The door swung open, and cold air blasted out.

"That's it," Dunrae told her, nodding at the door swinging above her head.

"I can't get up there."

"You have to. Here, climb on my shoulders, and I'll shove you up."

"What about you?" She could see the gray shapes of people creeping like smoke toward them. Ghost corpses, their dead faces gleamed like pale worms in wet soil.

"Just do it!"

He placed the blunderbuss down on the oily stone and cupped his big hands. Marei placed a boot inside, and he hoisted her up with alarming speed. She shot through the hole and crashed into something wet. She heard him cussing, and other noisome sounds surrounded him. Bessy roared, and next she knew, his head emerged from the ground.

He tossed the lantern and blunderbuss up, swung by his forearms, and pulled himself clear. He grinned at her and rolled to his feet.

"Yeah, that's it," Dunrae told her.

A dazzling glare. Marei blinked several times until her eyes adjusted, and she was amazed to see the ocean surging a few yards away.

Dunrae smiled, seemingly pleased. "We've crossed through."

She followed him along damp reeds fencing the gray water. Her mind was too dizzy to enquire where they were. Another dimension? She didn't want to think about that. The reeds parted and a river blocked their way. Shallow and broken by outcrops of rock.

"Now listen up. Their camp's on the other side," Dunrae Tarn told her.

"Whose?"

"The Kaa. We used the dimension-compass inside the Hall to find 'em. We'll ford this stream, and then you'll need to hide up while I go and take a look."

"I'll be coming with you."

"You won't, if you want to see that lad of yours again." He glared back at her, and she nodded.

The stream was icy, and the current pulling at her legs and the sand sucking. It took all her strength to keep up with the man. He allowed a short rest on one of the rocks before insisting they move again.

"There isn't much time," he told her. "Be light soon." She had no idea how he knew that.

They reached the far bank. Marei heard the surge of waves where river met ocean. There were dark shapes moving out there. Her eyes, having adjusted fully to the gloom, focused on three ships. Lean-hulled and sharp, their sails were furled neatly and bunched below masts. Nearer were tents or pointed huts. She saw firelight and glimpsed a face leering back at her.

"Fuck it—they've seen us." Dunrae stood and dropped Bessy into his hands. "Come on, lass, stick close and shoot anything that fucking moves." He ran forward yelling.

Marei yelled after him, then screamed as a face emerged from the reeds. A man, his head shaven and eyes shaded by dark tattoos, grinned at her to show neatly filed, steel-tipped teeth. He had bones in each ear.

She raised the crossbow and fired, and he disappeared. She crouched and cranked another bolt back. Another Kaa appeared, and she shot again, running on, stopping, crouching and loading again.

She heard Bessy roar and someone scream. Again, the blunderbuss blasted, and she saw bits of body spray the reeds ahead.

"Dunrae?" Marei crashed blindly into a man's back. He turned, a fish spear gripped in his hands. He grinned at her and grabbed her cloak. Marei swung about and rammed the crossbow into his mouth. She fired. The bolt cracked out the top of his skull. He dropped, and she stumbled on.

Again, Bessy roared.

"This way!" she heard him shout. She cleared more reeds and saw Dunrae standing inside a circle of tents. He was surrounded by skinny white-faced men jabbing hooked spears. She kneeled, cranked the crossbow, and fired, taking the closest in the back.

Two bolts left.

Two Kaa broke away to attack her as Dunrae struck out with the blunderbuss, cracking the nearest one's skull. There were more screams and shouts. He had a brand in his right hand and was waving it about.

The two Kaa were onto her, harpoons jabbing. She fired and missed, dropped the crossbow and reached for her knife. They laughed at her, and she knew it was useless.

"Dunrae!"

But he was surrounded by Kaa and couldn't get to her.

Marei kicked out at one's groin and swiped her knife arm in a vicious arc. The Kaa jumped back. A third arrived, grinning. She knew they were playing with her and taking their time.

"Bastards!" She jabbed again. This time, one caught her wrist and pulled her close. His mouth closed on her neck as he bit down.

Marei twisted free as sharp pain tore up inside her throat. The two ghouls were smiling. She felt blood dripping down her neck. She was weakening. They wouldn't have to wait long.

Dunrae.

A shadow appeared behind, and one of the Kaa gurgled and fell. Marei saw the fish spear sticking out of his mouth. Before the second could turn, the spear found his guts and he screamed, pitching forward into the boggy reeds.

Marei sliced wildly up at the last, the knife shredding his trousers and cutting off his balls. She stabbed again and again until she was too weak, then slipped to the ground barely conscious.

"Mother!"

A face emerged, and she faintly recognized her son.

"*Dafyd?* I must be dead. But it's good to see you."

She felt his strong arms pull her up.

"Mother, you're not dreaming *or* dead. And you've saved us, you and that man."

"Dafyd?" Her vision was fading, and she'd lost a lot of blood.

"We need to get going." She vaguely noticed Dunrae's shadow looming over Dafyd. His big arms were wrapped around a weeping child.

"You saved her."

"Told you I would. We need to get moving—they're

coming back. Take the babe." He passed the mewling child, Dalreen, across to her son.

Marei felt herself slipping.

"Mother … she's badly hurt."

Here, you worry about little 'un, and I'll look after ya mum." She heard his gruff voice, but her vision was blurry and she was slipping away.

"Mother …"

Marei's eyes closed. She felt her body lift and drift, feather-light, floating out across the ocean, saw a distant glimmer brightening the horizon. It rose, turned golden, and became a woman's beautiful smile.

"Rest in the arms of the Goddess." She recognized Jynn's voice. Then she saw Garland standing, sword in hand, and next to him a stunted, ugly creature. They were surrounded by fires. She drifted and floated out toward the smiling face.

Dunrae's voice reached her: "Not yet, Marei."

She saw the flames closing in on her lover. *I'm sorry, Garland.*

"He knows they're free, Marei," Dunrae said. "I told your man I'd save Dafyd and the child. In return for …"

His voice drifted off. She made out a blurry face. Dafyd, or Dunrae Tarn? Or perhaps Garland? Her mind floated, and she felt her body spreading and flattening. At peace.

It is time.

"It's not time yet, Marei. You've still many things to accomplish."

Her eyes opened and she blinked, recognizing Jynn's cottage, Rosey's warm happy smile, and the sleeping child in her arms.

"Dunrae Tarn brought you back here, Marei," Rosey said,

a tear tracing her eyes. "My Dafyd, and the baby, too. He said he couldn't have done it without you."

"I thought I was dead." She barely recognized her own voice, trembling as it was. Her mouth felt heavy, and she was desperately weak. But there was no pain.

"You almost were."

A new voice had spoken, silky and smooth. She turned and saw a slender, silver-haired woman with large green-and-yellow eyes smiling at her. Those eyes were familiar. Marei thought she knew who this was.

"You're the cat."

The woman nodded. "Sometimes I am, yes. You need to sleep, Marei."

"What about Dunrae—where is he? And my poor Garland?"

"Dunrae is needed elsewhere. As for Sir Garland ... he, at least, is not alone."

"He was surrounded by fires."

"He has help and will soon have more. His main task is about to begin. Worry not about the Journeyman. Your love will stay with him. You must rest. The tooth tear was deep and filled with Kaa poison, but you will recover thanks to Jynn and Dunrae Tarn. And the courage and quick thinking of your son."

Marei closed her eyes. "Will I see either of them again?"

The silky woman blurred, becoming a cat. The gray animal brushed against her face, and she felt a deep, warming calm.

"I expect so," the cat-woman's voice told her. "Either in this life, or maybe the next." The words reached her from far away. "Sleep in the arms of the Dragon, Marei. Know that you are safe, and the Dance has moved on."

And Marei slept.

24

ARIANE'S VOW

FOR ARIANE, the passage through had felt like an extension of last night's dream. A shifting pattern, where the skies had glowed silver through gold, before darkening to purple.

The Dreaming had found her. She'd risen above her bunk, seen herself lying there asleep. He'd been calling out her name in that booming, thunderous voice.

Your Betrothed. Sensuata.

The Sea God. The pledge must be made. The bargain cemented.

He has come to claim His prize.

She'd seeped through the window, a fret of mist and dreams. Outside, Ariane had seen the water changing hue, from dark green through shimmering gold. The ship faded behind her as His calls beckoned her come. She lifted and drifted out across those shifting waters.

As she glided, Ariane saw creatures writhing below the surface of that glassy brine. There were leviathans—great serpents that raised their purple heads. She saw krakens, squirting giant squids and, further down, the broken wreck-ages of ships.

She dropped stone-swift into the brine. The soothing water welcomed her like a strong lover's arms, swallowing her body and calming her mind.

She sank deep into the water. It felt blanket warm and sucked her down. The ocean's creatures surrounded her: small fishes, lobsters, giant squid, silver darting sharks, electric eels, and rays all serenaded her and guided her down.

Down and deep.

Into the forgotten watery dark. A name reached her from a memory.

Telimantua.

The name rang loud in her ears. A distant, watery gong. She saw a vision of emerald and silver. Tall pillars draped in weed. A city of floating gardens, of green-eyed statues and bubbling caverns, where big-eyed, steel-clad fish watched her pass.

Music filled her ears as she slipped down deeper, the pillar and stone ruins wrapping around her. She heard the soft notes of harps and distant organs.

Then she saw Him. Huge as a thundercloud.

Guised as a young man. He came to her, naked, his sex stirring and fathomless, stormy eyes smiling. He spoke, addressing her spirit, the booming voice causing the stones crack open at his feet. She saw weed tendrils writhe and shimmer swayed by His breath. The myriad tiny fishes vanished into hidden caverns, like a rainbow dance of flashing lights.

IT IS TIME TO FULFILL YOUR PART OF THE BARGAIN, ARIANE. DID YOU THINK THAT I'D FORGOTTEN?

No! I will not do this. I'm needed elsewhere.

The words had frothed from her dream lips. His smile faded, replaced by a frown. The terrible eyes turned cruel.

YOU DARE REFUSE ME?

Ariane's eyes opened, as a thud of wave struck the side of her cabin, knocking her from the bunk. She cursed as her arm struck the floor painfully.

Oh, shit …

She sat up, hearing someone rapping at the door. There were shouts outside her cabin.

"Highness, are you hurt?"

Cale's voice.

"I am well. What is happening?" She rubbed her arm and stood shakily.

"Rough night—we've come through some kind of vortex."

What's he talking about? "It's all right, come in."

The cabin door opened, and Cale's ginger grin showed— but it faded when he saw her holding her arm where she'd struck it on the floor.

"You *are* hurt?"

"It's nothing," she said, her mind shaken from the dream and head throbbing. "What hour is it? Seems calmer—has the storm passed?"

He sat on the bunk beside her. He looked exhausted, as though he'd not slept a minute last night. "I have no idea, highness. But it's … yes, *calm.* Thank the Goddess. And the sun is shining, so that must be good."

"You look shattered, Cale."

"A touch, aye."

"Crenna?"

In response, he laughed ironically.

"What's the matter with you?" Irritated, Ariane felt like

slapping him. She was badly shaken from the watery night-mare and didn't need any nonsense from her former squire. "Have we raised the cliffs of Crenna yet? If not, where the fuck are we?"

He looked at her sheepishly and shook his head. "Did you sleep through the entire performance?"

"Cale, if you don't start making sense, I'll hit you with something hard. Yes, I slept heavily last night, and woke moments ago when I fell out of bed. The jolt was caused by a bad storm, which happily has dissipated. What of it?"

"We've crossed over, highness."

The new voice belonged to Doyle. Garland's second was standing outside her cabin, his face pale, eyes worried.

Ariane felt her cheeks burning. "You had better explain, Doyle. Because this fool seems to have lost his wits."

Cale shook his head and Doyle nodded slowly. "We saw it all: Cale, myself, and Taic," he told her. "Fassyan and the crew went below. Taic didn't want his men worn out. And Fassyan …"

"A bad storm has taken us past Crenna? Out into the open ocean?"

"And back through time." Doyle matched her angry stare for a moment, before dropping his gaze.

Ariane stood shakily and glared at him. She ignored Cale, nodding his head emphatically beside Doyle.

"*What* did you say?"

"We've crossed some kind of vortex," Cale repeated.

Ariane switched her gaze to him, and back to Doyle.

"Vortex …?"

"While you slept, highness, we saw visions out on deck," Cale told her "I heard bells chiming, and there were faces moving in the sky. The sea turned to black, velvety glass, and strange fishes raised their scaly heads above the water. We saw this."

All right ...

Ariane seated herself on the bunk and gulped in stale air. Could it be true? After Rann's visit, they'd entered a fog—a dark fret that reminded her of the one raised by the Aralais wizard, Zallerak, as they fled the wrath of Crenna and its cruel pirate prince. She'd drunk heavily and tried to shake off Rann's memory, which was why she'd slept so well. She regretted that.

"Like the storm Zallerak conjured from the wind?" she asked Cale.

"Different. It wasn't sorcery or Aralais magic. We've crossed a portal through dimensions. The Goddess—it has to be Her." Cale stared at Doyle, who nodded again.

Ariane looked at them both long and hard. They held her gaze, Cale with raised brow and Doyle with jaw set. Finally, Ariane released them from her scrutiny.

"All right, I'm sorry I was angry. And I also regret having slept through what you witnessed. Is Fassyan ... the crew. Was anyone hurt?"

"No, highness. It wasn't a storm," Cale insisted. "More like a shifting and blurring, with music and booming noise. Ethereal. Especially the visions I mentioned. That last wave hit us as the sky changed, and we found ourselves sailing different waters."

Ariane chewed her bottom lip. "Thank you both. Leave me to my thoughts. I'll join you on deck in due course." They nodded, and Cale shut the cabin door carefully.

Ariane stared at the door for a moment and pressed her palms together. She mouthed a silent prayer.

· · ·

Goddess, I know you've helped us.

Please guide me hence. I feel like a lost child, and these men are my responsibility. Tell me Rann's visit and that nightmare were but echoes reverberating inside my worried head.

Please save me from Him ... you know that I had scant choice but to make that pledge.

Placate Your Brother and rescue your queen!

Ariane opened her eyes. She needed to move. Do something. Instinctively, she strapped on her swords and made for the deck, where bright sunshine shimmered on a pale-blue ocean.

Taic waved and joined her. His tanned face was grinning, the long blonde locks windswept and wild. "We've raised some foreign cliffs, highness."

"Where?"

"Northeast—lookout spotted them from the crow."

"Tack closer."

"Already doing it."

"Taic, did you ...? I mean, is what Cale and Doyle say right? We've passed through a portal?"

"Shit, yeah. Frigging marvelous. Err ... *sorry* ... But you slept through an interesting night, highness."

Mine was quite eventful, too, she thought wryly.

Two hours later Ariane stood by the wheel with Doyle, Fassyan, and Cale beside her. All watched as Taic guided *Kraken Girl* into a stone harbor.

Ariane saw people gazing across at their ship with curious expressions.

"We've been at sea but a week," Fassyan said behind her.

"Surely we can't be far past Crenna's west coast? I've never heard men speak of land out here."

"That's because we're nowhere near Crenna," Taic said, winking at Ariane.

Ariane smiled at Fassyan. "Apparently last night's mist carried us across the dimensions. I missed the event, as did you."

"I went below …" Fassyan looked ashamed.

"Doesn't matter," she told him. "The important thing is that the Goddess is aiding us, as I knew She would." She turned to Doyle standing beside her. "We will find your lost captain and the bow Kerasheva. I am certain of it." The bright day had almost driven away her nightmare. *Almost.*

Doyle nodded, his eyes filled with doubt. She didn't blame him. "Where is it you think we are, highness?" he asked.

"We passed those two islands earlier," she said. "You saw the trail of smoke rising?" He nodded. "Ashmali's Island, has to be. Taic and I studied the ancient charts of Gol and the surrounding lands. We think we've arrived at some harbor on the south coast of the Great Continent. Most likely Aketa in Zorne, or Siotta further east in Spagos."

Fassyan looked askance. "How can such a thing be possible?"

"I find drinking helps," Taic said, slapping the huntsmaster's back.

"It's true, Fass, old son. We're lost in the past." Cale rubbed his ruddy beard. "I've shared some weird experiences with you, highness. Have to say that this one tops them all."

"We crossed over last night," Ariane told Fassyan. "I've no idea how. These three talkative fellows can explain the fascinating details to you. I'd rather focus on what we're doing next."

"I was going to ask you that, highness. Are you expecting trouble?" Taic asked her, after glancing at her swords.

"Perhaps."

Ariane gazed across at the people watching, as *Kraken Girl* rounded the harbor arm. Helmeted soldiers gazed down from a round tower.

"Those guards seem friendly, or at least not hostile," she said. "By the size of this harbor, there's a lot of trading done here. They'll think we're foreigners from beyond their borders, which of course we are." She smiled. "Anyone asks, we're from an island beyond Gol. That's if we can make them understand us."

"I'll barter and get us some more grog and such," Taic said, whistling up to the crew to make ready for the quay.

Ariane watched with Cale, Doyle, and Fassyan as the sailors made busy with ropes. Taic guided the craft into the still waters surrounding the harbor wall. Fassyan stood on the prow, leaning heavily on his bow.

She studied the crowd gathered to watch their arrival. Dark faces, mostly men, but the odd woman. All were staring at them with curious eyes. On instinct, she waved across at them. They shook their heads and turned away. Ariane shrugged—she must have shocked them. They'd have to be careful not to offend these people.

Once moored, Taic leaped ashore with two of his crew. Cale and Doyle went with them, as Ariane remained on deck with Fassyan.

"How do you feel, Fass?" she asked, worried about him.

"Like a coward who's let you down."

"Don't be ridiculous, and you shouldn't feel ashamed. Cale, like myself, witnessed sorcery and magic during the Crystal Wars. Doyle—who knows what horrors he faced in the east lands? You've never left Kelwyn before accompanying us on this voyage. That took courage. I know what I asked of you. But the Goddess is guiding us, Fassyan. Hold on to that truth." She gripped his hand, and a moment passed between them.

"I feel … *unworthy*. Cale and Doyle are seasoned fighters. Taic and his men, too. I'm just a hunter. A bowyer."

"You're the best archer in Wynais, and throughout Kelwyn, too, I'll warrant. Don't sell yourself short, man. I don't know Doyle well, but he was just an errand boy before Captain Garland chose him to scout for the Bear regiment, those few who survived. As for Cale"—she laughed—"he was a guttersnipe thief when first I encountered him. Working for a rogue called Hagan. Besides, I'm sure we'll need your bow skills soon enough."

"Can anyone shoot this sacred emerald bow?"

"Perhaps, I don't know? We have to find it first."

"Stolen from the Goddess by a master thief."

"Have faith." She smiled at him, feeling glad he was with her. "This is meant to be. We don't have to understand, Fass, but rather trust in Elanion's wisdom. Oh look, here's Cale back already."

"THEY SEEM APPROACHABLE," CALE SAID, AS HE JUMPED down to join them. "Taic's already got us some ale."

"As though that's important." Ariane rolled her eyes. "Have you discovered anything useful?"

"We're in Siotta harbor, several miles south of the city. There's a market and a lot of bantering, and they actually speak our language. The accents are odd."

"Care for a stroll?" Ariane said to Fassyan, as Cale disappeared below decks. He'd been tasked by Taic to make space for supplies. Ariane suspected he'd help to drink those before they got stored.

She needed exercise and time to get away, though a bustling and curious crowd seemed hardly the place. Truth was, she was weary and alarmed by her dream. It had seemed so real, especially the woman the evening before. But Rann had been real. Her visit had happened before she'd slept.

My mind's addled.

She couldn't deny Rann had been there, however much she cared to.

Ariane had made a promise years ago. She remembered how Corin an Fol had raged at her for bargaining her soul for their safety. Baron's ship—the *Starlight Wanderer*—was beset by a kraken and sinking fast. Her prayer to Sensuata had saved them that day. But He'd had a price. Ariane would be his betrothed and dwell with Him beneath the ocean.

What choice had she but to agree to those terms?

Then the war with Caswallon took over, culminating in the Happening. The old gods perished or moved on. Ariane believed herself free of the bargain. But Elanion had returned from the ether, and that meant the Sea God was out there too, ready to claim His prize. At least two of the high gods were back, and she was in deep trouble with one of them.

Damn it. Stop thinking …

She walked the harbor wall, Fassyan brooding by her side. She couldn't deny the feelings she had for this quiet, gentle hunter. Honest and noble, he sometimes reminded her of Corin, which was ridiculous, because that mercenary had been nothing but trouble in those early days. She'd loved him, though, until cousin Shallan intervened.

Oh, what am I thinking about …?

They reached the harbor town, the busy marketplace jostling with traders, merchants and all manner of folk. She saw Taic yelling at someone and worried he'd start a fight, Northmen being what they were—and Taic one of the worst in his younger days.

He saw her and grinned. She nodded curtly and walked on, Fassyan flanking her with bow across his shoulder and eyes on every stranger.

There were soldiers, but these seemed indifferent to their being here. The men struck her as lazy. Ariane hadn't read much about Spagos. A small country wedged between Zorne in the west, and Lamoza. Beyond that lay the huge empire of Xandoria. They would have to pass that before reaching Rakeel and sailing on to Gol. A journey of weeks, unless the Goddess intervened again.

Ariane suspected she would. And hopefully She'd keep Her terrible brother at bay. She shuddered. The world was insane. What choice had she but to act when called upon? She thought about poor Raule back in Wynais. A good man and dear friend. But husband and lover?

She stopped and perused some wraps, feigning interest. The merchant showed his gold teeth and whistled to a boy to produce more. Ariane waved him back and continued her walk until the market and its noises faded, as they paced down a cobbled street.

"Highness, is this wise, wandering so far from the ship?"

"I needed the exercise, and that marketplace was making my head spin. Besides, I have my swords, you the longbow. Only a fool would cross us."

"Even so."

Ariane raised a finger stopping his protests. "Look, a

tavern at the end of this street. Looks clean. Let's go take a look."

Fassyan shook his head dubiously but followed her until she entered the low door of a brick building with lanterns glinting behind dark drapes.

The proprietor nodded and seemed friendly enough. He approached, rubbing his apron. "More foreigners? Siotta must be popular these days. What can I get you, lovely?" He ignored Fassyan.

"This is—"

"—Sssh, doesn't matter," Ariane waved a hand hushing her huntsmaster's protests. She smiled at the innkeep. "Have you any tea? Or, actually, a brandy would work better." He nodded, and she had a thought: "You've had other foreigners in the harbor, people like us?"

"Err, yes. And no. Two fellas. One was a decent enough sort. Big, well used. My age. Soldier, I'd say. Officer, maybe? Seen some things by the shadow in his eyes. Heavy sword at his waist. He paid good coin, so I can't complain. Now, I think about it, his accent was similar to yours."

It cannot be

"His companion?"

The innkeep spat on the floor. "I didn't much care for that one's look, to be honest. A cripple, I took him to be. Short and bent. He kept his face well hidden in a deep hood, but the eyes were black as midnight. Gave me the creeps. He carried a bent stick with odd symbols carved down its length."

"Sounds like a sorcerer or shaman," Fassyan muttered.

The innkeep looked at him for the first time and nodded. "I thought the same thing, matey. Strange fellow, for sure."

"When was this?" Ariane asked him, her mind sharpening.

"'Twas but an hour ago, miss."

"Where did they go?" She straightened, and he backed away seeing the swords at her hip, his eyes puzzled and wide.

"Back to the harbor, I'd guess. I overheard the soldier fellow mutter something about Rakeel. That's at the far end of Xandoria. Long way from here. Probably where they came from, I've heard Xandorians is odd folk."

"Thank you—that's most intriguing." Ariane made for the door and bid Fassyan toss the innkeep some coin. He complied begrudgingly and followed her outside into the hot sun.

"Your brandy, missy?"

"Drink it yourself," she said. "You'll need it before Ashmali arrives."

"Who?"

Ariane walked briskly back to the marketplace, her mind working overtime. Fassyan looked at her sideways but kept his thoughts to himself.

It can't be a coincidence.

It wasn't.

She had almost reached the ship, joining Taic and his crew, who were busy tossing bundles across on to the deck. She'd been about to shout a greeting when someone caught her eye.

A man in a shabby cloak was leaning against a rail, gazing out across the ocean. A smaller figure crouched with a twisted stick, poking it into the dirt. There was something about that smaller figure that made her skin crawl. Something familiar.

Urgolais.

One of them had survived.

Ariane reached for her swords. She stopped when the man turned and gazed directly at her. Her jaw dropped. It was

Garland, the lost captain she'd sent to find her cousin
Tamersane.

GARLAND FROZE IN ASTONISHMENT, SEEING HIS QUEEN
staring across at him from the dock. He heard Zorc mutter
something but ignored him. He raised his hand in greeting
before dropping it again. She was staring, her beautiful face
stunned, the expression a mixture of horror, disbelief, and joy.

"That woman doesn't like me," Zorc said.

"Stay here," Garland told him and walked over, his eyes
seeing nothing but her face. He stopped yards away, bowed
stiffly, and stood with hands clasped to his chest. Her eyes
flicked across to Zorc, who'd crept up behind him.

"He's not an enemy," Garland told her

"An *Urgolais?*" Her eyes shifted back and forth between
him and Zorc.

"Yes, but on my side."

"How is that possible?"

"Can I explain?" Zorc cut in.

"Shut up!" Ariane glared at him.

"You must be Queen Ariane," Zorc said. "*Charmed.* You
know this man dotes on you?"

"Be silent, Zorc," Garland snarled, without averting his
gaze from her. "My queen … I …" He stopped, seeing a group
of men watching. He recognized Cale among them.

"Why is that creature with you?"

"Zorc helped me."

"An Urgolais warlock? One of the vile sorcerers Caswallon
conjured form Yffarn. Have you lost your mind, Captain
Garland?"

"I've asked myself the same thing many times, highness. And I've failed you, too. Tamersane ..."

"Is dead, yes. I assumed that were so. Not your fault. I shouldn't have sent you on a fool's errand."

Garland saw Cale approach. Like Ariane, his eyes were incredulous and horrified by Zorc's presence.

"Is that what I think it is?"

"He's called Zorc, and he's not an enemy," Garland insisted. "Without his help, I would be dead."

"The Urgolais stays out here," Ariane said. "You, captain, shall accompany us back to Taic's ship. There's much to discuss. Before we start with any of that, you'll need to convince me why I shouldn't kill this fiend?"

"That's if we can," Cale muttered.

"Because Zorc's my friend," Garland said.

"Poor bugger's lost his marbles," Cale snorted to the queen.

Ariane's bottom lip quivered. "What happened to you, captain?"

"I don't know where to start, highness."

"At the beginning. Cale, go inform Doyle that his captain has joined our team, and we'll need an early supper before departure. I see no reason to linger in Siotta."

"What about Zorc?"

"I won't kill him until I've heard your tale."

"He needs to come with us."

Cale laughed, but Ariane pointed at Zorc. "You stay put, warlock. I don't know what vile spell you've put on this man, but you won't get away with it. Understand? The Goddess Elanion has chosen me for Her mortal vessel. I had thought your revolting kind eradicated from our world."

"Thanks for the warmth," Zorc said. "Enjoy your supper. I'll still be here when you're done talking."

Ariane turned away briskly and snapped her fingers for Garland to follow. Cale gazed at him and shook his head, as Garland nodded to Zorc and followed his queen, his mind ravaged by guilt and failure.

Doyle was waiting at the gangway. Garland saw tears staining his cycs.

"Captain ..."

"I've missed you, boy," Garland threw his arms around his lieutenant. He also recognized the blonde Northman Taic, who he'd seen once in Wynais.

"We're leaving on the hour," Taic said.

"Doyle, Fassyan, you others, help Taic," Queen Ariane told them. "I want to be alone with my captain. We will need brandy. A full bottle."

Garland smiled ruefully at Doyle and followed his queen across to the ship.

"In here." She pointed to a door and entered a spacious cabin with chair, lanterns and bed. She took the chair while he remained standing. Taic arrived producing a fat bottle and two goblets, then left them with a wink.

The queen stared long and hard at him, her dark eyes unflinching.

"You've aged."

"I do not doubt that."

"Tell me that creature hasn't bewitched you."

"I've been struggling with the same question, highness. But Zorc needs me, and he is not like the other Urgolais. At first, I didn't believe it myself. But now ..."

"We'll get to Zorc later. You saw my cousin, witnessed his end?"

"At the Castle of Lights in Rundali. Tamersane followed Teret across the void. A gift from the Jynn. They are at peace. Teret saved us all. My queen, I ..."

She sipped her brandy and ventured a smile.

"It's good to see you in one piece. Can you guess why I'm here with these adventurers?"

"Doyle reported my failure?"

"He did no such thing. I'll not hear nonsense like that. Understood?"

He nodded.

"I *own* the failure of your quest, captain. It's on your queen. I sent you on a fruitless, dangerous journey, on a whim. A dream. Hoping that I could save my poor cousin from himself. How can I be angry with you? A vassal, and brave soldier. As for Doyle ... that man has nothing but pride when he mentions your name."

"But if so, why are you here, highness? Is it because of the lost voyager, Carlo Sarfe?"

"The Goddess has spoken to you, too. That's good."

"Not Her. Urdei. Elanion's child saved me in Graywash Hall. She says we have to stop Carlo from returning home."

"I mean to do exactly that. You know of his whereabouts?"

"I saw his ship with Zorc's spell glass when we were on the Alchemist Isle. I saw yours, too, though that might have been a vison of the future."

Ariane nodded. "Be seated." She motioned the bed, and he sat perched, the brandy shaky in his hands.

"Relax," she smiled, and he complied. "Tell me everything that happened after Doyle left you and returned. You were in Laregoza? Largos City, is that right?"

PART III

DECISIONS

25

RAKEEL

THREE WEEKS of sailing had raised the cliffs of Xandoria and, beyond, the walls of Rakeel Castle. Carlo hadn't wanted to stop here. The brief time spent on Cazea had left him more anxious than ever. But the supplies were low, and despite the crossing to Gol being short, the sea could be tricky. It was fast approaching winter, judging by the geese he'd seen flying south from the Great Continent.

A short stay, restock and away. The last leg awaiting. He should be excited, but he dreaded the return. He'd spent days in his cabin, ignoring Stogi, Tai Pei, and Garland's men. He'd shared meals with Slim Tareel and Gurdey, even Gold Tar occasionally. The bosun was keen to get home and had proved less quarrelsome of late.

As were the crew. All in good shape, their journey's end in view. Carlo knew they didn't believe his tale but rather thought him bewitched in the Castle of Lights or the town they'd seen instead.

And perhaps he had been? The distance and time and strange happenings had given him cause to doubt everything, even Teret and the love he thought he'd felt for her. The uncertainty made him feel awkward around Stogi and the girl. But they hardly noticed, he suspected.

The pair had a new friend. Somehow—and he didn't recall exactly how—that stirring bitch, Jenada, had persuaded her brother, the Tisen of Cazea, to insist on her sailing with them.

To Gol.

Despite all her warnings and talk of catastrophe waiting. Why? He couldn't fathom what she was up to. If Gol was to sink and burn, Cazea could expect a tidal wave, perhaps a typhoon, but not obliteration. They'd survive, mostly. Why court disaster by sailing into the eye? She was up to something, and he didn't like it. Stogi and the others had been cold toward him since they left the Island States. Carlo suspected Jenada was to blame.

It wasn't important. He'd stick to his plan, sail home to Sarfania, and save his kin. His people. Warn them of what the future held. What else could he do?

As they neared the castle and harbor, Carlo watched from the prow, eyes shielded from the sun. He saw a white bird glide past and hover low. His memory jolted back to leaving the shore in Rundali. He'd seen two birds that day—a hawk and a swan.

The hawk was back. It settled on the figurehead and preened its feathers. As he watched, it shimmered and blurred into a man—a hooded figure whose single silver eye glinted out at him. Carlo turned to warn the crew, but he could no longer see them, nor the harbor, nor shoreline. A mist had covered the front of the ship. He stood alone with the hooded man.

"I know you from somewhere." A distant memory. One of

the old gods. He was in grave danger and barely held back a shudder.

"Indeed, we've met, Carlo Sarfe. Different time and place. Today, I've an offer for you." The voice was crow raw. "There's a way you can save your family."

Carlo felt sweat trickle down his back.

"What do you want in return?"

"It's complicated." The brief bark of a laugh revealed a grin. "You, mariner, wouldn't understand. But I can help you, and that's all that should matter."

"My kin and countrymen?"

"Will be saved, I promise."

"What must I do?"

"Accept the gift when its offered. That easy."

"Gift?"

"The bow, Kerasheva. The thief will offer it to you. With Kerasheva, you can hold back both the demon's ruin and Zansuat's wrath. It's that potent. The Emerald Bow has many qualities you could never understand."

"It belongs to the Emerald Queen."

"She lost it. She's always been careless. Absent-minded."

"You're Her Brother, aren't you? The one they call—"

"Irulan." He smiled. "That's the name I use in Gol."

"Well, sorcerer, god—whoever you are. How can I trust your word?"

"You can't. But neither can you watch your family burn in Dovesi."

"My father's home is in Sarfania, not Dovesi."

The crafty eye pinned him from inside that hood.

"You'll witness the whole catastrophe. He'll make sure of that—unless you prove helpful. You have everything to gain, boy. Your land, kin, and countrymen. These crew who've

suffered hardships few men could endure—all saved from a
terrible fate they don't deserve, if you take the bow when its
offered."

Carlo choked back the emotion rising inside. "What
about Stogi? The Shen girl, and the Garland's soldiers?"

"Collateral damage."

"Why? Can't I save them, too?"

"No. Because they don't exist in your world."

"I cannot do that—they are my friends."

"Then you'll watch your home being destroyed and family
butchered. Over and over, in Yffarn. And Estorien …" The
grin turned cruel.

"What of my brother?"

"The saddest thread of all. His fate will be indirectly
caused by the ancestor of your new friends. Lissane Barola."

"Barola? That family is a stain on the reputation of Gol. A
blight and scourge." Carlo felt anger replacing his dread. Was
this wily schemer playing with him? "What of the Barolan
girl? How does this involve my brother?"

"Accept the bow, Carlo Sarfe. You won't have long to wait.
Don't let me down. I want to help you—after all you've been
through."

The eye probed him one last time, before the hooded face
faded as the mist cleared. He glimpsed a white hawk lifting
and arcing over the castle walls. Carlo steadied himself with
the rail. He felt shaken to the core.

What new madness assails me?

"WHOA, SKIPPER, YOU BEEN DREAMING?" SLIM TAREEL grinned at him as he approached from aft and gazed at the approaching harbor.

"I was just thinking," Carlo said, evading his mate's gaze.

"I've been doing that a lot lately."

"We're need to get home, and fast. We'll disembark soon as Tar's got our supplies ready. I need you and Gurdey watching the ship as I purchase what we need in the marketplace."

"No problem, skip."

"Oh, and Stogi and Tai Pei stay on board. We want to keep this quiet. I don't like Rakeel or Xandorians—and they most likely won't like our friends much, either."

"Got that."

Carlo watched tensely as Gurdey guided the *Arabella* into dock. Gold tossed a bow line, and a docker caught it and tied off.

Twenty minutes later, he was walking briskly through the harbor with Gold Tar and two others alongside.

"Meat and water, ale and brandy. Keep it simple," Carlo told Tar after sharing what coin he had left.

"I don't know why we stopped here," Tar grumbled. "It's a short crossing. We're almost home, skipper."

"I don't trust the weather, especially near Dog Island. It could get rough and stall our arrival."

"That's not the real reason, is it?"

"Just go buy us some good grog, Tar. Leave me with the decisions."

"Right you are, skip."

Irritable, Carlo moved on through the harbor, passing the castle walls. He left the men behind to help Gold Tar and made for the center of the market, where the gold dealers and stock traders tended their wares.

There'd been a fellow he knew worked at the jewelry exchange—a useful contact who spent a good deal of his time in Galanais and Dovess. Carlo wanted news of what was happening back home, especially if it concerned his older brother.

He walked briskly, passing cheese sellers and hawkers shouting out their wares. He smiled when he recognized the chubby face and bald pate of the contact.

"I'm looking for a jade necklace for my lady. It's a special occasion." Carlo reached inside his cloak. "I've honest coin."

"Jade's rare. Expensive this time of year."

"Can you cut me a deal?"

"You'd best come inside, sir." The stocky jeweler ordered a young man to watch over the stall and disappeared inside the trading tent. Carlo followed him and the trader closed the tent flap, making sure no one had seen them enter.

"Carlo!" he flashed a broad grin. "A happy surprise seeing you here. Your family have been asking after you."

"Estorien?"

"Not him—young Kael. Your mother, too. I was in Reveal just last month. A lot has happening since you departed. By the gods, man, you've been gone for months."

"Tell me everything, Taske."

"Wine?" The round-faced trader offered Carlo a chair and pulled one up bedside him. He poured two large glasses of Rakeel Violet. Carlo thanked him and gulped a swallow. He sat leaning forward, his eyes pinning the jeweler.

"Where to start ...? There's news from east and west, you know."

"Start with the name Lissane Barola."

The trader looked shocked. "But how would you know about that?"

"She's involved with my brother?"

"Ha, *no* ... Goodness, man your imagination's on fire."

"I heard her name mentioned in the wind, alongside my brother's."

"Well, Estorien's most likely met the girl, as he spends half his life in Galanais. It's possible they ..." He looked awkward.

"Estorien is in Galanais? Why?"

"It's a known fact to anyone who hasn't been sailing off the edge of the world the last six months. Your big brother Estorien Sarfe was appointed as ambassador by your father. He has a home assigned to him in Galanais, complete with guards and servants. You know what those Galanians are like."

"Deceitful twats, alongside the Barolans."

"Doubtless why they formed the alliance."

"Galania has sided with Barola?"

"Eon Barola married his only daughter to that twisted prick, Varentin. I was in town during the wedding. A rushed affair, I heard. Your brother would have been an honored guest there."

Carlo said nothing, chewing his lip and sipping wine, his head spinning with the news. He needed to find Estorien and get him out of Galanais. So much to do.

"The east?" he asked eventually.

"Well, there's all sorts really, and little good."

"Wars?"

"As always, and we're winning. But those Lamozan turds are stubborn in surrendering. I wasn't talking about that endless bloody skirmish, though. I mean the fires blazing out there."

"Go on ..."

"*Demon fire*, they're calling it. A touch dramatic, but it does seem beyond bad. Devastating blazes. They started in Zorne, raged through Spagos and Ketaq, and I've heard are currently burning crops near the front in Lamoza. Terrible. Then there's the warrior wizard."

Carlo felt his heart thudding in his chest. "Ozmandeus."

"Yes, that's the name on the wind. But again—how do you know that? Were you in Zorne? If so, you ought to be telling me about the fires instead."

For response, Carlo stood shakily and pulled the tent flap open, making sure there was no one near. "Sell your stock, Taske. Buy gold and leave Rakeel. Make for the Island States. Don't go near Gol."

"What nonsense is this?"

"I have it on good authority that the fires coming will destroy this city, and most of Xandoria, too. The fires are caused by the demon Ozmandeus summoned. Gods, but I'm almost out of time." Carlo tossed a gold coin on the jeweler's lap and left him gaping at him speechless.

He left the tent and stall, seeing the trader and his mate watching him and whispering warily. He broke into a run, crashing through the market, receiving harsh stares and the odd shout.

Carlo caught up with Gold Tar purchasing meat. He caught his arm. "Grab what you've got, we're leaving right away."

"We ain't finished yet."

"Do it!"

Carlo left Gold Tar and the others cursing as he returned to the harbor and jumped on board the *Arabella*. He saw Stogi watching him suspiciously.

What has she told them?

Beside him, Tai Pei smiled, her arms folded. She wore new black leather wrist straps embroidered with golden cranes. Carlo stared at them, his mood darkening further.

"You've been ashore."

She shrugged.

Carlo cursed and ignored the pair as he hurried aft to join Slim Tareel.

"We need to move, Slim."

"I'm still waiting on Tar and the others."

"They're on the way. Get her ready to cast off."

"Aye, skip. You hear that, Gurd?" he turned, awarding the wheelmaster a wry grin.

"On it," Gurdey said as the pair stared curiously at their captain. Carlo ignored their gazes. Instead, he spotted the woman, Jenada, who'd mostly kept below decks. She was talking to Tol, who stooped over her, as though listening intently.

That bitch knows what's going on.

Carlo approached, and both Tol and the woman turned and smiled. His grin was friendly, whereas the Cazean seemed expectant.

Carlo waved Tol leave them. "Jenada, will you join me in my cabin?"

She nodded and followed him below. Inside the cabin, Carlo closed the door and poured two glasses of brandy.

She accepted the offered glass with a nod.

"Well …?" Carlo stared into those beguiling brown eyes.

She raised a quizzical brow. "Captain?"

"Why are you here, Jenada? And don't deny that you're turning Stogi and the others against me. What kind of spite drives the wedge your making?"

"It's only fair to warn your new friends that you mean to betray them."

Carlo was about to respond angrily but instead gasped in alarm. Her eyes had shifted color and a cold green-gold gaze held him trapped like butterfly in gossamer.

"Who are you, woman?"

"Not your enemy, Carlo Sarfe. Despite what you may think."

"We're leaving right away," he told her. "You, sorceress, can stay in Rakeel. Save me having to throw you overboard. I'm sailing to Sarfania, where I will warn my kin of what's coming. For I know it's coming, Jenada. It's already underway."

She nodded sagely. "Fire and flood."

"Get off my ship, Jenada, or whoever you really are—woman, witch or spirit. I won't say it again."

Her eyes darkened to angry slits of green and gold. Ancient eyes wrapped in irony and shadow. They locked on him and stole his breath. Eventually, the gaze softened and returned to Jenada's sultry brown. The stranger had gone. Instead, the Cazean nodded wearily, as though recovering from a seizure.

"I will do as you request, captain. But heed my warning. You cannot save your family from the fall of Gol, not without the most terrible outcome. The dice are cast. The new Dance is well underway."

"I would have thought that the death of my kin, my race, and destruction of the entire continent a terrible outcome."

"You don't understand. *Please ...* "

"Drink up and leave, lady—I'll have no more of your meddling."

She smiled wearily and stood, rubbing her hands together.

"As you wish, Carlo Sarfe. I tried. But hear me: If you accept the bow—and I know Irulan's already brokered that with you—you will damn us all to eternal dark."

"I must save my family."

"By sending their souls to Yffarn." She stared long and hard at him. "Goodbye, Carlo Sarfe." Jenada left the cabin with Carlo shaking in rage.

"You're staying in Rakeel? Why?" Stogi felt a stab of disappointment when he heard her plans to sail back to Cazea.

"It's down to you, Stogi. You have to stop him."

"I can't blame a fellow for wanting to save his family from disaster. And he's my friend."

"I don't blame Carlo," she said. "Indeed, I feel nothing but sorrow for his awful plight. But this is much *bigger*. If he accepts the bow, we've already lost. And by *lost*, I mean *everything*."

She placed a warm hand on his arm and smiled. "I'll see you soon, my friend. Watch Carlo carefully, and his crew—especially as you near Dog Island." The woman took the ladder across to the quay. She waved as Gurdey ordered them cast out.

Tol and Taylon joined Stogi as he watched her walking along the jetty.

"What was all that about?" Taylon asked.

"She had a fallout with the captain, I'd guess," Tol said.

Stogi stared at the pair. "You lads need to stay sharp. The next few days will test all of us. Keep your steel ready and well honed."

He left them and walked up to gaze at Tai Pei lurking on the crows' nest above.

"We need to talk," Stogi called up to her. For once, she complied readily enough and swung down gracefully.

"I'm sorry your sweetheart left," Tai Pei said. Stogi glared at her, and she shrugged. "I didn't trust her, Stodge, nor cared for her much."

"Jenada was trying to protect us."

"From Carlo, our beloved captain?"

"Something bad's going to happen near a place called Dog Island."

"You a mystic now, too?"

"She warned—"

"—obviously, and she's right, too." Tai Pei glared back at him. "I don't trust her, but Jenada's right about Carlo. He won't be able to resist what they offer. Especially when the thief arrives."

"How …? What do you know, Tai Pei?"

"That if you, or I, or those two …" She pointed over at Tol and Taylon. "If any of us from back there set foot on Gol, we will perish. Vanish forever, like dust in a hurricane. Not only our bodies—our souls, too."

"You agree with Jenada?"

"Yes, but she's not about helping you. Rather about controlling, as they always want to. Whereas I am your friend."

Stogi rubbed his earrings and stifled a yawn. He felt angry and perplexed, but that was nothing new. He summoned what little patience he could muster.

"What's the connection between you and Jenada? I know you studied astrology and such." He didn't want to mention the other woman he'd seen inside Jenada's face. Turned out he didn't have to.

"Urdei's sister links us. Didn't you think it strange that we haven't heard from the blonde child since leaving the hooded island? Vervandi came instead. They both know the stakes at play here. Hence, two of the Fates are involved."

"That's not good." Stogi twisted a ring in his ear, until it snapped off. He swore and glanced down at the blood on his finger. She looked at him sideways. "What do you mean to do?"

"Is it not obvious? Kill Carlo Sarfe and his crew."

"What …? *Why?*"

"Because you're too weak, Stogi. Too damn loyal and blighted with the biggest heart possessed by any man I've ever known. But I'm an ice-cold killer and good at what I do."

"But I thought you loved Carlo?"

"I like him, yes. Carlo's a good man. *Shame.* But that's not important. Besides, it's always been you, Stodge. Since the day we met in the Shen mines."

"You … *me? What?*"

"You daft, bow-legged, fat, hairy fool. I've loved you since the moment I first set eyes on your ugly face. That's why I've stayed around to keep you safe."

She placed a fleeting kiss on his lips and left him gasping for air like the hooked fish he was.

CARLO JOLTED WHEN HE HEARD THE KNOCK. HE OPENED the door and wasn't surprised to see Tai Pei standing there, a half-smile and glint showing in her dark eyes. Freshly kohled, and her long, sleek hair spilling loose. She looked radiant in green silk gown and trousers.

Gods, but I'm weary.

"You're angry about Jenada, I know." He bid her take a seat on his bunk as he slumped into his chair, the evening sun glinting gold through the porthole.

She shook her head. "She was Stogi's pal, not mine."

"Aren't you curious as to why she came? And why I made her leave?"

"Not my concern—you're the captain. The king of this ship." Her dark eyes glistened wickedly.

"Jenada warned me to stay away from Gol. Said that by trying to alter … what's coming … I would bring on disaster. As if a drowned continent wasn't portentous enough for her."

"You look drained—you should sleep while you can."

"I'll be fine. Just tell me why you're here, if it's not about the Cazean woman."

"I'm worried about you, Captain Carlo. What are your plans? You can no longer deny that disaster's coming to Gol. It must have sunk in that you can't save Sarfania."

"I can warn my kin and people. Take who I can in the *Arabella* and return to Rakeel. From there, maybe head north, avoiding the demon's breath and tidal wash. Or back to the Island States, though not Cazea."

She snorted derision. "You'll be lucky to cram twenty people on this tub. What about everyone else?"

"Reveal harbor is full of all manner of craft." Carlo knew he was floundering. "Aside that, people can journey north and cross at the isthmus, or take their chance on hiring a boat at Galanais. At least they'll be warned. That's all I can do. And I *will* save my family, Tai Pei."

She nodded, her eyes misting over.

"I'm sorry I disturbed you, captain. I will leave you be."

"No ... *stay*, please do." He smiled and offered her a glass of brandy. She declined, but sat neatly on the bunk, her lips slightly parted.

"I feel I've always been short with you, Tai Pei. I never understood why you joined us when you could have stayed in Shen. I know they were after you, but surely someone with your talent would be fine."

"I had my reasons," she said, her dark gaze probing his. She raised a brow and smiled. "Are you sure that you want me to stay?"

"I do," he said, and before he realized it, he reached across and kissed her mouth.

26

BEYOND DOG ISLAND

GARLAND WATCHED the shore blazing orange to the north. It was late afternoon, and for three days they'd sailed east with the winds picking up. It was dry and hot during the day, but the nights were colder, and he suspected autumn was nearly over.

He stood with Doyle on the prow as the ship bucked and cut through chop. The coast of Lamoza steamed like baked clay several miles to the north.

"Looks like our time's running short," his friend said, watching the distant fires.

"Aye, it's started. First demon fire. Next the flood." Defying the grim skies, he smiled at Doyle. "I'm glad you came here, boy. Never expected to see you again."

"What else could I have done? Queen Ariane summoned me—it wasn't like I had a choice."

"The Goddess has spoken to our queen, as She apparently did in the old days. Sent her to stop Carlo Sarfe from reaching his home. It's a tad fucking tenuous, Doyle."

"What did she tell you?"

"Very little. And I've not seen her since yesterday. But Ariane allowed Zorc to accompany us, though he's to stay put in my cabin."

Doyle shook his head. "An Urgolais. Cale, Fassyan, and most the crew think the foul creature has a hold over you."

"What about you, Doyle?"

"Nah, I don't believe it. You're the same stubborn-arsed hardnose I remember. I did worry about you in Laregoza, especially when that Rana woman got hold of you."

"Ah, the Rana. I'd almost forgotten about her. An interesting lady."

"Pash shouldn't have stirred things up the way he did."

"Pash is dead—the others, too."

"All of them?" Doyle's face was shocked.

"I believe so, though I'm not sure what happened to Tol and Taylon. Those fucking woods, Doyle. Rundali. Terrible place. You're fortunate you skipped that journey."

"She's on deck." Doyle said quietly, having glanced around.

Garland turned and saw Ariane standing by Taic at the wheel. She was looking at the blaze to the north, her face worried.

"I'll go see what she has planned," Garland told his former second, who nodded and returned his gaze to the distant shore.

"Highness," Garland dipped his head as he approached her. Taic grinned greeting and seemed casual as ever.

"It's already underway," she said, looking north.

"Since this morning," he said. "A constant blaze lining the hills."

"Lamoza. I've been studying old maps. Taic says it could be three weeks before we arrive at Rakeel."

"I think those flames will get there quicker," Garland said.

Ariane looked at him sideways. "You want me to ask your sorcerer for help, don't you? Well …? Be frank with me, captain."

Taic coughed and looked the other way.

Garland stared at her sheepishly and nodded.

"My head warns we should turn about and sail back west. Hope somehow, return to our own time. But the Goddess needs us to stop poor Carlo. The only way we can do that is by getting to Gol before he does. Before those fires or Sensuata Himself destroys the place. Perhaps the Goddess will help us?"

"We cannot presume. Elanion most likely can't intervene."

"Then what choice do we have, highness, but to take what aid is offered, however unsavory?"

"You are right. I'll talk to that … *fiend*. Go fetch it."

Garland bowed and went below, entering the squat cabin he shared with the Urgolais. Zorc was seated on an upturned bucket, blinking up at him in the candlelight. He'd placed a cloth over the porthole.

"You need some air."

"I'd sooner stay put."

"She wants to talk to you."

"She hates me."

"True. But this is your chance to win her over."

"Slim chance."

"It worked with me."

"You're a halfwit, soldier. She's the Goddess's favorite queen. A headstrong bloody zealot, and she has a loathing of my race."

"As does everyone else. Are you coming?"

Zorc grumbled and followed him back out on deck.

Ariane had seated herself on a brass-studded ebony trunk near the aft mast. She watched their approach, her dark eyes angry.

Zorc shuffled up behind Garland and attempted a low bow—a hideous gesture that made his knees click as he almost buckled. Ariane glared at Garland, who hoisted Zorc under an arm as he struggled to stand.

"It seems we need your help, Urgolais." The queen stared coldly at them both.

"At your service." Zorc attempted a bow again. Garland pulled a face.

"Stop that, for fuck's sake," she snapped irritably. "Captain Garland tells me you know a great deal about our venture."

"I know who your enemies are, queen. For they are my foes too."

"That's rich coming from an Urgolais warlock."

Zorc sighed. "As I said to Garland, I'm not like those others you encountered in the last war. They were corrupted by the warlock Morak, Shadowman curse his name."

"Says you."

"Because it's true," Zorc hissed, causing her to raise a brow at Garland.

"We'll award you benefit of doubt … if you prove useful," she said, again glancing at Garland.

He nodded. "You can't let me down, Zorc. I vouched for you."

Zorc glared at them both. "What would you have me do?"

"Find Carlo Sarfe and allow us to catch up with him. Garland says you have a spell glass that crosses through time and dimensions? Perhaps we should look at that first?"

Zorc fumbled in his coat and produced the cylindrical object. He passed it over to her. She glanced at Garland. He nodded.

"You have to twist the end," he said.

She gingerly placed the narrow lens to her eye and twisted the front. She squinted and cursed. "It's too fucking blurry."

"Keep twisting," Zorc said.

She tried again. "Oh, that's better. Where should I look?"

"To the east, probably, since that's where we're heading."

"You can't talk to her like that," Garland hissed, but Ariane hadn't noticed the sarcasm. She swept her gaze back and forth with the Urgolais glass.

"Any luck?" Garland asked her.

"Yes, *no*. I think I've found Gol. I followed the coastline, altering the focus, and it showed the mountains and Xenn City beyond. I recognized Rakeel by the ancient texts. The castle and harbor. Then the gulf beyond, and what must be Galanais."

She placed the glass down and looked excited. "My ancestor, Lissane—Kell's lover and mother of the first high king—she's in that city waiting for her lover, Estorien Sarfe. I'm seeing our past, Garland."

"Keep scanning," Zorc said, eyeing Garland wryly. "Try further south."

She lifted the glass again and turned the dial. "That must be Sarfania. A swamp. Oh, there are strange rocks resembling some sort of distorted castle. I think I've gone too far. Yes, open sea again."

"Steer clear from that castle," Zorc hissed. "Bad place. Avoid the Aralais's lair. Erun Cade won't have got there yet."

"What?" Garland blinked at Zorc, who shook his head. They waited as she gazed back and forth with the glass for several minutes.

"I think I've found him," she said at last, smiling with satisfaction, and passing the glass to Garland.

He placed his eye against the lens and again was shocked by the clarity. He could see a rocky island surrounded by clouds. Beyond that, a line of low cliffs flattened into a steamy marsh. He scrolled closer and saw what must be Reveal harbor surrounded by clear water and marsh. A hidden wooden-stilted fortress with secret pathways and snares.

"Do you see the ship?" she demanded.

"Not yet." Garland pulled his focus from the marsh and returned to the sea, sweeping back slowly toward the rocky isle. "There's an island. The glass keeps pulling my gaze there. Oh, now I see the ship."

Garland recognized the crimson sails as he twisted the cap and brought the sight closer. He saw the figurehead carving of a beautiful woman and read the words, *Lady Arabella* painted below. "He's steering too close to that island."

Ariane snatched the glass from him and pressed it to her eye. Zorc grinned. "She likes the spell glass," he said. "Perhaps I should offer it as a gift?"

"Sssh," Garland waved him quiet.

"That must be Dog Island. It lies west of Galania. He's almost home," she told them, her eyes shining.

Garland nodded and was about to add something when a distant shimmer caught his gaze. He touched Zorc's cloak, and the Urgolais's ruined lips drew back in fear.

"Time for me to go below," he said.

"What is that?" Garland asked him, while the queen still watched with the glass.

"Her." Zorc replied and left them fast as he could. Garland called after him, but the Urgolais vanished below decks.

The shimmer became a shape. A large white bird, floating on the waves, bobbing and drifting toward them. A swan. Pure and graceful, wings arched.

"Highness ..." He tapped her shoulder

Ariane withdrew the glass and glared at him.

"What? Where's Zorc gone?"

Garland pointed at the swan approaching with uncanny speed.

"Goddess ..." Ariane gasped and sank to her knees. Garland followed her lead. The swan glided close, and its shape shifted, becoming a tall woman striding through the waves.

Clad in diamonds, she stood over them and pointed east. Garland saw a rainbow spreading across the ocean, in its midst a vast arch opening on a different sky. Even as he watched, the giant woman faded and the swan disappeared. Instead, he glimpsed a white hawk circling high above and crying out in plaintive, shrill calls.

"You must sail beneath the arch," a familiar voice said. Garland turned and saw the child Urdei smiling at him. "That way, you'll arrive on the island before he does."

"Carlo's landing on Dog Island?" Baffled, Garland glared at the child. Ariane didn't seem to have noticed her. She was still gazing at the arch, as though trapped in a trance.

Urdei placed a finger to her lips and smiled. "Your queen doesn't know I'm here. Make for the arch. Sail beneath. And be careful—this Dog Island is not what it appears."

"What awaits us there?"

"Revealing that would spoil the fun," Urdei laughed and vanished from his sight.

Ariane shook herself and nearly dropped Zorc's glass.

"The Goddess spoke to me. Dog Island has shifted to the same dimension as Laras Lassladen and Graywash Hall. The thief is there—the bow, too. They are luring Carlo close. We need to get there first."

"I'll pass that on to Taic," Garland said shakily.

"Beneath the arch," she told him.

Minutes later, Garland watched with eyes wide as the ship drifted, as though pulled by hidden chains toward the huge, shifting golden archway. A thousand feet high it appeared, the stones and lintels shaped with mason precision. He heard music as they glided close, the soulful notes of a harp drifting up and merging with the pink clouds that swelled and bubbled around the arch's lofty crown.

Ant-tiny and insignificant as dust, the ship sailed beneath that mighty stone. Like two mile-high leaning pillars, the arch walls reared at either side. Garland saw faces carved on the stone.

Gods and demons—some beautiful, others hideous to behold. The faces gazed back at him, their eyes cold and piti-less, seeping into his soul. He looked away, focusing on the murmuring ahead. A wall of gray water rushing toward them.

"Going to get bumpy," he heard Taic yelling from behind.

"Highness, you'd best go below," Garland urged Ariane, who still seemed half in a dream.

She gazed back at him, her face lit by the gold of the Arch's shadow. "There is nothing to fear, Captain Garland. Elanion the Protector is with us."

The wall of water rose impossibly high. Garland worried they would drown, but he stood firm beside his queen. Watching and waiting, his heart thudding in his chest. Big hands on sword.

The wave broke around them and vanished. Garland heard bells tolling and saw huge creatures emerging, their triangular heads cresting the waves.

The arch had gone, as had the coast to the north. Instead, they clipped through a charcoal sea beneath the starry night sky. An island loomed a mile off to the right. A single light glinted out from a tall white tower.

"Make for that light," Ariane shouted back to Taic.

"Dog Island resembled a bare rock when I saw it with the glass," Garland said, not happy confronting sorcery again.

"That isn't the same Dog Island," she said. "We've shifted dimensions again. Or, rather, that tower has followed us here."

"You know this place, highness?"

"I believe I do. Surely that's Laras Lassladen, where Elanion holds court."

Her eyes were feverish with excitement. Garland wished he could share the emotion. He felt only dread.

"Kerasheva must be there. The thief never left Her island, and She has guided us to him. Carlo as well."

"But Highness, how can a mere thief defy Elanion so brazenly? Surely, this is a trap …"

"Sssh!" She waved him be silent, shaking her head and pointing off to the right. Garland saw the lanterns glinting over the crimson sails of Carlo's ship. The *Arabella* was making for the tower, too.

Trap or not, they would soon find out.

SHE'D LEFT AN HOUR AGO, CREEPING OUT WITHOUT A sound. Carlo had drifted off soon after she'd gone. He woke with a throbbing head, rolled from the bunk, and stood blinking and confused at the bright shaft of light shining in through the porthole.

Not sunlight. It flickered for a minute and winked out, replaced by gloom. Lightning? He didn't think so. He dressed quickly and clambered up onto deck. Dry Gurdey greeted him with a shrug.

"I saw lights—a storm, maybe? Another ship?"

"Nothing to report," Gurdey said.

Almost evening, steady chop. Carlo studied the chart by Gurdey's hut. "We should have raised Dog Island by now."

"Passed that while you were kipping."

"We're almost home." Carlo grinned at his wheel master, but Gurdey's' face had blanched.

"Fuck ..."

"What ...?" Carlo saw where he was looking. A dark wrack of cloud loomed over pointed rocks approaching fast, the sea frothing white around them. "Steer away, man!

Gurdey spun the wheel averting the rocks. "Those rocks shouldn't be here."

"You must have drifted off course."

"No way." They cleared the outcrops, but the darkness above seemed to follow them. Some kind of storm rising to the east. It didn't look promising.

The darkness reached out and cloaked the skies above. Carlo heard sounds, the drumming of rain drops on the sails, and what was that? The laughter of a child? The barely audible chime of a bell?

This storm isn't natural.

A thud and grind sent him sprawling. Gurdey clung to the wheel, cursing.

"You've hit a fucking rock, Gurd!" Carlo stared in disbelief as the dark mass of an island rose up to greet them. "I thought you steered clear?"

"I did, damn you." Gurdey wrenched on the wheel again, and the *Arabella* lurched to larboard. For brief moments, Carlo saw open water and escape before the wall of rock blocked their path yet again. "It's hopeless, skip. We're caught in a whirlpool that keeps turning us around. It's brought us back on Dog Island."

Carlo felt an icy cold trickle down his spine. "I don't recall seeing lights on Dog Island."

"What's that?"

"Over there, off starboard, half a mile."

"Looks like some kind of tower."

"There's no tower on the Dogs—just fucking crags. It's sorcery, damn it. Someone's blocking us," Carlo said. "Make for the light."

"Are you mad?"

"Do it, Gurdey."

The wheelmaster glared at him but turned the wheel toward the distant tower and found the resistance disappear, replaced by a helpful breeze guiding them closer.

The rocks circled and closed in around them, like crab claws. It was gloomy, almost twilight, the dark cloud floating above. They'd entered a deep cove of sorts. Carlo saw the tower rising needle-tall a mile ahead, standing remote on the crest of the highest rock.

Off to the right, lightning jabbed down. Carlo winced. For the briefest instant, he saw a man watching from the nearest outcrop. Clad in checkered tunic and trousers, his head covered with a three-pointed hat with bells on each corner. The face was masked in the guise of a golden owl. The jester figure leaned on a bow that gleamed emerald bright in the lamplight. Carlo sucked in a sharp breath.

Kerasheva.

The jester lifted the bow in both hands high over his head. He shook it and brought it down on his knees, and lightning struck the ground where he stood. A white bird settled by the checkered man, who lifted the bow high again. The bird changed, and Carlo saw cloaked Irulan staring at him with that chilling single eye.

"It is time, Carlo Sarfe," Irulan called across to him with his gravelly voice. "Master Keel has brought the bow. You must cast anchor where you are. Join us here and claim your destiny. Save your kin and country."

"The tower?" Carlo yelled back across the water. "Its light is seeking us."

"You must stay away from the tower." Irulan's voice reached him easily, despite the distance. Carlo felt the ship lurch and start dragging, as though caught in a riptide or sudden current.

"She's heading for the rocks again," Gurdey yelled in his ear. "I can't …"

"Gold Tar, drop the anchor," Carlo called across to the bosun. As he yelled, he saw Irulan's face lit up by lightning. The hooded figure motioned the checkered archer to step forward. The bowman bowed low and snatched a glittering arrow from the sky, and Carlo saw him pull back and loose.

He's aiming at us.

"Duck! Arrow!" He watched the shaft arc high and drop, stone-swift, striking the *Arabella's* deck amidships. The timbers exploded in his ears, splinters shot in all directions, Gurdey and the crew vanished, and Carlo found himself flying through cold, wet air.

A STRONG HAND CAUGHT HIM, AND SOMEONE SPOKE.

"He's alive, seems unhurt."

Carlo staggered and blinked. He opened an eye and stood shaking.

What the fuck?

Two strangers stared at him: a wiry-framed man with canny dark eyes, and a red-haired, hard-faced woman he vaguely recognized.

"Good to see you again, Carlo Sarfe," the redhead said, her fierce gaze a mix of gold and brown. Behind her, a huge, square rock swelled and manifested out of the gloom.

"You need to come with us, old son," the skinny man said.

"I know this place." Carlo felt his feet sinking into hot rock. The woman grabbed at him, but her face faded.

"Carlo … don't give in to them. You'll betray us all …" Her voice drifted away, as the rock rose around him.

They'd gone.

Instead, a horseman watched him in silence, a morning star thrust out from his saddle. Carlo gulped as he recognized Sir Valen the Gaunt by the greenish hue emitting from his armor. Surrounding the faceless knight were seven hounds, jaws slavering and blood-red ears glinting in the gloom. Sir Valen swung his mace, and Carlo saw pale figures with long harpoons surrounding him—other men, too. One had hard, glassy gray eyes, and another carried a double-headed axe.

Finally, the jester with the bow appeared smiling before him.

"You work for us now, Carlo Sarfe," the archer said, his voice cool and arrogant. "Come, claim your wages."

"Where is this place—am I back in Graywash Hall?"

The archer removed his pointed hat, shaking free his long silver hair. His eyes stared at Carlo through the owl mask. Green eyes, colder than a cat.

"I'm Keel," the archer-jester said. "I'm offering you this bow."

Carlo felt the hot rocks slither from his feet. The archer, Keel, reached out with both hands, the bow held level. Carlo felt Irulan's eye burning into his back.

"Take Kerasheva," the god told him. "Save your people. This is your chance!"

Carlo stepped forward and reached for the weapon.

Someone yelled, and a shadow crossed his path. He glimpsed Tai Pei's white face before the ground erupted and he found himself falling again.

27

AN ULTIMATUM

"Rocks!" Cale yelled the warning as Garland watched in dread alongside Queen Ariane, with Doyle and Fassyan huddled behind. The weather had changed suddenly as they approached the island, the stars smothered by dark masses of clouds and squally rain lashing down.

Taic and two others struggled with the wheel. It was hopeless. Some invisible current forced them toward the rocks, and quickly. The tower had disappeared behind a large outcrop. He could see the light filtering, searching. There was no sign of Carlo's ship.

Taic swore and put all his weight behind the wheel. *Kraken Girl* lurched and slid past the gravelly base of weed-strewn rocks. Barely, she scraped through. Garland winced, seeing the barnacles grind and tear the strakes.

A sailor cried out and tumbled as one of the stays snagged and snapped, tossing his body overboard.

Taic yelled for a rope, but it was hopeless. They'd passed the rocks, and no man could survive long in that current. Garland closed his eyes. The clouds closed in, and a fog filtered out from a dark line of shore, framed by more rocks. It had gotten almost dark.

"Where's the tower?" Cale yelled at Taic.

"I can't see shit," the Northman yelled back.

"It will find us," Ariane said behind him. Garland turned and nodded. "There are wicked forces at play here," she told him. "They want to steer us away from Laras Lassladen."

"I thought this island *was* Laras Lassladen?" Garland said.

She shook her head, but it was Zorc who answered him. "The tower is caught inside the rock. Don't you see?" The wretched Urgolais looked worse than usual, his coat soaked and battered, and his ugly face shrunken like a rotting apple, almost hidden inside the hood.

"What's it talking about?" Cale glared at Zorc.

"Graywash Hall," Zorc glared back at him from the hood. "It's all around us, fools. The clouds. Current and rain—all are working to its pattern. It's blocking us from the tower."

"That's too bad, but we need to find Carlo Sarfe. Did anyone see what happened to the *Arabella*?" Garland said.

"She's likely grounded and sunk," Taic said, not over-helpfully.

"Carlo's here," Ariane said. "They won't harm him."

"They?" Garland said.

"The Kaa, you dolt—have you been asleep all month?" Zorc's eyes bulged. "We crossed the dimensions again under that arch. The Kaa were alerted—Sir Valen, too. Graywash Hall was already closing on Carlo."

"Then why's that tower trapped inside?"

"Because Graywash Hall and Laras Lassladen are the same fucking thing," Zorc yelled. "Or, rather, two manifestations: dark side and light. The spinning coin, but which side will land face up?" He started cackling inanely.

"Shut up," Ariane told the Urgolais.

"Looks like we're grounding," Taic shouted. "Hang on, people."

Garland saw a thin, jagged line emerging through the treacle black. A stony beach. Mercifully, the rocks had parted, and *Kraken Girl* scraped and lifted onto gravel.

He gripped the rail, saw Zorc tumble, and scooped him up with his free hand. Behind him, Ariane swore, and Cale knocked his head against the boom mast.

"You all right?" Garland asked, as the ship skidded to a halt.

Cale grinned back at him. "Nothing in here worth damaging," he said, tapping his head.

"Her hull's breached," Taic said mournfully as he joined them. "We won't be sailing out of this cove anytime soon."

Ariane stared coolly back at him. "Do what you can, Taic. You and your men stay here. Cale and Fassyan will accompany me. We search for Carlo Sarfe. He has to be here somewhere. This place is a net to lure him. Garland, you and Doyle can accompany us, too. And you'd best bring him." Her eyes flashed to where Zorc sat shaking, his ruined fingers grabbling the torn coat around his knees.

Kraken Girl had listed to larboard, making it easy to clamber over the side and jump down. Cale went first, sword in hand, followed by Fassyan with his bow, an arrow nocked and ready. Ariane descended next, her eyes scanning the rocks as the mist pulled back, showing a faint path ahead. She wore her swords, the green cloak swirling around her legs as she strode.

Doyle dropped and walked behind, sword held ready. Last up, Garland took the rear with Zorc, a gloved hand resting on the heavy broadsword. Zorc, hobbling with his twisted stave, muttered incomprehensible obscenities beside him.

Cale shouted back, and Garland saw the mist had almost cleared ahead. The tower stood a half-mile to their right, crowning and dominating a windswept crag. The white light shone out over their heads, ranging back and forth.

"It's searching for Carlo Sarfe, too," Ariane called out. "Come on! We need to get to the tower."

"That's looking unlikely," Cale shouted.

"Aye, we've company," Fassyan called back.

Garland cursed, seeing Sir Valen appear out of the mist, guiding his green horse down the track leading from the tower. Surrounding the faceless knight were snarling dogs and half a dozen men. He recognized Shale's hard face as the brigand pointed at him and laughed.

Other figures rose from the fading mist at either side. Gaunt and pale, the skinny Kaa surrounded them with their long-barbed harpoons.

"Seems we're fucked," Cale said as Garland caught him up.

The Kaa blocked their retreat and pressed in on each side. Sir Valen spurred his horse and cantered closer as Shale and the other men yelled and followed behind. Ahead, the dogs jumped and snapped hungrily.

"Aye, we're definitely fucked," Cale said.

"Shut up," Ariane glared back at him. She had her sword held ready. "You and I have faced worse than these … whoever the fuck they are."

"That's unlikely." A new voice.

Someone had spoken from behind. Garland turned in shock, seeing a large figure emerge from the gloom. Where had he come from? A burly figure wrapped in a heavy woolen coat. He carried a long, metal, fluted tube over his right shoulder.

He'd seen the man before. It was the one who saved him from the sucking mud after he and Zorc fled the Beguiler on the beach.

Dunrae Tarn.

"Well, I'll be buggered," Zorc chortled. "The Avenger. It's good to see you."

"I'm not here to help you, Urgolais, toe-rag," the newcomer said in a rough accent.

The big man swung the heavy tube from his shoulders and glared at Sir Valen, who Garland noticed had stopped his canter and stood high in his stirrups, the morning star resting at his side. The Kaa backed away, though Shale and his men remained put. They looked wary, edgy. Even the dogs were quiet, their tails slunk below their legs.

"Who are you, stranger?" Ariane asked.

Dunrae Tarn looked at her casually, before switching his steely gaze across to Garland. "Journeyman," he nodded briefly. "We met briefly. Remember?"

"I do. You freed me from …"

"You stay put with me, old son. Zorc, you too. We'll keep 'em busy, us three. Queen, you and your men need to get inside that tower, and fast. The Sea God's coming, and He's not happy with you, my dear."

"What … *who are you?*" Ariane glared at him, her swords held level. Garland saw Sir Valen trotting in circles.

"Do as he says," Zorc hissed at her. "I know this man."

Ariane stared at Garland. He nodded. "Zorc's right. He's helped us before. And they seem wary of him, highness."

"But the way ahead is blocked," Cale said, pointing to where Sir Valen sat his horse.

"If you move, matey, I'll unblock it for you," Dunrae Tarn said, showing the ghost of a grin. "Stand aside."

They complied without further word. Garland watched, amazed, as the big man aimed the cylinder up the hill. He saw Shale and the other men duck. He blinked in astonishment as a flame flashed bright, followed by a roar and blast echoing out across the beach.

"Fuck …" Cale muttered, beside him.

Garland saw the path had cleared ahead.

"Go!" Dunrae Tarn shouted.

Ariane stared at him wild-eyed for a moment before nodding.

"Stay alive," she ordered Garland, before turning and running up the track with Cale, Doyle and Fassyan close behind her.

Garland saw them clearing the rise as the mist peeled back and the Kaa reemerged from the rocks, where they'd taken cover from Dunrae Tarn's booming deviltry.

"Zorc, you might need to work something out," the man in the coat said. "I need your friend here to find Carlo Sarfe before Valen's yobs get to him. Keep these bastards busy, Croaky. I know you've a few tricks up those rotting Urgo sleeves. Meanwhile, I'll deal with Sir Valen."

The knight had returned and sat his horse, the morning star swinging high over his head. Dunrae leveled the weapon again. This time, Garland covered his ears.

Tai Pei stood before Carlo, her eyes narrow with rage. The jester, Keel, had his knife around her throat. She'd acted fast, but he'd been quicker. Beside him, a glassy-eyed man held the bow, his hard gaze watching Carlo.

"Take the bow from Shale, and I'll let her live," Keel said. "Quickly—else she dies."

Tai Pei strained to speak, but he jabbed the knife into her throat. Carlo yelled, seeing her eyes bulge in horror.

"Stop!" Carlo held up his hands. "I'll do as you say, but remove the dagger from her throat."

"First take the bow."

"Not until you free Tai Pei."

"She isn't important." Keel flashed him a grin, as though he found the situation amusing. Perhaps he did, the evil bastard. Carlo channeled his rage.

I'm not sinking yet.

"I love her!" He forced the words out, glaring at the jester.

"Quaint," Keel's mask curled in a sneer. "But that's too bad. Because either way, you're shafted. I kill her and you lose everything—your family, kin and country. Take the bow, and she's doomed anyway, as are the others not of your time. Unless they accompany me to the Hall—everyone's welcome there. The Orb's not fussy. Including this sparky girl. We've always got space. Best I can offer." Keel glanced at his companion, who nodded and lifted the bow to offer it out. Carlo stepped forward.

Tai Pei was wriggling and making mewling noises. "Don't!" she spat, and he dug the knife deeper. Carlo saw blood streaking her neck.

"Release her, and I'll take the bow," Carlo said, feeling his heart thump as he saw the trickle bead on her white skin.

"It doesn't work like that." Keel's cruel green eyes pinned Carlo. He didn't notice the insect appearing above his head. Carlo did and felt a fierce surge of hope. A golden wasp with eyes the color of cornflowers. It droned, hovered, and dived inside Keel's owl mask, biting his left eye.

The jester cursed as blood covered his mask, clouding his vision. Tai Pei broke free and ran across to Carlo. The insect had moved to Shale and was biting him. Carlo could hear Irulan's crow voice booming from somewhere.

"Take the bow, Carlo. Before it's too late!"

The wasp was still biting the faces of the jester and his servant. Kerasheva lay in the dirt. Slowly, Carlo walked toward it.

"Don't do it," Tai Pei hissed, clutching the gash in her neck.

"I have to save my family, Tai Pei."

The wasp swelled and puckered, becoming a slender woman with slanted milky eyes standing before him.

"I'm Coristain, of Faerie. I've come back through time to help you, Carlo Sarfe, fulfilling a vow I made in your future. There is a way through this conundrum, but you must take the bow and come with me."

Before he could move, another figure emerged from the gloom. A smallish man with red hair and gold-flecked brown eyes.

The man stooped and quickly grabbed Kerasheva before Carlo could react. He flashed him a grin and vanished, reappearing by the water.

"I'm taking this," the redhead said. But before he turned away, Keel's gloved fist batted into the side of his head, knocking him forward.

Shale grabbed the bow and held it across for Carlo, as Keel and the red-haired stranger rolled and tumbled in combat.

Take it." Hooded Irulan emerged from the gloom and

stood beside Shale, his silver eye blazing at Carlo. "Now! I will not be thwarted."

The god's iron will worked upon him. Carlo stumbled and nodded slowly.

"I will do this for my family." He ran up and grabbed Kerasheva, lifting the emerald bow with both hands.

"No!" Tai Pei screamed as he glanced down, feeling the wonderful weapon in his fingers.

I have to ... He turned and stared at her, just as the dagger plunged into his chest. She twisted the blade and withdrew it quickly, her dark eyes wet with tears.

"I'm sorry," she said, and stabbed him again.

"Tai Pei ..."

Carlo dropped the bow and clutched his gaping chest, the blood seeping out. He felt no pain, only relief.

Not my problem anymore.

He sank to his knees and the world went black.

28

ALLIES AND ADVERSARIES

GARLAND FOLLOWED Dunrae Tarn through the dark mass of stone. He saw creatures writhing inside the rock. There were beady eyes watching him like trapped bugs, their stare cruel, alien, and wicked.

"Where are we going?"

One of the bugs leaped at his face. He swatted it back into the oozing stone. It sunk within and faded back to nothing.

"Away from the light," the big man said. "Time is short."

Garland saw lightning striking the sea ahead, and booms of thunder rolled past as storm clouds mustered like blue-flashing towers in the distance. He reached a precipice and almost fell. The big man gripped his arm, steadying him.

"Down here."

"Why are you helping us, Dunrae Tarn? How do you know Zorc?" Garland asked, his mind struggling to absorb what was happening.

"No time to explain, mate. Be happy that Marei is safe— the girl and her baby, too. They know I'm helping you."

Garland felt a flood of relief. *They're safe?* He wanted to ask further, but the man shook his head.

"Quit jabbering and follow me. You'll need to concentrate and watch your step." Tarn bid him follow down the steep shale slope. Garland started descended precariously, using the sword as a prop. Hard to see where to place your feet. Treacherous, slippery, and steep—almost dark under those broiling clouds. They slipped and slid for what seemed like ages as the lightning show lit up the sky and black oily water beyond.

"Where is he?" Garland shouted eventually, as wind rose chill, whipping his soaked hair around his eyes and almost stealing what little vision he retained.

Dunrae Tarn didn't reply but signaled him to hurry. Garland sighed with relief when they reached the bottom and trudged through a rain-filled valley, the lightning spears striking the path ahead like javelins tossed by some angry god.

Which is probably what they are, thought Garland grimly.

The rain worsened. Drenched, they reached a narrowing where the road tapered into a squeeze between two large rocks. Once through, Garland wiped the rain from his eyes, blinking at a stony shore and the wreckage of two ships bobbing beyond.

"We're gone full circle," he muttered, dismally.

Dunrae Tarn walked briskly off to the right. "This way."

Garland followed miserably. They were achieving nothing.

He stopped abruptly when he saw a woman. She was odd-looking—too thin, and yet beautiful. Her milky eyes had no pupils, and the disheveled hair was a cascade of silver streaked with gold.

Her skin was flawless and shimmered with a pale blue haze reflected in her silver gown. Garland saw the clasps at her breasts that resembled tiny butterflies, the diamond wings lifting and closing like clams in tides, as her secretive smile deepened. He thought of Ysaren, the blue witch he'd encountered back at the Lake of Stones. This woman appeared younger but had a similar look.

"Journeyman and Avenger. You heroes arrive too late." Her voice was dreamy, alluring, and full of sly promises.

"Lady Coristain." Dunrae Tarn warned Garland back. "Let me deal with this elf—she's beyond crafty," he said in a whisper.

"Elf?"

"Where's Sarfe?" Dunrae Tarn demanded, glaring the witchy woman.

Coristain rewarded him with a beautiful smile laced with irony. "I've already said you are *too late*, Avenger. We have lost him."

"Carlo's dead?" Garland asked her, but she ignored him.

"Where's the body?" Dunrae Tarn demanded.

The woman smiled sadly and faded from view.

Dunrae Tarn cursed and slung his cylinder down. "You know things are fucked when the elves appear."

"Where did she come from?"

"Same place we've got to go. The Void."

"What …?"

"That's where we'll find our sailor."

"She told us he's dead."

"I know what she said." He reached down and hoisted the weapon back over his shoulder. "Should have guessed this wouldn't prove easy. Grab my arm, Journeyman."

"Before that, promise me Marei is safe?"

He nodded, holding his hand out. "Aye, for the meanwhile. But we'll need to get back there. Everything's got skewed."

"As usual, I don't understand."

"Grab."

Garland gripped the offered hand.

"She called you *Avenger*, as did Zorc. Who are you? What part do you play in this … nightmare?"

"Shut up and hold on tight. Here we go, matey!"

Dunrae Tarn pulled him forward with a jerk. Garland felt a hot swirl of gas erupt around his face. Beneath him, the ground vanished, and cold fingers of steam reached out for him and pulled him down.

"Close your eyes," Dunrae Tarn yelled as they fell through the steaming gas. "That way, the Chaos creatures can't get inside your head and mangle your brains."

Garland did as he was told, holding back a scream as hot wind stung his cheeks and mouth. They were falling fast. He heard shrill laughter and the scraping of metal fingers on harp strings. The pain faded. He felt his body hit a soft floor, like mulched leaves in a wintry wood.

"Open 'em," Dunrae said from somewhere close.

Garland blinked. He saw the man standing staring off at a bland, empty horizon, the barrel weapon still slung casually over a shoulder. The long blue coat flapping without wind.

"This is the Void?"

Dunrae Tarn placed a finger to his lips. "You passed through it safely before. No questions—don't even think 'em. Keep your mind neutral, else they find us."

"Who?"

"Sssh. Follow me, and focus on my coat. Think of nothing. Create a mind wall that blocks them out. And *walk*."

Stogi crawled from the wreckage of the ship, his face bleeding badly, and he could see half the crew out there floating in the water dead. He'd seen the green arrow fall and strike the deck. On impact, it had exploded, tossing splinters and broken men skyward. He'd witnessed Taylon struck by an oar, and Dry Gurdey had been caught in his own wheel and left hanging upside down, his neck snapped and head lolling.

Stogi had drifted ashore, helpless, half-drowned, and feeble with loss of blood. Tol had found him and pulled him out the water. His friend's other arm was hanging limp at his side.

"It's broken," he'd told Stogi, his face contorted with pain.

"Tai Pei?"

"No idea."

"We have to find Carlo. Stop him getting to that bow."

"He's probably dead, like that lot," Tol nodded his head to the bobbing bodies floating around the fragments of the *Arabella*.

"He's alive," Stogi muttered. "Those bastards need him. That gaudy-clad archer and his friend. The Enemy. They'll make sure Carlo survives. Here, let me bind that arm."

"You're too weak, almost drowned by the look of you. Need rest."

"I'll be fine," Stogi lied. He felt the blood seeping inside his shirt. A belly wound. Not good. He had several hours, perhaps a day? The pain was terrible, but he couldn't afford the luxury of dying yet. Not with his soul at stake.

He helped Tol rip a section from his shirt, and together they managed to make a sling for his arm so he could walk unimpaired.

"Your turn." Tol gasped when he saw the gash in Stogi's

stomach. "There's still splinters in that wound. You'd best stay put. I'll go look."

"I'm coming with you."

"You're badly hurt, Stodge, old mate. Rest here, I'll report back soon as I know what the fuck is going on."

"I can manage." He made to stand but cried out and slunk back down. "We've got to find him, and Tai Pei."

"Leave it to me—just don't fucking die."

Stogi cursed as his friend staggered off behind the rocks. Moments passed, and the pain swelled like an acid ball expanding inside his stomach.

"Sod this …"

Stogi closed his eyes and gritted his teeth.

I won't just lie here and bleed.

He had to move. He tried again, and mercifully blacked out.

"I'VE TAKEN THE PAIN AWAY, AT LEAST FOR THE MOMENT."

Am I dead yet?

Stogi opened his eyes and saw the girl Urdei standing beside two strange ladies. They were tall, like sisters. One a touch too thin, with spiteful-looking and milky, orbless eyes. The other lady looked familiar. She appeared kindly, her green-gold gaze sorrowful—as though she'd like to help him but couldn't. Oblivious to that, Urdei was chuckling merrily between them.

"It's all got a bit messy, Stogi," she told him.

Who are …?

"You've not met my sister, Vervandi?" The child glanced up at the kind eyed woman on her right. That lady said nothing as she gazed down at him with those mesmerizing eyes. "And this is an old friend, Coristain. She was of Faerie but works for our Mother these days."

Faerie?

The woman, Coristain, nodded her head, and the slight curve of a smile lifted a corner of her lips. There was a cruelness to her the other two lacked. And something else—a malicious humor in her eyes. Her skin was blueish in tone. That didn't seem important at the moment. He worked his mouth and discovered he could speak.

"Carlo—we have to stop him ..."

"It's gotten complex," Urdei said, shaking her head.

"Tai Pei's killed him," the elf woman said, nastily in Stogi's opinion. "I tried to intervene, but she was too quick."

"Carlo's dead?"

Urdei smiled. "Perhaps he is. Hard to be certain, here at the nexus."

"Where am I? And Tai Pei ... is she ...?"

"This is the place between worlds, Stogi of Tseole." Vervandi spoke for the first time, her voice calm and soft yet resonating power. Stogi decided he liked her more than her little sister. "Here everything is possible, and time or distance have no meaning."

Stogi nodded wearily. *Now for the big question.*

"Am I dead too?"

"Death is but a fork in the road," Vervandi told him. Which wasn't really the answer he'd wanted. "But you live yet," she added with a smile. "And will recover, if you allow us to help you."

"Why wouldn't I?"

Vervandi shook her head, her gaze drifting off past the

others. "I must depart for a time—Urdei, too. Our mother needs us. Coristain here will watch over you."

Don't leave me with her ... Please ...

Urdei blew him a kiss, and the two sisters faded like water misting over hot glass. He shifted uncomfortably. Still no pain, but for how long? Coristain stared down at him with those cold, milky eyes.

"Are you friend, or sprite?"

Her lips curled with mischief as she crouched beside him, stroking his hair. Stogi felt sleepy, his mind drifting under that spidery touch.

"What do you think?"

"That I have to trust you, since they did. Still ..."

"You're a brave man, Stogi of Tseole." The smile was genuine. That surprised him. It seemed beneath that misty blue resided a real person. "Underrated," she said, the smile turning devious again. "Perhaps it's time someone appreciated you properly."

She leaned close and kissed his mouth.

He gasped, pulling back in shock and her eyes flickered angrily. "I'm mortally wounded—you shouldn't take advantage."

"You'll recover. See, your wound has dried up already."

"There were splinters—it will go bad."

"Gone. You'll be fine."

He looked down at his belly and shook his head.

"What happened to Tai Pei?"

"I don't know." She withdrew and seemed irritated by his question. Best he be careful here. "Nothing's decided yet. Come, relax, *poor* Stogi. Sometimes if you wait long enough, the answers arrive. And it's just we two ..."

"What do you want from me?"

"Is that not obvious?" She kissed him again, her musky scent filling his senses.

You shouldn't ... Stogi's mind wandered and tripped, drifting down, like snowfall into a dreamy, delightful daze.

If I'm dead, this isn't too bad.

ARIANE STARED UP AT THE SHIMMERING TOWER. FAR below, the sea rose in fury, and giant waves crashed and buried the rocks.

"Are we going inside?" Cale asked her.

They'd climbed for an hour until they reached the ridge where the white tower shimmered close, its searching light sweeping the lashing ocean beyond.

"We have to find Carlo Sarfe. For all we know, he could be inside."

"I don't see any doors," Fassyan said. Beside him, Doyle gazed back down the slope, his face strained. Ariane felt for him, doubtless worried about Garland. Nothing they could do. They had to trust the newcomer, Dunrae Tarn. Whatever his game, he was clearly no friend of her enemies.

The Urgolais, Zorc, had conjured a mist around them, allowing Ariane and her three men to escape the faceless knight and his hunters. They'd been climbing the first scarp when a loud boom had thudded in the valley below. The skies had turned black, and storm clouds soaked them with icy rain that had worsened as the minutes passed.

The tower was their salvation.

Laras Lassladen.

They'd be safe there. It seemed to float on the ridge ahead. The closer they got, the further away it appeared. Someone—

or *something,* she suspected—was determined to keep them from reaching the Goddess.

"We must keep walking," Ariane said, her heart sinking as they topped another ridge. The tower looked more distant than it had twenty minutes ago.

"Fucking sorcery," Doyle muttered. Cale's face was bleak, and Fassyan looked white.

Ariane was angry. "We have to get there first, worry what happens after that. Or how to get in. Courage, now—there'll be a way."

They walked on, the rain lashing their faces and a rising gale making progress slow. Another ridge rose ahead like a mirror image of the last. The white tower had slipped back again. They trudged for another fifteen minutes, stopping in alarm when they reached a sudden crack opening at their feet. A deep chasm spanned fifty feet with swirling gases oozing up from below.

I will not be defeated by your trickery. Ariane stood gazing down at that drop, her heart thudding. She'd almost fallen, had Fassyan not caught her arm.

A horn blasted behind them.

Cale slid the sword free of its scabbard. "We've company."

"There's a bridge," Doyle shouted and pointed along the ridge. Ariane saw a rickety-looking wooden structure, half-hidden by misty rain.

"I'd sooner not trust that," Cale muttered.

"What choice is there?" Fassyan said. "They're almost on us."

The faceless knight was riding full tilt toward where they stood, his hounds snapping and baying alongside.

"I thought that Dunrae Tarn fellow was going to deal with this bastard," Cale grumbled as Fassyan loosed his bow. Ariane saw the arrow pass through the rider's armor as though he were a shadow.

"Cross the bridge, you fools!"

Ariane saw Zorc emerge hobbling from the rain. She had no idea how the deformed creature had caught up with them. He leaned heavily on his stick, the soaked cloak hood plastered to his ugly face

"Come on!" she yelled, and they sped beside her toward the wooden bridge. The steel-cased rider circled his mount about and cantered down to where the Urgolais stood alone. She looked back and saw Zorc's cloak billowing as the rider fell upon him.

"Looks like Garland's ugly friend's done for," Cale said to Doyle as he reached the bridge. "I'll cross first." Ariane nodded. Doyle followed, and Fassyan bid she step on to the broken, rotting timbers.

"It's an illusion, Fass." She smiled as he followed her, and together they started crossing the gaping chasm. Ariane's words proved true when the bridge evaporated around them as they reached the middle.

Ariane fell beside her comrades as the cold air blasted her face and the yawning, belching chasm reached up to swallow them. High above and all around, the chaotic chorus of harp song and dark voices rang out.

She closed her eyes as the swirling gas sucked her in.

Goddess, help us, your servants...

29

THE OFFER

TIME'S NOTHING BUT A DREAM. You are outside of time …

They were home at last.

The *Arabella* glided through summer waters as the Sarfanian coastline revealed itself slowly. Creek, palm, and bay. Carlo recognized the marker at the head of the swamp. He yelled back to Gurdey, who turned the wheel to guide his ship into the intricate maze of mangrove waterways that hid their home from ocean and marsh.

They cleared the salt marshes and entered the channels, following the markers for a mile before the reeds parted, and Reveal emerged like a dream across the water.

He laughed seeing the distant lanterns.

I'm home … It was almost evening and the fireflies flickered gold as they rose in winking spangles above the misty water.

They docked. Carlo leaped ashore, bidding his crew farewell as they took horses from the estate stables and rode out to join their kin. He would catch up with them in a day or so.

First …

Carlo walked through the double doors of his ancestral home. He smiled warmly, seeing his mother playing with a new puppy. He called out her name, but she didn't respond.

"Mother, I'm back."

She was crouched combing the animal's matted hair, her brown skin gleaming in the last of the day's sun.

"Mother …" Carlo stood beside her. He reached down and stroked her hair, but felt nothing.

Mother…

I CAN BRING THEM BACK.

The voice drummed inside his head like stinging insects. Carlo turned slowly, terror shaking his lips. A man stood there, tall and elegant, clad in dazzling white with eyes the color of trapped night. The face was hard to define. He wore a flawless smile that reached out to Carlo, promising *everything.*

"Why can't she hear me?"

"Because you're dead." The man's smile surrounded him.

"I don't believe you."

"This will help."

The figure in white vanished. Carlo felt agony surging into his back. He looked down at the dagger and saw Tai Pei's face, her eyes wet with tears.

"I'm sorry," she said.

The vison past as swiftly as the pain. He stood on the deck of his ship, while the sea rose higher than a tower and swept toward them booming like thunder.

The man in white reappeared and stood beside him, a golden harp clutched in his hands.

"My watery Brother's work," he said. "Zansuat has scant patience. Even as He storms inland, the demon rages fire. Fire and water, Carlo Sarfe—and Oblivion. I brought you here to witness the final fall."

"My mother?"

"Lady Arabella perished in the blaze at Dovess Castle, as did your noble father."

Carlo sobbed. "I was too late. Estorien?"

"Murdered by Torlock, on the orders of the Galanians—his price for eloping with the Barola girl."

"If they're already dead and it's hopeless, why am I seeing this?"

"Because I can change the outcome, if you help me in return."

"Who are you?"

"Can't you guess?"

As he spoke, Carlo saw flies crawling and buzzing around his mouth. He strummed a chord on the harp. The black eyes narrowed cruelly.

"I am Futility and Ruin. The Prince of Pain. Master of the Orb that survived, despite their feeble efforts."

Carlo screamed as the rent in his chest erupted in fresh agony.

"I can make this last a lifetime. Or . . . "

The pain and flies vanished. He was perfection again—the smile kindly, black eyes wise.

"What must I do?"

Long white fingers capped in blood-red varnish traced the harp, and notes rose and danced around the featureless head. The half-face mocked him as the harp music rose and fell.

"You dropped the bow, Carlo Sarfe. You must return and pick it up. Finish what you started."

The wrecking waves were almost on them, but his crew seemed unaware.

"You'll save my family and friends?"

"I promise."

"What do you get in return?"

"Your souls …"

"I won't do it."

"*So be it.* There are other fools I can use. You gain nothing and lose all."

Carlo screamed as the pain tore him open inside. He saw the wave engulfing the *Arabella* and felt his body lifted like straw in a gale, hurled up into the rising, drenching wash.

"HE'S ALIVE."

The gruff tone came from far away.

"We need to move," the rough voice said. "You'll have to drag his body while I keep an eye out for the Kaa."

"Where are we taking him?"

"Inside the tower. The only way we can save him, and ourselves. Even Shorty cannot stop the power of the bow, once activated. He touched it—must have. It's why they're all dead."

Carlo opened his eyes. *This isn't real.* He'd died twice, and yet here he was alive again. A man crouched beside him, and another bigger rough-looking fellow gazed down, his hard, heavy face lined with frowns, the cloudy eyes ironic.

"Welcome back," the gruff stranger said.

Carlo looked at the other man. He seemed familiar, and after a moment he recognized Garland of Wynais, the soldier he'd met in the Castle of Lights.

"You're alive—I'm glad. Or is this just another dream?"

"No dream. A fucking nightmare. Been looking for you, boy," Garland said. "We need to get you somewhere safe."

Carlo laughed. "It's too late. The white one … he. *They're dead.* Gol … everything—"

"Likely so," the big man in the coat said. "Best you comply and come with us, old son."

"Who are you?"

"I've worked that out. Dunrae Tarn works for Jynn," Garland told him, as the other man turned away and gazed at the rising waters.

"We need to move," Dunrae Tarn said.

"I can walk," Carlo said, surprised at feeling no pain, only a numbness.

YOU CANNOT ESCAPE US.

For an instant, he glimpsed black eyes staring out from the rocks.

You don't exist

I DO, AND I'M WAITING FOR YOU.

The eyes flickered and vanished. Carlo turned away and followed the big man in the coat.

Stogi woke in a haze as the cold water lapped at his feet. He gazed down and saw the wound had gone. Instead, he felt rested, as though waking from a long sleep after a raging illness. His mind felt at peace, calm and content.

"My gift to you who made me happy, for the briefest time."

He looked up and saw the elf woman, Coristain, smiling whimsically at him. "Whatever the outcome Stogi, know that

I am your friend. Remember that always. The War of the Bow has begun. Carlo chose badly and has paid the price."

She flickered and vanished. Stogi rubbed his eyes and saw two wretched figures hobbling and leaning into each other as they approached where he lay. He sighed in relief as Tai Pei limped toward him, with Tol beside her. The man gasped when he saw Stogi sitting up, his wound having vanished.

"You're hale …"

"A lady healed me while you were gone. Don't ask me how —I was delirious. Where's Carlo?"

Tai Pei's eyes were filled with tears. "I stabbed him. It was that or lose you, Stodge."

"He's dead," Stogi nodded. "I'm sorry, but you had to …"

A stranger stood behind them, a huge metal tube on his shoulder. "He's not dead in the sense you mean."

"Who's this big bugger?" Stogi asked Tai Pei, who looked startled.

"Fucked if I know," she said.

"What now?" Tol asked. Tai Pei shrugged and stared at Stogi. She seemed unhurt, but her face was covered in blood.

"They were here," he told her.

"You're not making sense," Tai Pei said.

"You can't make sense of this," Stogi said. "There's a war raging all around us. The bow is the cause. Seek's involved. You remember the shaman?"

She nodded.

The newcomer coughed, turning their heads. "You people had best stop talking and follow me, if you want to survive the next few hours."

"Where did he come from?" Tol asked, seeing the man for the first time.

"Just part of the wonderful magic of this place," Stogi said, and the newcomer laughed as if his comment had been amusing.

"My friend Tol here's wounded, and the girl's shattered."

The man placed aside his heavy-looking tube and looked at Tol's arm. "I can fix that," he said, and turned to Tai Pei.

"Who are you, dark spirit?" she glared back at him.

He ignored her and placed a hand on her forehead.

"You're a tough-looking lass. I daresay you'll be fine. Now come on, you strays, we need to get moving."

Tai Pei glared at Stogi, who nodded and leaped to his feet, surprising himself as much as Tol.

"Can you find whoever healed you and ask her back here?" Tol said sheepishly.

"Doubt she'll come," Stogi said, as Tai Pei awarded him a quizzical glance.

"Why are we following this man?" she asked, as the stranger shouldered his odd-looking weapon and walked off. "He's most likely yet another sorcerer."

"He knows more than we do, for sure," Stogi said.

"I killed Carlo," she said. "Stabbed him, deep and true. This man's lying, and I don't know why."

"Let's go find out," Stogi said, resigned. She nodded, and Tol joined them painfully as they walked quickly to catch the man in the dark blue coat.

"Where are we headed?" Stogi asked him.

"Tower."

"What happens when we get there?"

The man stopped and turned. His grin was ironic. "We watch past become present, Stogi the Tseole. Witness the fall of Gol. Fire and water." He turned away again.

"Definitely a sorcerer," Tai Pei whispered, her eyes angry.

"'Spect so, but he seems to like us," Stogi said.

"What were you saying about a woman healing you?" she asked him as they walked. "Tol warned me not to hope, said you were dying from gut wound."

"An exaggeration. I was uncomfortable."

"A woman saved you?"

"I think she was a dream induced by the pain."

She raised a brow but let the matter rest.

They reached a cave entrance where the sea lapped inside.

"Wait here," the man said. He disappeared but returned moments later. "The way is clear to the tower, but we need to hurry."

Stogi followed the others inside the damp cave. The man in the coat held a lantern, casting shadow. He saw strange carvings on the walls. There were two men crouched nearby. One stood and called out Tol's name in a hoarse shout.

"Captain, it can't be!" Tol seemed to forget his pain as he rushed toward the shaggy figure and they embraced, though the stranger backed off when he saw Tol's arm.

"Taylon?" the man asked. Stogi saw Tol shake his head.

He turned to ask Tai Pei what she thought, but she was looking at the other man, her face ghostly pale and eyes terrified. Stogi turned slowly and saw Carlo Sarfe standing beside the big man's lantern, his eyes bright and face filled with a savage joy.

"It's almost time." Carlo's eyes were blacker than he recalled. The moment passed, and the captain of the *Arabella* seemed his old self, none the worse for Tai Pei's dagger.

"I stabbed you," she said.

He smiled back. "I know. Seems like it wasn't fatal."

"I watched you die," she said, her eyes switching to Stogi. "I don't like this, Stogi."

"Me neither," he said.

"We need to hurry, people." The big man with the lantern was walking into the shadows ahead.

"The tower awaits," Stogi said, nodding. "Hopefully we'll learn more inside."

"You think?" Tai Pei glared at him.

30

THE SEA GOD'S FURY

ARIANE WATCHED as lights rose and hovered around her face. It seemed like they'd been falling for hours. She'd glimpsed terrible faces swirling in gas, hearing screams, dark voices, wolf howls, and even once the sound of a melancholy harp.

Still tumbling, she watched as soldiers filed inside a city. There was fighting, the clash of steel. She saw bright banners and blood on shields as crows hopped and tore at mangled flesh. The Dreaming was back, filling her mind with portents as she fell.

The visions came and went, fading and flickering amid the scramble of sounds. Sometimes she glimpsed her friends falling beside her, their faces hidden by nothingness.

Is this death?

She didn't think so. There was no pain, at least after the initial fall. Her mind had screamed, but that had soon passed —replaced by a strange calm as she fell into that multicolored Void.

The Chaos Realms.

Part of her mind registered the thought. In that emptiness,

she saw men she'd known long ago. Among them, her champion Roman Parrantios and her father King Nogel. They faded back, crumbling like age-old parchment as she drifted past.

It comes down to this moment, where past and present collide.

She must have stopped without knowing. The voice had been close. A woman's, and familiar. She stood on a platform, a white light reaching out and lighting the world below.

A shadow drifted close. Ariane recognized Vervandi, who she'd known long ago and had been their guide through the Forest of Dreams, back when she first traveled with Corin an Fol.

Vervandi reached across and gripped her hand, the green-gold eyes urgent.

"Queen, come witness this shifting dance. Know that your greatest challenge will follow the events happening here."

"Where are we?"

"Inside Laras Lassladen. This tower is protected by your Goddess and can resist the Orb's evil gathering outside."

"My friends?"

"You will join them soon. They cannot see what you must, as it would destroy them. Come, the ledge."

Ariane followed Vervandi across to a platform of stone. She saw roses and other blooms nodding in a warm breeze. It felt like summer, but as she gazed up, she noticed three faint moons lining the velvet sky above.

"Where are we?"

"The tower moves through time and space, as it must. As Elanion's chosen, you are privileged to glimpse what only the gods and we sisters can witness. After the war, when the gods fought outside Kelthara and your city, the Order in the universe was re-arranged."

"I had believed the gods all dead."

"They were, as was I. And, in a sense, we still are. But part of us survived, like a tree struck by storm standing blasted and withered in a field but refusing to topple. Some, like dark Undeyna, eloped to the future, while others held back in distant galaxies, awaiting a signal from the Weaver or word of the next dance. There is no ending to the *dancing*. Existence comes in waves, Queen Ariane. Life and death, Past, Present and Future. Tides repeating the endless cycle which we call the *Dance*."

"Elanion spoke to my cousin, the High Queen. She needs me—it's why I set sail. But what task yet remains if the bow is lost?"

"The Goddess resides on distant Galenki and uses myself and others as her agents. She dares not return to Ansu. That is what He wants, the master of the Orb. And that traitor, the Sky Wanderer. Her husband, brother, and foe. My Father." Vervandi smiled sadly. "The gods are flawed like humans, Ariane. Only the Maker is without blemish.

"After the Happening, Elanion took hold of the witch Cille's mind, as She needed to keep a presence on the realms, to see if His shadow still stained Ansu. And, of course, it did —and does. For nothing can be destroyed utterly. A memory or zephyr will always remain. Especially in Limbo."

"What are you telling me? Evil thrives? That I know already."

"The Shadowman, or Old Night, is back in another form. The Orb is real. His true name I'll not mention, though you know it, too. That terrible being, my *Uncle,* was destroyed by the Weaver. And yet, Jynn the Maker could not unmake entirely. Evil will always endure. Such is the riddle of the universe."

"Jynn?"

"Creates but cannot destroy. Thus, the essence of Old Night's stain lingered on and festered. His dark mind became a place rather than an entity—a way to mirror and mock my Mother's refuge, Laras Lassladen, where alone She is invulnerable. That place is called Graywash Hall, its heart center the Orb. A concept, island, or castle—call it what you will. A living, breathing evil. All that remains of Him. The embodiment of Old Night. His malice and wickedness are trapped inside."

"Dog Island was part of that?"

Vervandi shook her head.

"Like Laras Lassladen, Graywash Hall can move through time and dimensions. Those inside seek to unravel the Weaver's Dance. My Father has joined them. He hates stability nearly as much as His eldest brother."

"You mean the old Wanderer? Leader of the Wild Hunt?" Ariane chewed her bottom lip. Corin had been haunted by that terrible entity. Oroonin, her Goddess's estranged husband.

"He has many names. When the Aralais made the thirteen treasures, they placed great powers in each. At the time, even the old gods feared this ingenious and powerful people. It was before the war with their Urgolais kin had all but destroyed their power.

"There was a time when the Aralais, with their artefacts and cunning, looked to overthrow the gods themselves, becoming the new masters of the universe. Even Old Night became concerned and leant His aid to the Urgolais, their bitterest foe. Thus, that secretive race turned to evil."

Ariane thought of Zorc but said nothing.

"The greatest Aralais treasures were the Crystal sword, Callanak, and the crown called the Tekara. You are familiar with both. But the third and final treasure was the bow Kerasheva—yet more potent. Their deadliest weapon had different powers—darker powers than the sword or crown, for these had been gifts to King Kell in return for his aid on arrival from Gol's ruin.

"Kerasheva is older, and as the bow was symbolic—their gift to the Goddess—an arrow fired from the weapon can alter time and shake the dimensions.

"Those three Aralais witches wanted it back to regain the power their kin had lost. Elanion intervened at great risk to Herself, stopping their ruinous schemes. The Castle of Lights witnessed their final demise, and the game shifted, as the thief stole the bow while the Goddess returned to Galenki."

"Who is the thief?"

"An old adversary. Someone who survived after bartering his soul. As did Sir Valen the false knight and, almost, the one they call the Avenger."

"I do not know these men you speak of."

"You recently encountered both, and you'll soon know more. Come, Queen Ariane, it's time to watch the *Dance* evolve ..."

Vervandi smiled and walked across to the lip. Ariane followed her warily. She stopped, gasping, gazing down through clouds for miles, seeing lands and seas far below and the distant stubble of mountains. Rivers wound like yarn thread coiling from a reel.

"You're seeing Ansu," Vervandi told her. "As the gods see our beloved green planet. It's time to go deeper. Come!" She grabbed her arm.

Ariane yelled, as they stepped off the ledge and drifted like kites down through the clouds, spiraling and twisting, until they arrived back in Dog Island.

They shifted in form, becoming two white birds waiting on a rock. Bird-Ariane saw Taic's ship, his men hard at work mending it. Further away, the wreckage of Carlo's vessel floated out into the night. Behind them, the white tower stood gleaming tall. Beyond its light, a dark shadow rose taller yet, morphing into a rival tower, its sleek walls black and oily. Ariane saw a beautiful face watching from a window in that dark tower—a man stood there garbed in gleaming white, his black eyes pinning her. She felt an icy terror.

"He cannot reach us here. Hold to courage. His soul, or Orb, cannot leave the confines of the Hall."

"That tower is Graywash Hall?"

"Part of the whole. Come! See with the Goddess's eyes. Let us take wing again. The players have gathered below. See how the wind rises in the east."

Ariane turned. Her Goddess-gifted fargaze saw flames crackling and rising in the west. In the other direction, she saw the seas rising. In their midst, she thought she could make out the figure of a giant striding naked through waves.

Sensuata.

Ariane felt an icy stab of fear.

Is he coming for Gol, or me?

Even as she watched, Ariane imagined she saw that terrible face staring back at her in anger. The moment passed, and Vervandi bid her look down to where the tiny figures of men faced one another far below. Her Goddess-enhanced vision took her closer.

"Who is that?"

"Mortals caught in the thread. Among them, Carlo Sarfe."

She saw a man stabbed by a girl as another woman tried to intervene. A familiar figure draped in checkers like a court jester fought another man with bright-red hair. The figures vanished. She saw the stabbed man alive and hale again, walking through lamplit caves with the murderous pale-faced girl and a stocky man beside him. She saw Garland with them and recognized the other man as one of his volunteers.

"Are they dead?"

"They seek our tower but cannot get in. Carlo must finish what he started."

"The bow?"

"Is waiting for him."

THE CAVES OPENED ON WARM SUN. CARLO BLINKED, seeing a tall woman greeting them.

"You others must go inside," she said, and she motioned him to stay. Carlo saw the mist lift, and a huge column of white stone rising above. He spotted a door leading to spiraling stairs.

"Why must I stay?"

"His stain is upon you," the strange lady said. "But fear not—we will help you. You are not alone, Carlo Sarfe. They are all here, and it is time you chose."

The shapes of men emerged, surrounding him. Carlo saw the rider with the faceless visor and scarlet plume. With him was the jester, his triangle hat and owl mask hiding his face again. The blood-eared dogs bayed, and the skinny pale faced hunters hoisted their harpoons.

The man in the checkered suit carried the bow again. Keel placed it on the ground at Carlo's feet as the dark host surrounded him. Carlo glanced back. His friends had vanished inside the white tower. They'd deserted him and followed the man called Dunrae Tarn.

"I am alone."

I'm with you, boyo.

He turned and saw a white hawk settle on a rock and preen its feathers. It became Irulan and flashed him a grin.

"He wants my soul."

"We'll work something out. What choice is there? Can't you see that your world is gone, Carlo. Look, the flames are rising! Rakeel is no more. And raging Zansuat attacks the coast of Barola. The game for Gol is almost played out."

"My kin and crew are already lost, spirit. I decline the bow. I'll not serve your needs. Damn you all to Yffarn."

He turned away but stopped when the archer appeared before him.

"It's not that easy," Keel said. He pointed, and Carlo's jaw dropped. His brother, Estorien, rode through a distant wood where men crouched low with bows.

Ambush.

He saw them fire, and his brother tumbled from his horse. A tall man cloaked in black rose out amongst them. He walked over with a long sword and sliced down.

"Estorien, no!"

Keel laughed and tossed the bow into Carlo's outstretched arms. "Save him with this," he said.

Without thinking, Carlo's fingers clasped around the bow. *HE HAS CHOSEN.*

The figure in white walked toward him, dwarfing all the others, and their shadows faded and flickered. Even Irulan seemed frail in comparison.

YOU ARE MINE, CARLO SARFE. THROUGH YOU,

I CONTROL KERASHEVA. COME, FOLLOW ME, AND
WITNESS THE FALL OF GOL.

But as the white figure turned away, Carlo saw another
bird—a bright swan gliding close.

"Kill that bird!" the joker, Keel, yelled at him. Carlo lifted
the bow, and Keel passed him a green arrow fletched with
emerald goose feathers. "Shoot it, damn you. Pass your first
test."

"Why must I?" Carlo clutched the arrow and placed nock
on bowstring, his hands shaking badly.

"Shoot!" Keel yelled at him as the swan glided closer.

He pulled back but stopped, gasping as the bow burnt his
fingers like heated coal.

The swan settled on the churning mass of water and gazed
directly at him. He tried to shoot the bird, but his fingers
blistered.

"I can't hold it, I ..."

*Drop the bow, Carlo! There's still a way home for you. But
only if you defy them. Cast aside Kerasheva.*

The pain faded, as the woman's clear tone drilled inside his
head. He gazed down and saw his fingers smoking.

"Don't listen to that bitch." Irulan's raw croak sounded
desperate.

Drop it and come to me.

"Augh," Carlo threw the smoking bow at the joker's boots.

"That's too bad," Keel said, scooping up the weapon,
passing it to the glassy-eyed man behind him. "Go hide this
somewhere, Shale. We'll find another use for Kerasheva."

YOU FAILED. TIME TO SUFFER.

The white figure rose like a tower of hate.

Carlo screamed, as fresh pain lasered between his eyes.

Stop!

The pain vanished again.

He is not yours, Saan. You lack the power you once had, Eldest Brother. Your Orb shell is cracking and cannot protect you forever. Be gone! And you, Husband, Brother. This is My planet. My peoples. GO!

The white figure laughed, flickered and vanished.

Irulan reappeared, his blazing silver eye locking on Carlo.

"You win this round, Elanion," he muttered. "But we'll be back, Saan and I. And Keel's boys will hang on to your bow for the time being."

Flee, Husband. You have no influence here anymore.

"Neither do you, Wife. We're supposed to be dead. Did you forget that? And I'll be seeing *you* soon, Carlo Sarfe." Irulan croaked a laugh and vanished.

Carlo choked and staggered. He shielded his eyes as the sky erupted around him. The clouds had shifted. Gone was the dark, replaced by a diadem of shooting stars and moons.

He saw a woman's face gazing down through shifting starlight. Beautiful, yet stern, with golden hair surmounted by a crown of black swan feathers. Then her visage faded. Through the gap, the swan drifted toward him.

The joker and his men had vanished. Carlo stood alone, his legs trembling and heart pounding. The bird approached smoothly over flawless blue water, the soft ripples lapping the shore at his feet.

You are saved, lost mortal. Come, while there's yet time to ride the heavens.

The green-gold swan eyes beckoned him climb upon her wings. He did so swiftly, and she bore him off up into the night sky.

"What happened? He accepted the bow?"

"We tricked them," Vervandi explained to Ariane as she saw Carlo's body lifted high on the swan's back.

"How?"

"Urdei called on Our Mother to intervene. Risky, as the other two were there. And they're all three banished from Ansu by my Grandfather. And … if Carlo Sarfe had shot the swan …" She shook her head. "A rash gamble, but that's Urdei and Mother for you. Paid off. Carlo's soul is safe, and the Enemy checked for the moment. Yet they retain the bow. Too bad. Time for us to leave here. Your comrades await you in the tower. Carlo Sarfe's part in the strife may be over. Yours, Queen Ariane, is about to begin."

Garland saw the sea lashing the rocks as Tol leaned against a pillar. Above them, the white tower rose, tall and needle-sharp. He saw two birds circling, then settling on the tower's crown.

The woman had placed salve on Tol's arm. Her name was Coristain, and she'd appeared for brief moments before fading back into the cave walls. Hard to know what had happened in there, but at least they were out and back beneath clear skies. The sea raging below, the white tower standing proud above.

He glanced at the people gathered around. Dunrae Tarn stood looking up at the tower, while Stogi and Tai Pei argued. Tol still leaned—the salve the strange woman gave him had worked miracles.

He'd barely stayed awake in the cave tunnels, and Garland had had to help him out. It was good to see one of his men had made it through, though hearing about Taylon's demise had saddened him. Doyle would be overjoyed seeing his friend. Tol had been the most popular of the volunteers who'd accompanied Garland all those crazy months ago.

"Where's Carlo?" Garland heard Stogi ask the big man. He looked about but saw no sign of the sailor. The Shen woman, Tai Pei, looked relieved, but Garland worried Carlo Sarfe had been pulled back into whatever nightmare had claimed him before.

At Dunrae Tarn's signal, they entered the door leading into the white tower. Inside, the walls shimmered like seashells, and soft flutes piped music from immeasurable distance.

The stairs wound up in concentric spirals, lifting into light. Garland felt a change of atmosphere, as though he were higher than the clouds, like he had been after escaping from Graywash Hall that first time.

As they got higher, he saw rooms leading off. Inside them, Garland glimpsed wide scenes—sometimes he saw rivers winding around wooded valleys, while tall mountains reared in others.

I'm looking in on worlds.

Once, he saw a castle with seventeen walls, wrapped around a stormy ocean.

"The rooms are gateways into different realms," Dunrae Tarn explained, after joining him, the others climbing up ahead.

"See, that one leads to distant Galenki." He pointed to a wide expanse that opened through a floating door, which had emerged to his right. Garland saw a strange sky lit by two orange suns.

"What is the secret of this tower?" he asked the heavyset man.

"Laras Lassladen lies both within and without the universe. From here, all things can be seen at the same time."

"Those enemies from Graywash Hall. You're part of that business. You know them."

"I know some of them, as do you," Dunrae Tarn said. "The Hall's central Orb gathers those who favor Chaos, much as Laras Lassladen harbors heroes and those with high destiny. People such as you, Journeyman, and your young queen."

"Where is Ariane?"

"Above. She has the best view."

"And Carlo Sarfe—what of him?"

Dunrae Tarn shrugged. "This way."

He pointed to a door that had appeared. Garland followed, and his jaw dropped as he recognized Marei's valley.

Marei!

He saw the woods and hills surrounding Torrigan's Tavern, and the mountains beyond, the path winding over. The city rested in haze at the far side.

His mind travelled the other way. He saw the sea, the river winding into that gray water. The village, its smoke rising. *And* ... no Graywash Hall. The hill where the castle had stood lay bare and stark. A single standing stone rose above cropped grass, like a warning finger. He saw a one-eyed crow perched on the tall stone.

"The Hall ... it's gone."

"Aye, we drew it away by making all this noise." Dunrae Tarn chuckled. "Your Marei's safe, Journeyman—her family too. The Jynn kept his word."

"How do I get back there? Surely my task here is done."

"Not yet, old son. The bow is still missing."

"I thought Carlo Sarfe took the bow."

"Mercifully, only for a minute. Kerasheva is back in the hands of Sir Valen's turds."

"The quest to recover the bow has failed. What now?"

He smiled at Garland. "It ain't over. Guess where we're going, Journeyman."

Garland scowled. "Back to Yffarn."

"Smile—the game's just picking up."

"Why do they call you the Avenger?"

"I'll tell you on the way through."

"To where? The Void?"

"You ask too many questions."

Garland wiped sweat from his brow and sighed. Perhaps it was better not knowing the answers. He followed the big man into another room. This time, the views spanned distant moons and blue space. Garland saw stars studding the firmament and huge figures striding above electric clouds.

"Not the Void this time," Dunrae Tarn said. "Gwelan, where I have a hunch your friend Shale took Kerasheva on the sly. And my enemy, Sir Valen the Gaunt, has since joined him. He'll call on the Grogans for help. Going to get busy out there."

"What of Marei—and the children?"

"You'll see her in time, boy. But not soon, I'm afraid. You're taking the long way home. That's why Shorty and me call you the Journeyman."

"You mean Randle the miller?"

"Aye, Shorty I call him. The Jynn. Your new boss." The man in the blue coat barked a wry laugh and shouldered his heavy weapon. "Time, we got going, old son. Ready?"

"Always."

"You had best go nudge your goblin pal. 'Spect he'll want to join us, too."

S{mallcaps}TOGI WALKED INTO THE SWEEPING HALL OF LIGHT, AS Tai Pei gripped his hand in hers. She'd been silent since they'd entered the tower. She seemed sad, her dark eyes filled with guilt. Neither of them believed that Carlo had returned. Whoever that had been in the caves was not their friend.

Tai Pei whispered in his ear, and he looked up as a smallish woman glanced his way. She was garbed in hunting green, three men beside her. Two appeared to be soldiers, the other a hunter carrying a longbow in his hands.

She smiled as they approached. "You must be Stogi and Tai Pei."

Tai Pei looked puzzled, but Stogi nodded.

"We think we are, but it's been a tad confusing lately."

She nodded. "Tol told me all about you. He's with Doyle. Both are Garland's men. I sent them on a fool's errand to find my cousin. Seems like an age ago."

"You're Queen Ariane," Stogi felt a rush of blood to his face. Tai Pei glanced at him curiously.

"I am she."

"Lord Tam was my *friend*."

"Lord *Tam*?" She crooked her neck and glanced at him sideways. "You mean my cousin, Tamersane?"

"We journeyed together and shared many adventures, before he ..."

"You'll have to tell me all about that. Come, it is time."

"Time for what?" Tai Pei muttered in his ear as he watched the small figure of Queen Ariane fade into the shimmering distance.

Ariane had felt the glistening of a tear after speaking with Stogi. She returned to the ledges where she'd stood with Vervandi, her men, and Tol. Together, they waited as Stogi and the pale, fierce-eyed girl caught up with them and watched the sky change below.

"Where is Captain Garland?" Doyle asked Ariane.

She shook her head. "I don't know."

"Dunrae Tarn is missing, too, and the Urgolais Zorc," Cale said.

Ariane had felt a pang of guilt, thinking about Zorc. The Urgolais conjurer must have perished saving them.

Too bad.

"They must have been delayed," she said, and turned to watch the skies again.

Marei stoked the fire as Rosey tended little Dalreen, who giggled as she tickled her ribs. Dafyd came inside, his arms laden with logs.

"Winter's here," he said, grinning.

She nodded. "There's been more customers today and for three days running, despite snow blocking the passes."

"The last group came from the coast," Rosey said. "The village is full of the talk. The Kaa have gone, and the …"

"Hall, too," Marei said. "Impossible as that seems."

"Nothing is impossible."

They turned sharply at the voice. Marei gasped, seeing yellow-green eyes gazing back at her from inside the fire. Fenglegrim the cat leaped out from the flames and jumped into Dafyd's lap as Jynn emerged and rubbed his chubby hands together.

"You are safe for a good while, my children," he told them. "But Shale will return, and the others. Keep one eye on the door."

"What about Garland?" Marei asked him, as he rubbed his hands over the flames.

"With Tarn the Bagman. The Journeyman's helping my Avenger. Our game has moved out to distant Gwelan. But you'll see Sir Garland again, have no fear."

"I'll hold you to that, Piper," she replied.

THE SWAN BORE CARLO UP INTO HIGH CLOUDS BEFORE drifting low and gliding over flat green water. They entered Reveal harbor, and this time his mother cried out and ran to him with arms held wide.

"Is this real?" Carlo asked the swan, but the bird had vanished. Instead, his people gathered around him and smiled their excited greetings. Later—much later, when he was alone on the wharf, his parents and young Kael having taken to their beds—Estorien approached him, and they shared the pipe.

"That's some tale, brother. You've been gone months, not years. And ... as though I'd go near a fucking Barolan wench. You should know me better than that."

Carlo said nothing. He watched the fireflies drift close as Estorien laughed and joked beside him. One firefly hovered and dipped, settling in his hands. A woman's smiling face gazed back at him with eyes of green and gold. She became the laughing girl, Urdei, and then another.

The swan-crowned Goddess Elanion smiled at him.

"This is Our Goddess' gift to you, Carlo Sarfe. Your voyage is over at last."

Home …

Ariane saw the seas rise into impossible towers, striking the shoreline, tearing and ripping through fields, drowning cities and lands. She witnessed men fleeing, their tiny bodies ripped away into the watery maelstrom.

North a way, a trail of fires blazed in a towering inferno, marching south to meet the floods. She saw cities crumble and tall towers buckle. The fires met the rising flood outside a castle on a causeway.

She witnessed three ships battling that tumult, departing as the quay was ripped away. The fiery demon's face rose high above the clouds, but the Sea God stood taller and drenched the fires, His waves lashing and churning until no land remained and a single whirlpool spiraled into a black hole of plunging, vanishing dark.

The Sea God stood and surveyed his powerful work. She could see the tiny speck of the three ships far out to sea. Sensuata, who the men of Gol had called Zansuat, turned His terrible face toward her.

Ariane bowed.

I am ready to keep my part of the bargain, she told him.

The Sea God vanished, and the destruction of Gol ebbed slowly from her mind, replaced by a warm breeze and open blue seas. A gull weaving high above.

"Any idea where we are?" Cale asked Ariane the morning after.

"Deep in Sensuata's realm. I doubt He'll let me escape this time."

"He'll have us to worry about." Cale said.

"What about the bow? Did anyone recover it?" the fierce girl, Tai Pei, asked.

"The thief, Keel, gave it Shale to hide. He's one of Sir Valen's people." The voice came from behind them. Ariane turned and saw Vervandi walking down the gunwale.

"Keel? I know that name," Ariane said as Vervandi joined them.

The woman smiled sadly. "You should, yes. He used the name when he killed your father at Caswallon's bidding. The thief is the former Assassin of Crenna."

"Rael Hakkenon survived? How? Corin an Fol said he'd died in Laras Lassladen—jumped from the world tower."

"He was damaged by that fall, but not broken," Vervandi said. "His face is ruined, and his dark soul no longer his own. Rael is the Orb's creature, like Sir Valen the Gaunt and Shale. There are others. The irony is that Laras Lassladen protected Rael as nowhere else could have—until the searching, reaching tendrils of Graywash Hall found a new and willing servant."

Ariane chewed her lip. "We'll have to find him again and put an end to his suffering. Recover the bow for good. And achieve that before Sensuata comes for me."

"Good luck with that." Vervandi touched her hand lightly.

"Will you help us?"

"Perhaps I shall."

"Oh, well … you did say that you were bored back in Wynais," Cale offered a smile.

"Yes, I believe I was," she said, and laughed.

"Where are we heading, highness?" Taic called down.

"Ask her," Ariane replied, but Vervandi had gone again.

She smiled at Cale. "Guess we'll find out soon enough. Care for a brandy?"

"Think we've earned one," he said, as the two of them went below.

GARLAND WATCHED THE FACELESS RIDER APPROACHING, his silver helm glittering dull green, the scarlet plume nodding, and a banner tied to his long lance. Beside him, Dunrae Tarn slung the blunderbuss into his hands and leveled the weapon. The rider circled and pointed.

"Name the place," Dunrae Tarn called across.

Garland saw other figures appear, Shale among them, carrying a bundle which resembled an unstrung bow.

Shale nodded, seeing Garland. "We'll await your joining us in Gwelan," he called out. "The Grogans will be pleased to see you."

The figures faded, and the horseman reared his stallion and turned it about, disappearing back down the hill.

"You don't have to accompany us," Dunrae Tarn told the hunched figure in the shabby cloak.

"Your new friend here has a promise to keep," Zorc glanced sideways at Garland.

"Aye, so I do, Zorc. To Gwelan it is. Lead on, Avenger!"

*Here concludes the story of Carlo Sarfe. Queen Ariane, Garland the Journeyman, Stogi and Tai Pei will return in **Journeyman Book 3**: **The Sea God's Women**, and their dance concludes in **Journeyman Book 4: Archer's Moon***

AUTHOR'S NOTE

THE HIERARCHY OF GODS AND ANSU MYTHOLOGY

The **Weaver/Maker** weaved the World-Thread. **Ansu** was the first world, beloved and gifted by His children the **High Gods**. Home of **Oroonin** and **Elanion** before they fell out

The First Born, **Saan**, persuaded His siblings that the Weaver was negligent of Their needs, having moved on to create other galaxies. Saan led a rebellion against the Weaver, but it was crushed. The Weaver, although angered, forgave His wayward children and moved on to fashion yet more worlds in His timeless **Dance**.

Most of the gods were chastised and ashamed of Their rebellion, but Saan was vengeful, deeming Himself ill-treated and forgotten. He raised an army of acolytes and started a second rebellion. This time, the other gods sided with the Weaver against **Cul-Saan,** as they named Him, meaning Overproud. But **Crun Earthshatterer** and **Undeyna of the Shadows** sided with Saan.

Again, the rebels were defeated. This time, the Maker was wrathful. Undeyna escaped to weave a web of protection around herself in **Darkvale**, a forgotten forest in Ansu's midst. Crun was punished and chained to an island that shifted through the five dimensions. Cul-Saan was renamed **Old Night** and punished severely, his limbs dismembered and head cut off. Each body part was stored on a separate world; the head resided in Ansu, beneath a mountain in the jungle region of southern Yamondo. A demon was charged to watch over it.

But the stain that seeped out as Saan's blood caused a canker that spread throughout Ansu, and Evil rose again. The **Aralais** and **Urgolais** voyagers had arrived from distant worlds. Ancient rivals, the Aralais were proud, and their enemy/kin envious and sly. The **Urgo** were great miners and were trapped by Saan's stain. Thus, they became evil and His slaves, but also learned much dark lore and were powerful sorcerers. The Aralais were known as the **Golden Ones** and fought their hideous kin for three thousand years. That war ended suddenly with both races exhausted, and it culminated with the timely arrival of the mortal hero, **Kell** from the recent fall of **Gol.**

After falling out with her Husband/Brother Oroonin, Elanion was chosen as **Guardian of Ansu.** She settled in the **Forest of Dreams** and warded the lands against any Urgolais survivors and Her enemy Undeyna, who had killed her beloved niece, and Undeyna's twin **Simiolanis**, out of jealous spite, thus earning the eternal animosity of Elanion. She gathered the **Faen** (a sort of elves) around her. Undeyna followed suit and gathered those Faen drawn to the dark. These became known as the Dark Faen. Meanwhile, the stain of Old Night filtered into the kingdoms of men after this new race was introduced to Ansu by the Maker—much to the dismay and chagrin of the High Gods and other beings.

Mankind thrived, and the time of Faerie and the gods dwindled into twilight. But some were vengeful. A mortal wizard, **Caswallon**, conjured long-dead Urgolais spirits up from **Yffarn** (the underworld). These he bargained with and gained great power, murdering the High King and usurping his throne, an action that resulted in a third and final war of the gods. The newly risen Urgolais leader, **Morak**, brandished the spear **Golganak** and used the fell weapon to raise the damaged shade of Old Night. Thus, with an army of winged goblins (**Soilfins**), the dragon **Vaarg**, and the **Groil** (flesh-eating creatures that resembled their Urgo masters), Caswallon's powerful allies sought to take back Ansu.

Queen Ariane and mercenary **Corin an Fol** led an army against Caswallon. Aided by some of the gods, Corin was destined to become High King, having almost drowned in a shipwreck as a babe. He did not know his father was the High King's brother, and himself heir to the throne. **The Tekara** (a sacred Crystal Crown) was shattered, allowing evil to return to the Four Kingdoms. After recovering that in **Permio**, Corin requested the blind Smith God, **Croagon**, to reforge the crown. With this done, he joined the war and sought **Callanak**, the hallowed sword of truth on **Laras Lassladen** where Elanion dwelt when She wasn't in Ansu. With Callanak and the crown, Corin, Ariane, and their armies could face their enemies, both mortal armies from Permio and **Ptarni** as well as the dark forces waking under the shadow of Old Night, who men called the **Shadowman**. A final battle took place outside **Kelthara**, where Queen Ariane and company witnessed the gods destroy each other in what became known as the **Happening**.

Old Night was broken forever. Undeyna escaped again and turned up as the Ice Witch **Sheega**, first in **Dunnehine** and later in **Valkador**. Elanion and Oroonin eloped to **Galenki**, a nearby planet where They quarreled and plotted. Most the other High Gods were slain, but some new ones arrived in Ansu and became known as the New Gods or **Northern Gods**. These fell out frequently, and a new war erupted between Undeyna/Sheega, **Faerie**, the servants of **Chaos**, the **Traveler** (Oroonin), **The Emerald Queen**, and a mortal berserker called **Jaran Saerk.** During this latest upset in the Cosmic Order, a thief stole Elanion's bow, **Kerasheva**, which recently had been recovered from the Castle of Lights in Rundali. The bow has the power to change both future and past. Kerasheva once belonged to the missing goddess **Argonwui**—She who was lost during the second war of the gods.

PANTHEON

THE WEAVER.

The High Gods:
   Cul-Saan – First Born, **Old Night**, the **Shadowman**.
   Elanion – The **Guardian**, The **Emerald Queen**, **Scaffa**, also known as **Laniol**.
   Oroonin – also known as the **Wanderer, Traveler, Gurn**, the **Ferryman, Irulan**.
   Borian of the Winds.
   Telcanna the Sky God, also known as **Talcan.**
   Croagon the Smith.
   Sensuata Sea God, aka **Zansuat.**
   Lesser Gods
   Crun Earth Shatterer – a giant
   Undeyna aka **Sheega** the Ice Witch
   Simiolanis, Her twin sister.
   Argonwui the Virgin, long-lost eldest daughter of Elanion and Oroonin.
   The Fates
   Urdei – Past

Vervandi – Present

Scolde – Future

The Northern Gods

The **Traveler**

Tyho the War God

Kullaan the Wind God, His twin brother.

Lofhi the Cruel

Peoples of Ansu

The Faen – original inhabitants of Ansu who served the Goddess Elanion.

Dark Faen – those Faen who turned against Elanion because they hated mortals and served Undeyna instead.

The Aralais – The Golden Ones, proud warrior-wizards who arrived in space ships from a distant time and place, seeking to continue their age-long war with their Urgolais cousins.

The Urgolais – Cousins to the Aralais and immortal wizards from a distant galaxy

The Elementals – a race of bodiless Faen who dwelt in Gol

Soilfins – flying goblins who served Cul-Saan.

Groil – Urgolais foot-soldiers and flesh-eaters fashioned by sorcery in their likeness.

Faerie Realms

Telimantua – home of Sensuata and His Consort/Daughter, **Rann**, beneath the Oceans

Yffarn – the Underworld

Urdheim – Land of the Stone Giants

Swartzheim – The Dwarfs' Realm.

Aelfheim – Home of the elves.

Limbo and Void – The Chaos Realms, the endless nothing from where the steel **Grogans**, the **Kaa**, and **Vaarg** the dragon came to punish the nine worlds.

READ ON FOR AN EXCERPT FROM
LEGENDS OF THE LONGSWORD

"Got your attention?" The poniard quivered on the table top, and twenty pairs of eyes looked his way - including the proprietor, who'd been ignoring him these last ten minutes. "Good. Hate to think you were avoiding me." Hagan smiled, removed the dagger and thrust it back in his sheath.

"We are busy today," the innkeep looked worried. For good reason. Rough tavern, wrong side of town. And some local gang members already well into their cups.

Hagan glanced casually over to the corner table where four big swarthy individuals turned their heads away and continued with their dice game. "Not sensible, drawing attention to yourself, stranger," the innkeep said, his worried glance on the mark left by Hagan's dagger.

"I think you're worried enough for both of us," Hagan yawned snatched the ale from the proprietor's sweaty hands and downed three-quarters. "That's better." Thanks. Been a long week." He managed a rare smile.

The man nodded and turned to another customer, but Hagan grabbed his collar checking him. "Name?"

"Rezala," the innkeep mumbled. Hagan let go and the man dusted down his collar. He looked alarmed – stressed.

"And this place?"

"*The Crimson Moon*. Did you not see the sign above the door?"

"No," Hagan said draining his tankard and shoving it on the table. "Another. *Please*." He smiled again—rare that. *I must be in a good mood. Won't last—never does.*

"You can go now," Hagan winked at innkeep Rezala. "Customers waiting," he pointed to the far side of the room where three large men had just appeared. They looked as thirsty as Hagan had been. They also looked violent and angry—ready for trouble.

Hagan loosened the sword by his side. He'd greased the scabbard this morning, the sort of thing that's saved a man's life. Hagan sipped this second ale. Strange life. *I'm an exile. A...renegade.*

It hadn't sunk in. His departure from Morwella had been rushed. No time to dwell on niceties. Too busy dodging arrows, stealing boats, stowing away on merchantmen. *And here I am...*

Permio. A tavern, in the worst corner of a very bad city, Cappel Cormac. Hive of every cutthroat, cutpurse, and murderous whore imaginable. A place where, he, Hagan felt quite at home.

But he was angry. He felt wronged—they'd exiled him. The Duke, his people. *And for what?* A bit of raiding and robbing. Hagan the Highwayman. Hagan liked the thought of that. But it was the principle. The word *exile* tasted bad. Lacked honor. *I didn't deserve that.*

Others had done far worse and they hadn't suffered such a punishment. They'd been hanged, a few hung, drawn and quartered. But he'd been *exiled*—the dishonor was a stain on his family's name. Not that that mattered as they were all fucking dead. But the Delmorier family had once been wealthy merchants, before Hagan's grandfather had squandered every penny, except the few his only surviving son lost in the vice dens. Father choked on his ale one night—selfish bastard, served him right. Didn't leave much for the skinny boy he'd abandoned, Hagan's mother having left them years earlier.

He'd grown up poor—survived the streets of Vangaris. Had nothing except his family's name.

But a name was important. A name meant—*everything.* Until now. Way down here he was just another villain, another killer with a grudge.

Hagan sipped his second ale, his mood darkening as he thought about how they'd wronged him back there in the north. A thousand miles away. *I can never go back—see home again.*

Didn't matter, Morwella was a shithole anyway. Taxed and squeezed not only by lofty Duke Tomais, but by the High King over in Kella City.

At least he was free now. Almost spent of coin, no horse, no home—*but free.* Hagan smiled a third time. *It's becoming a habit.* Then turned his head as fighting broke out near the door.

The newcomers had rounded on those gang members at the table. Old score by the look of it, Hagan wasn't interested. Just glanced over, saw the bottle broken and rammed into the fat one's eye. *Messy, that.* Hagan, mood shifting again, chugged down his drink and stood up. He needed somewhere to sleep out the afternoon, and food. That too.

The fight settled almost as soon as it had started. Two dead on the floor, the fat one screaming as blood streamed from his ruined face. The gang had fled, the three big lads were seated at their table. They wore broadswords, Hagan noted. Northerners like him.

Mercenaries.

One glanced his way as Hagan waded through the crowd, smoke, and perfume of whores as he aimed for the door. That swung open again, creaking, the hot afternoon sun blinding Hagan for a moment.

A man stood there. Tall, long shaggy hair, and a huge sword swung across his shoulder. He barreled in, clearing a space through to the taproom where Rezala still sweated and grumbled.

"You're banned," Hagan heard Rezala say. Glancing back, he saw Shaggy-Hair reach over and grab Rezala's collar. Not the innkeep's day.

"Shut up, and pour me a large one." The accent was odd but familiar. Another northerner. Hagan was intrigued, and he noted how the three big men at the table were also staring at this longswordsman. They looked angrier than before. And one reached for his blade. The tall fellow didn't notice; he was watching Rezala fill a tankard.

"Better enjoy that," Rezala said. "Last one you're getting."

Hagan saw the innkeep nod to the nearest mercenary.

"That him?" The sellsword asked. Rezala nodded. The longswordsman seemed oblivious, cradled his ale and sighed, as though he was sharing a tender moment with his lover, no one else around. Hagan wondered if he were soft in the head.

All three were on their feet. Big, angry, and well balanced. Confident. *Professionals.* They shoved sweaty bodies aside heading for the place where Shaggy-Hair was making love to his beer. Men grumbled and swore, the odd one spat. But they parted like palm leaves in summer storm letting the three large figures through.

Hagan scratched his face where a mosquito had bitten him. He hadn't cared about the earlier fracas, but was interested now. Why were these northerners here? And who did they work for? He needed to know, could be useful later.

"Outside." Hagan saw Rezala hint the door as the nearest mercenary stormed up behind Shaggy-hair. "Don't want another mess in here."

The man ignored him, and slowly slid his broadsword free for maximum effect, men parting either side to allow him room to swing.

"Put that back or I'll shove it up your arse," the accent was almost Morwellan. The lead mercenary paused, sword half out of scabbard, his fellows hustled close behind.

A mistake.

Shaggy-hair turned, and with a speed Hagan had seldom witnessed, slammed an open palm hard into the leading mercenary's face, cracking the small bone in his nose. He crumpled, sunk from view. The other two leaped forward.

And were knocked back.

Elbow to face, fist on balls, boot stamping on ankle. Shaggy-hair grinned as he grabbed the pair by their ears and slammed their heads together. They slid to join their comrade on the floor.

Shaggy-hair turned away and started on his ale again, ignoring the swarm of eyes and hostile glances.

"And you said *I* was drawing attention to myself," Hagan muttered to Rezala, who had glanced his way briefly before crouching low, whispering to a boy. Hagan watched the lad vanish out a back exit, the bright glare dazzling him a second time.

"Off to get the Watch I should imagine," Hagan said, as men resumed their seats, apart from the three sprawled on the floor. They showed no sign of moving any time soon.

"Expect so," Shaggy-Hair turned slowly and noticed Hagan for the first time. "Don't know you."

"Just arrived," Hagan said. "Think I'm going to like it here."

"No one likes it here," Shaggy-Hair said.

"Friends of yours?" Hagan hinted the three on the floor.

"Not really. They work for his boss," Shaggy-hair leaned over the counter, grabbed an empty tankard and hurled it at Rezala - catching him on the back of the head and knocking him from his feet.

He turned and grinned at Hagan. "I was banned anyway," he said, draining his tankard and striding from the room, a wave of bodies parting to let him through. Hagan suspected most had hands on daggers, and some would be following.

He chose to tag along.

"Wait," Hagan said, and the longsword stopped, turning slowly to stare hard at Hagan. *A man like me—a killer.* Someone with a grudge.

Steely eyes, the hue of northern oceans. Lean face, long bones, wicked scar above right brow. Black leather tunic and trousers. Silver studded belt, and battered mail shirt showing beneath.

"Name's Hagan Delmorier."

"Corin."

"From where—I can't grasp that accent."

"Fol—I'm Corin an Fol," he replied as though that were significant.

"Isn't that a province of Kelthaine?"

"Fuck off—it's a free country," the man called Corin said. "Nothing to do with Kelthaine, or the fucking High King."

"Sorry," Hagan shrugged. "Just curious."

"So are they," Corin said. Hagan turned and saw at least a dozen men had followed them out into the swelter of a Cappel Cormac afternoon. They stood in a circle surrounding Hagan and his new friend.

"I would leave if I were you," Corin said. "Me they want."

"I've only just arrived," Hagan yawned—past time for his afternoon nap. The stomp and scrape of boots in the distance, getting nearer. Shouting too. "Sounds like the Watch."

"Time I left," Corin said, and whirled around planting a fist neatly on the jaw of a bystander who'd got too near. He stepped sideways, slid the huge sword from its scabbard and shoved it point-first into the hot dry mud that served as a street in this shithole of a city.

The watch filed in looking nervous, tense, and very angry. "Your move," Corin said, flashing them a grin. They shuffled, glanced sideways at each other. A captain of sorts pushed his way through. Rezala yelled at him, holding a wet cloth to his bleeding skull.

"I barred him," Rezala said. "He's a troublemaker."

"All your punters are troublemakers," the captain looked pained, not wanting any of this. He pointed to Hagan. "And who is this?"

"I'm Hagan—just arrived."

"Well you'd better bugger off," the captain of the watch said. "Else we nab you for collusion."

"I only stepped out to enjoy the sunshine," Hagan said. No one was moving: captain, innkeep, the watch, tenants from the inn, and now bystanders and street vendors and even the odd, scarf covered whore—everyone had eyes on that two-yard sword, and the wild-eyed northerner leaning on it.

The captain approached Hagan, while staring at the other northerner. "I said go," the watch's leader hissed in Hagan's ear, then turned and yelled at his men. "Get him!"

Three spears levelled and poking, their owners thrust forward without too much enthusiasm. Bad mistake. *You have to do something properly, or not at all.* Hagan stepped away from the captain and blinked as metal glinted, there was a whoosh and a meaty thud. He saw a man's head rolling in the mud. A second joined it, then an arm.

"Time to run!" Corin shouted across to him.

Past time. Hagan turned on his toes, cat-graceful he pounced at the captain and kicked him in the groin, following up with an elbow to the face as the watch leader crumpled. Hagan grabbed an arm, swung the captain around into the next man attacking him. Both sprawled. Hagan saw Corin was loping down the street with that huge sword whirling like a windmill.

For fuck's sake... Thanks for waiting. Hagan stepped back, slid his rapier free and cut left and right. Swift clean strokes. They backed away. A gap appeared. He ran through just in time to see Corin vanish into a side street.

Would you trade your soul to save your life?

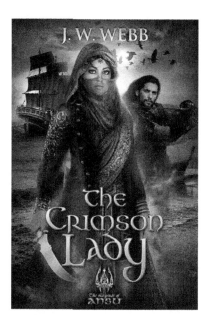

The Crimson Lady knows that her soul may be the price she has to pay to get revenge.

If you enjoyed *Blood Feud,* you will love this new tale, *The Crimson Lady.* It's available free for newsletter members only. Don't miss out! Join our fun newsletter the JW Webb VIP Lounge. *Subscribe today!*

ENJOY THIS BOOK? THEN HELP SPREAD THE WORD!

Reviews are one the most powerful tools in my arsenal when it comes to getting readers for my books. Much as I'd like to, I don't have the financial muscle of a New York publisher. I can't take out full-page ads in the newspaper or put posters on the subway.

(Not yet, anyway.)

But I do have something much more powerful and effective than that, and it's something that those publishers would kill to get their hands on:

A committed and loyal bunch of readers.

If you have enjoyed this book, I would be so grateful if you could spend just a few minutes leaving a review, wherever you bought it. And I'd love if if you'd like to email me a link to the review! ansureviews@gmail.com

Thank you so very much!

ALSO BY J.W. WEBB

THE LEGENDS OF ANSU

GOL: The Series Prequel

THE MERCENARY TRILOGY

Gray Wolf (Book 1)

Legends of the Longsword (Book 2)

Wolves and Assassins (Book 3)

THE CRYSTAL CROWN TRILOGY

The Shattered Crown (Book 1)

The Lost Prince (Book 2)

The Glass Throne (Book 3)

THE JOURNEYMAN TRILOGY

The Emerald Queen (Book 1)

The Voyage of Carlo Sarfe (Book 2)

THE BERSERKER TRILOGY

Blood Feud (Book 1)

The Giant's Dance (Book 2)

Shadow of the White Bear (Book 3)

ABOUT THE AUTHOR

J. W. Webb is an English writer living in Georgia. Mostly he writes fantasy, though sometimes diverts in even stranger directions. His epic saga , The Legends of Ansu, blends the mystic grandeur of JRR Tolkien with the gritty realism of GRR Martin. Webb's characters are three dimensional and flawed, their world a tapestry of vivid color and constant motion. All the books feature beautiful bespoke sketches by the late Tolkien illustrator, Roger Garland.

Printed in Great Britain
by Amazon